Praise for *Bad Monkey*

'Outlandish and hilarious, *Bad Monkey* confirms Hiaasen's reputation as the comic laureate of crime'
Mail on Sunday

'From the opening page, there is a confidence, economy and enjoyability to *Bad Monkey* that give the impression of a writer back in love with his franchise ... a novel that is as enjoyable to read as it seems to have been him to write'
Guardian

'He is a comic genius. *Bad Monkey* sees him on top form ... the energetic way he skewers venality and venery is laugh-out-loud funny'
Evening Standard

'I loved *Bad Monkey*. Hiaasen at his funniest and most thickly plotted. Like Chandler with a sense of humour ...'
John Niven

'A rum-soaked romp, brimming with shifty characters and razor-sharp dialogue'
Sunday Mirror

Carl Hiaasen was born and raised in Florida, where he still lives. He is a prize-winning journalist with a regular column in the *Miami Herald* and many articles in varied magazines. He started writing crime fiction in the early 1980s and has recently branched out into children's books; he has also had several works of non-fiction published.

Bad Monkey

CARL HIAASEN

sphere

SPHERE

First published in the United States in 2013 by Alfred A.Knopf,
a division of Random House, Inc.
First published in Great Britain in 2013 by Sphere
This paperback edition published in 2014 by Sphere

5 7 9 10 8 6 4

A CIP catalogue record for this book
is available from the British Library.

ISBN 978-0-7515-4334-6

Printed and bound in Great Britain by
Clays Ltd, St Ives plc

Papers used by Sphere are from well-managed forests
and other responsible sources.

MIX
Paper from
responsible sources
FSC
www.fsc.org   FSC® C104740

Sphere
An imprint of
Little, Brown Book Group
Carmelite House
50 Victoria Embankment
London EC4Y 0DZ

An Hachette UK Company
www.hachette.co.uk

www.littlebrown.co.uk

For all the flying fishermen of the apocalypse,
especially Jimmy

One

On the hottest day of July, trolling in dead-calm waters near Key West, a tourist named James Mayberry reeled up a human arm. His wife flew to the bow of the boat and tossed her breakfast burritos.

"What're you waiting for?" James Mayberry barked at the mate. "Get that thing off my line!"

The kid tugged and twisted, but the barb of the hook was imbedded in bone. Finally the captain came down from the bridge and used bent-nose pliers to free the decomposing limb, which he placed on shaved ice in a deck box.

James Mayberry said, "For Christ's sake, now where are we supposed to put our fish?"

"We'll figure that out when you actually catch one."

It had been a tense outing aboard the *Misty Momma IV*. James Mayberry had blown three good strikes because he was unable to absorb instruction. Dragging baits in the ocean was different than jigging for walleyes in the lake back home.

1

"Don't we need to call somebody?" he asked the captain.

"We do."

The hairy left arm was bloated and sunburned to the hue of eggplant. A cusp of yellowed humerus protruded at the point of separation, below the shoulder. The flesh surrounding the wound looked ragged and bloodless.

"Yo, check it out!" the mate said.

"What now?" James Mayberry asked.

"His freakin' finger, dude."

The victim's hand was contracted into a fist except for the middle digit, which was rigidly extended.

"How weird is *that*? He's flippin' us off," the mate said.

The captain told him to re-bait the angler's hook.

"Has this ever happened out here before?" James Mayberry said. "Tell the truth."

"You should go see about your wife."

"Jesus, I'll never hear the end of it. Louisa wanted to ride the Conch Train today. She did *not* want to come fishing."

"Well, son," the captain said, "we're in the memory-making business."

He climbed back to the bridge, radioed the Coast Guard and gave the GPS coordinates of the gruesome find. He was asked to remain in the area and look for other pieces of the body.

"But I got a charter," he said.

"You can stay at it," the Coast Guard dispatcher advised. "Just keep your eyes open."

After calming herself, Louisa Mayberry informed her husband that she wished to return to Key West right away.

"Come on, sugar. It's a beautiful morning." James Mayberry didn't want to go back to the dock with no fish to hang on the spikes – not after shelling out a grand to hire the boat.

2

"The first day of our honeymoon, and *this*! Aren't you sketched out?"

James Mayberry peeked under the lid of the fish box. "You watch *CSI* all the time. It's the same type of deal."

His wife grimaced but did not turn away. She remarked that the limb didn't look real.

"Oh, it's real," said James Mayberry, somewhat defensively. "Just take a whiff." Snagging a fake arm wouldn't make for as good a story. A real arm was pure gold, major high-fives from all his peeps back in Madison. *You caught a what? No way, bro!*

Louisa Mayberry's gaze was fixed on the limb. "What could have happened?" she asked.

"Tiger shark," her husband said matter-of-factly.

"Is that a wedding band on his hand? This is so sad."

"Fish on!" the mate called. "Who's up?"

James Mayberry steered his bride to the fighting chair and the mate fitted the rod into the gimbal. Although she was petite, Louisa Mayberry owned a strong upper body due to rigorous Bikram yoga classes that she took on Tuesday nights. Refusing assistance, she pumped in an eleven-pound blackfin tuna and whooped triumphantly as it flopped on the deck. Her husband had never seen her so excited.

"Here, take a picture!" she cried to the mate, and handed over her iPhone.

"Hold on," James Mayberry said. "Get both of us together."

Louisa watched him hustle to get ready. "Really, Jimmy? Really?"

Moments later the captain glanced down from the bridge and saw the mate snapping photographs of the newlyweds posed side by side at the transom. Their matching neon blue Oakley wraparounds were propped on their matching cap visors, and their fair Wisconsin noses practically glowed with sunblock.

Louisa Mayberry was gamely hoisting by the tail her sleek silvery tuna while James Mayberry wore the mate's crusty gloves to grip his rancid catch, its middle finger aimed upward toward the puffy white clouds.

The captain dragged on a cigarette and turned back to the wheel. "Another fucking day in paradise," he said.

The phone kept ringing but Yancy didn't answer it. He was drinking rum, sitting in a plastic lawn chair. From next door came the offensive buzz of wood saws and the metallic pops of a nail gun. The absentee owner of the property was erecting an enormous spec house that had no spiritual place on Big Pine Key, and furthermore interfered with Yancy's modest view of the sunset. It was Yancy's fantasy to burn the place down as soon as the roof framing was finished.

He heard a car stop in his driveway but he didn't rise from the chair. His visitor was a fellow detective, Rogelio Burton.

"Why don't you pick up your phone?" Burton said.

"You believe that monstrosity? It's like a goddamn mausoleum."

Burton sat down beside him. "Sonny wants you to take a road trip."

"Miami?"

"That's right."

"I'll pass." Yancy glared at the construction site across the fence. "The house is forty-four feet high – I measured it myself. The county code's only thirty-five."

"It's the Keys, man. The code is for suckers."

4

"Deer used to come around all the time and feed on the twigs."

Yancy offered his friend a drink. Burton declined.

He said, "Andrew, it's not like you've got a choice. Do what Sonny wants."

"But I'm suspended, remember?"

"Yeah, with pay. Is that Barbancourt?"

"My last bottle. Tell him anywhere but Miami, Rog."

"You want me to ask if you can go to Cancún instead?" Burton sighed. "Look, it's a day trip, up and back."

"They always screw me on the mileage."

Burton knew this wasn't true. Yancy had issues with the Miami Police Department, from which he'd been fired in a previous era of his life.

"Chill out. You're just going to the ME's office."

"The morgue? Nice."

"Come out to the car," said Burton.

Yancy set down his drink. "This ought to be special."

The severed arm had been bubble-wrapped and packed on dry ice in a red Igloo cooler. To make it fit, the limb had been bent at the elbow.

"That's all they found?"

"You know how it goes," Burton said.

"John Doe or Juan Doe?"

"Rawlings says white male, mid-forties, heavyset, black hair."

Dr. Lee Rawlings was the pathologist who served as the chief medical examiner for Monroe County. There were relatively few murders or accidental deaths in the Florida Keys, but Rawlings never complained. He filled his free time with golf, and was rumored to have whittled his handicap down to five strokes.

Yancy knew the sheriff was sending the arm to Miami because Miami was the floating-human-body-parts capital of America. Maybe they'd luck out and find a match, although Yancy thought it was unlikely.

"Traumatic amputation," Burton said.

"Ya think?"

"Charter boat brought it in yesterday. We checked our missing persons, all three of them. Nobody fits the description."

Yancy noticed the upraised finger on the end of the arm. "A sour farewell to the mortal realm?"

"Random rigor mortis is what Rawlings says. He took a picture anyway."

"Of course he did."

"Look, I'm late for my kid's soccer game."

"Absolutely." Yancy put the lid on the cooler and carried it up to his porch.

Burton said, "Sure you want to leave it out here all night?"

"Who's gonna jack an arm?"

"It's evidence, man. I'm just sayin'."

"Okay, fine." The island was plagued by opportunistic raccoons.

Burton drove off and Yancy moved the cooler into the house. From a kitchen cupboard he retrieved the Barbancourt bottle and ambled to the deck and poured himself one more drink. Next door, the construction crew was gone. Yancy's watch said five p.m. sharp.

For the first time all day he could hear seabirds in the sky.

The new sheriff of Monroe County was a local bubba named Sonny Summers who won office because he was the only candidate not in federal custody, the two front-runners having been locked up on unconnected racketeering charges eight days before the election. Sonny Summers's opponents were unable to post bond and therefore faced a strategic disadvantage during the campaign's final debate, which was conducted via Skype from a medium-security prison near Florida City.

During his sixteen years as a road patrol officer, Sonny Summers had received numerous commendations for not fucking up on the job. He was well-groomed, courteous and diligent about his paperwork. One year he led the whole force in DUI arrests, a highly competitive category in the Keys. His spelling on arrest forms was almost always legible, he never took any of his girlfriends on dates in his squad car and he smoked pot only on his days off.

Upon becoming sheriff, Sonny Summers arranged a series of get-acquainted luncheons with business leaders up and down the islands, from Key West to Key Largo. A recurring theme of these meetings was the fragility of tourism and the perils of negative publicity. The BP oil spill was often invoked, although not a drop of crude had ever reached South Florida beaches. Sonny Summers was sympathetic to the business owners, whose support he would need for future elections. Under no circumstances did he wish to be blamed for scaring customers away.

With that in mind, Sonny Summers ordered his public-information officer not to divulge any information about the severed arm that had been brought in aboard the *Misty Momma IV.* It was the new sheriff's worry that floating body parts would be bad for tourism, particularly the waterfront trades. This was laughably untrue, as any marina owner in Miami could have assured him. Nothing

7

short of a natural disaster discouraged people from going out on (or into) the water. One particular beach on the Rickenbacker Causeway got spunked regularly by raw sewage, yet squads of riot police couldn't keep the swimmers and kiteboarders away.

In any case, Sonny Summers was fighting a lost battle. A crime-scene van had been waiting for the *Misty Momma IV* when it docked, so news of the icky discovery spread quickly. Worse, the boneheaded angler who'd reeled in the dead arm was showing the pictures on his cell phone to everybody at the Chart Room. There was even a rumor that he'd posted a photo on Facebook.

"I'm counting on you," the sheriff said to Yancy, after Yancy finally answered the phone.

"How so?"

"I'm counting on you not to come back from Miami with that you-know-what."

Yancy said, "What if there are no matching limbs at the morgue up there?"

"I need some optimism from you, Detective. I need some can-do mojo."

"The Gulf Stream flows north."

"Duh," said Sonny Summers.

"Also, the prevailing breeze this time of year blows from the southeast."

"I was born here, Yancy. Get to the point."

"Factor in the wind and currents, the odds of that arm floating from Miami all the way down here are pretty damn slim – unless it was paddling itself."

The sheriff was aware of Yancy's employment history. "You don't want to drive up to the big coldhearted city, that's all."

"What if they won't take the case?"

"See, I'm depending on you to persuade them."

"I can't just leave a limb at the ME's office if they don't want it."

Sonny Summers said, "Tomorrow I'm announcing that the investigation has been turned over to the appropriate authorities in Miami-Dade County. That's the game plan, okay? This is officially no longer our headache."

"I would wait a day to be sure."

"Know what happened this morning? Some dickhead from Channel 7 calls up and says he heard that mangled corpses are floating up in Key West harbor!"

"Did you tell him to fuck off?"

"Call back tomorrow is what I told him. Wait for the media statement."

"Our victim's probably a rafter," Yancy said. "Drowned on the crossing from Havana and then got hit by a bull shark or a hammer-head."

"There you go!" the sheriff exclaimed brightly. "Aren't most rafters on their way to Miami to meet up with family? So that's where the goddamn arm belongs – Miami! End of discussion."

"It's not really up to me, Sonny."

"Let me put it another way: There will be no human remains on my watch. Understand? *No human remains.*"

Those close to Sonny Summers sensed that he was sometimes overwhelmed by his elevated responsibilities. The transition from writing speeding tickets to commanding a recalcitrant law enforcement bureaucracy had been bumpy. One aspect of the new job that Sonny Summers did enjoy was putting on a blazer and schmoozing with the chamber-of-commerce types.

Yancy tried to suggest that an occasional severed limb was no cause for panic.

"Really? The two-day lobster season is next week," the sheriff said. "We're expecting, like, thirty thousand divers."

"A sea of reeking turds wouldn't keep those lunatics off the water. What are you worried about?"

"We'll speak again tomorrow," said Sonny Summers.

Yancy said, "I'll drive up there on one condition: You lift my suspension."

"Not until after the trial. How many times do I have to tell you?"

"But it's such bullshit, Sonny. I didn't even hurt the guy."

The sheriff said, "Talk to Bonnie. She's the problem."

Bonnie Witt, Yancy's future former girlfriend, was prepared to testify that he'd assaulted her husband of fourteen years with a portable vacuum cleaner, specifically a tubular attachment designed for upholstery crevices. Clifford Witt had required some specialized medical care but he was more or less ambulatory within a week.

Sonny Summers said, "Of all the women you had to get involved with. Swear to God, Andrew. All the women on these islands."

"Our love was like a streaking comet." Yancy paused. "Her words, not mine."

"Did you take a look at it? The . . . ?"

"Arm? Yes, Burton insisted."

"Any theories?"

"No," said Yancy. "But it makes a dandy back-scratcher."

"Call me on your way back from Miami. I want some happy news."

TWO

A clawing heat settles over the Keys by mid-July. The game fish swim to deeper waters, the pelicans laze in the mangroves and only the hardiest of tourists remain outdoors past the lunch hour. Yancy's unmarked Ford was well air-conditioned but he still brought a box of Popsicles, which he positioned beside the disjoined limb in the cooler on the passenger side.

He was a pathologically impatient driver, and sucking on iced treats seemed to settle him. Bonnie had started Yancy on the Popsicle habit because she'd found it terrifying to ride with him on Highway 1. Mango was Yancy's favorite flavor beside Bonnie herself. These were the sorts of side-car thoughts with which he tormented himself.

The drive to downtown Miami usually took ninety minutes, but Yancy had stopped along Card Sound Road to purchase blue crabs, as there was still room in the cooler.

"Is this your idea of wit?" asked the assistant medical

examiner, a serious brown-eyed woman whose name tag identified her as Dr. Rosa Campesino.

"Help yourself to a Popsicle," Yancy told her. "However, the crabs are off-limits."

He summarized Rawlings's findings while Dr. Campesino removed the arm from the ice and carefully unwrapped it. She placed it on a bare autopsy table without commenting on the vertical middle digit.

"I suppose you've seen some winners," Yancy said.

"And you brought this all the way from Key West because . . . ?"

"The sheriff thought it might belong to one of your victims."

Dr. Campesino said, "You could've emailed some photos and saved yourself a tank of gas."

"Want to grab lunch?"

Finally, a smile. "I'll be back in a minute," she said.

Yancy ate another Popsicle. Unless you happened to be deceased, there were worse places to hang out than a morgue in the summertime. The thermostat was turned down to about sixty-three degrees. Very pleasant.

Dr. Campesino returned with a printout of the county's current inventory of body parts, listed by race, gender and approximate age – three partial torsos, two left legs, a pelvis, three ears, seven assorted toes and one bashed skull. None of the items belonged to a chunky, hirsute white male in his forties.

"I knew it," said Yancy.

"Maybe next time."

"Are you hungry?"

"My husband's a sniper on the SWAT team."

"Say no more."

"Did you notice this?" Dr. Campesino pointed the eraser end of a pencil at a well-delineated band of pale flesh on the wrist of the darkened arm. "His watch is gone," she said.

"It probably fell off the poor fucker while the shark was mangling him."

Dr. Campesino gave a slight shake of her head. "Often in upper-arm amputations the victim's wristwatch remains attached. Not so much in homicides. The bad guys either steal it to pawn, or they remove it to make the ID more difficult."

Yancy was certain that Sheriff Sonny Summers wouldn't want to hear the word *homicide*. "Then why wouldn't they swipe the wedding ring, too?" he asked.

"You're right. It looks expensive."

"I'm betting platinum. The guy's wife would be sure to recognize it."

Dr. Campesino leaned closer to study the damaged stump of the limb.

"What now?" Yancy said.

"The end of the humerus is hacked up pretty bad."

"Maybe he fell into the boat's propeller."

"That would be a different style of wound."

Yancy said, "You're killing me."

From a tray of instruments the pathologist selected a pair of hemostats, with which she extracted a pointed tooth from one of several puncture holes in the upper biceps. She dropped the smallish gray fang into Yancy's palm.

"I'm no shark expert," said Dr. Campesino. "Some marine biologist could tell you what species this came from."

Yancy pocketed the tooth. He asked how long the arm had been in the ocean.

"Five to seven days. Maybe longer." The young pathologist took some photographs that she promised to upload in case another part of the same corpse turned up in her jurisdiction.

"Can't you keep the damn thing here?" Yancy asked. "Honestly, it would save me all kinds of grief."

"Sorry. Not our case." Dr. Campesino was mindful of the blue crabs when she returned the orphaned arm to the cooler. "I'll call you if we get something that looks like a match."

Yancy was aware that the Miami-Dade medical examiner's office sometimes assisted other jurisdictions in difficult cases. He was also aware that his boss hadn't sent him to Miami to initiate a murder investigation.

"Can we call it an accident? I mean, if you had to guess."

"Not without a more thorough exam," said Dr. Campesino, peeling off her latex gloves, "which I'd be happy to do if we had an official request from Monroe County."

"Which you won't get."

"Can I ask why?"

"I'll tell you over a strictly platonic lunch."

"Nope."

"Fine," Yancy said. "So what would you do if you were me?"

"I'd go back to Key West and advise Dr. Rawlings to pack the arm in his freezer. Then wait for someone to show up looking for a missing husband."

"And what if nobody does? It's a cold business when true love goes south. Take my word."

"Can I ask you something? Did you bend his middle finger up?"

"God, no! They found it that way!" Yancy moved the arm aside as he pawed through the cooler in search of another mango Popsicle. "Dear Rosa, what kind of sick bastard do you take me for?"

The person responsible for Yancy leaving the Miami Police Department was a sergeant named Johnny Mendez, who at the time was working with the Crime Stoppers hotline. To augment his salary Mendez would recruit friends and relatives to call in with tips on crimes that had already been solved, providing detailed information that detectives already knew. Then Mendez would backdate the tip sheet and personally sign off on the reward money, half of which he took as a commission.

Yancy had discovered the scam when he'd read a *Herald* story about a bus driver who'd received forty-five hundred dollars from Crime Stoppers for providing "crucial information" leading to the arrest of a man who stuck up a pedicure salon in Little Havana. Yancy himself had busted the robber, with no guidance whatsoever from the general public. The suspect had helpfully dropped his fishing license at the crime scene, and two days later Yancy jumped him while he was waxing the hull of his Boston Whaler.

The bus driver who'd phoned in the bogus tip turned out to be a second cousin of Sergeant Mendez's. One morning Yancy boarded the cousin's bus and sat in the first row and opened a notebook. After thirty-three blocks the driver spilled the whole story. He said Sergeant Mendez was upset to have opened the newspaper and seen the item about the reward, and had punished him by pocketing all but a grand.

That night, after too many rum and Cokes, Yancy decided it would be fabulously clever to dial the Crime

Stoppers number and report Sergeant Mendez for grand theft and embezzlement. Mendez wasn't a big fan of irony, and in any case he'd been busy covering his tracks. Yancy was eventually accused by Internal Review of making up lies about a fellow officer and of trying to extort money from Crime Stoppers. Yancy's position was weakened by the transcript of his phone call to the tip line, in which he suggested that a reward of fifty thousand dollars would be appropriate for the "courageous and upright deed" of exposing a crooked cop.

Yancy had delivered that line in a snarky and facetious tone, but the review board never got to hear the original tape, which had been mysteriously damaged by magnets while in Johnny Mendez's possession. Suspended without pay, Yancy quickly ran out of money for his lawyer and had no choice but to resign from the department, in exchange for not being indicted. Sergeant Mendez denied all wrongdoing but was quietly reassigned to the K-9 division. Soon thereafter he was bitten in the groin by a Belgian shepherd trainee named Kong, and he required three operations, culminating in a scrotal graft from a Brahma steer.

Mendez retired from the police force on full disability at age forty-four. He lived on Venetia Avenue in Coral Gables. Parked in the driveway was a silver Lexus coupe undoubtedly purchased with Crime Stoppers proceeds. One solution to the severed-arm dilemma would be for Yancy to plant the limb in Mendez's car, perhaps strung to the rosary that hung from the rearview mirror. Yancy discarded the idea – if by some chance Mendez overcame his panic and called the police, the arm would end up at the county morgue, where it inevitably would be traced back to Yancy based on information provided by the exquisite Dr. Campesino.

Over the years Yancy had conjured many irrational revenge fantasies about Johnny Mendez. For a time he considered seducing Mendez's wife until he realized he'd be doing Mendez a huge favor. Mrs. Mendez was an unbearable harridan. Her features were a riot of futile surgeries, and she laughed like a mandrill on PCP. Yancy once bought her a margarita at the InterContinental, and for two solid weeks he'd slept with the lights on.

Now he was parked down the block from the Mendez marital nest. A fat Siamese was primping on the hood of the Lexus. Yancy assumed the animal belonged to Mendez, who seemed like a total cat person. The man's inability to control K-9 candidates was further evidence.

Before Yancy could make up his mind about snatching the Siamese, his cell rang. It was the sheriff, probably seeking confirmation that the severed-arm transfer was complete. Yancy let the call go to voicemail.

On the drive back to the Keys he phoned Burton and gave him the bad news.

"They didn't want the damn thing. Now what do I do?"

"Lose it somewhere," Burton said. "That's my advice."

"Listen to you."

"Seriously. Take 905 back through North Key Largo – there's a dirt road about halfway that leads to an old cockfighting ring."

Yancy wasn't sold on the plan. "My luck, some birder will find it."

"Not before the ants and vultures do."

"What the hell's wrong with Sonny, anyway? This is no big deal."

Burton said the sheriff freaked when Channel 7 called.

"Anyway, he already gave a press statement saying the case had been turned over to Miami-Dade."

"I warned him, Rog."

"Just ditch the fucking arm and come home."

"Let me think about this."

"I wish you wouldn't."

Yancy boiled the blue crabs and served them on hearts of palm, sprinkled with lemon pepper and Tabasco. Bonnie brought a bottle of Bordeaux. The fine vintage was wasted on Yancy but the gesture seemed rich with promise. Still she said: "I shouldn't have come."

They ate dinner on the back deck, where a world-class sunset was being ruined by the vulgar structure arising next door, spears of light slanting harshly through a checkerboard of window spaces and door frames.

"Where's the good doctor?" Yancy asked.

"Lauderdale. He's got a meeting tomorrow with our bankers."

"It must be nice to have bankers. As a couple, I mean. 'Here's our Christmas tree. Here's our minivan. And, oh, last but not least, here are our bankers.'"

"Shut up, Andrew," Bonnie said. Her frosted hair was in pigtails, and a touch of pink gloss had been applied to her lips.

"He's sixty, you're forty. I remain at a loss." Yancy threw up his hands.

"Don't try to flatter me. I'm forty-two and you know it."

She kicked off her flip-flops and crossed her smooth tanned legs, which stirred in Yancy's chest a longing that almost incapacitated him. He and Bonnie hadn't slept together since the night before the vacuum-cleaner incident.

Yancy said, "The sheriff would lift my suspension if you and Cliff agreed to drop the charges."

"So that's why you invited me tonight."

"I ask you over three or four times a week, but you always say no."

"Cliff won't budge," Bonnie said. "He wants to see you punished."

Yancy pointed out that a trial would be humiliating for all parties. "Especially the alleged victim."

"Alleged? There were three hundred witnesses, including yours truly."

The assault had occurred at high noon at Mallory Square, which was packed with cruise-ship passengers. Fourteen amateur video clips of admissible clarity were in the hands of the prosecutor.

"Nobody calls you a whore and gets away with it," Yancy said.

"Well, I *was* cheating on him, as you'll recall. And I believe he used the term 'tramp,' not 'whore.'" Bonnie balanced a plate of crabs on her lap. With a silver fork she probed for morsels amid the ceramic debris. "These are pretty darn tasty," she said.

"Talk to him, darling. Please. I need my badge back."

"Why didn't you just punch him like a normal person? Why'd you have to go and sodomize him with a Hoover?"

Yancy shrugged. "You always said he had a bee up his ass. I was only trying to help."

"Are you seeing anybody?" Bonnie had no talent for changing the subject. "I don't think you're ready yet. I think you're still recovering."

"It's true, I'm a portrait of frailty. Tell me again why Cliffy isn't divorcing you."

"He adores me, Andrew."

"Even after catching us together."

"Yes," said Bonnie impatiently.

"On his own boat."

"We've been over this a hundred times."

"In the tuna tower, for Christ's sake! His own wife and another man, lewdly entwined." Yancy inserted a crab claw in his mouth and bit down violently. "We must've looked like the fucking Wallendas up there."

The boat was a seventy-two-foot Merritt with all the bells and whistles. Dr. Clifford Witt had recently retired from the practice of medicine, having invested in a chain of lucrative storefront pain clinics that dispensed Percocets and Vicodins by the bucket to a new wave of American redneck junkies.

Bonnie said, "I wouldn't be here tonight if I didn't care."

"Yet still you intend to testify against me."

"I'll take no joy from it, Andrew." She looked down, tugging at a loose thread on her cutoffs. "Of course, you could cut a deal. Spare us all from the messiness of court."

Yancy frowned. "And lose my job? That's automatic after a felony conviction."

"Suppose I got Cliff to go along with dropping the charge to a misdemeanor? Between you and me, Dickinson's office would be thrilled."

Billy Dickinson was the local state attorney, and he had no appetite for ventilating scandals.

"Sonny could still fire me," Yancy said, "or bust me down to deputy." Still, a misdemeanor wasn't insurmountable, career-wise.

"What do you think of the wine?"

"Yeasty," said Yancy, "yet playful."

Their affair had started on a Saturday afternoon in the produce section at Fausto's, the two of them reaching simultaneously for the last ripe avocado. From there they beelined to Bonnie's car and sped up the highway all the way to Bahia Honda, where they spent the night, hiding from the park rangers and humping madly on the beach, carving their own private dunes. For breakfast they split the avocado.

Yancy had been aware of Bonnie's marital status; Cliff Witt was his dermatologist at the time, always ready with a frigid zap of liquid nitrogen whenever Yancy burst into the office to present a new, ominous-looking freckle. Yancy appreciated Cliff Witt's accessibility but knew of his reputation as a horndog perv and pill peddler.

Still, guilt fissured Yancy's conscience when he began undressing the man's wife. It was his first encounter with a Brazilian wax job, and rapture soon blinded him to the manifest hurdles in his path. Usually he avoided married women.

"I suppose I should go," Bonnie said, rising. She had pale blue eyes and reddish lashes that looked gold-tipped in the light.

Yancy suggested a detour to the bedroom, and she said no. "But I'm a little drunk. Maybe a shower would wake me up."

"There's an idea."

It was just like old times, Bonnie's bare bottom slapping against the wet tile while Yancy's heels squeaked in joyous syncopation on the rubber bath mat. Somehow they broke the soap dish off the wall and also spilled a bottle of Prell, which played havoc with Yancy's traction. Afterward they toweled each other dry and fell into bed, and there Bonnie made a peculiar revelation.

"I am wanted in Oklahoma," she said.

"You're wanted here even more."

"I'm serious. That's why I married Cliff. I was a fugitive. *Am* a fugitive."

Yancy wasn't always a good post-coital listener, but Bonnie had gotten his attention. She said, "My real name is Plover Chase."

"Ah."

"*The* Plover Chase?"

"Okay," Yancy said.

"I can't believe you don't remember the case! Stay right here."

Naked she bounded from the sheets, returning with a French handbag that Yancy judged to be worth more than his car. From a jeweled change purse she removed a newspaper clipping that had been folded to the size of a credit card. As Yancy skimmed the article, he recalled the crime and also the steamy tabloid uproar.

Plover Chase was a schoolteacher in Tulsa who'd been convicted of extorting sex from one of her students in exchange for giving him an A on his report card. The boy was fifteen at the time; she was twenty-seven. On the day of her sentencing she'd disappeared.

"The judge was a shriveled old prick. I was looking at ten years," Bonnie recapped. "So instead I hopped a plane to Lauderdale. Cliff's medical office was advertising for a receptionist, and the rest is history."

"Does he know the truth?" Yancy asked.

"Of course." Which explained why Bonnie had stayed with him.

22

Yancy eyed the headline on the article: WARRANT ISSUED FOR TEACHER CONVICTED IN SEX-FOR-GRADES SCHEME. He wasn't sure whether he should act shocked or jealous. Certainly he had nothing as sensational in his own past.

He said, "May I offer a couple of observations? One, you're even more beautiful today than you were then."

"That's a mug shot, Andrew. And, FYI, a dyke named Smitty had just given me a full-on cavity search, which is why my eyeballs are bulging in that photo."

Yancy plowed on. "Number two, 'Bonnie' is so much sexier than 'Plover.' I don't think I could ever be intimate with a Plover – it's just not a name that can be seriously howled in the heat of passion."

"Cody had no trouble," Bonnie said.

Yancy raised an eyebrow. "The teenage victim of your seduction?"

"Yeah, some victim. He knew more positions than I did."

"Actually, Cody's a good sturdy name. He would be, what, about thirty now?"

Bonnie said the young man had sat in the front row of her AP English class. "I have no defense for what happened. He flirted with me, fine, but so did lots of the boys. Our . . . whatever . . . only lasted a couple of weeks, and of course he blabbed to everybody. His mother was the one who went to the cops."

"Even after you gave him an A?"

"There was no trade! Cody was an outstanding student."

"I assume he took the stand."

"His parents threatened to sell his Jet Ski if he didn't testify. Apparently he'd kept a journal of everything we did and how many times we did it. His writing was quite jaunty and explicit – I should never have turned him on to Philip Roth."

"So what was the final tally? How many trysts?"

"The jury was a horrid bunch, Andrew, leering like gargoyles."

Yancy said, "I can only imagine."

"Anyway, I wanted you to know the full truth, now that we're closing the book on each other's lives."

Like a buzzard coasting through clouds, the thought crossed Yancy's mind that his lawyer might be interested to learn that the wife of the man Yancy was accused of assaulting – and a key witness against him – was herself a fugitive from a sordid felony rap. He let the notion glide away.

"Whatever happened to Cody?" he asked.

"How the hell would I know? He was a dumb mistake, that's all."

"We all make 'em."

"I'll talk to Cliff again tomorrow. Promise."

Yancy said, "Thank you, Bonnie. I like being a detective."

"In the meantime you're still getting a paycheck, right? So go fishing or something." She returned the newspaper article to her purse. Then she stood up and stepped into her denim cutoffs. "I need some ice in my wine. How about you?"

"I'm good."

Yancy lay back on a pillow and watched Bonnie button her blouse. She always did it without looking down, her gaze clouded and faraway and dull. After she left the room, he shut his eyes and tried not to think about the supernatural frequency of erections enjoyed by fifteen-year-old schoolboys.

"Andrew!"

He lifted his head and through the doorway he saw Bonnie rigid in the glow of the open freezer. Her fists were pressed to the sides of her head.

"My God!" she said.

Yancy sat upright, thinking: *Oh fuck.*

"Andrew, what have you done?" she cried. "What on earth have you done?"

Three

After that night, Bonnie refused to come back to Yancy's house. From her line of questioning it became depressingly clear that she thought him capable of murdering somebody and hacking the corpse into pieces. Yancy took this as a sign that he'd failed, over their time as lovers, to showcase his best qualities.

He told Bonnie that the severed limb was evidence in an unsolved missing-person case and that he was storing it at home as a personal favor to Sheriff Sonny Summers, which was nearly true. Sonny didn't know Yancy still had the arm because Yancy hadn't told him, not wishing to upset the man who would soon be deciding Yancy's future in law enforcement.

Some nights, when it seemed as if Bonnie would never again be available to him, Yancy found himself wishing he'd followed Burton's advice and dumped the dead arm in the mangroves. That remained an option, of course, and perhaps one of these days he'd do it.

After a telephone plea featuring abject begging, Bonnie

finally agreed to meet him for breakfast at a diner on Sugarloaf. Afterward they made love in the back of her 4Runner, sharing the cramped space with her husband's smelly golf shoes. From Yancy's vantage it was impossible not to notice that Bonnie was no longer waxing.

"We're moving to Sarasota," she explained. "Cliff's burned out on the Keys."

"But what about the trial?"

"There won't be any trial."

In jubilation Yancy rubbed his chin back and forth across her pale stubble. "You're an angel!" he chortled.

"Whoa, cowboy. It doesn't mean you're off the hook."

"No? Then what?"

"I tried my best, Andrew."

Yancy sat up quickly, bumping his head on the roof. "But they *are* offering me a deal, correct?"

"Yes, and you'll take it," Bonnie said, "because Cliff doesn't want to go to court and you don't want to go to jail. Hand me that bra, please."

"What about my suspension?"

"Look, I'm not even supposed to be talking about this. I honestly *did* try my best." She finished dressing and nimbly vaulted back to the driver's seat. "Out," she commanded Yancy. "I'm late for a facial."

He exited by the rear hatch and hurried around to her window. "I'm going to miss you," he said. When he leaned in for a kiss, she offered only a damp cheek.

"Good-bye, Andrew."

"Good-bye, Plover."

Yancy went back to his car and called Montenegro, his attorney at the public defender's office. "How soon can you be here?" Montenegro asked.

27

"Give me something to chew on. What the hell's going on?"

"Dude, you know how things work in this town."

Yancy sagged and said, "Damn."

"It's a good news, bad news scenario. I'm around till noon."

There was a bad wreck at Mile Marker 13, a head-on between a gravel truck and a southbound rental car that crossed the center line – somebody's Key West vacation done before it started. The fire department was still hosing the gasoline and blood off the pavement when Yancy inched past the scene in his Crown Vic. He lost a half hour in the traffic jam, but Montenegro was still waiting when he got to the office.

"What's their offer?" Yancy said.

"Just sit down and take some deep breaths."

"I need a lawyer, not a goddamn Lamaze class."

Montenegro smiled and popped a Diet Coke. He was unflappable and beyond the reach of insults, as the job of a public defender required. Although he won his share of trials, few were the days when he didn't have to deliver unwelcome, life-changing tidings to some hapless shitbird. Occasionally he had the pleasure of counseling an innocent client, although Yancy didn't quite fall into that category.

"The good news, Andrew, is that you won't have a felony on your record. Billy Dickinson's agreed to drop the assault charge to misdemeanor battery. Six months' probation, court costs and of course you'll reimburse Dr. Witt for his out-of-pocket medical." Montenegro always looked drawn and pasty. His head was as slick as an eggshell, and he peered at the world beneath veined saggy eyelids.

But the sonofabitch was sharp.

Yancy said, "Okay, get to the bad news."

"Not so fast," the lawyer said. "In addition to reducing the charges, the state agrees not to object if you continue working as a pensioned employee."

"Fan-fucking-tastic!" Yancy sat forward to give Montenegro a high-five, which was returned with a mild pat.

"However—"

"Here we go," said Yancy.

"—Dr. Witt, the victim, strongly feels that you're unfit to be a police officer." Montenegro paused for a slurp of cola. "I don't happen to agree, but I'm not the one who had a suctorial attachment inserted up his rectum."

Yancy slumped in the chair.

Montenegro went on: "Dr. Witt consented to this plea deal under two strict conditions. First, you stay away from his wife. Second, you resign from the sheriff's office. I advise you to do both."

"Let me tell you something disturbing about Mrs. Witt, something I just found out."

"Doesn't matter, Andrew. Sonny's made up his mind. He wants this mess over and done and out of the media."

Yancy said, "No, Monty. Let's go to trial."

"You'll lose," Montenegro said mildly. "You'll be mauled. Slaughtered. Eviscerated. The jury will despise you. And guess what? They won't need testimony from a naughty spouse. They've got the injured victim and, literally, a boat-load of eyewitnesses. You've seen those videos taken by the cruise-ship passengers, right? Dude, you're toast."

The fact couldn't be disputed. Yancy said, "Forget what I said about Bonnie."

"Forgotten. But I'm not done with the good news."

"Your words, not mine."

"You've still got a job, Andrew, at almost the same salary." Montenegro lowered his voice. "Sonny arranged it. Be sure to thank him."

"A job doing what?"

"This is where I'm counting on you to keep an open mind."

"Oh boy," said Yancy, laughing softly in despair.

It had not been his finest moment. He'd found a shaded parking spot under a banyan tree on Front Street, where he'd spent an hour tidying up the Crown Vic. The vacuum device at issue wasn't a Hoover, as incorrectly reported by the newspapers, but rather a 14.4-volt Black & Decker cordless model with a rotating nozzle and superior suction.

Nor had the assault been premeditated. Yancy, having spotted Bonnie and her husband walking down the sidewalk, hunkered low in the front seat to avoid being seen. As they passed, he overheard arguing. In a reedy voice Dr. Clifford Witt called his wife either a tramp or a whore, at which point Yancy was certain Bonnie let out a wounded sob. She later would dispute the reason for her tears, blaming a dubiously documented allergy to night-blooming jasmine.

In any event, a misplaced sense of chivalry launched Yancy from the car and – with the vacuum in hand – he followed the quarreling couple to Mallory Square, where they began shouting at each other. Yancy later insisted that Clifford Witt had raised a fist toward his wife although Bonnie, somewhat unhelpfully, denied it.

The attack was swift and Witt was caught flat-footed. Being younger and stronger, Yancy easily pinned the doctor and yanked down his linen trousers. Tourists from the cruise liners assumed the two men were rowdy buskers, for which the city docks are famous, and whipped out cell phones to record the amusing playlet. Despite the authenticity of Witt's screams, nobody moved to disarm Yancy. The Black & Decker snorkeled mercilessly until its batteries petered out.

As officers led him away, Yancy watched Bonnie tend to her fallen husband. A local juggler offered a festive beach umbrella, which was positioned modestly over the appliance sprouting from Clifford Witt's marbled buttocks. Afterward Yancy felt truly awful.

"I admit it – I went totally batshit," he said to Sonny Summers. "It'll never happen again."

"Dr. Witt thought a trial would be embarrassing for everybody – him, his wife, you and the sheriff's department. He did us all a huge favor by going along with this plea."

"Except I lose my badge."

"But not your freedom. You should be celebrating. Monty told you to take the deal, right?"

"Please don't fire me, Sonny."

"What you did to Dr. Witt – I'm sorry, but that's totally unacceptable behavior for a detective, especially in a public venue," the sheriff said. "Did you see the editorial in the *Citizen*? They'd rip me to shreds if I cut you a break."

"But you owe me one, remember? For taking that rotting arm all the way to Miami, just 'cause you didn't want to deal with the case."

"I appreciate that, too. Which is why I made sure you have another job."

"So I lost my mind for five lousy minutes. You've seen

what Bonnie Witt looks like? Now imagine her dancing around your kitchen wearing nothing but dive booties. Sonny, I was possessed!"

The sheriff shrugged one shoulder. "Her husband's connected, Andrew. He's biopsied half the county commissioners. You were lucky Dickinson didn't charge you with sodomy."

"What if I told you the On switch got stuck."

"It took us a month before YouTube agreed to pull those nasty clips."

"Fine, I get it." Yancy surrendered to the inevitable. "So, what's my new gig?"

"A good one, under the radar."

"But just until things cool off, right?"

"Sure, Andrew."

Yancy surveyed the items on the sheriff's desk: a glass leaping-dolphin paperweight from the Kiwanis Club, an oversized Rubik's Cube, a MacBook, a coffee mug from *America's Most Wanted* and a half dozen photographs featuring Mrs. Summers and their three children, the youngest of whom wore in every frame the hollow stare of a future serial killer.

"Do you enjoy a good meal?" Sonny Summers said. "The reason I ask is you're pretty thin. Unlike some of us, right?" He patted his gut and chuckled.

"I like to eat, sure."

"But you probably go out a lot, being single and all. You know where I'm headed with this?"

"No fucking clue, Sonny."

"Your new job – it's an enforcement position."

"But not *law* enforcement."

"Next best thing," the sheriff said.

Yancy said, "I'm begging you."

Sonny Summers winked. "Restaurant inspector – it's like a paid vacation, Andrew."

Yancy's jaw made a popping sound. "Roach patrol?"

"They had an opening, so I made a call. The other fella, he got sick and quit."

"He died, Sonny."

"Okay, he died. But first he got sick."

Yancy rose slowly. "I really don't know what to say."

"Thanks is enough. By the way, we'll need your Glock and the keys to the Crown Vic."

Because Sonny Summers technically was no longer his boss, Yancy thought it might be entertaining to tell him the truth about the severed arm – that the Miami medical examiner had rejected custody and now it reposed back in Sonny's jurisdiction, among the Popsicles and grouper fillets in Yancy's kitchen freezer.

Instead, all Yancy said was: "When do I start?"

He was born in South Miami and raised in Homestead. His father was a ranger at Everglades National Park and his mother worked in the dock store at Flamingo. Yancy grew up on the water and dreamed of becoming a backcountry charter guide until he realized it would require almost daily contact with tourists. When Yancy was eighteen, his dad put in for a transfer to Yellowstone and Yancy chose to stay behind. The young man was anchored to Florida, for better or worse. A passion for tarpon fishing prolonged his education but eventually he earned a degree in criminal justice and wound up with the Miami Police Department. His marriage to a robbery detective named Celia expired when she accepted a job in Ann Arbor and again Yancy refused to move. They had no children, only a hyperactive border collie that had failed to bond with Yancy despite his earnest efforts. Usually dogs adored him so he was glad to see this one go, though not so much his wife.

For consolation he bought a secondhand Hell's Bay skiff with a ninety-horse outboard. He still had it, and after his dispiriting sit-down with the sheriff he spent the afternoon poling down the oceanside flats. The tide was all wrong but Yancy didn't care. A light sea breeze nudged the boat across crystal shallows, past eagle rays and lemon sharks and an ancient loggerhead turtle, half-blind and thorned with barnacles. It was a perfect afternoon, though he didn't cast at a single fish.

When Yancy returned home he saw a cream-colored Suburban parked in front of the soon-to-be mansion next door. A well-dressed man, stumpy in stature, stood in the future portico. He was slapping at bugs and speaking with agitation into a cell phone. Yancy recognized him as the owner.

The man, whose name was Evan Shook, soon came to the fence. "Excuse me," he said.

Yancy was hosing the salt rime off his boat. He nodded in a false neighborly way.

"There's a dead raccoon in my house," Evan Shook reported with gravity.

"Not good," Yancy said.

"It's huge and it's starting to rot."

Yancy winced sympathetically.

"Could you help me dump it somewhere? I've got people on their way to look at the place. They flew all the way from Dallas."

"Did you call Animal Control?" Yancy asked.

"Lazy pricks, they won't come out here till tomorrow. I could seriously use a hand."

Yancy shut off the hose. "Here's the thing. It's really bad luck to disturb a dead animal, and I can't afford any more of that."

Evan Shook frowned. "Bad luck? Come on."

"Like a Gypsy curse, which is not what I need at the moment. But you can borrow my shovel."

"The damn thing reeks to high hell!"

Yancy changed the subject. "That's quite the Taj Mahal you're building."

"Seven thousand square feet. Tallest house on the island."

"I can believe it."

"You know anybody who might be looking to buy, now's the time to go big!" Up close, Evan Shook's cheekbones appeared to have been buffed with a shammy. When a black Town Car rolled up to the cul-de-sac, he said, "Oh shit."

The driver opened the rear door and out came an older couple, ruddy and squinting. Evan Shook hurried to intercept them.

Yancy wiped down the skiff and went inside. The Barbancourt was gone so he poured himself a Captain and Coke. He wasn't in the practice of collecting roadkill but he'd spotted the misfortunate raccoon that morning along Key Deer Boulevard. Why leave it for the birds?

From the refrigerator he took a package of hamburger patties and two ripe tomatoes, which he placed on the counter. He turned down the AC, cranked up Little Feat on the stereo and looked out the kitchen window.

Next door, Evan Shook was attempting to herd the perplexed Texans back to their Town Car. Apparently the tallest house on Big Pine was not being shown today.

Four

Yancy received his first bribe offer at a tin-roofed seafood joint on Stock Island called Stoney's Crab Palace, where he had documented seventeen serious health violations, including mouse droppings, rat droppings, chicken droppings, a tick nursery, open vats of decomposing shrimp, lobsters dating back to the first Bush presidency and, on a tray of baked oysters, a soggy condom.

The owner's name was Brennan. He was slicing plantains when Yancy delivered the feared verdict: "I've got to shut you down."

"A hundred bucks says you won't."

"Jesus, is that blood on your knife?"

"Okay, two hundred bucks," said Brennan.

"Why aren't you wearing gloves?" Yancy asked.

Brennan continued slicing. "Nilsson never gave me no trouble. He ate here all the time."

"And died of hepatitis."

"He ate for free. That was our deal. Six years, never

once did he step foot in my kitchen. Nilsson was a good man."

"Nilsson was a lazy fuckwhistle," Yancy said. "I'm writing you up."

Working for the Division of Hotels and Restaurants was the worst job he'd ever had. His appetite had disappeared the first morning, and in three weeks he'd lost eleven pounds. It was traumatizing to see how many ways food could be defiled. His first sighting of maggots put him off rice pudding forever. The opening of lobster season brought no joy because Yancy couldn't bring himself to order from a menu a crustacean of unknown provenance; all he thought about, day and night, was salmonella.

The only reason Brennan wasn't arrested for attempted bribery was that Yancy didn't want to wait around for a deputy to show up. He couldn't clear out of Stoney's fast enough. For lunch he drove home and boiled a potato.

Rogelio Burton stopped by. He looked Yancy up and down and said, "God, what do you weigh?"

"I'm down to a buck sixty."

"And you're, what, six foot two? That ain't healthy, bro."

Yancy picked up a fork and went to work on the potato. "You want half?"

Burton pulled up a stool at the kitchen counter. "The reason I came, Sonny sent me. What'd you ever do with that . . . you know . . . arm?"

"I made it into a weathervane. It's on top of my roof."

"Andrew, this is for real."

"I've still got the damn thing."

"Good. That's what I figured."

"How is that good? I'm breaking about a half dozen laws."

Burton said, "A woman came in the other day to report her husband missing in a boating accident. He fits the general description."

"Took her long enough."

"She was in Europe for a month. Her old man was heading to the Bahamas to meet some buddies on a fishing trip. The Coast Guard found debris from his Contender a few miles off Marathon. A friend of the widow's had caught the story on Channel 7 about the *Misty* snagging a body part. Anyway, you see the problem."

Yancy did see the problem. He had a human arm in his freezer that shouldn't be there. "So, take it back to Dr. Rawlings," he said. "He can swab for DNA and close the case, or not."

"Way ahead of you. Rawlings saved a tissue sample from the day it got caught. Definitely the same dude. The wife brought in some shavings from her husband's nose-hair trimmer – Rawlings said it's a ninety-nine percent match."

"So what's the hitch?"

Burton took a beer from the refrigerator. "She wants the fucking arm, Andrew. She wants a church service and a formal burial, the whole show."

"And that she shall have." With a screwdriver Yancy began chiseling the limb from the freezer, where it was wedged among a pile of Stouffer's dinners. He placed the frosty appendage on the countertop in front of Burton and said, "All yours, amigo."

The detective used an elbow to push it away. "Rawlings won't take it back because the paperwork says it's at the coroner's in Miami. Now you get the picture? The widow went up there and, of course, they had no body pieces that belonged to her husband."

Yancy heard a door slam and looked outside. A van from Animal Control had parked in front of the half-finished house next door.

"The sheriff was highly pissed with you," Burton went on, "till I explained what happened, how the ME up there wouldn't take the case. I told him there was a chance you kept the arm."

"Lucky I did," Yancy said.

"For safekeeping."

"No, Rog, for taxidermy practice."

"Let me call him." Burton finished off his beer and went out the front door to phone Sonny Summers.

Yancy returned the severed member to its chamber among the frozen entrées. Whenever he'd thought about getting rid of it, the cop in him had said no, what if there'd been a murder, not an accident? Or what if it *was* a drowned Cuban rafter, and somebody's brother or sister in Hialeah was waiting for word? Now that the mystery was solved, Yancy was glad he hadn't followed Burton's advice and discarded it. An arm wasn't much for a wife to bury, but anything was better than an empty casket.

Through the window Yancy noticed unusual activity at the empty construction site. A uniformed officer was dragging a heavy black garbage bag across the pavers toward the Animal Control van. The officer wore a white medical mask, protective goggles and blue rubber gloves that came up to his elbows.

Burton came back inside and said everything was cool. "Sonny's telling the widow that you're the 'authorized custodian' of unclaimed remains. He said just give her the thing."

"That's it?"

"And try to behave, Andrew. She just lost her hubby."

"You ever eat at Stoney's?"

"Man, I love that place. The widow's name is Stripling – here, have her sign this."

Burton produced a Release of Property form that had been conceived with more prosaic items in mind than a severed limb – wallets, car keys, jewelry, eyeglasses, articles of clothing. Somebody had already checked the box labeled "Other."

"Does she keep a copy?" Yancy asked.

"Hell, no. In fact, once she's gone, throw away the paper. It's just for show."

"Gotcha."

Yancy said, "I get major brownie points for this, right? Sonny knows I saved his ass from a major lawsuit, not to mention some ugly press. Losing a dead man's arm!"

"You gotta stay cool."

"Tell him I want my desk back. Tell him I'm wasting away on roach patrol."

"He hasn't forgot about you," Burton said.

"Randolph Nilsson fucking died from this job!"

"Eat lots of yogurt, Andrew. Find a flavor you like."

His next stop after lunch was a Burger King. Compared to Stoney's, the place was as immaculate as a surgical suite. Yancy saw one of the cooks sneeze into a Whopper but the manager made him throw it away, so Yancy didn't write him up.

After a half-hearted inspection he sat down in a booth, where he aimed to kill the whole afternoon. With dull resolve he re-read the state's lengthy checklist of critical code violations.

Did the restaurant obtain its food from an "approved" source? Was it cooked at the proper temperature? Stored at the proper temperature? Handled with minimum contact? Did the employees wash their hands after taking a dump? Were all the restrooms equipped with self-closing doors? Was there toilet paper? Did they wash the dishes in hot water? Did they properly clean and sanitize all food contact surfaces? Were there signs of rodents or insects? Unsafe electrical wiring? Uncapped toxic substances? Did the restaurant have a current state license, and was it prominently displayed?

The manager of the Burger King hovered fretfully. He brought Yancy a cup of coffee, which Yancy insisted on paying for.

"Everything okay?" he asked.

"Relax, sport," Yancy said. "You passed with flying colors."

"Yes!" The manager, who was all of twenty-five, pumped a fist and spun a circle on one heel.

Yancy asked if he'd heard the sad news about Nilsson.

"Who?"

"The guy that had this job before me."

The manager shrugged apologetically. "We never saw him, sir."

"Of course not," Yancy said.

"What happened?"

"He passed away. Mind if I hang out for a while?"

Yancy took out a Margaret Atwood paperback Bonnie had given him. It was highly entertaining, and every now and then he would come to a dog-eared page upon which Bonnie had scribbled comments in the margins:

So funny!

So true!

Why can't I be like this?

Foolishly, Yancy dissected every marked passage in the hopes of finding clues to Bonnie's innermost feelings. On some pages he'd spy a slanted notation, always in lavender ink, that referred to their own relationship, or to him by name.

Sounds like something A.Y. would say.

Pure Andrew!

Just like a certain man I know.

No matter what the context, Yancy was warmed to be in Bonnie's thoughts, and also to know that she obviously wasn't sharing the book with her husband. On a whim he dialed her cell phone and left a lustful message that he hoped would make her blush. She hadn't spoken to him since that quickie in the 4Runner.

The manager brought a plate of fries, which Yancy accepted along with a refill on the coffee. By Keys standards it could hardly be considered a payoff. His phone thrummed and lit up, and so did his heart.

But it wasn't Bonnie calling.

"My name is Eve Stripling. Are you Detective Yancy?"

"Actually, it's Inspector Yancy." As in roach inspector.

"Sheriff Summers gave me your number."

She sounded fairly young. The accent was flat, midwestern.

Yancy said, "I'm sorry for your loss, Mrs. Stripling."

"Yes, it's awful, just awful. Where's the best place to meet up?"

Before Evan Shook's bulldozers razed the lot next door, Yancy went outside almost every evening to watch the white-tailed Key deer nibble on the hammock scrub and red mangroves. They were fantastically small and delicate-looking; even a buck was no bigger than a golden retriever. Only a few hundred of the deer remained, roaming a handful of islands. Big Pine and No Name Key had the most, but the animals were hapless when it came to avoiding cars, especially at night. Every year the *Citizen* published a gloomy scorecard of roadkills as the species teetered toward extinction. Not everyone shared Yancy's fondness for his four-legged neighbors; signs urging motorists to watch out for the critters were sometimes found spray-painted as rifle sights.

Ninety-two hundred acres had been patched together as a refuge for the remaining deer. Being unable to read, they frequently meandered beyond its boundaries. Some had become recklessly tame, mooching handouts from tourists and losing all fear of humans. Yancy never fed the small herd that appeared at dusk on the land beside his own. He didn't snap pictures, or whistle, or make up cute names for the fawns. He just sat there sipping rum and watching the deer do their thing.

Now they were gone, and Evan Shook's spec house was fucking up the sunset.

Yancy trudged inside and transferred the severed arm from his freezer to the Igloo cooler. He then toted the cooler to his personal 1993 Subaru – the roomy Crown Vic having been reassigned to a working detective – and drove to the Winn-Dixie supermarket. There he purchased two large bags of ice to make sure the limb belonging to Eve Stripling's late husband didn't thaw during her drive back home, wherever that might be.

She arrived at the store a half hour late driving a generic

Malibu. To Yancy it looked like a rental. He was leaning against the front fender of his car, sporting a red baseball cap so she could locate him in the parking lot.

"This feels like a dope deal," she said with a nervous smile. "You *are* Inspector Yancy, right?"

"And you must be Mrs. Stripling."

"Eve is fine." She was in her mid-thirties, slightly on the heavy side. The outfit was gold-strapped sandals, tight white jeans and a long-sleeved blue cotton top. Her auburn hair was tied back and her pale nose was freckled. All this Yancy could see by the light of the grocery store.

"Guess I should have a look," she said.

"You sure about that?"

"It's all I got, all that's left of my sweet Nicky."

Yancy set the cooler on the warm hood of the Malibu and removed the lid. Fortunately, the parking lot wasn't crowded. He untaped the bubble wrapping to expose the arm.

The upraised middle finger was the first thing to greet Eve Stripling.

"Who's the comedian?" She was clutching her elbows to her midsection, as if trying to stop herself from spinning into orbit.

"That's how they found it," Yancy told her. "Weird, I know."

She managed a brittle laugh. "Maybe it was Nicky flipping off the sharks."

"Is that his wedding band?"

"I'm pretty sure." She held her breath and leaned close to examine the stiffened purple hand. "You got a flashlight?"

Yancy had one in the Subaru. The batteries were weak but he shook it until the bulb lit up.

Eve Stripling gave a heavy nod. "That's his ring. It's most definitely him."

She didn't comment on the etiolated band of skin where her husband's watch had been, which surprised Yancy. Earlier he'd received a phone call from comely Dr. Campesino in Miami. Apparently the pathologist wasn't completely put off by Yancy's incompetent flirting, for in her spare time she'd digitally enlarged her photograph of the rectangular outline on the wrist of the phantom limb. In that way she was able through online resources to identify the missing watch as a limited-edition Wyler Genève Tourbillon, distinguishable by a unique clasped crown shield and also for its suggested retail price of $145,000. Yancy had assumed that the loss of such an expensive timepiece would catch the notice of a widow, even in the throes of grief. But Eve Stripling said nothing, so Yancy left the subject untouched.

A radish-eyed old geezer in hiking books walked by, pushing a grocery cart. He saw the two of them looking into the cooler and piped, "You catch some fish?"

"Lobsters," Yancy said.

"How much you want for 'em?"

"Not for sale."

"Don't be a dick."

Yancy took out the dead arm and waved it at the old man, who shuffled off quickly. Eve Stripling wore an expression of suppressed dismay. After repacking the limb, Yancy placed the cooler in the trunk of the Chevy.

He said, "What was Nick's line of work?"

Now on a first-name basis with the victim.

"Oh, he's retired."

Just like Johnny Mendez, Yancy thought, although Nick

Stripling probably hadn't made his fortune looting a Crime Stoppers account.

"Did they ever find his boat?"

"Just some cushions and spare gas cans," Eve Stripling said. "Also a deflated life raft – they said it must've got popped by fish hooks."

"Was there a fuel slick?"

"Yeah, five miles off the Sombrero Lighthouse. His body floated south, obviously."

"Anybody else on board?"

"No, just Nicky. He was on his way to Cay Sal to catch up with some friends."

A mosquito was feasting in a dimple on Eve Stripling's chin. Under more casual circumstances Yancy would have reached over and flicked it away. Instead he said, "The bugs are out of control tonight. Let's sit in the car."

"I should really be going."

"This won't take much longer."

"But the sheriff promised—"

"Just a couple more questions. All routine." That's what detectives did, they asked questions. Yancy meant to stay in practice.

He opened the door for Eve Stripling, then went around and got in the passenger side. The new smell confirmed it was a rental.

"How far's your drive?" he asked.

"Miami Beach."

A short hop not to bring your own wheels, Yancy thought, but he let it go. She'd probably rented the Chevy because she was afraid her husband's dead arm would stink up the Jaguar. "Was Nick a good swimmer?"

"So-so. He loved that damn fishing boat, though."

46

"How old was he?"

"Forty-six. We've got a condo on Duck Key," Eve Stripling said, "but I was in Paris when it happened."

"When did you learn he was missing?"

"The France trip was a present from Nicky. I wasn't worried when I didn't hear from him because he hardly ever calls from the islands. The cell service over there is suck-o. He was supposed to get home the Sunday after I did. When he didn't show up, I just figured the fishing must be super good and he'd decided to stay. Why aren't you writing any of this down?"

"Like I said, it's just routine."

"So, anyway, Wednesday comes and still no Nicky. That's when I started calling around and the Coast Guard told me what they found. They said it was super rough that weekend and his boat probably swamped."

"That happens."

"He called it *Summer's Eve*," she said fondly, "after me."

Also the name of a douche, thought Yancy. But, hey, it's the thought that counts.

"Are we done?" she asked.

"Almost." From a breast pocket he took the Release of Property form that Burton had given him. Eve Stripling switched on the dome light so she could read it.

"How long were you married?" Yancy asked.

"Seven years in February." She turned her head to show him the diamond studs in her ears. They were substantial. "He bought me these for our anniversary."

"Sweet. Do you have children?"

"Nicky has a grown daughter." She signed the paper and handed it back to him. "This still doesn't seem real," she said in a raw, whispery voice.

"When's the service?"

"Day after tomorrow."

"Soon, then."

"The funeral home says there's not much to do. Being it's just, you know, an arm."

"They can fix that middle finger, no problem."

Eve Stripling looked puzzled.

"Not that you'd have an open casket," Yancy added. "But just in case . . . "

"Oh, right. Good idea."

He got out of the car. "Again, I'm sorry for your loss."

"Thank you, Inspector."

Behind the wheel Eve Stripling appeared smaller and almost contorted. With a shudder she hunched forward, squeezing her eyes closed, and it was Yancy's impression that she was trying very hard to cry.

Five

Miguel was no beekeeper; he made that clear. He was an exterminator of bees, a highly trained assassin.

"Tell me what you've got," Yancy said.

"There's an old wood house on Ramrod, the whole east wall. I am ripping it apart tomorrow."

"I hope the hive is large."

Miguel laughed, flashing a gold-tipped incisor. "The hive is a motherfucker, Andrew. You cannot believe how big."

"But how are you going to move the damn thing?"

"Don't worry. It is what you hire me for."

"And the bees will follow? That's the part I don't understand." Yancy had a vision of Miguel's truck weaving down Highway 1 while enclouded by a seething swarm.

"They sleep at night," Miguel said. "I got a system."

"Dead bees won't do the trick. They have to be alive."

Miguel gave a sigh he reserved for thick-skulled gringos. "For sure, Andrew. Alive."

"How much do you charge?"

"For such a fucked-up job? Three hundred, plus gas."

"I can probably swing two-fifty."

"Bullshit," Miguel said. Then: "Okay, two-fifty."

Yancy handed him a piece of paper with the address. Miguel glanced at it and said, "Who lives here?"

"Nobody. It's under construction."

"Excellent, my friend. Where you want me to put the hive?"

"The master bedroom would be lovely. It's on the top floor, facing the Gulf."

"No problem." Miguel took the cash from Yancy and counted it. "Here is the thing, Andrew, because I am what you call a straight shooter. When they find that mother-fucking hive, the people that own the house, I'm the one they gone to call first."

"Well, who else?" Yancy said.

"'Cause I'm the top bee guy from here to the Redlands."

"Everybody knows that, Miguel. Everybody." Yancy envied the man's pride in his work. "Shook is the owner's name. When he calls, I'm thinking maybe you could be tied up for a while – let those poor honeybees have some fun."

"I got so much fucking jobs right now, my wife she is ready to kill me."

"All right, then. Mr. Shook can wait." Yancy gave Miguel another twenty-dollar bill.

"You want, I'll email to you some pictures, Andrew. For proof."

"Not necessary, amigo. I'll know when it's done."

Miguel was grinning as Yancy got in his car. "You look sharp, man, all pimped out. Must be some world-class pussy waiting up on the mainland."

"Actually," said Yancy, "I'm going to a funeral."

*

50

A short death notice had been posted on the *Herald*'s website: Nicholas Joseph Stripling, age forty-six, of Miami Beach. Survived by his loving wife, Eve, and one daughter, Caitlin Cox. Private services to be held at the Neo-Pentecostal Church of Faith, followed by interment at the St. Lazarus Gardens and Water Park in North Miami.

North Miami!

The drive took almost four hours in manic traffic, Yancy cussing humanity most of the way. He owned one dreary black suit that he'd bought years earlier for his mother's service, and he hadn't worn it since. Now the coat hung too loosely on his frame, Yancy having dropped so much weight since becoming a restaurant sleuth. The paradox wasn't lost on him – he'd worked many bloody crime scenes and never once felt queasy, yet the glimpse of a desiccated rat carcass in a vat of stale muffin mix left him poleaxed with revulsion.

So far, the only good thing about the job was that nobody complained if he didn't show up. The restaurant owners were relieved not to be inspected, and they made no inquiries to Yancy's supervisor regarding his whereabouts.

His decision to skip work and attend Nicky Stripling's burial was out of character for two reasons. First, Yancy had always been a punctual public employee and, second, he strenuously avoided graveyards. A morgue full of chilled stiffs was no problem, but for some reason a field of sunlit tombstones gave him the willies.

Ever since meeting Eve Stripling, Yancy had been sleeping poorly, nagged by the missing pieces of her story – a story of no evident interest to anyone but him. It was an easy matter to feed Nick Stripling's name through the state crime computer, revealing a single arrest and conviction at the age of twenty-seven. The colorful details were in a file at the courthouse.

Young Nicky had had a minor role in a common Florida insurance scam in which fraudsters would intentionally crash cars into innocent drivers and then submit mountains of phony medical claims, which the victims' insurance companies almost always paid off. Stripling acted as the driver and was skilled at directing each staged collision with such finesse – front bumper angled into a rear rocker panel, the impact buffered by a subtle last-second deceleration – that neither he nor any of his co-conspirators received so much as a knot on the head. Whiplash was the faked injury of choice because of its domino cascade of serial billings and easy profits. The lineup of complicit health-care providers included an alcoholic chiropractor, a senile orthopedist, an unlicensed radiologist and a battalion of nonexistent physical therapists. Nick Stripling's take for each crash was relatively paltry, so he'd turned state's witness at the first prodding from investigators. He ended up getting ninety days in the county jail and five years' probation.

From such inauspicious beginnings Stripling was somehow able to retire in his forties. Yancy was curious to know the secret of the man's prosperous turnaround.

No more than fifty hardy souls showed up for the funeral in a baking summer heat that undulated off the bright green grass. Yancy feared he might sweat through his suit. Eve Stripling wore a black dress, black heels and a veil. She sat in the shade under the canopy before a walnut coffin piled with wreaths. Yancy wondered if the mortician had pro-rated his embalming fee, since there was only one limb to bury.

A young blond woman, also dressed in black, sat at the opposite end of the first row. Yancy assumed she was Caitlin Cox, Nick Stripling's daughter from a prior marriage. From her body language Yancy perceived that she wasn't enamored with her father's current wife. Wearing saucer-sized sunglasses, Caitlin Cox fanned herself and every so often whispered to her buzz-cut husband, who was built like a stevedore.

Yancy kept well back from the mourners and remained standing. Shielding his eyes from the sun, he noticed he wasn't alone; two other men were maintaining a practiced distance, and their suits were charcoal gray, not black. Law enforcement of some sort, Yancy guessed. They were sweaty, too. August in the city could wilt a soul.

A generic silver-haired preacher rose and said saintly things about Nick Stripling before the coffin was lowered. Eve Stripling stood up and thanked everyone for coming. She said she'd placed in Nick's casket a childhood Bible and his favorite speargun. To Yancy it seemed a bold hobby – spearfishing – for a mediocre swimmer, as Mrs. Stripling had described her late spouse when she came to collect his left arm.

After the mourners broke into small groups and headed for their cars, Yancy approached the two cop types and said, "Friends of the deceased?"

No response except barracuda stares. Both of the men had brown hair, light eyebrows and cinder-block chins.

"You must be feds," Yancy remarked.

"Don't be an asshole," said one.

"That's bad luck, swearing in a cemetery. Like a Gypsy curse."

The men turned to leave.

"Or maybe it's blowing each other in a cemetery," Yancy said. "I forget which."

He found himself dodging Eve Stripling, although she probably wouldn't have recognized him in a suit and a tie. While waiting for her limousine to depart, Yancy drifted off among the sun-bleached headstones. Almost immediately he came across some unlucky bastard who'd been born on Yancy's very own birthday and now lay six feet under. Yancy's respiration shallowed and his palms moistened and his skin felt like it was crawling with centipedes. He stumbled a few plots farther, dropped to one knee and upchucked on the final resting site of one Marlene Suzanne Moody, who by Yancy's quick calculation had passed away at age ninety-nine and was now safe from indignity.

After wiping his cheeks and smoothing the wrinkles from his pants, Yancy made his way back to the funeral canopy. Only Caitlin Cox and her husband remained at the grave. They stood shoulder to shoulder, saying nothing.

Yancy walked up and offered his condolences.

"Were you a friend of Dad's?" she asked.

"I'm Inspector Yancy, from the Keys. I was in charge of your father's remains."

He presented one of his old detective cards. He figured what the hell – his cell number hadn't changed. Caitlin's husband asked Yancy why he'd come to the burial.

"Sometimes, in these cases, the family has questions. I just wanted to be available."

It was a smooth response, caring yet professional. Yancy had polished the wording while waiting for the funeral procession to arrive.

Caitlin put his card in her handbag. A pair of cemetery attendants hung back on the edge of the shade. They weren't allowed to start shoveling the dirt over Nick Stripling's coffin until all the mourners were gone.

His daughter said, "I do have a question, Inspector."

Yancy liked the Scotland Yard-ish ring of his new title. "I'll do my best," he said.

"We peeked at it in the funeral home – Dad's arm."

Jesus, Yancy thought. *Don't tell me they were too lazy to fix the finger.*

"It happened during rigor mortis," he said.

Caitlin Stripling Cox seemed puzzled. "What on earth are you talking about?"

Her husband spoke up. "She means the wedding ring. Tell him, sweetheart."

"Eve switched it out," she said.

"The one I saw on your father's hand looked like platinum," Yancy said.

"That's right. And the one he's wearing now is yellow gold. Fourteen karat, *maybe*." The downgrade was reported with somber disdain.

"Is it possible Eve decided to keep the original ring for sentimental reasons?"

"Lots of stuff is possible." Caitlin frowned down at the casket. Yancy hoped she wasn't expecting him to pry open the lid and appraise the substitute wedding band.

"Why don't you ask Eve about it?"

"Because she hates me and I hate her. She's a vicious cunt, by the way."

Caitlin's husband said, "Sweetheart, please." His shirt collar was soaked, and a crystal droplet of perspiration clung to one of his earlobes. Yancy didn't stare.

"A vicious greedy lying cunt," elaborated Stripling's daughter.

"It's a rough time for everyone," Yancy said.

"Is that legal – taking his ring?"

"As his wife, she's entitled."

"She probably stole his goddamn watch, too!"

Caitlin Cox was in her early twenties. Yancy figured she must have been a baby when her old man was staging auto accidents to rip off insurance companies.

He said, "The watch was already gone when they found your father's arm."

"Are you still on the case, or what?"

"I was in charge of delivering the remains. Unless some new information turns up, there's not much else to be done."

Caitlin laughed acidly. "I told you so, Simon," she muttered sideways to her husband. "Nobody wants to investigate."

"Investigate what exactly?" Yancy asked.

"Eve killed him, Inspector. She murdered my father."

Simon Cox put an arm around his wife. "Okay, that's the Xanax talking. Let's go home, baby."

Yancy offered to meet with them later in private. Caitlin said there was no point. "Don't you see? She already got away with it!"

Her husband steered her away from the grave, Yancy following.

"What makes you think she killed him, Caitlin?"

"Oh, please."

"Did your dad say something about Eve? Was he unhappy in the marriage?"

Caitlin pulled free of Simon and spun around. "How the hell would I know if he was happy or not? I haven't talked to the sonofabitch in years."

*

56

The captain of the *Misty Momma IV* was Keith Fitzpatrick, a fourth-generation Conch. His father had smuggled ganja from Jamaica, his grandfather had shipped rum from Havana and his great-grandfather had salvaged wrecked schooners that had been lured by deviously placed torches to the unforgiving reefs of Key West. Keith Fitzpatrick himself was a renowned fish hawk, booked years in advance, and therefore satisfied to abide the law. He made good money because he ran a thirty-eight-footer with only one mate.

Yancy met him for a beer at the Half Shell Raw Bar on the harbor. The motto of the place was "Eat It Raw!" Tourists went berserk for the T-shirts.

Fitzpatrick said, "Andrew, I heard Sonny canned your ass."

"Temporarily."

"That sucks." Fitzpatrick's face was boot brown except for a white goggle stripe from his sunglasses. His forearms were like glazed cudgels, his hands scarred and scaly.

"They got me doing restaurant inspections," Yancy said.

"No way. You aren't the one that shut down Stoney's?"

"Listen, man, that kitchen – it was crawling with *every-thing*. So gross."

"I love that place," said Fitzpatrick.

Yancy placed the small gray shark tooth on the bar.

Fitzpatrick picked it up between a thumb and forefinger and turned it in the light. "Nuthin' special," he said.

"What kind is it?"

"Looks like a bonnethead. Maybe a baby lemon."

"But not a bull shark or a tiger, right?"

Fitzpatrick shook his head and chuckled. "Not this little runt, no."

"That's what I think, too," said Yancy.

Bonnetheads, the smallest species of hammerheads, averaged only about three feet in length. It was unlikely that any shark so small would be far offshore feeding on a human body, competing with the monsters.

"Where'd the tooth come from, Andrew?"

"That arm you snagged."

"No shit?" Fitzpatrick examined it once more. "Don't make sense, unless the dead guy's boat sunk in the shallows. Which I heard he went down off Sombrero Light."

"Let's say he drowned in deep water and the body washed up on a flat."

"*What* flat?"

"Let's just say."

"Still don't explain how his whole arm got twisted off the way it did," said Fitzpatrick. "I never seen a bonnethead could do that. You?"

"Nope. I don't believe it's possible."

"So what is it you think happened? Tell me."

"I'm not sure."

"But Sonny's keepin' you on the case."

Yancy gave a misleading wink. "Let's not advertise it. Want another beer?" He ordered a couple more Budweisers.

Fitzpatrick asked if other body pieces had been found. "A leg or a head? Whatever."

"Nothing but that arm."

They were interrupted by a pushy fellow in a papaya polo shirt who recognized Fitzpatrick from a fishing website and wanted to go "load up" on mahi the next day. Fitzpatrick said he was booked until the Second Coming, but he provided the name of another charter captain.

When they were alone again, Fitzpatrick turned to Yancy and said, "How you doing on roach patrol? It's got to be different."

"Look at me." Yancy flapped his shirt collar to display his new pencil neck. "Every time I walk into a joint, all I can think about is maybe some guy in the kitchen is greasing his ass with the pizza dough. Crazy shit like that, swear to God. I can barely stand the sight of food."

"Come on, man, you gotta eat. Let's get some conch fritters."

"Go for it. I'm full."

"Promise me you won't shut this place down, too. I'm dead serious – you'd start a damn riot."

Yancy said, "You knew Randolph Nilsson, right? The last guy who had my job."

"Yeah, he was married to my second wife's third cousin. Or maybe it was my third wife's second cousin. Anyhow, I'm the one scattered his ashes out by the Mud Keys. He was only fifty-three at the end. But life ain't fair, right?"

"No, Keith, it's not."

Two more bottles of beer appeared on the bar counter, along with a platter of raw oysters. Fitzpatrick turned to scout the room, which had filled with lobster people and locals. His gaze fixed on a rangy, black-haired kid sitting beside a hard-looking blonde at a corner table. The kid wore a tight T-shirt and a scraggly pubic goatee. In his mouth bobbed an unlit cigarette, and both arms were extravagantly tattooed in a Neptunian motif. He gave Fitzpatrick a smirking salute, and the captain nodded back.

"Who's the Tommy Lee impersonator?" Yancy asked.

"He used to mate for me," Fitzpatrick said, "till a couple weeks ago."

"What boat is he on now?"

"The S.S. *Jackoff*."

"Gotcha."

"Mr. Charles Phinney, he don't need to work no more. Or so he informed me the night he quit. This was after I chewed him out for not hosin' off the tackle and wipin' down the teak. He says, 'Fuck you, old man, you can stuff this shitty job.'"

"Now he's buying you beer and oysters," Yancy said, "and dating hookers."

"Showin' off is all. He said he come into serious money, but that could mean he won eighty-five bucks on the Lotto scratch-off. Now all of a sudden he's Donald fucking Trump."

Yancy was fond of shellfish but he couldn't even look at the plate. It was tragic, what his new job was doing to him. "Was Phinney working on the *Misty* the day you caught the dead arm?"

"He was," Fitzpatrick said. "That useless sonofabitch couldn't even get it unhooked."

When Yancy looked back, the kid and the prostitute were heading for the door. Fitzpatrick slurped an oyster. He said, "Took me a month to teach that fucking retard how to rig a bait."

"You'll hear from him again."

"Don't say that, Andrew."

"When the money runs out, he'll come begging to get back on the *Misty*."

Two gunshots rang out from the parking lot. A woman began shrieking Phinney's name.

"Or maybe not," Yancy said.

Six

The typical Key West murder is a drunken altercation over debts, dope or dance partners. Premeditated robbery-homicides are rare because they require a level of planning and sober enterprise seldom encountered among the island's indolent felons.

Charles Phinney was already dead when Yancy reached his side. He lay fish-eyed and soaked with blood, the pockets of his black jeans jerked inside out. His companion, who turned out not to be a hooker, said the killer rolled up on a blue moped, shot Phinney twice, stole his cash and took off. She said the man wore a camo sun mask and a red or orange rain poncho, which would have drawn notice anywhere except Margaret Street on a Friday night.

Because of the location of the crime, the city police – not the sheriff's office – would be handling the investigation. Uniformed officers taped off the intersection at Caroline and kept the crowd back while a paramedic pounded for show on Phinney's chest. Keith Fitzpatrick, whose leathery face had drained to gray, hung around until the kid's body was loaded into an ambulance. Then he said he was going home to drink himself to sleep.

Yancy remained at the scene with Phinney's girlfriend. Her name was Madeline and she worked at a T-shirt shop on Duval. She said the shop was owned by Russian gangsters, and that's who killed Phinney.

"They must've heard him braggin' about the money," she said.

Yancy asked how much he was carrying.

"Thousand bucks, maybe."

"Where'd he get it?"

"A job." Madeline sniffed and looked away. Tears streaked her chalky makeup.

Yancy said, "What was he dealing – coke? Meth?"

Madeline turned back with a narrow look. "You a cop or something?"

"I'm on sabbatical." Which was true enough.

She wiped her eyes. "I never seen anybody get shot before. Goddamn." She said she and Phinney had been dating only a month or so. "He was selling pot," she added.

Yancy noticed her reading his reaction, trying to figure out if he believed her.

He said, "So what happened was he made a big score and quit his job on the *Misty*."

"Yeah. Exactly."

"And you really think your bosses killed him for a grand?"

Madeline seemed to be reconsidering her theory. "Will I have to, like, go to court?"

"If there's a trial, sure."

"Thing is, Charlie was talkin' all over town. The Russians

weren't the only ones knew he had a wad." She shrugged. "Could've been anybody that shot him."

Yancy overheard one of the city detectives say that the blue moped was a rental. It had already been found, abandoned in an alley off Southard.

"I can't afford to lose my job," Madeline said. She wore her bleached hair in a spiky crop. Her hands were rough and her eyes were old-looking. Yancy figured she had fifteen years on Phinney.

"You got a smoke?" she said. "I'm comin' apart here."

"I quit a long time ago. Sorry."

"Oh. You're one of *them*."

Yancy picked a virgin Marlboro off the pavement. It was the same one Phinney was mouthing when he'd walked out of the oyster bar, the one he had paused to light when the robber on the moped shot him.

Madeline took the dead man's cigarette from Yancy's hand and said, "Why the hell not?"

That same night, 264 miles away, a man on the eastern coast of Andros Island lightly tapped on the door of a woman known as the Dragon Queen. When she let him in, the man, whose name was Neville, said, "I need some woo-doo on a white mon."

The Dragon Queen sat down in a flaking wicker chair. "What de hell's wrong wit your boy dere? He dont look right."

"Dot's not my boy," Neville said. "Dot's a monkey I look ahfta."

He'd won the animal in a game of dominoes with a sponger from Fresh Creek. The sponger told him it was the same monkey from the Johnny Depp pirate movies, which were filmed nearby in the Exumas. Neville named his new pet Driggs and he fed him too much deep-fried food. Before long the monkey got wrinkled and tufts of fur began falling out. He defiantly refused housebreaking so Neville made him wear disposable baby diapers with holes cut out for his tail. Now the nearly hairless creature was hugging Neville's left leg and chittering in dread of the voodoo woman.

She rocked forward to squint. "He sure dont favor you, suh. Bettuh talk to de missus and find out who she been messin' wit, ha!"

Neville let it go. The Dragon Queen was either far-sighted or wasted, possibly both.

"Who dis white devil you wish to be rid of?" she asked.

"He go by de name Chrissofer."

Neville presented a bottle of Bacardi 8, which he had traded for a bucket of conch meat and two hogfish with the captain of a yacht anchored in the South Bight. It was well known that the Dragon Queen was partial to good rum.

"You got any ting belongs to dis mon?"

"Piece a shoyt." Neville unfolded a teal-colored part of a sports shirt of the vented style that American sportsmen wore to the bonefish lodges. Neville had recovered the fragment from Christopher's garbage can.

He said, "I want you pudda spell on 'im."

The Dragon Queen had a pink batik scarf swirled round her head, and a necklace strung with polished bivalves. She took the piece of the white man's shirt and sniffed it.

"I do dis ting fuh you, he might go'n die," she said.

Neville thought about it. "Whatever God's will."

"Where de white mon aht?"

"Bannister Point. Dey said yestuhdey he go eat lunch aht de conch shack in Rocky Town. 'Im and his woman."

"He like dot place, huh?" The Dragon Queen opened the rum and filled a stained coffee mug. She didn't offer any to Neville, which was fine. He was nervous being in the same house, her house, because of her reputation as a wanton man-eater. Three of her much younger boyfriends had fallen dead under murky circumstances. A fourth had fled Andros, supposedly to Cuba. Neville concentrated on avoiding the Dragon Queen's gaze, which was said to bewitch even the strongest of men.

She asked about Christopher's woman. "A white lady?"

"Yeah," Neville said. "She come 'n' go."

"Wot her name?"

"I dunno. She keep to huhself, same as 'im."

"So, tell me why you wish bod fuh dis mon." The Dragon Queen was smiling now. She had a mashed-up nose and the overbite of an ancient tortoise.

Neville said, "Juss so he get off de island, no matter how."

"All right, suh."

She traced her callused brown fingers along the strip of fabric, which was coiled like a boa in her lap. "He not a Bahamian, dis white devil. He not from Freeport or Abaco."

"No, ma'am, dot's true. He from de States."

"Den woo-doo must be extra strong. Cost more, too, you unnerstahn."

"All right."

"Bring me nodder bottle a rum."

Neville nodded. "Dot I will."

"And next time, you stay 'round to keep me comp'ny. But not tonight." The Dragon Queen pointed to the door.

Neville's heart was hammering as he got on his bike and pedaled away down the scraped coral path. The diapered monkey, riding on Neville's head, maintained his perch by clinging fiercely to Neville's ears. His tiny fingertips were moist and the nails felt sharp. Neville was grateful for the moonlight that helped him find his way.

Desperation had driven him to visit the voodoo lady. The white man named Christopher was planning to put up a resort for rich tourists on a stretch of waterfront where Neville lived, where his father and grandfather had lived before him. Recently Neville had been ordered to pack up and move. A letter was delivered saying his half-sister in Canada had sold the family property on Andros and upon closing would send Neville his share of the proceeds, which he didn't want.

What he wanted was to live and die on the beach, under the shade of casuarinas.

Nobody at the government office in Lizard Cay or even Nassau could straighten out the situation, so with trepidation Neville had turned to the Dragon Queen. He was unaware that his problem lay beyond her supernatural powers and was in fact connected to faraway criminal events in the Florida Keys, including the cold-blooded murder that very evening of a foolhardy boat mate named Charles Phinney.

Neville's bicycle jounced off a rocky divot as he coasted downhill, and a sharp pinch of pain caused him to cry out. "Bod monkey! Bod monkey!"

But the frightened animal kept his teeth buried in Neville's scalp until they skidded to a stop in front of the house.

Yancy got home around midnight and rolled a joint. The stuff was called Trainwreck yet it failed to knock him into a proper stupor. Although he'd seen a number of dead gunshot victims, he remained disturbed by the pooled emptiness in Charlie Phinney's eyes.

A check of his cell phone revealed, to his surprise, three messages from three different women. It had been eons since such a fine thing had happened.

The first caller was Bonnie Witt, formerly known as Plover Chase, who'd called from Sarasota to leave the following voicemail: "Hey, it's me. Don't get all hot and bothered, but I've been thinking impure thoughts about you. Cliff hasn't touched me in ages because he's experimenting with autoerotic asphyxiation – you know, where guys beat off while they're faux-strangling themselves? Very classy. Anyhow, he's a total klutz, as you know, so I'm pretty sure he's going to hang himself to death one of these nights in the broom closet. Twice already I found him passed out on the floor, blue as a jellyfish. And yesterday he showed me how to use a portable defibrillator, just in case he screws up. I guess what I'm saying, Andrew – and God knows I don't expect you to wait around – I think there's a fifty-fifty chance I'll be single again soon. Anyway, give me a call."

The second voicemail was from Dr. Rosa Campesino, whom Yancy had texted during an idle period at the crime scene, while detectives were interviewing Phinney's girl-friend. The pathologist sounded very interested to hear that the shark tooth she'd tweezered from the severed arm belonged to a small specimen, possibly an inshore species:

"That definitely raises the possibility of foul play. This boat captain you spoke with, would you consider him an expert? Just to be sure, you should send the tooth to the Rosenstiel School at the University of Miami. They've got some of the top shark people in the world. Maybe you could keep me posted on how this all sorts out, okay? Also . . . well,

I want to apologize for telling a small lie the day you came to the office. I'm not really married to a sniper on the SWAT team. Actually, I'm not married at all. Sorry I jerked you around – just wasn't in the mood for lunch."

The last message was from Caitlin Cox, estranged daughter of the late Nicholas Stripling, who said: "Sorry to hassle you on a weekend, *Inspector*, but remember what I told you at the funeral? About my stepmother, that greedy hose monster? Well, now I've got proof! Seriously, it's a lock. So call me right away. I mean, if you want to be a big fucking hero and solve this case."

It was an avalanche of information for a stoned person to absorb. Yancy kicked off his flip-flops and stretched out on the kitchen counter and blinked up at the curled ceiling panels. A mental picture of Dr. Clifford Witt masturbating bug-eyed with a noose around his neck caused Yancy to wonder if Bonnie's husband had actually enjoyed the vacuum-cleaner assault that had cost Yancy his detective job. The phone message gave him no reason to believe Bonnie would come rushing back to the Keys, even if freed by widowhood from Clifford's grasp. Yancy leaned toward the hard-edged view that she was regretting her tipsy confession and was angling to keep his hopes for romance alive so that he wouldn't spill the beans about her fugitive status.

The call from Rosa Campesino was more intriguing, as it opened a door to future communications and possibly a date. At least that's how Yancy chose to construe her words. He'd never wooed a coroner and wasn't sure how to read the signals. He would replay radiant Rosa's message tomorrow, when his head was clear.

Finally, there was Caitlin Cox. Yancy doubted that she had absolute proof her father had been murdered, but she might have stumbled across something worth knowing. He decided to meet with her, and not just because he was bored out of his skull on roach patrol. Yancy felt a cop-like responsibility to sort out the truth about Nick Stripling, whose severed arm had been the centerpiece of Yancy's freezer during all those days when nobody had wanted it.

Furthermore, Yancy perceived – even under the woozy sway of ganja – an opportunity for redemption in the event that Eve Stripling really had killed her husband and tried to make it look like a boat accident. If Yancy, riding solo, was able to nail the widow for homicide, what else could Sheriff Sonny Summers do but reinstate him to the force?

That was Yancy's last fanciful thought before floating to sleep on the kitchen counter, and awaking hours later to the sound of a scream.

Seven

Woodrow and Ipolene Spillwright owned three houses. The first was a spacious plantation-style spread in their hometown of Raleigh, North Carolina, where Woodrow had retired from an executive position with R. J. Reynolds. The second was a ranch-style home near Tempe, Arizona, where the arid climate was said to benefit those with pernicious lung disorders of the sort that afflicted Woodrow, a brainlessly faithful consumer of his employer's tobacco products. The third Spillwright residence was a two-bedroom lakeside cottage in Maine, where the deer flies were so bloodthirsty that Ipolene (or "Ippy" as she was known in Raleigh social circles) would spool her pudgy bare ankles with Glad wrap before scuttling to the mailbox in the morning.

In Ipolene Spillwright's opinion, three houses were two too many for a couple pushing seventy. However, her husband had recently visited Florida with his country-club buddies and managed to land a seven-pound bonefish, a seemingly prosaic event that robbed him of all common sense. He'd returned to North Carolina and proclaimed his desire to purchase a winter home in the Keys, where he could hone his skills with a saltwater fly rod. Mrs. Spillwright told Woodrow that he'd lost his marbles but he refused to give up the quest. Their arguments were brief (for he quickly ran short of breath) yet animated. Finally, after Woodrow agreed to sell the Maine cottage and place the Arizona house in a rental pool, Ipolene said she would accompany him down to "Hemingway country" to look for a place on the water.

Property in Key West was stupendously overpriced so Woodrow had Googled his way up the island chain to a place called Big Pine, where someone was advertising a multistory spec home with "breathtaking sunset views."

Ipolene Spillwright said, "It'd better have an elevator, Woody, because you don't have the strength for all those stairs. And what in heaven's name are we going to do with seven thousand square feet?"

Her husband entertained a vision of himself basking on a pearl-colored chaise, accepting a margarita from a smoky-eyed Latina housekeeper. He said, "Let's go have a look, Ippy. What's the harm?"

When they emerged from the Miami airport, the first thing Ipolene Spillwright remarked upon was the gummy, sucking heat, which she predicted would kill them both before they made it to the Avis lot. Woodrow rented a white Cadillac coupe and pointed it south. He reminded Ippy that they wouldn't be staying in Florida during the summer months and, besides, Raleigh was also a steaming armpit in August.

It was a long drive to the Lower Keys, and the Spillwrights didn't resume speaking until they crossed the Seven

Mile Bridge, where Ipolene grudgingly remarked upon the view, a twinkling palette of indigo, turquoise and green stretching to all horizons. Woodrow Spillwright was practically levitating with joy.

They went directly to Key West and checked into a bed-and-breakfast a few blocks off Duval Street. Although Woody was whipped, he gassed up on bottled oxygen and took Ipolene strolling through Old Town, an excursion that nearly ended disastrously when he ambled off a curb in front of a speeding ambulance. His wife pulled him out of the road and led him back to the B-and-B as the night filled with the wailing of sirens. Another tourist couple informed the Spillwrights that a man had been robbed and shot outside a popular dockside bar, prompting Ipolene to spear her husband with a reproachful glare.

The next morning they were up at daybreak, racing up the overseas highway toward Big Pine Key. The island's many side streets confused the Cadillac's GPS unit, so Woodrow and his wife resorted to a map. At one point they passed a white-tailed deer so small that it had to be genetically defective. Ipolene decreed it was a sure sign of toxic waste spillage, and that she wouldn't be surprised if the humans living on the island were similarly stunted.

They were met at the spec house by the owner who, while short of height, was hardly circus material. He introduced himself as Evan Shook.

Mrs. Spillwright peered straight past him and said, "But the place isn't even finished yet!"

"I've brought all the plans with me. You're gonna love it."

Woodrow immediately inquired about the angling. "Bonefish is my game," he said.

Evan Shook grinned, then winked. "You, my friend, just died and went to heaven." As a precaution he'd arrived early to scout the downstairs for random carrion. He didn't want a repeat of the bloated-raccoon fiasco that had ruined his prospects with the Texans.

"The bugs are chewing me alive," Ipolene complained. "Can we please go inside? Such as it is."

The tour of the unfinished house took a while, due to Woody Spillwright's diminished lung capacity and his wife's endless questions. Sidestepping stacks of drywall and raw lumber, Evan Shook remained chipper and upbeat, at one point even volunteering that he could be flexible on the price. He was eager for the Spillwrights to experience the spectacular vista from the master bedroom suite – lush green mangroves veined with azure creeks and gin-clear tidal pools. And beyond: the Gulf of Mexico.

It was Evan Shook's belief that Mr. Spillwright would be so blown away by the exotic seascape that he would make an offer on the spot, providing he didn't collapse in a wheezing phlegm-fest before reaching the top of the steps.

Eventually they made it, Woodrow's wife shouldering him up to the final landing. After a recuperative pause, they entered the suite like wide-eyed pilgrims. Even Mrs. Spillwright seemed dazzled as she stood in the plywood frame of the unfinished bay window, a soft salty breeze on her cheeks.

"Well," she said. "This is really something."

Evan Shook wore the smile of a barracuda. "Didn't I tell you?"

"It's paradise," croaked Woodrow Spillwright. Dreamily he took in the cries of the terns and gulls. "How soon will it be finished?"

"Depends." Evan Shook cocked a hopeful eye toward Ipolene. "Would you two be interested in a custom kitchen? I can show you some sketches."

Later, after the Spillwrights had been stabilized at the emergency room in Marathon, Evan Shook would ask himself how in the name of Jesus B. Christ he'd failed to notice the humongous beehive on the suite's interior east wall. The oozing honeycomb was immense, at least six feet high and half again as wide. Yet the bees must have been calm when Evan Shook led the Spillwrights into the bedroom – of that he was certain. Otherwise he would have heard them buzzing, there were so damn many. Thousands? Millions?

Evan Shook speculated that the swarm must have been agitated by the scent of Ipolene's perfume, which smelled like rotting orchids. Or perhaps the insects were roused by the heat of the morning sun. For whatever reason, the savage little bastards went ballistic.

With gravity now his ally, Woodrow Spillwright descended the stairway in a humping blur, his wife yowling on his heels while slapping the bees out of her hair. Evan Shook lagged behind to flail uselessly at the angry intruders. Barely a week had passed since he'd been up to the fourth floor, but evidently enough time had passed for the bees to construct a Vegas-style hive. If only his contractor worked half as fast, Evan Shook mused bitterly, the goddamn house would have been finished a year ago.

Although he got stung thirteen times, the pain was negligible compared to his distress at losing the sale. The Carolinians hit the ground running. By the time Evan Shook caught up, they were already locked inside the Cadillac, feverishly trying to make sense of the keyless ignition. Evan

Shook was tapping plaintively on the glass when the engine revved to life, and he was forced to leap clear as old Woodrow peeled out. Through the tinted windshield Ipolene could be seen shaking a bee-bitten fist.

In the driveway next door stood Andrew Yancy, a newspaper tucked under one arm. He waved amiably as the Spillwrights sped off.

"Go on. Try it," Lombardo said.

Yancy dubiously eyed the plate. Brennan was standing by their table, waiting.

"It's yellowtail," he said.

"I believe you." Yancy took a small bite. The fish had been fried whole until crispy, Cuban-style. It tasted all right.

Brennan folded his arms. "See? Ain't it the best?"

Lombardo said, "Give us a few minutes to talk."

When they were alone, Yancy said, "It's not exactly fresh, Tommy."

"Yeah, but it's not spoiled, right? It's not fucking *contaminated*."

"Last time I was here, that asshole tried to bribe me."

"For God's sake, Andrew, it's the Keys. Eat your lunch."

Yancy's official job description was "sanitation and safety specialist." Tommy Lombardo had been assigned to train him, more or less. Lombardo was FDA-certified but he was also a local. Shutting down a restaurant for code violations – not cool. In his entire career on roach patrol, Lombardo had never ordered an emergency closure. He wanted Yancy to let Stoney's Crab Palace re-open that afternoon.

"They have a thing planned for that kid who got shot. Phinney? A fund-raiser to pay for his burial. There's a country band lined up and everything," Lombardo said. "Have a fucking heart."

"The food service area is a maggot festival."

"No, they cleaned it up. Why do you think I had you drive out here on a Saturday? Brennan, he's been working like a dog."

"Which is probably what he's serving for an appetizer," Yancy said.

Lombardo was exasperated. "See, this attitude of yours? Man, just 'cause you used to be a cop. . . . These are hard-working people. You can't treat 'em like criminals."

"The law says no vermin in the kitchen."

"The law says? Okay, Andrew, the law also says you're supposed to be certified by the state fire marshal. Are you? Nope. The law also says you're supposed to take the food manager's exam before you can work as a state inspector. Did you do that? Nope. You got this job because the sheriff made a phone call, which is no big deal, but all I'm sayin' is let's not get carried away with what the law says and so forth. Brennan's a good guy who's just tryin' to make a fair living."

Yancy pushed the plate away. "There was a used rubber in the oysters."

"Yeah, I read your report."

"How does that even happen?"

"It's not all Brennan's fault," Lombardo said. "The employment pool down here, it's sketchy. As a cop you should know."

Yancy stood up from the table. "Well, let's go have a peek."

The kitchen was much cleaner, he had to admit. No rancid shellfish or rodent droppings were on display. Yancy swabbed the food preparation surfaces and checked the temperature in the refrigerators and salad cooler. Brennan, who was cracking stone crabs, proudly showed off his new hairnet. Yancy dropped down and shined a flashlight under the stove, where Brennan had apparently unloaded two or three cans of Raid. Yancy scooped up a handful of dead German cockroaches and a tick, which Lombardo shrugged off.

"There's bug parts in your fucking raisin bran," he whispered. "The government says it won't hurt you."

Brennan piped up: "Nilsson was crazy about my food."

"He *died* from your food," Yancy reiterated.

Lombardo shook his head. "No, no, it was something else."

"Tommy, I read the autopsy. Hepatitis A."

Brennan said, "Then he must've caught it from that sushi pit on Cudjoe. That place is naaaasty."

Yancy nodded toward the fresh stone crabs piled on the cutting board. "Those are beauties."

"Aren't they?"

"Too bad they're out of season until October."

Brennan brought the mallet down on his thumb and yipped. "But these claws are imported from Panama. No – Mexico!"

"I think we're just about done here," Lombardo said.

"Wait a minute." Yancy walked over to the stand-up freezer and pointed with the toe of his shoe. "Is that a tail? Tell me that's not a tail."

"Goddammit," said Brennan.

Someone had slammed the freezer door on a rat.

"Least it's not alive," Lombardo observed. He was very much a glass-half-full breed of civil servant. "Come on, Andrew, have a heart."

Yancy grunted in capitulation. Snooping for *E. coli* didn't make his adrenaline pump. He was way more interested in discovering how Nicholas Stripling got rich, and what Mrs. Stripling stood to gain from her husband's death.

Lombardo gave Yancy some forms to sign, and Stoney's was back in business. Brennan embraced Lombardo and extended an ungloved hand to Yancy, who shook it tepidly and headed straight for the restroom to scrub off the crab drippings.

When he returned to the dining area, he found Lombardo alone at a table, polishing off the remains of the yellowtail and a pitcher of sangria. Brennan stood at the bar talking to Madeline, Phinney's hard-luck girlfriend, who had come to arrange the memorial fish fry.

"Be right back," Yancy said to Lombardo.

"Hey, take your time."

As soon as Madeline spotted Yancy approaching, she bolted out the fire exit. He hurried after her but she was already on her bicycle, pedaling like a maniac down Shrimp Road.

Lombardo came out the door squinting into the sunlight. "What'd you do to scare that poor woman?"

Yancy truly had no idea. He took a ten-dollar bill from his wallet and placed it in Lombardo's hand. "Put this in the jar," he said, "for the kid's funeral fund."

"Where are you going? Brennan wants you to try the chowder."

"Not until they find a vaccine," said Yancy, and jogged for his car.

"This is exactly what I'm talking about!" Lombardo yelled after him. "You gotta work on your fucking people skills!"

Caitlin Cox stepped off the airplane in Key West without her husband. Yancy couldn't get much out of her on the drive to the Marriott – small talk about the asinine security lines at Miami International, the bumpy flight, the sweaty Canadian dude sitting next to her.

Yancy waited at the hotel bar while she checked in. Twenty minutes passed, half an hour. He felt like a cop again. Maybe she was getting a massage.

He was about to go upstairs and pound on her door when she finally made her entrance, having changed into a tank top and black capri slacks. She wore the same jumbo sunglasses that she'd had on at the funeral. She sat down on the bar stool beside Yancy and said, "You ready? Don't you have a notebook or something?"

"Just tell me what you found out."

"Dad had a two-million-dollar life insurance policy. Guess who's getting it all?"

"Doesn't mean she murdered him," Yancy said.

Caitlin looked annoyed. "That's a shitload of money, Inspector." She ordered a Grey Goose martini.

Yancy asked why she and her father hadn't spoken to each other for so long.

"What difference does that make?"

"Was it because of Eve?"

"She told him I had a drug problem, which I did. Ancient history. She also told him I was stealing from him, which I wasn't. Don't you want a drink?"

"Iced tea, thanks. How old are you, Caitlin?"

She laughed. "Almost twenty-four. I know what you're thinking."

"How long have you been straight?"

"Two years. Okay, nineteen months." She picked up a menu. "How's the swordfish?"

Yancy said, "I honestly wouldn't know." One of these days he'd be inspecting the hotel's kitchen. "Most guys like your father own big life insurance policies. That's not unusual."

"Eve told him I was snorting heroin, which was none of her business. I was a model, okay? That stuff was everywhere. But I never stole a nickel from Dad. Now, did I run up some credit card bills? Yeah, but that's not the same as embezzlement or fraud, whatever. Anyway, Dad cut me off so I told him to go fuck himself, and that was it. He never called me back, and I never called him. Do I feel shitty about that? Yeah, but I can't change what happened."

The bartender brought a tall glass of tea and some cocktail nuts. Yancy was reaching for a pecan when he thought he saw it move. He yanked away his hand and, with a straw, cautiously probed the bowl for lurking insects. None were to be found, of course. These days he was imagining crawlers everywhere, a dispiriting occupational hazard.

Caitlin said, "You some kinda germ freak?"

Yancy selected a different pecan and, in hopes of appearing normal, popped it gaily into his mouth. "Have one," he said.

"Uh, no thanks."

He chomped down forcefully with his molars to pulverize the nut, just in case. Caitlin checked her iPhone for messages. "There was this girl, back when I was modeling? She was from Austria, natural blonde, and she had a germ thing,

80

like you. Every night she filled the bathtub with Purell and soaked for, like, an hour. Seriously."

"Did you know your dad had retired?" Yancy asked.

"Is that what my stepmother told you? That lying thundercunt. Dad wouldn't ever quit working, not ever."

"But how would you know? You hadn't spoken to him in years."

She glared. "Whose side are you on anyway?"

"Nobody's. Tell me what he did for a living."

"Eve didn't clue you in? He sold electric scooter chairs to old folks that can't walk very good. So they can motor themselves from the kitchen to the bathroom, whatever. Haven't you seen those infocommercials?"

Caitlin ordered another martini, and seemed pleased when the bartender belatedly asked to check her ID.

"They're fast little buggers, those scooters," she went on. "Dad mopped up, too. I mean – Florida? Hullo? There are *so* many geezers down here."

Yancy had seen the TV ads late at night. In addition to the chairs' compact turning radius, a main selling point was that elderly customers didn't have to pay out of their own pockets; Medicare covered the cost.

It was possible that Nick Stripling had retired honestly, Yancy thought, but more likely he'd been running a scam and shut it down before the feds nailed him. That could explain the two plainclothes Ken dolls at the graveside service.

"How do you know your father didn't just pack it in and go fishing? Sounds like a sweet retirement."

Caitlin was adamant. "Not Dad. No way."

"There were a couple guys at the funeral who looked like federal agents," Yancy said. "Was Nick having any problems with the law?"

"No! I mean, I don't think so. You should go ask Eve. Ha! Good luck with that."

"Nobody from the government ever spoke to you?"

Caitlin fidgeted. "A few years back, when Dad and I were still tight, he had some hassles with the IRS. I mean, who doesn't, right? But he got it all straightened out."

Yancy asked how she'd met her husband, and she seemed perturbed that he'd changed the subject.

"Simon worked security on some of my fashion shoots. He's the one who got me off dope. He used to be an MP in the army, did a couple tours in Iraq. But getting back to Eve, here's something else: She's already trying to get the court in Miami to declare Dad legally dead! That's how bad she wants to get her slutty paws on the insurance. But Simon says it takes five years in a missing persons case."

Yancy said, "Not if they find something."

"Even just an arm?"

"Any persuasive evidence of death. An airplane crashes, sometimes all that's left of a victim is a burned wallet or a shoe or a shred of skin. That's enough for most judges. They won't make a family wait five whole years."

Caitlin was getting more peeved. "What the fuck is your problem? Everything I say, you knock it down. How much did Eve pay you?"

"I'm holding out for new Michelins on the Subaru."

"She murdered my father for two million bucks, okay? Any jackass can figure that out."

"Dial it down," Yancy said. He nodded at the bartender, who smoothly retreated. "I'm not saying you're wrong, Caitlin. I'm saying you need more proof if you want the cops to get fired up."

She raised her hands. "I thought *you* were the cops."

Yancy made up something about following chain of command. Caitlin would be on the next flight to the mainland if she knew he was assigned to restaurant inspections.

"What about the boat sinking?" she demanded. "That story was so bogus."

A week earlier, the hull of Nick Stripling's boat had been located under seventy-five feet of water off the coast of Marathon, in the same area where the debris had been recovered. There was no money in the local Coast Guard budget to raise the *Summer's Eve*, even if investigators had wanted to. The official report said the vessel likely had capsized in rough seas.

"Somebody pulled the plug," Caitlin Cox asserted, "after Dad was already dead."

"So, hire a salvage company," Yancy said.

"How much would *that* cost?"

"A lot. It's a major job."

"Shit."

Yancy decided it was too soon to mention what he knew about the small shark tooth removed from Nick Stripling's arm. "Eve told me your father wasn't much of a swimmer."

Caitlin slammed her drink on the bar. "Are you kidding me?"

"Yet she put his favorite speargun in the casket, which seemed weird," Yancy said. "Most spear divers I know can swim like a fish."

"Dad was a damn porpoise, I'm not kidding. He could hold his breath forever. *Now* do you believe me about Eve? The reason she said he was a shitty swimmer was to make it seem like he just gave out and drowned after the boat went down. Which would never happen."

"Besides the insurance money, did she have any other reason to kill him?"

Caitlin leaned close. "Try a hot boyfriend."

"Go on," said Yancy.

"In the Bahamas!"

"You know this for a fact?"

"Let's move to a booth," she said.

Eight

The salesman at the Ford dealership informed Eve Stripling that the import duty on a new SUV in the Bahamas was seventy-five percent, a figure she made him repeat. After doing the math in her head, she realized that the new Explorer she'd been eyeing would cost, like, sixty-five grand.

"That's robbery," she observed.

"But I'm afraid it's the law," the salesman said sadly.

"My boyfriend'll never pay that much."

Eve walked off the lot thinking how strange it sounded when she said the word "boyfriend," strange but also sort of exciting. She took a taxi back to town, complaining to the driver about the outrageous tariffs on automobiles. The driver said he'd paid almost fifty-two thousand dollars for his cab, a used Dodge minivan he'd located on Craigslist in Hialeah. Eve was genuinely outraged on his behalf.

Stopping at an outdoor bar, she ordered a Nassau Nemesis, one of many colorful rum beverages concocted for tourists. Parked on the street was a yellow Jeep Wrangler with a hard top instead of canvas. A For Sale sign was taped to the windshield. Eve inspected the vehicle, which appeared to be in good condition except for a thumb-sized rust spot on the hood.

She drank another Nemesis and asked the bartender to play some UB40. Then she ordered fried grouper fingers and carelessly dribbled hot sauce on the crotch of her white jeans. Normally she would have been mortified, but the booze was kicking in hard. She tucked a paper napkin over her lap and asked for a basket of fried shrimp, which she was heartily demolishing when the owner of the yellow Jeep showed up carrying groceries. Eve hurried to the street, her napkin flapping.

"How much you want for it?" she called out.

The woman set her bags in the Wrangler's back seat. "Toidy towsend," she said to Eve.

"No way. Twenty-five."

"Wot!"

"Plus we need it barged down to Andros," Eve said.

"Twenty-eight if you pay'n cash. Where you ship it, dot's your prollem."

Eve went to see the Bay Street banker who was their new best friend and withdrew the money for the Jeep, which she drove sinuously to the waterfront. There she connected with a craggy white Bahamian who agreed to barge the car to Victoria Creek for a thousand dollars. Eve haggled briefly and without much starch. Her mission had been to purchase wheels and, by God, that's what she'd done.

On her way to the airport she called him in Miami. "You'll like it," she said. "It's super sporty!"

"What do you mean?"

"It's bright yellow, honey. I'm gonna call it Yellow Bird, like the song."

"And this is your idea of what a new widow should be driving? Something sporty?"

Eve sighed. "Where we're goin', who's gonna know? A whole new life is what you said. Isn't that the whole point?"

"The point is not to stand out like a couple of dumbass expats. Staying under the radar, understand? Yellow Jeep, might as well ring a fucking cowbell every time we drive to town."

He sounded on edge. Eve couldn't blame him, all the pressure he'd been under. Both of them, actually – though at the moment she was feeling exceptionally smooth and ironed out, thanks to the rum buzz.

She said, "Honey, everything's gonna be fine. Take a deep breath."

"How much did they stick you for?"

"Twenty-eight even."

"Automatic or stick?"

"You are too much."

"White would have been a smarter color. Black even."

"Boring. We're islanders now, remember? You with the orange poncho."

"When are you leaving?" he asked.

"Soon as Claspers fuels up the plane."

"Tell him to hurry."

"Does that mean you miss me?"

"I can't wait to get the fuck outta here is what it means."

Eve laughed drowsily and said, "See you soon."

A government man came all the way from Nassau to inform Neville that it was time to move. The sale of the family homestead to the white American named Christopher was official, the closing documents filed. Neville held no voice in the matter because his half sister, Diana, was the legal trustee. She lived full-time in Toronto with her acupuncturist fiancé and rarely came back to Andros, not even for homecomings. The government man told Neville he'd soon be receiving a cashier's check for $302,000 Bahamian, which was half the property's purchase price minus the broker's commission, bank fees, lawyers and so on.

When Neville replied that he had no use for the money, the government man thought he was joking.

Neville didn't have a wife but his three girlfriends heard he was about to become rich and started making demands. To get away he took his boat down to Mars Bay and went fishing for a few days. His only companion was Driggs the almost hairless monkey, whose unnerving resemblance to a psoriatic human delinquent served to keep both friends and strangers at a distance.

The patch reefs were teeming with groupers and mutton snappers, but Neville's mood remained morose. He was deeply disappointed that the Dragon Queen's voodoo spell had failed to waylay the mysterious Christopher and his lady friend. Currently the couple was renting a private home on the water near Bannister Point. Neville had yet to lay eyes on the man, who was rumored to wear a bright poncho and carry a gun.

As for the woman, Neville saw her for the first time when she stepped off a private seaplane at Rocky Town. She was kind of chubby though pretty: dark reddish hair and fair skin, with a spray of cinnamon freckles. The doctor flies attacked her hungrily, and both legs were trickling blood by the time she made it to the car.

Neville didn't know anybody who knew her name. He didn't know it, either.

What Christopher intended to do with the beach-front property had been the topic of many rumors, but the government man confirmed to Neville that an exclusive resort was planned, a private club offering time shares to be rented out as luxury hotel suites. The marketing would aim at wealthy Americans, Brits and Asians. There would be a geisha-style spa, two freshwater pools, a tiki bar and a four-star Caribbean restaurant. Also: cabanas, kayaks, paddleboards, snorkeling – even clay tennis courts!

The first phase of construction would be twenty-five units. Andros being the largest and most undeveloped island in the Bahamas, the prime minister himself had promised to fly in for the groundbreaking.

"Dey gon call it Curly Tail Lane," the government man told Neville.

Curly-tailed lizards were common throughout Andros. The stout little reptiles were bold and quick, and their twitchy courtship dance was always a hit with little children and tourists. Although Neville had no quarrel with the lizards, he thought Curly Tail Lane was a stupid name for Christopher's building project.

"Green Beach is wot my grandfahdda always call de place."

"Maybe once 'pon a time," the government man said.

"Dis some bullshit," Neville told him.

"Mon, you got a poymit fuh dot sick-ass monkey?"

Neville said, "Get off my land."

He spent two extra days down at Mars Bay because an east wind blew twenty knots, and Driggs was prone to sea-sickness. The ice in the cooler melted, so Neville ended up giving all his fish to the cook at an eco-lodge in exchange for another bottle of rum, with which he hoped to recharge the Dragon Queen.

However, upon returning to Lizard Cay, Neville saw that Christopher's crew had ripped out his wooden dock, every damn piling. He anchored his boat behind a neighbor's place, leashed Driggs's to the porch rail and hurried bare-foot down the rocky cratered road. A new chain-link fence surrounded his land, complete with a padlocked gate and a No Trespassing sign. Neville scaled the fence and ran through the trees until he came to a rubble of blue cinder blocks where his family house had stood.

He fell to his knees and, because he was alone, sobbed freely. Then he pulled himself together, walked over to Christopher's backhoe and urinated copiously into the fuel tank.

Yancy's father was retired from the National Park Service though he still lived in Gardiner, Montana, at the north entrance of Yellowstone. Every summer Yancy would fly out to fish for cutthroats on Slough Creek, or do a float down to Yankee Jim Canyon. He looked forward to these visits but this year he couldn't go.

"I'm working on a big case," he told his dad on the phone. "A possible homicide."

"Well, sure. I understand."

"Sorry, Pop."

"Maybe I can come down to the Keys and throw at some tarpon. I'll stay out of your hair."

Yancy said, "It's just not a good time."

He didn't have the spine to admit that he'd lost his detective badge and gotten busted down to roach patrol. Too well he remembered his father's heartsick reaction after he was canned by the Miami Police Department, a crushing setback that had occurred shortly after Yancy's mother was lost to cancer. Yancy couldn't bear to hear such disappointment in the old man's voice again.

"Maybe we can fish together in the fall," he said.

"I'm going on a steelhead trip to BC. You'd have a ball, Andrew."

"Sign me up."

Somebody was knocking on Yancy's door. It was Miguel, the bee guy. He was wearing a full-on beekeeper suit, including a hooded veil.

He winked behind the mesh at Yancy and said, "Excuse me, sir. Tonight we will be removing a serious motherfucking honeybee hive from the structure next door. Until then perhaps you should stay inside. Unfortunately, the bees have been disturbed."

"I appreciate the warning."

Miguel winked again and cut his eyes toward the construction site. Evan Shook was watching from his Suburban, in which he had sealed himself against the ruthless swarm.

"A risky situation," Miguel said, "but we are utmostly professionals."

"That I can see."

"Your neighbor, Señor Shook, he was stung many times. Lucky for him he is not allergic."

"Nor am I," Yancy said.

"Still, I would not take chances. Do you have any pets? Smallish children? You understand I must ask these questions. Would you be owning a pacemaker?"

Yancy was happy to play along. "No, sir. And I live here all by myself."

"Excellent. We will be done by midnight." Miguel went through the motions of handing Yancy a business card. "In case you are ever likewise troubled with bees. You can phone day or night. Also I am on Skype."

"Good luck with that hive," said Yancy.

"Vaya con Dios."

"Seriously?"

Miguel smiled. "Shut your fucking windows, Andrew."

Yancy buttoned up the house and headed down to Key West, where he'd set up lunch at a terrific Cuban place on Flagler with an ex-Border Patrol agent now working for Homeland Security. The man owed Yancy a favor and he stepped up big-time, bringing a printout that detailed the recent foreign travels of Mrs. Eve Stripling.

Caitlin Cox had said her stepmother was in the Bahamas, not Paris, at the time her father's boat went down off Marathon. Caitlin's proof was Eve's phone bill, which showed numerous roaming charges from a wireless company based in Nassau. To Yancy, Caitlin had admitted stealing the bill from the mailbox at her father's home in the hope of establishing the identity of Eve's secret lover. Caitlin was certain such a man existed because she'd spotted her stepmother buying a swimsuit and designer flip-flops at a Bal Harbour boutique, two days before Nick Stripling's funeral. Caitlin was there shopping for a black dress.

Mindful of her motive, which was gaining access to her late father's wealth, Yancy nonetheless found the tip intriguing. Caitlin's suspicions seemed to be partially confirmed in the records provided by his Homeland Security connection – Eve Stripling had in fact gone to Paris, although for only a week. Then she flew back to the United States, clearing Customs at JFK before taking a nonstop to Nassau. It was nineteen days later that she returned to South Florida on a private seaplane that landed at Watson Island. There she paid duty on thirty-four hundred dollars of women's clothes and a ten-karat-gold men's wedding band, which, according to her declaration documents, had cost a whopping one hundred and ninety-nine bucks. Yancy assumed it was the same gold band Eve had switched out for Nick Stripling's expensive platinum one before burying his abbreviated remains.

Interestingly, she'd bought the replacement ring in the Bahamas before returning to Florida and reporting her husband missing at sea. The purchase made no sense unless she'd already known that Nick was dead and that his ring finger had been recovered, attached to his floating arm.

Yancy felt so energized by this disclosure that he picked up the twenty-eight-dollar meal tab, even though he'd barely touched his *picadillo* due to a suspicious-looking olive. Of late he was subsisting mostly on Popsicles and so-called energy bars, which came hygienically machine-sealed in foil although they settled in his stomach like bricks of industrial glue.

His friend from Homeland Security got up and said, "Thanks for lunch, Andrew. But anybody asks, we never talked."

Yancy grinned. "Hell, I don't even know your name."

A squall blew across the island and Yancy drove around Old Town waiting for the rain to quit. On Fleming Street he passed Fausto's grocery and thought of Bonnie, a.k.a. Plover Chase. With improbable ease he rejected the impulse to dial her number. Perhaps he was finally, at age forty-two, growing up.

He parked on Eaton Street and made his way to Duval. Even in the dead of summer it was crawling with overfed tourists courtesy of the cruise ships, which Yancy considered a vile and ruinous presence in the harbor. After grabbing a beer at the Margaritaville café he began searching the T-shirt shops for Madeline, girlfriend of the late Charles Phinney. He found her at a place called Chest Candy, which aggressively catered to strippers, transvestites and aspiring nymphomaniacs. The display window featured a blond-wigged mannequin wearing a diaphanous tank top with sequined lettering that said: CUM TOGETHER.

Again Madeline spooked when she saw Yancy, only this time there was no place to run. She yelled for the store manager, a sallow twit named Pestov who vanished as soon as Yancy inquired about his immigration status.

After locking the front door behind himself, Yancy cornered Madeline and asked what the hell was going on.

"I got a lawyer! So watch it."

"Why do you need a lawyer?"

She said, "You told me you weren't a cop."

"I said not at the moment."

Some dork wearing Teva sandals and black socks started rattling the doorknob. Yancy shooed her away. "Tell me what's going on," he said to Madeline.

"The cops think I set Charlie up to get ripped off."

"Where'd you hear that?"

"Three times they had me in for questioning. What'd you tell them? Jesus, I need a smoke."

Yancy said, "The police never even interviewed me."

Madeline's hands were trembling as she lighted up. "I'm gonna lose my damn job."

"They'd be doing you a favor."

She said, "I wouldn't never hurt Charlie. He treated me good."

"I believe you, Madeline. But I can't help unless you tell me the truth. So let's start over, okay?"

"Not here," she whispered, glancing behind her. "The Russians, man!"

"Screw the Russians." Yancy poked his face into the back room and said, "Yo, Madeline's taking the afternoon off."

"Is fine," Pestov muttered sullenly from a closet.

"Thank you, comrade. And God bless America!"

Yancy drove Madeline out to Stoney's, which naturally had been her and Phinney's all-time favorite restaurant. They took a two-top in a corner and from the unkempt server Yancy was pleased to learn Brennan was away in Homestead, probably stocking up on frozen tilapia that would later be promoted to fresh swordfish on the menu.

Madeline asked for a vodka tonic and Yancy ordered a Coke.

She said, "I lied. I don't really have a lawyer."

"They tend to charge a fee."

"Which I have about forty bucks to my name."

"What have the cops told you?" Yancy asked.

"I got a record is the problem. Grand theft a long time ago, shoplifting, whatever. Plus they found out I'm way behind on my Visa card and also my rent, so I guess they think I lined up someone to shoot Charlie and take a cut of the cash. But I didn't!"

Yancy believed Madeline, for he knew more about the murder investigation than she did. One of his fishing pals was a city police lieutenant who'd told him that the rented moped used in the robbery had been wiped totally clean of prints, even the gas cap and side mirrors, demonstrating an attention to detail not common among the local dirtbag element. The killer's weapon hadn't been found but the .357 shell casings and bullet fragments belonged to 158-grain Winchester hollow points, a premium load for a low-rent street crime.

Yancy said, "Tell me again how much cash Phinney was carrying."

Madeline paused before answering. "Maybe twelve hundred bucks?"

"Last time you said it was a grand."

"Well, I didn't go through his fucking wallet and count it!" She took a slurp of vodka.

"You also told me he got the money from a dope deal." Yancy was watching her eyes, which flitted everywhere but in his direction. "Who was he selling to, Madeline?"

"I never met the dude. What difference does it make?"

"Maybe Charlie overcharged him. Or maybe the stuff turned out to be stinkweed and the customer got pissed off."

"No, no, that's not it," she said. "Everybody in town knew Charlie was carrying that money. He wouldn't stop talkin' about it. They probably followed us to the Half Shell that night and waited outside."

Over the years Yancy had interviewed enough witnesses to know when one was winging it. Usually they were just trying to cover their own asses, a practice also favored by law enforcement professionals although Yancy had never quite gotten the hang of it. He told Madeline she had two minutes to come clean, and right away she began to shake and cry. Yancy scooted his chair closer and put an arm around her.

"Everything I told the cops is true except about the cash," she said. "Charlie didn't get it from sellin' grass."

"Did he steal it from someone?"

"No! He would *never*." Her breath was stale and her hair smelled like an ashtray.

"Then where'd he get the money, Madeline?"

She pawed at her eyes with a cocktail napkin. "It's pretty fucked up," she said.

"I need to know before I can help."

"But you're not even a real cop."

Yancy gritted it out. "I'm on loan to another department, that's all. Temporarily assigned. Now tell me the whole story."

And Madeline was right. It was fucked up.

On the charter docks of South Florida there had evolved among a handful of unscrupulous captains a method of duping inept out-of-towners for extra money. The key prop in the scam was typically an Atlantic sailfish, caught on a previous trip and stored on ice in an aft hatch inaccessible to the paying clientele.

Once the boat was at sea, a mate first baited the outriggers and then the flat lines, which were trolled closer to the boat and often enhanced with a skirted plastic lure. Thus began a sporting day, with high hopes among the unsuspecting anglers. When the time was right, one of the mates would distract them with a clamorous false sighting of jumping porpoises or a cruising hammerhead shark, which the customers always pretended to see as they didn't wish to be regarded as clueless rubes.

Binoculars were handed out and the anglers were directed to the bow of the ship in order to improve their view. At this juncture the mate would remove the dead sailfish from the cold hatch and covertly hook it to one of the flat lines. Once the jelly-eyed corpse was dropped in the water, the forward motion of the boat carried it back into the frothy wake.

A cry of "Fish on!" would go out, and one of the hapless sports – usually a hungover husband – would come lurching back to the cockpit, snatch the rod from the mate's grasp and begin reeling like a madman. The boat's towing of the limp billfish created enough natural drag to test the flabby muscles of most novices. Later they would brag to their pals back home that they'd whipped the sonofabitch in five minutes flat. As further testament to human vanity, no suspicions would be voiced over the odd fact that their trophy sailfish, a species renowned for its acrobatics, never once jumped out of the water.

At boatside, the mate would cap the charade by pretending to wrestle the prize into an unlocked fish box, where the entire party of numskulls could peek at it and snap pictures to their hearts' content. The coup de grâce would occur back at dockside when the captain persuaded the lucky angler to have his catch mounted, later to be displayed on the paneled wall of his real estate office or perhaps in the family den. A tidy deposit would be forthcoming, divided by the captain and mates, and a few months later the client would receive via UPS an exquisite six-foot sailfish, painted cobalt blending to indigo and airbrushed with lateral dashes of silver and gold. The replica, manufactured by the taxidermist from a standard plaster cast, would be fixed in a lifelike leaping pose, its sharp bill aimed toward the clouds and its tall dorsal fin regally flared.

Of course by then the real sailfish had been recycled profitably and eventually dumped overboard, having decomposed to chum after five or six fake captures. It was a scam to be saved exclusively for the most witless of tourists, but it worked often enough to have been passed along over decades among a certain low-pirate class of sportfishing crews.

Charles Phinney didn't learn of the trick from Captain Keith Fitzpatrick but, rather, from a stranger who'd approached him one evening at the Garrison Bight Marina while he was hosing down the *Misty Momma IV.* There was, however, a twist.

"It wasn't a dead sailfish they wanted him to hook on the line," Madeline told Yancy. "It was a dude's cut-off arm!"

"Jesus."

"I told Charlie it was the grossest thing I ever heard and he'd be crazy to do it. But he was gonna make three thousand cash."

"Three grand?"

"I'm not shitting you," said Madeline. "So he said okay."

"And got paid?"

"Same day, in hundred-dollar bills. He made me swear not to tell anyone. He said they told him it was only a practical joke, no big deal. The arm came off a dead body from some mortician school."

By now she was lapping a third vodka tonic. Yancy felt like having a stiff one, too, but he wanted to be able to remember every word. He'd write it all down as soon as he got home.

"The night before," she said, "in Charlie's apartment? We were so fucking nervous we got stoned out of our heads. I mean *baked*, okay? He had the . . . you know . . . in this big ice cooler, I'll never forget—"

"Wait, Madeline, who gave Phinney the arm?"

"Someone brought it to the dock that same night, when

he was alone on the boat. Anyway, the cooler – Charlie asks do I want to see the you-know-what and I said no freaking way, you asshole. But he takes the thing out, right? And it doesn't look real but at the same time it's too gross to be fake. And we both, I don't know why, we just start laughing. He's swingin' the thing around like a baseball bat and I've got this half-calico kitty cat, Sheeba, all the fur on her back is stickin' up. Charlie and I both just fell out, it seemed so damn funny. Sounds pretty fucking twisted, I guess, but it's not like we put it up on YouTube or nothin'."

"So it was really good pot," Yancy said. Bonnie Witt's reaction to the severed limb had been not so jolly, though, in retrospect, they hadn't laughed very much as a couple. Again he asked: "Who brought the dead arm to Phinney?"

"Here's the worst," said Madeline. "We're so trashed, Charlie grabs the middle finger on the hand, right? The bird finger? And he bends it up like this, so it looks like the dead dude is flippin' us off! I 'bout peed my panties. But then he stuck the thing in the freezer and next morning it was all iced up, and he couldn't bend the finger back 'cause he was afraid it would snap off. So that's how it stayed when he took it on the *Misty*."

"Captain Fitzpatrick didn't know anything about this, right?"

"You kidding? He would have gaffed Charlie in the nut sack."

She wanted another cigarette so Yancy followed her outside. He stood upwind and gulped the salty fresh air. The inside of Stoney's smelled like fried sweat socks.

"Who else did Charlie tell about the arm?"

"Nobody but me," Madeline said emphatically. "Soon as he sobered up he got semi-paranoid about it. But the money, you know, that was different. The night after he got paid he took me to Louie's for dinner and bought a round for everyone at the bar, two hundred bucks." She dragged hard and then flicked the butt into a rain puddle. "Nobody said he was Alvin Einstein."

Yancy thought it was fortunate that Phinney and Madeline hadn't pooled their genes. He said: "Who got Charlie to do this thing? Didn't he mention the guy's name?"

"Wasn't a guy," Madeline said. "It was a chick that brought him the cut-off arm, Charlie said. He didn't know her name but she's the one who paid him, too. A white chick in tight white jeans. Is that wild or what? Like she was on her way to the damn mall."

Yancy patted her hand. "You need to get out of town."

Nine

They didn't call ahead, just showed up one evening at the door. Shark-gray suits, flat expressions. They told Simon Cox they needed to speak alone with Caitlin. Simon, who practically got a boner when he saw their federal shields, obediently disappeared into the small bedroom he used as a gym.

The interview only lasted twenty minutes – the agents could plainly see Caitlin wasn't living like a Kardashian, or even like the daughter of a wealthy dead medical-supply executive. She was creeped out because they knew the humiliating balance of her checking account, down to the penny. They knew Simon's car was paid off, and hers wasn't. They knew the amount on her American Express card. They even knew about one of her rehabs.

And now they knew what her house looked like, all fourteen-hundred square feet. Lebron James had closets that were bigger.

"What're you guys after?" she asked.

"Money," said one of the agents.

"Dad didn't pay his taxes again? That figures."

"It's more complicated than that. Did he ever discuss his business with you?"

"We weren't speaking for a long time. So no is the answer."

The other agent said, "Did he give you any instructions, in the event of his death?"

"What did I just say? The two of us weren't talking. He didn't even put me in his will is what I heard."

"Looks like his wife gets everything," the first agent said, "all twelve thousand dollars."

Caitlin laughed in disbelief. "Twelve grand?"

The second agent said, "Now you understand our interest."

"Dad had a shitload of money."

"That's our information, as well. However, the only American bank account with his name on it held twelve thousand and change when he passed away – basically enough for the funeral. So, we were hoping you might know what happened to the rest."

Caitlin glared at the agents. "Eve's the one you should be talking to about the money. Ask her if she killed my father, while you're at it. Because she did! Don't you guys do murders?"

"If you have hard evidence, you should call the police right away."

"Done deal," Caitlin declared. "I got a detective in the Keys working the case full-time. Yancy is his name."

The FBI men showed no reaction, no interest.

One of them said: "We tried to interview Mrs. Stripling

about your father's finances, including his life insurance policy. She asked to be left alone."

"And that's what you did?" Caitlin asked incredulously.

"She's not under subpoena, Mrs. Cox."

"Good, then leave me alone, too!"

As soon as the agents were gone, Simon came out and asked Caitlin what they'd wanted. She told him it looked like Eve had ripped off her dad's estate.

"Big surprise, right?" she said. "All Dad's money is missing – who knows how much."

"They'll find it," said Simon confidently. The feds were absolutely the best.

"He was a fool to marry that greedy whore." Caitlin was still livid. "I hope they throw her ass in jail for a hundred years."

"Did they leave a card?" Simon asked, meaning the agents. He was thinking he would ask them out for a beer. Bring along his résumé.

The phone rang and Caitlin picked it up. She looked surprised by the caller. Lowering her voice, she turned her back on Simon, which he didn't appreciate.

The moment she hung up, he said, "Who was that, sweetheart?"

"You won't believe it – my former stepmother, all sweet and friendly."

"Eve?"

"Swear to God." Caitlin wore an odd smile. "She wants to get together, just her and me. A girls' day."

"That's messed up. What did you say?"

"I said, Are you paying?"

*

For once Yancy didn't mind driving to Miami. Dr. Rosa Campesino had agreed to meet for lunch. On the Eighteen-Mile Stretch he got stuck behind a minivan with a CHOOSE LIFE bumper sticker.

"Choose the accelerator! How's that for starters?" Yancy was shouting, pounding the horn.

He didn't mind if people advertised their religious views on their cars, but those who did invariably were the slowest, most faint-hearted drivers. It was uncanny, and all road cops knew it to be true. If God was *my* co-pilot, Yancy once groused to Burton, I'd have the fucking pedal to the metal soon as I left the garage.

Rosa arrived in her morgue scrubs at the restaurant, and she looked fabulous.

"What happened? You're so skinny," she said. "I'll order for both of us."

They were seated at a café on Miracle Mile in Coral Gables. The menu was promising, but the night before Yancy had dreamed about Stoney's Crab Palace – mouse tracks on a Key lime tart.

"I've been fighting a stomach flu," he said.

Undaunted, Rosa ordered them veal with penne pasta. She wore a fresh touch of lipstick but no other makeup, which Yancy found wildly beguiling. This he recognized as the onset of infatuation.

"Did you get fired? Tell the truth," she said.

He felt his neck get hot. "It's more like a probation."

"No, I've been checking up. You're quite the renegade, Andrew." She was smiling, thank God. "I've heard of Sergeant Johnny Mendez, by the way. Not a good guy."

"A congenital crook," Yancy said. "Disgrace to the uniform, et cetera."

"Still, you could have handled it better. Now, what happened down in the Keys?"

"That I'd rather not discuss."

"Too bad," Rosa said. "My life coach told me not to sleep with anybody who harbors a murky past."

"What about a murky present?"

"I don't really have a life coach, Andrew. However, I do believe in full disclosure."

He coughed up the whole story with a facsimile of contrition. His crude assault on Dr. Clifford Witt didn't seem to shock Rosa, but then again she was a coroner in an urban combat zone.

"Last week I did a post on a man who had a clarinet up his colon," she reported. "That's not what killed him, by the way. It was a single gunshot to the head from a jealous lover. She played the oboe."

"Shakespeare was born too soon."

"So you lost your detective job and now you're inspecting restaurants for rat poop and bacteria. Not exactly a lateral career move."

Yancy said, "I'm righting the ship, even as we speak."

The pasta and veal arrived. It was delicious, but he backed off after a couple of bites. Rosa asked for an update on the severed arm, and he told her what he'd found out. She was intrigued by the dead-sailfish scam.

"That's a classic," she said.

"I'm thinking the wife and her boyfriend killed Stripling, or had him killed."

"Before or after they sunk the boat?"

"Doesn't matter. They chop off one arm and take the expensive wristwatch, but they leave the platinum wedding band as part of the act, so that Eve can make a show of

106

identifying it later. Then they put the arm in the shallows off some secluded beach so the bonnet sharks can gnaw on it, purely for appearance."

"How'd she pick this Phinney character to smuggle that nasty thing onto a boat?" Rosa asked.

"You hang around the docks, it's not hard to find somebody who'd sell their own mother's kidney for three thousand bucks. Once that tourist on the *Misty* reeled in Stripling's arm, Eve was golden."

"Until Phinney started blabbing about the money."

Yancy nodded. "That's why he got shot. It wasn't a robbery. Hell, he'd already blown through most of the dough."

"You said the shooter was on a moped? That's like Bogotá in the old days."

"Mopeds are all over Key West. This one was a cash rental on a stolen driver's license – somebody hired by Eve, I'm betting. Or possibly it was the boyfriend himself who pulled the trigger."

"Whose name you don't know."

"Hey, I'm just getting started."

Rosa said, "Eat your lunch, Andrew. It's sinful to waste good food. I thought you said the widow's love hunk was in the Bahamas."

"That's what I was told. It's a quick flight to Florida."

"There must be a record of that. He'd have to clear Customs."

"Only if he's an upright, law-abiding citizen," Yancy said. "A seaplane could fly in low and land anyplace. It's risky, but so is murder."

Because of the poor condition of Stripling's arm, determining the precise date and time of his death was impossible. The crime had probably occurred when Immigration records showed Eve to be in Nassau. However, with access to a floatplane and an outlaw pilot, she could have flown straight to the Keys, killed her husband, staged the boat accident and been back in the Bahamas by nightfall.

"Super bold," Rosa said.

Yancy ordered a cup of coffee that was so strong it made his eyes water. For dessert Rosa had the tiramisu.

"So, you're investigating this elaborate homicide in your leisure time? Off the reservation, as they say." She was giving him an amused, sideways appraisal.

"I want my badge back, Rosa. If I can just nail down this case—"

"Are you kidding? It doesn't work that way."

"Maybe not in Miami, but Key West is small-time. I'm tight with the sheriff."

"Oh, Andrew."

He didn't mention that he'd never before worked on an unsolved murder. During his time with the Miami police he'd been assigned to burglaries and the occasional armed robbery. In the Keys he'd been called to a total of three killings; all were domestic scenarios featuring on-scene confessions by impaired roommates.

"Now it's your turn, Doctor," Yancy said. "Tell me what led you to the cheery, life-affirming specialty of forensic pathology."

"It was either that or trauma care. I prefer patients who hold still."

"Plus you get to play cop, too."

Rosa laughed. "Some days I do."

She gave Yancy the short version of her biography: Born and raised in New Jersey; daughter of Cuban immigrants; undergrad at FSU, med school at the University of Miami;

divorced, no kids, lived alone with a tank full of tropical fish. In the fall she would turn thirty-nine, and she planned to treat herself to a spa day at the Mandarin.

"Darkest secret?" Yancy asked.

Rosa thought for a moment. "Okay, this *is* dark. Once I made love on an autopsy table at the morgue."

Yancy was overjoyed to picture the scene. "How do you top that?" he said.

"Late one night, me and this guy I was dating. Those rooms are really, really cold."

"Your idea or his?"

"Mine," Rosa admitted, blushing. "Mark – my friend – he got semi-freaked. I never saw him after that. He just stopped calling."

"One of these days he'll be out of therapy."

"I love my job, but I'm pretty sure it's screwing with my head."

"Tell me about it," said Yancy. "I've dropped, like, fourteen pounds since they put me on roach patrol. I have these nauseating nightmares about filthy, putrid-smelling kitchens – bugs in the goddamn custard."

Rosa frowned and pushed away the tiramisu. Yancy paid the check and walked her to her car, some sort of sensible sedan. "I meant to thank you again," he said, "for figuring out the brand of Stripling's missing watch. That was impressive."

"Oh, I'm full of tricks." She elbowed him playfully and got in her car. "That woman whose husband you molested – are you still involved with her? This is a test, by the way."

"Bonnie has moved to Sarasota."

"Answer the question."

"No, that tawdry chapter of my life is closed. I'm in the process of rebooting." Yancy smiled hopefully.

"Maybe some night I'll come down and cook for you," Rosa said. "I bet I can make you hungry."

Then she drove off.

Midwest Mobile Medical Systems had been located in a bland office park in Doral, west of the Miami airport. The occupancy rate of the complex was only twenty percent and the few tenants no longer included Midwest Mobile, which had closed down upon the retirement of its young president, Nicholas Stripling. His daughter, Caitlin, had eagerly provided Yancy with the name and former whereabouts of the company.

The door lock was of inferior quality, surrendering to Yancy's screwdriver on the first pry. Inside the suite were eight identical cubicles, stripped bare except for the desks, IKEA knockoffs that gave the place the appearance of a tele-marketing boiler room. Stripling or his staff had hauled away the files, printers and computers and, judging by a trail of white confetti, even brought in shredders.

In one desk Yancy found a color brochure advertising the "Super Rollie," a personal sit-down scooter that promised "the comfort and agility of a motorized wheelchair combined with the traction and durability of a world-class riding mower." The Super Rollie Power Chair was available in three-wheel or four-wheel models that could cruise up to nine miles per hour. Options included a headlight, a touchpad sound system and a captain's seat that swiveled 180 degrees. Prices ranged from eight hundred dollars for the basic package to four thousand for a candy-red chariot with a dashboard glucose meter. Medicare patients were assured that the vehicles could be obtained "with little or no cost to you." The main requirements were a doctor's prescription and federal form CMS-849, a Certificate of Medical Necessity for Seat Lift Mechanisms, which Midwest Mobile Medical would helpfully fill out on each customer's behalf.

"Take a ride on our Super Rollie," the brochure urged, "and recapture your independence!"

Yancy pictured himself careening down the Seven Mile Bridge aboard one of the zippy power chairs, Rosa Campesino riding on his lap.

A jowly security guard peeked in the doorway and said, "I thought you guys were done with this place."

"One more pass," said Yancy. Following his lunch with Rosa, he'd put on a necktie and a drab coat jacket to make himself appear more cop-like.

"You ever gonna arrest somebody?"

Yancy gave a thumbs-up. "Count on it, brother."

He waited until the guard was gone before he resumed searching. Probably federal agents were the ones who'd been snooping there before. Unfortunately, Nicholas Stripling had died before they could indict him.

A crumpled paper that had escaped shredding by Stripling – or confiscation by the FBI – proved to be a handwritten note: "Nicky – Dr. O'Peele says he never got paid for last month. Wants you to call him."

On his smartphone Yancy was able to access the website of the state health department, which revealed that only one medical doctor named O'Peele was licensed in Miami-Dade County. Also available online were records of the property appraiser's office, which listed a Gomez O'Peele as the owner of a three-bedroom condominium in North Miami Beach. An hour later Yancy was standing in the lobby of a high-rise, buzzing the doctor's unit number.

"Whoozair?" asked a groggy voice from the speaker box.

"Inspector Andrew Yancy."

"Oh shit. What?" Then, after a pause: "Come on up."

O'Peele was wearing a stale nappy bathrobe and one moleskin slipper when he answered the door. His eyeballs were bloodshot and his hair appeared to have been groomed with salad tongs. "Can I see some ID?" he said.

Yancy flashed his lame restaurant-inspector credentials, which drew a foggy squint from the doctor.

"Izzit morning already?" he asked.

Yancy brushed past him. "That's an unusual name, Gomez O'Peele."

"My mother's Cuban. She divorced my dad and remarried a mick. Are you FBI?"

"I'm not at liberty to say." Yancy delivered the line with a straight face. He would never have tried it on a sober person.

"How'd you find me?" O'Peele said. "Never mind. I know my rights."

The condo was piled with dirty laundry and fuzzy pizza boxes. O'Peele shambled to the disordered kitchen, which showed evidence of an active cockroach colony. Yancy found himself scanning the floorboards for signs of movement. The doctor downed a shot of bourbon and announced he had no intention of doing prison time.

"Tell me what you think you know," he said, "and I'll tell you if you're on the right track."

"Fair enough," Yancy said.

"But only if I get immunity."

"That's up to the prosecutors, not me."

"Then you'd better go. My lawyer is mean as a timber wolf."

Yancy took a safe-looking can of ginger ale from the refrigerator. He popped the tab, sat down at the kitchen table and waited patiently for Dr. O'Peele to start gabbing.

"My training is orthopedic surgery. I had a damn good practice in Atlanta – sports medicine mostly – but then there were some personal setbacks. Nothing that reflected on my work, but that medical board, what a bunch of cold-hearted pricks! Finally I just said screw it and moved down here and connected with Nick."

"You never set eyes on an actual patient for Midwest Mobile Medical, did you?"

"That's true," the doctor admitted hoarsely. "All I did was sign prescriptions and fill out the 849s. A nobody is what I was. A worker drone."

Yancy said fraud was fraud. O'Peele looked wobbly. "I've got substance issues," he confided. "This is not the arc I mapped out for my life. May I sit down?"

"Of course. Let's hear more about Mr. Stripling."

O'Peele shook his head so violently that his cheeks flapped. "Request denied!"

"Then at least clue me in on how the scam worked. Where did Nick get all those Medicare numbers?"

"He bought a list of, like, ten thousand names," the doctor said. "Some clerk that worked at one of the hospitals. Mount Sinai or Baptist, I don't remember which."

As Yancy had suspected, Midwest Mobile Medical was a ghost-patient operation, billing comical sums to Medicare for electric power chairs, stair lifts, walkers and other durable home-care items that would never be delivered. The senior citizens whose IDs had been hijacked remained in the dark because the government checks were mailed directly to Midwest Mobile.

Such fraud was epidemic throughout South Florida and practically risk-free, thanks to Medicare's stupendously idiotic policy of paying out claims before asking questions. By the time the FBI zeroed in on a brazen cheat such as Nicholas Stripling, he would have already shut down his operation, banked a few million and scurried on. Had he not been killed, he by now would have resurfaced with a new storefront and a new company logo, working the same easy swindle.

"How much did he pay you?" Yancy asked O'Peele.

"Hundred bucks for every Rollie prescription."

"And you weren't the only doctor signing them."

O'Peele chuckled drily. "I was the only *live* one. The other docs, they'd been dead from old age since forever. Somehow Nicky got hold of their filing numbers. There were two girls in the office, they did all the forgeries."

Yancy had mixed feelings about what he was learning from the strung-out physician. While pleased to confirm his suspicions about Stripling, he also understood that solving the murder of a despicable felon wasn't good for as many brownie points as solving, say, the murder of a beloved Little League coach or a department-store Santa. Some people might even endorse the view that Eve Stripling had performed a service to humankind – or, at the very least, to the Medicare trust fund – by ridding the world of her larcenous spouse. A similar thought had occurred to Yancy, though he wasn't inclined to walk away from the case. Eve belonged in prison, if not on death row. She'd murdered her man for the money.

O'Peele slugged down another shot. "How much do you people pay your informants these days?"

"Not my department," Yancy said.

"A thousand dollars sounds ballpark. For all the inside

stuff I just gave you? And I've got plenty more. We're talking mother lode."

When Yancy asked Gomez O'Peele how he'd heard about Stripling's death, the doctor stammered and said he couldn't recall. From a foul cranny of his robe he produced a bottle of white pills, three of which he placed under his blistered tongue.

"Sorry," he said to Yancy.

"Yes, you are."

"I used to be board-certified, Inspector. One time I got a paper published in the AMA journal."

"Wild guess: It was a woman who lured you down this squalid path."

O'Peele bared his grungy implants. "Who are you to judge?"

"A voice of experience," Yancy said. "Go back to bed."

He had one more stop before heading back to the Keys.

The phantom power-chair racket had been good to the Striplings. Their house was a Spanish-style remodel on Di Lido Island off the Venetian Causeway. It had four bedrooms, four baths, a heated lap pool, a dock on Biscayne Bay and a view of the city skyline. The landscaper was an overzealous admirer of sea grape trees and Malaysian palms.

According to the MLS website, also easily accessed by Yancy's phone, the property was listed for $2 million and had been on the market only a short time. As was sometimes the case in such upscale neighborhoods, no For Sale sign had been planted in front of the Striplings' home. This was a Realtor's ploy designed to make prospective buyers believe that they were privy to an exclusive showing, and that the owners weren't especially motivated to sell.

Yancy drove twice past the entrance and then parked in some shade down the street. While he might have been dressed like a working detective, the motley Subaru betrayed him as a civilian. He had no itch to explain his presence on Di Lido to the real police, who wouldn't be impressed by his roach-patrol ID. And although he still had good friends in Miami-Dade law enforcement, none of them were placed highly enough to spring him from a jam.

What Yancy should have done was drive home, but he loathed the evening rush hour and knew the southbound turnpike would be, in the parlance of hard-core commuters, a goat fuck. Therefore he had some time to kill. Enough time to get lucky.

It was easy to find a house that had been shuttered for the summer, and that's where Yancy left the car. He removed his coat and tie and donned a yellow hard hat that he was supposed to wear while probing the storage lofts and crawl spaces of pest-infested restaurants. Add the toolbelt and he looked somewhat like a utility-company employee.

Walking down the street, he tried to simulate the gait of an overworked stiff who'd been busting his hump all day in the blazing sun and had one last job on his ticket sheet. As he approached the Stripling residence, he spotted a cable-TV service box halfway up the property line. Each corner of the house was equipped beneath the eaves with a security camera, so Yancy pushed the hard hat low on his head in order to obscure his face while he dismantled the cable box and pretended to repair the wires.

He was hoping to catch a glimpse of the widow's boyfriend, or at least a sign of male presence – swimming trunks tossed on a patio chair, a cigar butt in a poolside ashtray, whatever. It was possible that Eve Stripling was too careful to bring her lover to the house, but in Yancy's experience lust usually triumphed over prudence. Besides, Eve would have no reason to believe she was suspected of murder unless Nick's daughter had confronted her, which seemed unlikely.

From the back of the property wafted pleasant fragments of an old song. To Yancy it sounded like the Eagles or maybe Poco, piped through outdoor speakers. He was kneeling near the concrete pad for the air-conditioning unit and pool pump, and the motor noises made it hard to follow the melody. Unfortunately for Yancy, the motors also drowned out the low-frequency growl of the neighbor's chow-cocker-rottweiler mix, which charged from behind and clamped its jaws on his left buttock.

Later he'd recall twisting his torso while spastically attempting to whack the animal with his hard hat, at which point he must have toppled sideways and struck his head on the slab. It was dark when he awoke with a roaring skull, his pants seat shredded and sticky with blood. The Satan-hound, having lost interest, was nowhere in sight.

Yancy lay there for a while, staring up at the sky. It was a clear night, though the starlight was washed out by the vast amber glow from the city. He remembered camping many times in Everglades National Park with his father; they'd arrange their sleeping bags to face west, 180 degrees away from Miami, so they could scout for constellations on a backdrop of natural darkness. Yancy decided that, once he got back his regular job, he'd invite his dad to fly down and they could paddle kayaks along the Shark River, or maybe through the backcountry of Chokoloskee. Winter was a better season, anyway; the nights cooled off, and there was plenty of dry tinder for a fire. And no goddamn bugs! Yancy recalled his mother's aversion to insects, which made his dad's posting in the Glades somewhat of a tribulation. But she'd hung in there, even through the blast-furnace days of summer when the mosquitoes were so thick you could inhale them into your lungs.

A door slammed and Yancy blinked himself back into the present. He was surprised to feel a tear slipping down his cheek. He rolled over and crawled through a bed of manicured bushes and then along the base of a stucco wall, toward the pool patio. Peeking around a corner, he saw Eve Stripling, crammed like a pepperoni into her white skinny jeans, standing on a lighted stone path leading to the boat dock. She was speaking to a taller hatless man beside her, his features obscured by the shadows. Although Yancy couldn't hear their conversation, the elevated pitch of both voices suggested a crisis in progress.

No more than a hundred yards away, rafting like a ghost pelican in the water, was a seaplane.

Ten

Evan Shook believed that only a masochist or a moron would stay in the Keys all summer. The humidity was murderous and the insects were unshakable, yet here he was. His sons were jacking off at a soccer camp in Maryland, his wife was on an Aegean cruise with her book club and his mistress was camping at a bluegrass festival in Vermont, probably balling some goddamn banjo player.

Meanwhile the construction project on Big Pine Key loomed as one of the stickier problems in Evan Shook's untidy world. He'd purchased the lot after the real estate market tanked and two years later he broke ground, anticipating a rebound in the demand for high-end island getaways. He was mistaken. The spec house wasn't done and already he'd been forced to drop the price four times. Most buyers with real money wanted a place closer to Key West, so they could safely patronize the eateries and multitude of bars. The farther one had to drive from Duval Street late at night, the higher the risk of a costly DUI pullover. Big Pine was twenty-nine miles up the road.

Still, Evan Shook had gotten promising nibbles before this bizarre stretch of foul luck – first the dead raccoon, then the hive of killer bees. He stormed the county offices to complain, but he couldn't find anybody in authority who would even write down his name. Eventually he was steered to some dweeb at the agricultural extension.

"They should spray the island to wipe out all the bees and wasps," Evan Shook declared. "And pay some trapper to kill those fucking raccoons. Fifty bucks a tail."

"That's not funny," the young agricultural agent said.

"Do you have any idea how much tax I pay on my property? More than you make in a year!"

"Here's some advice: Do a better job of securing the job site."

Evan Shook snapped, "Thanks for nothing, junior."

The unfinished house suffered from the absence of windows and doors, which were essential to sealing the structure from marauding wildlife. Before ordering the expensive impact-resistant glass that was required for new construction in hurricane zones, Evan Shook had been hoping to line up a buyer who'd spring for custom hardware.

As he drove back to the property, he again considered turning the whole damn thing over to a Realtor and flying home to Syracuse. However, due to a slender and ever-dwindling profit margin, Evan Shook remained opposed to paying somebody a commission to sell his spec house. Who needed a real estate agent when you had global internet?

Two potential buyers were coming to Big Pine that very morning – a middle-aged gay couple from Oslo. One of them owned a firm that manufactured drill equipment for deep-water oil rigs, and Evan Shook smelled a cash deal.

In his emails he'd laid it on thick about the "balmy Florida winters" and "laid-back tropical lifestyle" and "picture-postcard sunsets."

Typical Nords, the two men had arrived early for the showing. When Evan Shook pulled up, he saw them standing at the fence and conversing with his eccentric neighbor, Yancy. It was impossible not to notice that Yancy's pants were bunched around his ankles, and that the Norwegian couple was soberly contemplating his bare ass.

Evan Shook experienced a flush of dread. *What the fuck?* He remained inside the climate-controlled Suburban to mull the possibilities.

Yancy definitely liked women but perhaps he was bisexual. In that case, his presence next door might be a selling point for the spec house, should the Norwegians find him attractive. Evan Shook decided not to interrupt Yancy's private exhibition, just in case. He fiddled with the stereo dial and pretended to be talking on his cell. In the rearview mirror he inconspicuously checked his face for residual bee stings, and he was pleased to see that the welts were fading.

Soon Yancy pulled up his trousers and returned to his house. Evan Shook got out of the SUV and crossed the unsodded lot to greet his guests, whose first names were Ole and Peder. They were fit and fair-skinned, and they spoke better English than he did.

"I see you've met Mr. Yancy. An unusual guy."

"Yes," Ole said. "He is fortunate to be alive."

"Oh?"

The Norwegians exchanged clouded glances. Peder said, "Didn't he tell you what occurred last night?"

"No, I haven't talked with him," Evan Shook said, thinking: *This can't be good.*

"He was attacked while jogging," Ole reported.

"Yancy jogs?" Evan Shook decided it could be true. The man looked as scrawny as a scarecrow. "Did he get mugged or something?"

"Bitten," said Peder, "by wild dogs."

"A pack of them," Ole added.

Evan Shook was speechless. He'd never heard of feral hounds roaming the Keys. The Norwegians said the animals had "mauled" Yancy's rear end.

"He fought them off before they could reach his throat," Peder said.

"Where did all this happen?" Evan Shook asked.

Ole pointed. "Right there. At the corner of your street."

"That's awful," mumbled Evan Shook. *Awful in every imaginable way.*

"Mr. Yancy said it's not the first time. Usually he carries bear spray but last night he forgot."

Evan Shook bobbled helplessly. "Bear spray. Really?"

The Norwegians cast not a glance toward their future four-story island vacation house with the picture-postcard sunset view. They were grimly scanning the street for bloodthirsty canines.

"Let me assure you," Evan Shook said, "I've never seen so much as a stray Chihuahua on this island."

In the maddeningly neutral manner of Scandinavians, Peder shrugged. "Mr. Yancy showed us the bite wounds. It was a serious aggression."

"Well, I hope he's notified Animal Control. And if he hasn't, *I* damn sure will. Those mutts will be rounded up and gassed, I promise. Now, please, let me give you a tour of the palace."

Ole shook his head apologetically. "We don't wish to waste your time, Mr. Shook."

"You're not wasting my time. Are you kidding?"

Peder said, "I'm afraid we're no longer interested. This location, really, it isn't what we had in mind."

"Although your house looks quite airy and nice," Ole added. "It will make an excellent vacation home for somebody, I'm sure."

Evan Shook felt like his spine was being tapped. "Look, the price isn't locked in stone. Let's go inside and get out of the sun. The construction crew won't be back till noon."

"We have cats," Peder said. "So, you see, this neighborhood would be out of the question."

Ole elaborated politely. "They are too old to outrun a horde of dogs. Inge is eleven and Torhilda is thirteen."

"That's a pity," said Evan Shook. He sounded like a tire going flat.

The Norwegians firmly shook his hand and departed in their rental car. Evan Shook glared across the fence, where Yancy was leaning against the rail of his cedar deck. He had what appeared to be a shotgun under one arm, as if standing guard against another wolfish onslaught. Evan Shook spat on the ground and slouched off toward the chill of his Suburban.

Dr. Rosa Campesino, who insisted on examining it for herself, said: "Andrew, that's the nastiest-looking butt I've ever seen on a live person."

"The dog was a mutant brute!"

"Just hold still."

She swabbed the pulpy bite marks with Betadine while

Yancy pondered the sublime irony of being wounded in the same nether region where he'd targeted Bonnie Witt's husband.

"Looks like Fido got a mouthful," Rosa remarked, "and you didn't have much to start with."

"I have other noteworthy attributes." Yancy was flat on his belly in bed. When he reached out to squeeze Rosa's leg, she swatted his hand.

"Actually, you could use a few stitches," she said. "I brought a surgical kit, just in case."

"To cap off a truly humiliating second date."

"Hush, Andrew."

The drive back from Miami had been more nerve-grinding than usual because he'd had to tilt sideways behind the wheel, in order to keep weight off his mangled left buttock. It was worse than one of Bonnie Witt's nutty yoga positions. Contorted for nearly three hours, his brain pounding from the smack on the concrete, Yancy had emerged like an arthritic crab from the Subaru.

The next morning he'd phoned Rosa to tell her what had happened at Eve Stripling's house. She said she'd come straight down as soon as she finished the final autopsy on her schedule, a routine suicide. Yancy passed the time on his feet, because sitting was too painful. Liquor helped somewhat. He also distracted himself by initiating a useful conversation with a pair of Norwegians who were waiting to tour the monstrous spec house next door.

Rosa looked irresistible as she walked up Yancy's front steps, but he was in too much discomfort to make a move, even after she changed into a devastating sundress.

While she inspected the knot on his skull, he said, "Know what? We'd make a great crime-solving duo."

"How much have you had to drink?"

"Have mercy, woman. I ran out of Advil."

"Well, I don't sleep with drunken guys. Period."

Yancy sighed. "So many rules."

She took notice of the shotgun propped in a corner, and Yancy told her restaurant inspections could be dangerous. She informed him that for dinner she was doing blackened grouper with mashed sweet potatoes and a grilled Caesar, and that he was going to finish every bite or never see her again.

"I also stopped in Key Largo and got some homemade carrot cake," she said.

"From where?"

"What's the difference?"

"Rosa, you don't understand. I see all the health reports. I know the dirt on every kitchen."

She ordered him to be quiet while she sewed up his gnawed butt cheek. To take his mind off the intimate unpleasantries, Yancy told the story of how he was conceived during side one of *Abbey Road*.

"You mean side two," Rosa said. "The medley."

"No, side one. According to my mom, the big moment happened during 'Maxwell's Silver Hammer.'"

"It's all starting to make sense," said Rosa.

After trimming the last suture, she made Yancy stand up and drink an entire pitcher of cold water. When his head began to clear, he told her about the seaplane parked behind Eve Stripling's house.

"I ran the tail numbers on a flight-tracking website. It's a Cessna Caravan that's leased from a company in Boca Raton. Flew in from Congo Town the day before and cleared Customs at Opa-locka, all legal and proper."

"Where on earth is Congo Town?" Rosa asked.

"Bahamas." Yancy jerked a thumb toward the east. "Andros Island."

"Andrew, you'd make a darn good cop."

"That dog bite still stings like hell. You sure you know what you're doing?"

"My other patients never complain. They are, however, deceased."

That's when she kissed him. It was a good one, bordering on unforgettable.

"Only because you're injured," she said, and kissed him again.

He pulled her close. "How's this going to work with all these stitches? Do I have to keep standing?"

"Well," whispered Rosa, "I suppose you could kneel."

Yancy lifted her sundress. "You're the doctor."

The Dragon Queen asked, "How much you take fuh dot pink boy?"

Neville said he wasn't for sale.

"Too bod."

"And dot's a monkey, madam, not a boy."

"He got a name?"

"Driggs." Neville opened the brown bag. He handed her the fresh bottle of rum and a box of cheroots. "Dot woodoo dint woyk on Chrissofer," he said. "He supposa be gone but he ain't."

"Wot!"

"Mon tore down my house!"

"Maybe den he drop dead."

"No, madam, he come in again dis morning. Got offa plane wit his woman and drove 'way." Neville had received

126

the upsetting information from a cousin who worked at the airport.

The Dragon Queen struck a match on her bare heel and lighted one of the cigars. She assured Neville that she'd put a hideous, unshakable curse on the white devil. "Juss you wait. He be gone from Andros in due time."

"I cont wait fuh due time," said Neville. "Soon dot fella gon start puddin' up his damn hotel."

Neville had been hiding in the pines while Christopher's workers had replaced the fuel filter on the backhoe into which Neville had pissed. He asked the Dragon Queen what type of voodoo she'd used on the white American.

"Dot piece a shoyt you brought tuh me. Any minute now, his skin be fallin' off his body. Maybe his balls, too."

She twisted open the rum and took a husky slug, careful not to dribble. Then she sprang up from her wicker throne and began to dance, clapping her hands and swirling her long red-and-yellow dress. Neville glanced anxiously at the door, which he'd left ajar in anticipation of a speedy exit. Driggs bared his yellow teeth and bounded onto Neville's shoulder. It was the middle of the afternoon, broiling hot and not a murmur of breeze. The windows of the woman's shack were open and the doctor flies buzzed throughout, targeting the bald patches on the monkey's hide.

Neville was disappointed that the Dragon Queen's spell had failed, and increasingly skeptical of her claims. He'd returned to try once more only because of her considerable reputation for dark magic. He told her that stronger voodoo was needed to neutralize the man called Christopher. The Dragon Queen replied that she had needs of her own, and flapped the flowing dress up over her head. Neville was mortified to be flashed in such a crude manner. Driggs began to shriek and twitch and claw at his diaper.

"Madam, please," Neville protested.

"Wot's wrong wit dot ugly boy of yours? Am I de first grown woman he ever seen naked as God made us?"

Neville lied and said he was late to meet a boat mechanic in Rocky Town. He dug into a pocket and came up with twenty-one Bahamian dollars, which he counted out and placed on the table next to the rum. The Dragon Queen sighed, tucking the bills into her damp bony cleavage.

She said, "I will need some udder poysonal tings belonging to dis mon. Dot shoyt is all boined up."

Neville told her he'd come back with something better. That evening he would snoop in the trash cans outside the big oceanfront house that Christopher was renting. That's where he'd found the piece of shirt.

"Now, put dot sweet pink boy on my knee," she said, jabbing a dirty fingernail toward Driggs. "Lemme have a squeeze."

"No, madam, he bites."

"Wot!" She craned forward like a buzzard, studying the face of the trembling animal. "I tink someone pudda bod coyse on dis youngstah long time ago. But, see here, I kin make 'im good as new. Juss leave 'im wit me."

The monkey hissed and vaulted out of her reach. Neville followed him out the door.

Dinner was superb. Yancy cleaned his plate for the first time in weeks. Afterward he took Rosa out on his skiff. She asked why he hadn't remarried after Celia left him. He told her he'd come close twice. Rosa's own marriage had lasted three years and fizzled with nobody to blame, or so she said.

The truth was more depressing, laid bare by Google Earth. It happened on a rare slow day at the Miami-Dade morgue, when she had only one autopsy scheduled – an elderly female tourist who had straightforwardly drowned at Key Biscayne, a tragedy witnessed by fourteen blood relatives, none of whom could swim a lick. Why a family devoid of water skills chose to vacation at a seaside resort was beyond Rosa's scope of inquiry. The postmortem was completed by lunchtime and she had the afternoon to kill.

That's when a blood tech named Gaylord showed her the Google Earth app, which he downloaded to Rosa's office desktop. Soon she was enjoying aerial views of the Hoover Dam, the Malecón in old Havana, and even – more impressively – her parents' home in Union City. From thousands of feet in the sky she could still make out the old sycamores lining each side of the driveway, the rectangular outline of her mother's flower garden and a blurred image of her backyard swing set, which her father sentimentally refused to dismantle.

Next Gaylord loaded Google Maps with a street view, which sent Rosa eagerly cruising the roadways of her youth. There was the Ferraro house – Bobby Jr. had asked her to the junior prom; the shutters were now periwinkle blue, not white like before. The two-story where Angie Fernandez and her sisters had lived looked deserted, a sign planted in the dead lawn saying the place was up for sale by some bank. Also gone were the Sotos, who'd come from Cuba with Rosa's parents; the new owners had erected a tall wooden fence and nailed up a Beware of Dog sign embellished with the silhouette of a snarling pit bull.

It was only natural for Rosa to check out her present Miami neighborhood and the dwelling she shared with

Daniel, her then spouse, who worked as a teak carpenter on yachts. The driver of the Google camera truck had chosen a sunny morning to map the streets of Morningside, and Rosa thought their small home looked tropical and welcoming – the red barrel-tile roof, the green ivy nibbling at the bright stucco walls; in the front yard, ponytail palms, crimson bougainvilleas and a birdbath carved from limestone.

The only thing out of place that day, when the Google crew with their roof-mounted cameras rolled by, was a car Rosa didn't recognize in the driveway. The car was parked next to Daniel's Ram pickup, and it appeared to be a late-model Camry or an Accord; who could tell the difference? Dark blue was the color, though, definitely. The car had a Florida license plate that was partially fuzzed in the video – Gaylord surmised that Google did that on purpose because of privacy concerns – although upon enlargement Rosa was able to identify the prefix, which was LRW.

She would never forget those three letters because, as events unfolded, they came to stand in her mind for Low Rent Whore. Having nothing better to do on that slow afternoon, Dr. Rosa Campesino fed the tag information to a cop friend, who ran a statewide computer check and found one and only one blue Honda Accord registered with a tag beginning with LRW. It came back to a Sandra Jane Finn, white female, age twenty-nine, who was known to Rosa as a freelance hotel lifeguard and stand-up paddleboard instructor. For Daniel's birthday Rosa had purchased for him a ten-foot Dragonfly and three private lessons, which had evidently evolved to include floating blow jobs on the Intracoastal Waterway.

That night Daniel broke down and admitted to the affair,

lamenting his wretched luck that the Google vehicle had rolled past the marital homestead on one of the rare occasions when Sandy happened to be there. Usually they met at her place, he added ineptly. Rosa evicted him at scalpel-point, and over time she'd successfully swept him into a tiny moldy corner of her memory.

"You still talk to your ex?" Yancy asked.

"He's deceased," Rosa said, "but even if he wasn't, I wouldn't call."

A pod of dolphins rolled in the channel and Yancy patted softly on the water to draw them near. Rosa said she wasn't sure if she wanted to have children because her job presented such a depressing outlook for the human species. Yancy understood how she felt. Bonnie Witt had once tearfully begged him to impregnate her; the fact that he'd briefly considered the request was proof that he'd been crippled by romantic self-delusions. Their offspring would have been eternally fucked up, prime fodder for Dr. Phil.

The dolphins moved on, swimming leisurely with the tide. Yancy poled the skiff up on a grassy flat and staked off from the stern. He felt all right as long as he didn't sit down. A colossal thunderhead bloomed to the west, smothering the sun but spreading a lavender veil of light.

"Tell me about the other patient you saw today," he said to Rosa. "The one who didn't whine and squirm."

"You mean the suicide? It was a doctor, believe it or not."

Yancy briefly thought of Clifford, but he remembered that the Witts were in Sarasota. *Unless there was a medical convention in Miami . . .*

"Please tell me he didn't strangle himself with his pecker in his fist."

"No!" Rosa said. "And, by the way, that wouldn't be a

suicide. That would be an autoerotic miscalculation. This fellow did the job with a handgun."

"Messy, but less embarrassing."

"He was also drunk out of his gourd, and probably loaded on oxycodone. They found prescription bottles all over his condo. We'll know for sure when the lab finishes the toxicology."

Yancy had stopped admiring the sky. "He wasn't an orthopedist, was he?"

Rosa turned in the bow and looked up at him. "How'd you know?"

"His name was Gomez O'Peele?"

"Yes, Andrew, but how on earth—"

"I went to see him yesterday, after you and I had lunch. He used to work for Nick Stripling."

"Jesus, maybe the guy freaked out after you braced him."

"That's not the reaction I got. He wanted cash money for being an informant. Did they find a note?"

Rosa shook her head.

"Then how," Yancy said, "can you be sure he killed himself?"

"Point-blank wound, right temple. His prints on the weapon. No sign of forced entry, no sign of a struggle. His brother said he'd lost his job at a clinic and had financial problems, booze issues, drug issues." Rosa raised her hands. "It's textbook, Andrew."

"Except maybe it's not."

"Did you see a gun when you were there?"

"No. What did he use?"

"A .357 Smith."

"Let me take a guess on the ammo," Yancy said. "Hollow points, 158-grain."

"Okay, stop."

"Just like the ones that killed Charles Phinney." Yancy unstuck the pole and started pushing the skiff off the shallows. "When did this happen?" he asked.

"One of the doctor's neighbors heard a bang around seven-thirty, eight o'clock. She knocked on the door, got no answer. Didn't call the police because she had company – not her husband." Rosa was frowning. "This morning a rabbi who lives in the building found blood spots in his parking space. They'd dripped from O'Peele's balcony, where the body was found."

Yancy was disturbed to think his visit had in some way precipitated the doctor's death. Had somebody been surveilling the condo? Or maybe the shooter had followed him there. He thought of Eve and her boyfriend, their hushed and agitated conversation in the backyard on Di Lido Island. Had they been talking about O'Peele? Had they already shot him?

But why bother killing the guy, since Nick Stripling was dead and unreachable by prosecutors? A murder only made sense if Eve herself feared being indicted as a conspirator in the scooter-chair scam, and if she feared O'Peele would testify against her.

"I'll hold off signing the death certificate," Rosa said. "It should be easy to compare the bullets that killed O'Peele and Phinney. Meanwhile you should tell the homicide cops in North Miami Beach what you know. Tell them you were at the doctor's condo a few hours before the shooting and he seemed okay."

"I'm not telling anybody I was there."

"Andrew, this is serious shit."

"So is saving my career."

On the ride back to the boat ramp, Yancy mentally replayed his brief time inside O'Peele's place. He was fairly certain he hadn't left a trace of himself, besides fingerprints on a ginger ale can that the cops were not likely to dust since he'd tossed it in a Dumpster in the parking lot. Fortunately, he hadn't given the doctor one of his expired detective cards or even a phone number.

Still, there remained a slender chance that, despite the Percocets and bourbon, O'Peele had been sufficiently alert to have noted the name when Yancy flashed his restaurant-inspector ID. What if O'Peele had scrawled it down somewhere after Yancy had gone? *That* could be a problem.

Back at the house, Rosa inspected his stitches and predicted scar-free healing. Yancy attributed her unwavering Hippocratic detachment to the sorry sight of his gnawed, calorie-deprived hindquarters. When he asked her to spend the night, she declined.

"I'd never make it to the morgue on time."

"So, take the day off," Yancy said, belting his pants. "Join me on roach patrol. Tomorrow it's a gyro shop owned by Rastas who supposedly sell ganja out the back door. Lombardo thinks mice are nesting in the stash, which means they're the world's mellowest *rodentia*. Still, I could use a backup."

"Sounds like a dreamy third date," said Rosa, "but I'll take a rain check."

"When you talk to the homicide detectives in North Miami Beach, ask them if they found a cell phone on Dr. O'Peele."

"They did. In a pocket of his robe."

"I'd love to know the last number he called."

Rosa said, "Let me see what I can do." She delivered another toe-curling kiss and headed out the door.

Yancy took his time washing the dishes because standing was pain-free, making it easier to focus on the murder case. He was certain that Eve Stripling was responsible for her husband's death, yet he couldn't rule out the possibility that she'd had nothing to do with the shootings of Charles Phinney and Dr. Gomez O'Peele. Whoever said there's no such thing as coincidence never worked as a cop. The young boat mate could have been robbed and killed by some random dirtbag who'd heard him blabbing about his windfall, just as the pathetic orthopedist could have spiraled into a drug-induced abyss and ended his own life. Smith & Wesson was a popular brand of handgun in Florida, and plenty of unreliable characters favored .357s.

Like most police officers, Yancy had never in the line of duty fired his own service pistol, a lightweight Glock .40 that he'd been forced to turn in along with his resignation. At first he'd felt naked without a holster under his arm, but that had passed with time. For home protection he maintained a double-barreled 12-gauge Beretta loaded with buckshot, a habit left over from residing in greater Miami. For life in the Keys, such a substantial weapon served mainly as a decorative fixture. Yancy would never have thought to carry it while rolling his garbage can out to the street, which is where he was ambushed by a masked bicycle rider wearing a blaze-orange poncho, no more than an hour after Rosa Campesino had kissed him good-bye.

Eleven

Yancy remembered exactly when he decided to become a police officer: It was the day of his grandmother's funeral. A gang of burglars who specialized in scouting obituaries had looted his Nanna's apartment while she was being buried. Yancy's family was sickened when they walked in on the mess, which included gratuitous defecation not uncommon in such break-ins. His mother's knees buckled and she dropped to the floor, sobbing. His father made her stay by the door while he and Yancy searched to make sure the thieves were gone. Stolen were his grandmother's television set, her wedding ring, some heirloom jewelry worth maybe two grand, and an oxygen tank that had been left by her bed.

The Homestead cops snapped some photos and told the family not to expect any miracles. Watching his mother cry while his father cleaned up the intruders' shit, Yancy experienced an overpowering anger. That such a small, shabby crime could cause so much heartache was a revelation, and he thought of how often it happened every day. The jam-packed conditions in Florida prisons seemed proof that the majority of felons eventually fucked up and got busted. Yancy imagined it would be profoundly satisfying to participate in that process, although later he'd look back on his thinking as naïve.

Still, until his third or fourth year as a detective, he continued to fantasize about capturing the assholes who'd trashed his grandmother's place on the day of her funeral. In his daydreams the burglars wildly resisted arrest and were always dealt an agonizing lesson, their window-prying fingertips crushed to pulp by a squad-car door or the butt of a pump gun.

In real life those apprehended by Yancy usually surrendered without resistance, aware that their period of confinement would be brief and only nominally tuned to their actual sentence. Savvy thieves understood that the court system went easy on the unarmed and that violence was for fools. Yancy had occasionally tackled or Tazed a fleeing suspect, but never had he been forced to fight off an attack. Although he'd punched his way out of a couple of bars, he held no special skills in self-defense or the martial arts, having quit karate classes at age twelve because they'd cut too onerously into his fishing time.

It didn't really matter, because the cyclist caught him completely by surprise.

As Yancy was placing the trash can by the road, he heard the swish of air through spokes and he turned to look. A stretch mask obscured the face of the approaching rider but the orange poncho shone even in the deepening dusk. The bike knocked Yancy to the ground, and when he looked up, the stranger was standing over him. The last image to register was a downward-swinging arm with a bulky, ornate wristwatch.

Later, as a throbbing consciousness returned, Yancy surmised that he'd been struck with an old-fashioned sap or possibly a sock filled with coins. The blow landed on the opposite side from the bruise he'd incurred at Eve Stripling's house, leaving his head with conforming knots, like raw antler nubs.

Now the man in the poncho was dragging Yancy by the collar through the lot next door, past Evan Shook's spec house. Yancy's rear end was afire with pain, the friction against the ground having shredded Rosa Campesino's delicate web of sutures. The far side of Evan Shook's property fronted a canal, and Yancy sensed what was coming next. His limbs hung uselessly, however, and failed to respond to urgent brain commands. He half-shut his eyes and pretended to be coldcocked.

The masked stranger was grunting and huffing by the time he reached the canal. Awkwardly he tried to heave Yancy headlong, but Yancy's toes snagged on a ridge of coral rock, leaving him half in and half out of the water. Swearing, the attacker kicked at the soles of Yancy's feet until Yancy slid like a comatose otter down the bank.

He knew that the man who was trying to kill him – the same man who'd murdered Charles Phinney and probably Gomez O'Peele – would be unable to see him swimming in the murky canal if he went deep enough. His arms and legs didn't awaken for several harrowing seconds, and his lungs were searing by the time he began to make progress. Fortunately the waterway was narrow and the opposite shore was fringed densely with mangrove trees. Skinny as he was, Yancy managed to slither into the embroidery of roots and poke his head up for air. He was no more conspicuous than a floating coconut or an orphaned lobster buoy.

The burly figure in the poncho stood on the other bank, staring hard in search of bubbles and scanning the length of the canal to make sure that the victim of his beating hadn't surfaced. Yancy clung to the barnacled mangroves and braced his knees, trying not to create ripples. His bruised skull clanged, and hot pulses of nausea raised the annoying prospect of a concussion. Mosquitoes swarmed his ears and eyes, but he couldn't slap them away for fear of causing a telltale splash. Eventually his attacker turned and hurried off.

Five minutes was as long as Yancy could tolerate the insects. Gingerly he extricated himself from the roots, dog-paddled across the canal and crawled out. The thick night air seemed almost as heavy as the salt water. Approaching his house, Yancy saw a light go on in the living room, revealing through a front window the masked killer in the poncho. He was handling Yancy's shotgun, checking to see if it was loaded, which of course it was.

Yancy ducked into Evan Shook's place and groped his way to what must have been a closet. The door had yet to be hung but still it was a refuge of sorts, a recessed cubby where he could hide and dry out. Maybe take a nap. The closet smelled like raw pine, and Yancy felt sawdust under his feet. His forearms and knees stung from where the barnacles had grated the skin. He touched his scalp and found a syrupy wetness. There arose an urge to strip out of his sopping clothes, and the effort exhausted him.

As he drifted away, a familiar tune entered his woozy head. It was a rocking John Hiatt number, "Master of Disaster."

*

Evan Shook insisted on meeting the Turbles at the Key West airport and he personally escorted them to Big Pine. The couple rode together in the second seat of the Suburban so they could snuggle. With the loss of the skittish Norwegians still fresh, Evan Shook would have donned a topcoat and chauffeur's cap if he'd thought it would help sell his godforsaken spec house.

Ken Turble, who preferred to be called Kenny, had made such a killing in the commodities markets that he remained revoltingly wealthy after losing two-thirds of his fortune in a divorce. His new wife, Tanya, was eleven years younger than the youngest Turble offspring. Kenny proudly shared this information with Evan Shook early in the car ride. As a way of backfilling, Tanya yipped, "I got a business degree from Kaplan."

By Mile Marker 7, it was clear to Evan Shook that the marriage was doomed. Behind him the Turbles were cooing and murmuring so insipidly that they couldn't possibly have anything in common. Still, Evan Shook was pleased to see the crusty old coot derailed by lust; obviously he'd buy anything for his nubile bride, including a half-finished vacation chalet in the Florida Keys. A friend in the advertising business once told Evan Shook that Viagra was the only thing keeping Tiffany's and Porsche afloat, and Evan Shook thought the same might hold true for high-end real estate. A glance in the rearview mirror confirmed that Tanya Turble was now giving her husband a peppy hand job, which could only serve to prime him for Evan Shook's sales pitch.

"Eyes on the road," Kenny Turble warbled rapturously.

"Yes, sir," said Evan Shook.

Tanya inquired if there was a Kleenex in the vehicle. Evan

Shook reached back and presented his handkerchief, which happened to be monogrammed. "Keep it," he said.

She laughed. "Duh."

"I think you're gonna fall in love with this house."

"We saw a gem on Marco Island. Right, baby?"

Kenny Turble said, "Gorgeous place. Except I don't golf."

"Honestly, I can't see you two on Marco," Evan Shook commented. "The average age is, like, eighty-four. Don't get me wrong – my mother lives there and she's happy as a clam – but you don't strike me as the bridge club-and-shuffleboard type."

"Or golf," said Kenny.

His wife rolled down the window and let fly the sticky handkerchief. "They had a cool gym in town," she said.

"Do you enjoy fishing? We've got some incredible offshore action – tuna, mahi, even blue marlin."

"Kenny loves that stuff. Me, I just like to lay out."

"Sun we've got," Evan Shook said. "Three hundred and twenty-five days a year." It was a statistic he'd invented for the occasion; for all he knew, it might have been accurate. However, the line about his mom living on Marco Island was bullshit; she had a town house in Scottsdale.

"We almost there?" Tanya asked.

"Hey, check out the deer," Evan Shook said as they passed a doe and two fawns.

"Oh, sweet. And they're so little!"

Ken Turble grunted. "When's the season open?"

"November through January," Evan Shook replied, another lie. You could go to prison for shooting a Key deer, but he didn't want to queer the deal by telling that to Kenny, obviously an avid hunter.

Nothing seemed amiss when they got to the property; no sign of creepy Andrew Yancy in the vicinity. Tanya Turble headed for the spec house while her husband quizzed Evan Shook about windstorm insurance and flood-elevation certificates. Kenny also wanted to know if he could put in a dock, and how deep the water stood at low tide. The two men strolled to the bank of the canal, where Evan Shook was disturbed to see a discarded liquor bottle, a spinning rod and a gamey pair of flip-flops.

"What's the matter?" Ken Turble said.

"Let's go inside so I can give you and your wife the grand tour."

But the tour fizzled quickly. Upon entering the house they came upon a nude man sprawled on the floor of the future living room. He was face-up in a splayed, post-crucifixion pose. His head glistened with lumps, both knees showed fresh scabs and his outflung arms bore gashes and scrapes.

Evan Shook blurted, "Yancy, what the fuck!"

"Those dogs, man. You didn't see 'em?"

Tanya Turble stood off to the side with slender arms folded. Her husband couldn't help but observe that she was staring at the naked intruder's crotch.

"Who the hell is this character?" Ken Turble demanded. "Is he on drugs or what?"

Yancy raised his head to cough. "They went berserk again. I was lucky to get away."

Evan Shook was trembling as he hurriedly gathered Yancy's damp clothes from the bottom of the closet and threw them at his feet.

"I live next door," Yancy said, sitting up slowly.

Tanya said, "What kinda dogs?"

Kenny elbowed Evan Shook. "That's his house right there? Oh great."

"I was putting out the trash last night," Yancy continued, "and the pack was on me so damn fast, I barely made it to the canal." He rose and wriggled into his damp pants. "Soon as I got out of the water I ducked in here to hide."

In the hope of boosting Yancy's stock as a potential neighbor, Evan Shook informed Ken Turble that Yancy was a police officer. Who wouldn't feel safer with a cop living on the block? A spark came to Tanya's green eyes, which again her watchful husband detected.

"What kinda cop?" she asked.

"I'm not free to say." Yancy steadied himself against a wall. "Sorry about all the blood," he said to Evan Shook. "Your crew will be painting over it anyway, right? One of these days."

"Did you go fishing on my property last night?"

Yancy sighed. "Jesus, do I look like I went fishing?" He turned to Tanya Turble. "Wild dogs on the island. They only come out at night."

"You mean like werewolves."

"No, darling," said Kenny, stepping to his wife's side, "just a bunch of stray mutts."

Evan Shook spoke in toneless desolation. "I've never laid eyes on these animals. Not once."

Young Tanya addressed Yancy. "Would they eat a collie?"

"Are you kidding? They'd eat a fucking Clydesdale."

She pursed her lips. "Well, we could keep Barney locked up – that's our dog."

Ken Turble was wishing the cop would put on a shirt so that he might recapture his wife's attention. "No, sweetie,

Barney needs open space to run. We can't leave him cooped indoors all day."

Evan Shook asked, "Don't you want to see the view upstairs?"

Kenny said no thanks. Tanya suggested they summon an ambulance for the injured police officer.

"No need," said Yancy, toddling toward the door. "My girlfriend's a doctor."

It hurt so badly that he actually screamed in the shower. Rogelio Burton arrived with nine tubes of Neosporin, the entire inventory from the local Walgreens. While Yancy gooped his multiple lacerations he told Burton everything that had happened since Eve Stripling had come to claim her husband's severed arm.

Burton said, "You need to clue the sheriff in right away."

"Not until it's a lock."

"That's insane, Andrew. You're gonna get yourself killed *and* blow the case. How did this asshole find you? The guy who tried to drown you."

"I have a guess," Yancy said.

He surmised that Gomez O'Peele had a better memory for names than most junkies. The doctor had probably phoned Eve with a shakedown in mind soon after Yancy left the apartment. Told her he'd just been questioned by a cop – how much was it worth to her for him to keep his mouth shut about the Medicare scooter scam? Eve had told him to sit tight and she'd bring some money. Instead she sent Poncho Boy with his .357. Once he pried Yancy's name out of O'Peele, he put a bullet in the poor slob's noggin.

Tracking Yancy to his house would have been easy for Eve, who already knew he lived somewhere on Big Pine. An online check of property records would have produced the address. Google would have given her a flawless road map and, as a bonus, the news stories about Yancy's recent departure from the sheriff's office. From Eve's point of view, a disgraced ex-cop wasn't such a risky target for killing. After all, she and the boyfriend had made her husband's murder look like an accident; why not the same fate for Yancy?

"Call Sonny," Burton implored again.

"Sonny does *not* want to know about this."

"You're putting me in a helluva shitty position."

"What position? You just stopped over for a beer. Big deal." By now Yancy was shining from the ointment. He looked like an abused gummy bear.

"The widow's boyfriend jacked my shotgun last night," he informed Burton. "Oh, and here's a clever touch: He left an empty booze bottle and one of my spinning rods down by the water, so everybody would think I got drunk and fell in, whatever."

"Works for me." Burton had begun to pace. "Phinney's girlfriend is missing."

"She left town."

"Man, could you please put on some clothes?"

"I'm too sticky," Yancy said. "Hey, Rog, if I slipped you the tail numbers off a seaplane, could you find out who chartered it? I mean without sending up a goddamn flare. I'll give you the name of the leasing company."

Burton said, "I've got my job to think about, Andrew. A wife plus two kids that might want to get off the rock and go to college someday. Why do I want to get dragged into a mess like this? Look at your victims and tell me who gives a shit. Let's see – there's a low-life Medicare scammer, a dock rat and a crooked doctor with a dope habit. Before you come close to making a case, Stripling's wife and the poncho dude will be long gone. Disappearing is no problem in the Bahamas, *mon*. You know how it goes."

"I know that anybody can be found."

"And who's gonna pay for your hotels and plane tickets, Andrew? The health department? Are they doing extraditions now, too?" Burton raised his hands. "What's the fucking point?"

"Catching a couple of murderers, that's the point," Yancy said. "Hell, it's something to do in my spare time. The tarpon run is over." He grabbed a towel from the bathroom and wrapped it around his waist. "Did I mention that Eve gave the dead husband's fancy watch to her boyfriend? He was wearing it last night when he clocked me."

Burton said, "What if Stripling was killed in Miami? You think the homicide guys up there will give you credit for solving the case? Never in a jillion years. Your name won't even be in the reports, Andrew, unless you change it to C. Informant."

"Do me a favor," Yancy said. "Next time you come over, just bring chicken soup."

"For Christ's sake, I'll check on the seaplane."

After Burton was gone, Yancy realized he should have asked to borrow a gun. Eve would be scouring the *Citizen*'s website for news of Yancy's tragic drowning. When she didn't find the story, she'd probably send the boyfriend back to Big Pine to try again. Yancy called Rosa Campesino at the morgue to tell her about his action-packed evening, but the secretary said Rosa was in the middle of an autopsy. Next Yancy tried Caitlin Cox and left a message on her voicemail.

Hearing a knock, he peeked through a window and saw

a sallow, thickset fellow who was dressed like a plainclothes cop, which he was.

"John Wesley Weiderman," the man said after Yancy let him in. "Oklahoma Bureau of Investigation."

"You're shitting me."

"Can I have a glass of ice water?"

"Did you fly into Miami International?"

"Yes, sir."

"Then hard liquor is in order."

"Tap water's fine, thanks." John Wesley Weiderman opened a briefcase and took out a years-old mug shot of Plover Chase, a.k.a. Bonnie Witt. "Do you know this woman? Her husband said we might find her down here."

Yancy sat down across from the investigator. "I haven't seen her in a while. Can I assume she's in trouble?" He was wondering why Clifford had ratted out his beloved Bonnie.

"Ms. Chase is a convicted sex offender. For years she's been a fugitive."

"Well, we did have an affair, a romance, a fling, whatever you call it back home. But in no manner did she victimize me, John – may I call you John? I was a willing participant. Recklessly enthusiastic, to be truthful. But I'm sure Dr. Witt filled you in. Here in the Keys she called herself Bonnie, not Plover. I'd never sleep with a woman named Plover."

The investigator said, "What's the matter with you?"

"In general? I don't know where to start." Yancy readjusted his towel, which kept slipping off his hips due to the medicinal sheen on his skin.

"Were you in a fight?"

"There's a pack of mad dogs in the neighborhood, I'm sorry to say."

"Those don't look like dog bites."

147

Yancy shed the towel, spun around and bent over to display the tooth wounds inflicted by the mixed-breed fiend that lived next door to Eve Stripling. The investigator from Oklahoma took a slight step back.

"And what happened to your head?"

"I took a tumble," Yancy said, "while running for my life." He refilled John Wesley Weiderman's glass with water. "Are you folks really going to prosecute Bonnie after all this time? Hell, the bail bondsman's probably dead from old age."

"Dr. Witt said you used to be a detective."

"Tell me something – when you spoke with Clifford, did you happen to notice any rope burns on his neck? Because he likes to choke himself while he whacks off. Not that I'm passing judgment, but it's important for you to know that your complainant has oxygen-deprivation issues."

John Wesley Weiderman said, "Hey, I'm just doing my job."

Although Yancy had never been to Tulsa, he imagined any civil servant there would jump at the offer of a trip to Florida, even in the dead of summer. The investigator gave Yancy a business card, but not before asking point-blank if Plover-slash-Bonnie was the person who assaulted him.

"John, get serious."

"But it wasn't really wild dogs, was it?"

"What did she do to piss Clifford off? Or, should I say, *who* did she do?"

"Please call me if she shows up. To us, this isn't a joke."

Yancy began pawing through the open Neosporin containers on the table. "Man, the last thing I need in my life right now is a fucking staph infection." He found a tube that wasn't empty and said, "Would you excuse me for a minute?"

"Actually, I've got an appointment in Key West." John Wesley Weiderman stood up. "Can you recommend a place for lunch? The guy at Hertz said Stoney's was real good."

Yancy smiled in resignation. "So I hear."

Widowhood was a grind.

Eve Stripling thought she'd prepared herself, but there was much more paperwork than she'd expected. Also, the endless condolences – her friends, Nicky's friends, random clergy, relatives she didn't know existed. Except for Caitlin they all meant well, although Eve was ready to strangle the next person who brought her a damn casserole.

The problem was she had limited grieving experience to draw from. On numerous occasions she sensed crying was expected of her, yet the only way to make it happen was by remembering a pet turtle she'd owned when she was nine. Flash was the turtle's name; he was the size of a silver dollar. One day he trundled out of the house and her mother backed over him with the Delta 88. Eve was bereft for a week. She accused her mom of squashing Flash on purpose, the so-called accident occurring soon after a tense family conversation about bacteria on pet-store reptiles. A burial was held under a lime tree in the backyard, Eve bearing the compressed remains of her companion upon a Teflon spatula.

Years later, at Nick's funeral, all the time Eve stood sobbing by the coffin she was actually thinking of poor little Flash, whom her parents had coldly refused to replace. Every tear she shed that day was for her lost turtle, not for her husband.

Her most important task, besides mourning, was to persuade a Miami judge to declare Nicky dead. It should have been a routine order, the severed arm being more than ample evidence of his tragic demise. The hurdle was Nick's daughter, who'd been spreading a vicious whisper that Eve had murdered him and chopped off his left arm to fit a bogus story about a boating accident.

Hiring a lawyer to threaten Caitlin Cox with a slander suit might have been sound strategy for an innocent widow, a woman with nothing to hide. For Eve Stripling, the wiser course was to reach out with a peace offering – or a *piece* offering, as it happened. From past experience she knew Caitlin's hostility could be dissolved by a gush of money. At first Eve couldn't bring herself to make the phone call, but soon it became clear there was no other choice. Her nightmare scenario was Caitlin showing up at the court hearing, telling the judge that her rotten stepmother had bumped off her beloved father.

Whom she hadn't seen in years because she was a selfish, pouty, greedy—

Deep breath, Eve had said to herself before dialing Caitlin's number.

Lunch is the way to go, someplace quiet where we can talk business, neither of us having to pretend we can stand the sight of the other.

Suck it up, Eve told herself, *you're the only one who can pull this off.*

And she did.

They'd met at a small Brazilian restaurant in the Design District. Caitlin came right out and asked her if she'd killed Nick, or paid to have him killed. Eve swallowed hard, bowed her head and refocused her thoughts on Flash, her precious childhood buddy, stuck like a patty of brown chewing gum to the left rear tire of her mother's Oldsmobile. It worked like magic – Eve quickly began to cry, blubbering that she'd loved Nick Stripling more than anyone, anything in the world. He *was* her world!

Caitlin was taken aback. "Then what about that boyfriend of yours in the Bahamas?"

At which point Eve could feel the color rush from her tear-streaked cheeks. Somehow she managed to keep it together, cooking up a story about an elderly uncle that seemed to temporarily appease Caitlin. Eve then steered the conversation to the less precarious topic of money, specifically the generous benefits of Nick's life insurance policy, half of which he'd wanted his only daughter to have despite their heartbreaking estrangement.

In addition, Eve went on – Caitlin practically drooling in suspense – there was an offshore bank account that Nick Stripling had opened for the benefit of future grandchildren.

Caitlin, suddenly sentimental: "Simon and I are trying to get pregnant!"

So the deal got done. Eve ordered a bottle of white wine, which Caitlin depleted single-handedly before the food arrived.

"I didn't kill your dad," Eve said solemnly, reaching across to touch Caitlin's hand. "He died when his boat sank, just like they said."

"I know, shit, I know." Caitlin had achieved that level of alcohol-induced volubility where no thought goes unspoken, no secret goes unshared.

And that had been when Eve Stripling learned her stepdaughter had been talking to Andrew Yancy.

Twelve

After Neville's home on Green Beach was demolished, he went to stay in Rocky Town, where he alternated sleepovers with his girlfriends. The backhoe Neville had attempted to sabotage was running fine again, joined by a bulldozer that had arrived on a barge from a bankrupt development on Chub Cay.

To watch over the Curly Tail Lane construction site, the rich American called Christopher recruited some pinheaded brute from Nassau. The fellow had a high crinkled forehead and small malformed ears that looked like fetal fruit bats. People said he used to work at Fox Hill prison but got fired for brutalizing inmates with a marlin billy. Christopher put a rusty, camper-style trailer on the property, and that's where the new man slept. Occasionally Neville spotted him in town, eating at the conch shack, but he never lingered.

On the same day Christopher's new earth-chewing machine appeared, Neville went back to see the Dragon Queen. He presented to her a man's black nylon sock that he'd snatched from the same garbage can as the shirt fragment, outside the house rented by Christopher and his woman. The Dragon Queen frowned when Neville handed her the sock, which had a hole in the heel.

"Dis all you got fuh me?"

"Please, madam. I dont have much time."

"Look how big dis mon's feet be! No wonder my udda coyse dint woyk."

Something about the Dragon Queen seemed different, and at first Neville couldn't figure it out. Then, when she reached over and deftly snatched a doctor fly from his arm, it struck him: The woman was dead sober. The hairs on Neville's neck prickled when she plucked one wing off the fly and then watched it spin helplessly across the warped plank floor.

He said, "I kin go bok and look fuh sum ting more. Wot is it you want?"

The Dragon Queen grinned. She had perhaps seven teeth in her whole mouth. "Wot do I want? I want *you*, suh."

It was a moment Neville had been fearing; the Dragon Queen's rapacious appetite for men was legendary. Not wishing to become her next doomed lover, he'd prepared a defense.

"No, madam, I got de clap."

"Lemme have a peek." She rocked in her wicker chair and lit a cigar.

Neville shook his head. "Dot's not proper."

The Dragon Queen was firm: No sex, no more voodoo curses on Christopher. Neville was angry but he held back. Instead he said, "De mon already rip down de house where my own fahdder was born. He toyn it into a heap a goddamn rocks."

153

She spat and said, "White devil."

"Den help me take 'im down."

"You don't got de clap. Drop off your pants, bey, so I kin see your ting."

"Wot else you take fuh pay? All I got is foity dollahs."

The Dragon Queen chuckled and shut her eyes and blew a wreath of smoke that smelled like rancid mulch. "Mistuh Neville, where's dot little pink boy a yours?"

"He's outside. Why you ask?" Neville had leashed Driggs to the handlebars of the bike.

"So, den, here's wot we do." The Dragon Queen cracked one eyelid. "You give dot boy to me, as my own, and I'll pudda coyse on dis white devil Chrissofer make 'im dread sorry he ever set foot on dis island. Maybe even kill de mon, fuh true. Dot's all I want from you. No money, no fucky, juss Driggs."

"Madam, I tole you. Dot's not a real boy."

"So you say."

"Why you want 'im fuh?"

"It's lonely here on dis dusty hill. I gotta pull de wings off flies juss so dey stay 'round to keep me comp'ny. Dot ol' Driggs, he could dance hoppy circles 'n' make me lof all night long. Nodder ting, I kin teach 'im how to pour my rum drinks and rub my feets."

"But—"

"Dot's my final offer, suh. If you want sum bigass woo-doo, either gimme de boy or every fine inch a your manhood." The Dragon Queen stubbed the cigar and dropped it inside the black sock that Neville had taken from Christopher's trash.

"Madam, he's not a very good monkey."

"Oh, I know."

154

Neville wasn't sure why he cared about Driggs, who had a corrupt streak and no appreciation for Neville's many acts of kindness. The animal was dexterous and conniving, but discipline was almost impossible because Driggs retaliated with filthy bites to soft-tissue targets such as calves and thighs. Even when unprovoked, the creature traveled with a septic disposition. On the streets he shrewdly singled out white tourists and approached them for handouts. Those who balked might be punished by a rabbit punch to the genitals, or the nasty twist of a nipple. On one occasion, a German teen who tried to snap a picture of the animal was flogged with her own bikini top.

Driggs's noxious attitude baffled Neville, although he suspected a dietary deficiency. He'd become worried when his little sidekick started molting, yet all efforts to wean the monkey from conch fritters and johnnycakes were vehemently rebuffed. Neville's girlfriends were scared of Driggs and demanded that the scabby demon remain tethered outdoors during Neville's nocturnal visits. The monkey's response was to dig both hands into his diaper and hurl handfuls of feces at the windows, a raucous spectacle that had pitched Neville's love life into a stall.

"He smot. Dot I kin tell," said the Dragon Queen. "I teach 'im some prime woo-doo moves."

"Butchu ain't gon hoyt de fella, right?"

"Wot!" Indignantly she flapped her hem up and down, Neville turning away.

"Hoyt dot little fella?" she cried. "Come back in a few days, see if you don't find de hoppiest pink boy in all de world. Under my roof he gern live like de Prince a Wales!"

Neville said Driggs was worth eight hundred dollars,

which was what he'd been told by the sponger who'd given him the monkey years earlier at the domino game.

"Eight hundred! Dot's crazy talk," said the Dragon Queen.

"He was in de movies wit Johnny Depp. It's no lie."

"Cap'n Jack Sparrow? You fulla crap. Your boy played de bod monkey?"

"Yes, madam, in all dose pirate movies. And he *is* a monkey," Neville reiterated.

The Dragon Queen crowed uproariously. "You bring me dot boy Driggs fuh payment, I put a jumbo coyse on your white devil."

Neville was torn. "Led me tink wot to do. I come right bok."

Outside, Driggs squatted on rash-covered haunches beneath the gumbo-limbo tree where Neville had left him. It was a repugnant scene that would alter both of their lives. The Huggies diaper lay shredded on the ground, and Neville's bicycle seat was slathered with fresh shit.

Neville's outrage swelled as he appraised the stinking mess. "I fed up wit your foolishness!" he snapped. "Come den, let's go see your new momma."

The monkey stopped gnawing on his leash and looked up. His upper lip wormed into a reflex sneer, but his rosy bald brow furrowed in consternation.

"Dot's right," Neville said. "Dis is good-bye."

The owner of Big Luke's Lobsteria was Luke Motto, a former Thoroughbred jockey who stood five-two. He was called Big Luke because he was the tallest among six siblings.

The Lobsteria was Yancy's first official stop after a ten-day sick leave (ordered by Lombardo), during which Yancy went fishing alone every morning. For privacy he chose the Content Keys, and wore only his boxers while poling the skiff. The salt air hastened the healing of his gouged ass and also the mangrove scrapes on his limbs. His headaches ceased shortly after the bruises disappeared. As a treat he landed several good bonefish and an eighty-pound tarpon. Twice Rosa drove down after work and stayed the night.

"You double-clicked that fucker," Big Luke said accusingly.

"I'm afraid not."

They were arguing about German cockroaches, which Yancy was required to count during all restaurant inspections. The pest census was a challenging aspect of the job although Tommy Lombardo, Yancy's instructor, had provided little guidance. For reasons unclear to Yancy, the state of Florida required that live roaches and dead roaches be tabulated separately. Perhaps a deceased roach was deemed less repellent to diners than a crawling one, but in truth the contamination differential was negligible – insect parts versus insect droppings.

Yancy himself favored dead roaches because live ones were too quick, a coppery flash disappearing beneath a shelf or baseboard. During his first week on the job, and uncertain of protocol, Yancy included in his live-specimen tallies only those he was able to corner and kill. Many others escaped, and he was nagged by a sense of falling short in his duties.

So, to the dismay of unsanitary proprietors such as Luke Motto, Yancy developed a method of herding and capturing live roaches that allowed a more precise accounting. In his right hand he wielded a billiard cue to which he'd bolted the head of a badminton racket. In the other hand he carried a

DustBuster, a lighter, updated version of the device he had ingloriously deployed against Dr. Clifford Witt in Mallory Square.

One brisk pass through the kitchen of Big Luke's Lobsteria filled the vacuum with a pulsing, melon-sized mass of roaches that Yancy neutralized by vigorously shaking the filter compartment until the captives were too addled to mount an escape. He then dumped his catch on a butcher-block cutting board, and got down to business with tweezers and a thumb-activated ticket counter he'd bought on Amazon for $2.99.

"That one right there – you did him twice!" Luke Motto insisted.

The total of live roaches was up to sixty-eight, which in Yancy's view qualified as an infestation. "And I haven't even checked the pipes under the sink," he remarked through his hospital mask.

"Don't!" Luke Motto bleated.

"I got five bucks says we break two hundred today."

"And I got a C-note and a free shrimp hoagie says you cut me some slack."

"If you had half a brain, Luke, you'd spend that money on an exterminator."

With every click of the counter, Yancy dropped another dizzy roach into a large Ziploc baggie. Lombardo hadn't instructed him to preserve the insects as evidence, so he didn't. Customarily, after presenting his inspection report to the disgruntled owner, Yancy would dispatch the roaches by placing the baggies under a tire of his car and flattening them on his way out of the parking lot. It wasn't an authorized technique for disposal, but so far none of the restaurateurs had lodged a complaint.

"You can't just barge in here and shut me down!" Luke Motto protested. "This ain't Nazi Russia!"

Yancy tuned him out while completing the order for a temporary suspension. He offered the phone number of a Marathon pest control company and told Big Luke he'd be back in three days for a re-inspection. Then he squashed the roaches with his Subaru and drove to Duck Key to view the condominium belonging to Eve and Nicholas Stripling.

The building superintendent gave up the key as soon as Yancy displayed his health department credentials. For a weekend condo it wasn't bad. The living room featured a balcony view of the Atlantic, while the bedrooms overlooked a polyp-shaped swimming pool with a slightly discolored kiddie pond. In the closets of the condo Yancy found men's and women's outdoor clothes, fishing rods, spearguns, flippers, dive masks, snorkels and a roll of clear Visqueen poly sheeting of the type used to protect carpet and furniture from splatters while a room was being painted – or a human body was being chopped to pieces.

The second scenario occurred to Yancy after he spotted a hatchet, scoured clean, inside the dishwasher. It made sense that if a woman was involved, the hatchet would have been rinsed of gore before being placed in a dishwasher rack amid wine glasses and salad bowls. Yancy reached into the opening of the garbage disposal and carefully probed the movable blades. All he recovered was the fractured chip of an olive pit.

Next he went to the double shower in the master bedroom and unscrewed the drain cover. He employed a bent coat hanger to explore the pipe, which yielded a clot of jet-black hair. Ensnared in the yucky clump were three sharp-edged, whitish fragments no larger than kitten's teeth.

Yancy deposited the entire tangle in another baggie, locked up the condo, put the key under the mat and returned to his car. There he phoned Caitlin Cox and said, "I believe I know where they murdered your father."

Her reply caught him by surprise: "Actually, Inspector, we need to talk."

Yancy cranked up the Subaru's fitful AC and waited.

Caitlin said: "Look, I was wrong about Eve. There's no hot boyfriend in the Bahamas – she stopped there on the way home from Paris to visit one of her uncles. And Dad's wedding ring? The only reason she swapped it out for a cheapo? She didn't have the heart to leave it on his hand inside the coffin. She got a jeweler in Bal Harbour to hang it on a necklace and, God, I feel like such an a-hole. The more I think about it? Seriously."

Yancy was miffed at himself for not seeing it coming. "Caitlin, listen to me. Eve bought that replacement wedding band in Nassau before anyone told her your dad was missing, much less dead, which means she already knew. And, just so you're up to speed, the nonexistent boyfriend tried to kill me the other night. I'm pretty sure he was wearing your father's wristwatch."

"That's crazy."

"Okay, I made it all up. Because, truly, I've got nothing better to do."

"Look, man," she said. "I'm super sorry I got you involved, but I was so bummed about losing Dad I guess I didn't want to believe the truth. He swamped his boat and drowned, end of story, just like the Coast Guard said. I mean, bad shit happens to fishermen all the time, right? The perfect storm, whatever."

Yancy told her about the plastic sheeting and the hatchet

he'd found in the condo. "And also some white bony fragments in a shower drain."

"Oh please," said Caitlin. "Broken stone crab shells, probably."

"What about the hand axe?"

"Dad used the flat side to crack the claws. Just a couple of taps is all it took."

Yancy knew he couldn't bring Caitlin around, but he was curious to learn how the deal went down. "So you're not mad anymore about Eve getting the whole two million from his life insurance?"

"No way."

Then came the edgy pause. Yancy smiled and put the car in gear.

"Anyhow," Caitlin continued, "turns out Eve and I are what you call co-beneficiaries. We split the money fifty-fifty. So I guess Dad wasn't so pissed at me after all."

"When did you find all this out? Because last time we spoke, you expressed the view – and I'm quoting more or less faithfully – that your 'greedy slut of a stepmother' was screwing you over."

Caitlin said, "Because I was super upset, okay? I wasn't thinking straight."

"Until?"

"I saw Eve, and there was Dad's wedding ring on her neck. Then she told me about the insurance policy and other stuff."

"Other stuff?"

"You know. Inheritance stuff."

Yancy thought: *All that's missing is a winning Lotto ticket.* "And where did this healing conversation take place?" he asked Caitlin.

"She took me to lunch."

"Yes, I can picture it. Where are you now?"

"At the courthouse."

"Let me guess: Where you just finished telling the judge you totally agree with Eve – your dad should be declared legally dead."

"Yeah, so?" On the other end, Nick Stripling's daughter seemed to be clearing a chunk of cactus from her throat. After the guttural delay she said: "What the hell's wrong with you, anyway? You never heard of closure? Families are supposed to come together, no matter what."

"And nothing says closure like a million bucks."

"Dad died when his boat sunk, just like they said. Let it go, dude."

"Not possible, Caitlin. We'll chat again, you and I."

"Why? No, we won't!"

"Then tell me his name."

"Who?"

"The mystery uncle in Nassau."

Caitlin said, "You're such a dickhead."

Yancy tossed down the phone and gunned his car toward a gap in the traffic, heading up the Overseas Highway.

Thirteen

When Yancy was younger, he'd briefly considered joining the U.S. park service, like his father. "Why didn't you?" Rosa Campesino asked.

"I was too lazy. And the pay sucks."

"Andrew, you're full of shit."

"Look at it this way. If I'd become a ranger in the Everglades, we would never have met."

"Unless an alligator got you, and I was assigned to do the post."

"Assuming there was something left of me," Yancy said.

"Oh, there would be. Gators are sloppy eaters. By the way, you've healed magnificently."

"I was hoping you'd notice."

Rosa was massaging him on an autopsy table. It was half past midnight at the morgue and they were alone in the main suite, which had twelve forensic workstations. Each narrow table was made of eighteen-gauge stainless steel. Rosa had spread some towels, removed the headrest and instructed Yancy to lie still on his belly.

"What happens if somebody walks in?" he asked.

"Just play dead. I'm serious."

She was wearing a lab smock, rubber-soled white shoes, and nothing else. In theory Yancy should have been wildly aroused, but the venue creeped him out. He'd made love to women in all sorts of odd places – with Bonnie Witt, of course, high on the tuna tower of her husband's boat, but there had been other memorable trysts inside a windmill on a putt-putt golf course, the second-to-last car of a Metrorail train, an unoccupied toll booth on the Rickenbacker Causeway and a self-photo kiosk beside the manatee pool at the Miami Seaquarium. He understood the thrill of semi-public sex, but doing it among the deceased seemed more dark than daring.

The Miami-Dade morgue had been designed with a contingency for a worst-case airline crash; its five coolers were made big enough to hold all the passengers and crew from a fully loaded jumbo jet – a total of 555 bodies. Tonight there were only sixty-six in refrigeration. Yancy had declined Rosa's offer of a tour. It felt good when she pressed her knuckles into the meat of his back, but he was having trouble unwinding. The cold filtered breath of the morgue didn't smell like death, but it wasn't exactly a breeze off Monterey Bay.

"Roll over, Andrew."

"Then I can't play dead if we're caught."

"And why not?" Rosa said.

"Because dead guys don't get boners."

"Do what the doctor says."

She turned off the overhead light and climbed on top of him. The autopsy platform wasn't comfortable but it was sturdy. Soon Yancy loosened up and his thoughts began meandering, which sometimes happened when a smooth physical rhythm was established. It was no reflection on his partner; he had an incurably busy brain. Rosa herself seemed happily diverted, so Yancy kept pace while sifting through the day's events.

Except for a colorful exchange of profanity with a meth-head tanker driver on the turnpike, the ride to Miami had been uneventful. Yancy had first stopped at the Rosenstiel marine lab on Virginia Key, where an earnest young master's candidate examined the shark tooth extracted from Nick Stripling's severed arm and confirmed the species as *Sphyrna tiburo*, a common bonnethead that typically feeds inshore. The finding proved that Eve Stripling and her accomplice had placed the stump of her husband's limb in the shallows and chummed up some resident predators in the hope that their gnashing would add verisimilitude to the drowning story.

The pale shards Yancy had plucked from the shower drain at the Striplings' condo were definitely pieces of human bone, not stone crab shells as Caitlin Cox had claimed. Rosa made the determination visually over a paella at the Versailles, Yancy introducing the fragments in the same funky nest in which he'd found them. Rosa promised to order DNA tests on both hair and bones, and compare the results to the swab taken from Stripling's arm by Dr. Rawlings in Key West. Yancy had no doubt of a match. The hatchet, presumed instrument of dismemberment, he had discreetly conveyed in a Macy's shopping bag.

Later, over flan and Cuban coffee, Rosa had presented him with the only number dialed on Dr. Gomez O'Peele's cell phone the night he died. She'd obtained this key information from a North Miami Beach detective who was striving to seduce her. The call had been made minutes after Yancy had left O'Peele's apartment.

Yancy took down the number and went outside to make a call of his own, and soon he had a name: Christopher Grunion, no middle initial. The billing address on the telephone account was a post office box in South Beach. When Yancy returned to the table, he swept Rosa into his arms and kissed her exuberantly until the other diners broke into cheers. He was soaring because Christopher Grunion was the same name that Rogelio Burton had found on the charter contract for the Caravan seaplane Yancy had seen behind the Striplings' house on Biscayne Bay.

Although Grunion had no criminal record, and not even a Florida driver's license, Yancy felt certain he was Eve's secret boyfriend and co-conspirator. O'Peele had likely phoned him to demand hush money after Yancy's unexpected visit, and got shot for his greedy play. "It's Poncho Boy!" Yancy had exulted, waving a mango Popsicle while he and Rosa were driving to the morgue. "The guy who killed Phinney – the same fuckweasel who tried to drown me!"

The massage on the autopsy table had settled him a bit. Now, as he was boosting Rosa up and down with his hips, she reached up and fastened her hair into a primly perfect bun, an Elizabethan effect that revealed the flawless slope of her caramel neck and shoulders. For all her lithe athletics she stayed remarkably quiet, as if she were afraid to awake somebody in the building, which would have been quite a trick.

One advantage to fucking on immovable steel was that it didn't squeak, unlike Yancy's sagging bed at home. The first time they'd had sex there, Rosa was so distracted by the noise that she couldn't make it happen. She said the box spring sounded like a chipmunk being skinned alive. Now, astride him on a slab where hundreds of homicide victims had been meticulously disemboweled, she shuddered suddenly, smiled and teetered forward. Pressing a moist cheek to his chest, she said, "Okay, this is pretty warped. I should probably get some counseling."

"Well, I thought it was fantastic."

"Don't lie, Andrew."

"Are you kidding? I came like Vesuvius."

Rosa sighed. "It's a freaking HBO miniseries. All I need is fangs."

Yancy kissed the top of her head. "I would've been a worthless park ranger," he said. "Disappearing for weeks at a time with just a tent and my fishing rods. The other thing? Poachers. If I caught some asshole jacklighting a fawn, I'm not sure I could restrain myself, arrest-wise. My dad, he's a very disciplined guy. I did not end up with that gene."

"I definitely don't want children," Rosa murmured. "Does that make me a selfish rotten person? Never mind. Not a fair question while you're still inside me."

"Christ, you cut up dead people for a living. Don't be so tough on yourself."

She sat up sleepily. "I should really make an effort to put on my clothes."

"Do you have video in this place?"

"Of course." Rosa pointed to a small camera mounted above the table. "Don't fret, Andrew, it has an Off switch. I'm not *that* twisted."

"Some weekend we should go camping down at Flamingo, just the two of us."

"You're very sweet," she said. "Now let's get out of here."

*

Yancy drove back to Big Pine the next morning and was surprised to see a car in his driveway – an old Toyota Camry with a crooked Oklahoma license tag. He took the tire iron out of his Subaru and ran through a hard rain toward the house.

Bonnie Witt stood in the kitchen, scrambling eggs. She was wearing a Sooners jersey, and her toenails had been painted gold. The fugitive life had taken a toll on her tan.

"I've still got a key," she said pertly.

"Another oversight on my part."

"I can explain everything, but first I want you to meet someone special. Honey?"

"Hey yo." A shirtless man was sprawled on the couch watching ESPN. He looked up and gave Yancy some sort of faux bro salute.

Bonnie said, "Andrew, say hello to Cody. Cody, this is my dear friend Andrew."

Yancy propped the tire iron in a corner and shook Cody's waxy hand. Whatever he might have looked like in high school, back when Bonnie was blowing his mind, the kid had grown up to be a lump – mottled skin, thinning hair and a gut that hung over unstrung board shorts. Yancy insisted on taking over breakfast duties so that the two of them could share their love story, which he anticipated to be a high point of his day.

"I just couldn't stop thinking about him," Bonnie said, "so one day I said screw it, life's too short. Got up at four in the morning and drove nonstop from Sarasota to Tulsa, nineteen hours. This was after I'd found him on Facebook—"

"But she didn't even friend me first," Cody cut in. "One night she just shows up by the salad bar and, you know, holy shit."

"He was the number two man at the Olive Garden—"

"My boss was a major dickbrain. It was time to move on."

"When Cliff found out I was gone," Bonnie said, "he went postal. Called the OSBI and totally sold me out."

The OSBI was the Oklahoma State Bureau of Investigation, which, after Dr. Witt's tip, had dispatched Agent John Wesley Weiderman to interview Yancy about the elusive Plover Chase. Unfortunately, the lawman's investigatory mission to the Keys had been cut short when he was stricken with shellfish poisoning after eating contaminated mussels at Stoney's Crab Palace on Stock Island. Yancy felt somewhat responsible, and he looked forward to ambushing Brennan with another surprise inspection.

"So I quit my job," Cody said, "and Ms. Chase and I went seriously outlaw."

Bonnie blushed. "He still calls me that, after all these years – Ms. Chase! The police were looking for the 4Runner so we switched to Cody's car."

"Except there's no XM Radio. Bummer," he said.

"Last night we camped on the beach at Bahia Honda." Bonnie favored Yancy with a fond-memory wink. "A raccoon swiped our marshmallows."

Cody said, "I chased after him but he got away."

Yancy loaded two plates with eggs and bacon, and he slid them across the counter. Cody inquired about the possibility of a bagel.

"Cream cheese or marmalade?" Yancy asked.

The young man beamed. "Hell, yes!"

Solemnly Bonnie said, "I never stopped loving him, Andrew. You know that."

Yancy knew no such thing, but he was savoring the plot line. "Does Clifford know Cody's back in the picture?"

"Lord, no! He thinks you and I ran off to the Seychelles. That's what I wrote in my good-bye note, just to throw him off."

"For God's sake, Bonnie."

Cody glanced up from his plate. "'Bonnie'? So who came up with *that* one?"

Yancy was wishing that Cody would put on a shirt. His tufted breasts were droopy and mole-covered, and Yancy spied what appeared to be a fresh bite mark above his left nipple. It was increasingly difficult to keep an open mind.

"The night before I left Cliff," Bonnie was saying, "I walk into the bathroom and there he is, dangling from the shower faucet, flopping and gurgling and jerking on his little weenie. For a noose he used one of my Hermès scarves! I mean, seriously, Andrew, enough's enough."

"An intolerable situation," Yancy agreed.

Through a cheekful of mulched bacon Cody said, "Hey, Ms. Chase. If you're gonna be Bonnie then I'm changing my handle to Clyde!"

She laughed and squeezed his pudgy elbow. Yancy pried a scorched bagel from the toaster and dressed it to Cody's specifications.

"So, where are you two heading?"

Bonnie said she was hoping they could stay with him. "Until the heat's off? Please?"

Yancy told her about the visit from Agent John Wesley Weiderman. "It's not safe here," he added. "Also, my girlfriend wouldn't go for it."

"Whoa." Bonnie hitched an eyebrow and put down her fork. "Andrew has a new lady," she said to Cody, who was using a green-tinged thumbnail to remove a sesame seed from his teeth.

"She's a doctor," Yancy said.

"What kind of doctor?" asked Bonnie.

"Well, a surgeon."

"Does she have a specialty?"

"She operates on pretty much everything." It wasn't a lie; when Rosa did an autopsy, she diced up the whole works.

"Funny," Bonnie said.

"You don't believe me."

"No, I meant it's ironic: I just dumped a doctor and here you've taken up with one."

Through the window Yancy saw no sign of the construction workers next door. Wet weather was his ally.

Cody said, "Ms. Chase told me how you butt-plugged her hubby with a DustBuster. That's some awesome man-shit right there."

He reached across the counter to honor Yancy with a knuckle bump. Yancy tried to visualize the kid's photograph in the school yearbook. From Cody's present condition it seemed inconceivable that he could have made himself attractive to Bonnie at any age. Perhaps he had quieter charms, such as a nine-inch cock.

"May I ask you something?" Yancy said. "It's about Ms. Chase's trial. I read where you testified against her."

"A suck move. Mom and Dad made me do that."

Bonnie gently interrupted, suggesting a change of topic.

Cody went on: "The important thing is we're back together again. Right?"

"You kept a hot little journal of your romance is what I heard," Yancy said.

"Hey, I was fifteen. I thought I wanted to be a writer."

Proudly Bonnie chipped in: "He was wild about *Portnoy's Complaint*."

171

"Well, sure." Yancy smiled. "Cody, are you keeping a journal now?"

He reddened. "No! I mean, what for?"

"In case you two get caught. Bonnie goes to jail, all the tabloids would line up to pay big bucks for your story. But I'm sure you wouldn't do anything like that. Who wants coffee?"

After they were gone, Yancy walked over to the spec house and set up a Santeria shrine in the future living room. Improvising, he'd chosen a handmade doll of the warrior god Changó, and for sacrificial offerings included apples, tamales, copper pennies, a dead rooster collected on Simonton Street by Animal Control and a saucer of cat blood left over from a spaying performed by a veterinarian friend. These items were laid out upon a crude satanic pentagram that Yancy had drawn in red Krylon paint on Evan Shook's floor slab. In the center he placed a rat skull, ominously marked with the numerals 666. Students of the occult would have discounted the scene as an amateurish juxtaposition of unconnected superstitions, but Yancy believed that maintaining cultural authenticity was less important than creating a vivid first impression for potential home buyers.

At lunchtime he drove down to Stoney's and confronted Brennan, who disclaimed responsibility for Agent John Wesley Weiderman's emergency trip to the hospital. "The man's got a family history of diverticulitis!"

Yancy said, "I hope he sues your ass off."

"Sit, Andrew, sit. Try the oysters Rockefeller."

"I want to see the kitchen. You know the drill." Yancy was carrying his vacuum-equipped roach-catching device.

"I'm glad you're here." Brennan fumbled to fit on a

hairnet. "Somebody came by askin' where you been. Jesus, is that a fuckin' gun on your belt?"

"Absolutely." After being nearly murdered by Eve Stripling's accomplice, Yancy had purchased a used Glock to replace his forfeited service weapon. He would have preferred another 12-gauge but that was out of his price range.

Brennan seemed agitated. "Nobody on roach patrol packs a piece! Nilsson didn't even carry a damn pocketknife."

"This can be treacherous work," Yancy said.

"The way some people do it, yeah. You got a carry permit?"

"Who was in here asking about me?"

"That girl," said Brennan. "Phinney's girl."

"Madeline? She's back?"

"For 'bout a week now. Come on, man, try the fuckin' oysters."

"Where's she staying?"

"In Old Town, with some pimple-faced Russian d-bag. Hey, are you leavin' already?"

"It's your lucky day," Yancy said, and made for the door.

Defiantly Brennan tugged off the hairnet. "I got nuthin' to hide here! Drop in anytime!"

Madeline was working at the same skanky T-shirt shop on Duval, Pestov lurking ferret-eyed among the inventory. She told Yancy she'd returned to Key West because the police no longer considered her a suspect in Phinney's murder. Yancy noticed that she'd chopped her hair even shorter and dyed it a shade of chartreuse that was popular for tarpon streamers. In addition she was sporting fresh ink – her dead boyfriend's initials, tattooed on her left wrist.

He said, "It isn't the cops I'm worried about. That's not why I wanted you to get out of town."

"Then who? Why would anyone want to hurt me?"

"Because – hold on, I'll be right back." Yancy went to the rear of the store and chased the scuttling Pestov out the door. Then he went back inside and informed Madeline that the man who'd shot Charlie had tried to kill him, too.

"Poncho Boy's feeling some heat," Yancy said.

"But he's got no cause to kill *me*. I don't know zip about zap."

"You know where Charlie got all that money."

Madeline said, "Stop tryin' to scare me. And what's with the gun?"

Yancy remembered her saying she had a sister in Crystal River. "Go stay with her until this is over. Please, Madeline."

"Millie got born-again last October."

"Oh."

"For the third fucking time. All she does when I visit is preach Jesus Christ our Lord 'n' Savior in my face, twenty-four/seven. One of her stupid cows got fried by lightning and she said it's God's will. No way can I be under the same roof with that psycho. She threw my Kools down the garbage disposer!"

Yancy said, "There must be somewhere else you can go."

"The Russians won't let anything happen to me. I already talked to Pestov."

"Pestov is a barn maggot."

"Dude, I need this job."

"Really? All the T-shirt shops in the world?"

Yancy hung back while two dancers from Teasers came in to browse for the latest in nipple clips. After they left,

Madeline smiled at Yancy and said, "I'm okay here. It's kinda cool that you care, but I'll be fine."

When he returned to Big Pine, the rain had quit and the sky was clearing. Evan Shook stood on the street in front of his spec house, addressing a horseshoe-shaped gathering of the construction crew. Yancy interpreted Evan Shook's gesticulations as beseeching. Some of the workers apparently had been unnerved by the sight of the Santeria altar or the rodent skull in the pentagram, possibly both. Yancy purposely had designed the display to touch a broad socio-religious spectrum.

He was rocking to Dave Matthews an hour later when Evan Shook pounded on the door, somewhat discourteously in Yancy's view. He hid the Trainwreck he'd been smoking, unplugged his earbuds and straightened the shiny blue necktie he'd taken to wearing on restaurant inspections; the pattern on the fabric was a lateral skein of tiny silver handcuffs.

By way of a greeting, he said: "Is there news of the wild dogs? Please come in."

Evan Shook remained on the front stoop, seething in the compressed manner of small men accustomed to bullying. Clearly he was inhibited by Yancy's height, and also the hip-mounted firearm.

"Have you been in my house again?" he asked somberly. "Somebody . . . "

"Yes?"

"Somebody defaced the downstairs."

"Good Lord. When did this happen?"

"Just this morning."

"That's unbelievable. In broad daylight? Kids, I'll bet." Yancy was counting on the conservative neckwear and police-model handgun to work in his favor, your average vandal being untidy and unarmed. The smell of pot, however, imperiled his credibility.

"I've been working all day," he said. "Just got home."

"So your answer is no, you haven't been over there." Evan Shook wondered if Yancy was too stoned to lie.

"Was anything stolen?" Yancy inquired. "You should hurry and hang those doors and windows, get the place buttoned up. Not just for security – it's hurricane season."

"Right." Evan Shook plainly had more to say, but his gaze kept dropping to the black butt of the Glock. The bracing accusations he'd had in mind, the harsh warning he'd composed – these would remain undelivered.

"The neighborhood's gone to hell," Yancy said supportively. "It used to be so safe and quiet."

"If you see anything unusual going on over there—"

"Of course, of course." Yancy craned his head out the doorway, as if warily scouting for a rabid dog pack or rampaging delinquents. "I'll try to keep a closer eye on things, Mr. Shook."

"Thanks."

"There used to be deer on your property, did you know that? Every evening around sundown. But now they don't come."

Evan Shook nodded witlessly. The damn mosquitoes were eating him alive.

"When I first moved here, it was mostly small houses," Yancy went on, "what you might call bungalows. Nothing as grandiose as your place. What is that, four floors?"

"I've gotta get to the hardware store," said Evan Shook, "before it closes."

Yancy stayed up listening to his iPod while the television

was tuned to Animal Planet. The effect was enthralling: wildebeest migrations accompanied by Joni Mitchell and the Strokes. Yancy took no delight in Evan Shook's tribulations but wrong was wrong – the mansion was a fucking abomination. Yancy's objective was to prevent it from being sold and finished.

He ate three energy bars and weighed himself: 162 pounds, a string bean. He was surprised that Eve Stripling hadn't sent her stud muffin Christopher back to the Keys to properly finish killing him. By now she'd surely learned from Nick's daughter that Yancy wasn't drowned and that he intended to keep pursuing the case. He flipped the channel to Conan and unplugged one ear for the monologue. Afterward he turned off the TV and searched the kitchen cupboards for evidence of vermin. In some ways his roach patrol duties weren't so different from police work – the quarry was nocturnal, and unfailingly left a trail.

Marinating in a lukewarm bath, Yancy smoked the rest of the joint and dozed off. At some point he was rousted by Dr. Rosa Campesino's voice. It was rising from his cell phone, which he had apparently grabbed off the toilet seat and answered in a haze.

"Andrew, I need you here right away."

"Wadizzit? You awright?"

"Wake up!"

"Take it easy."

"That damn arm is back!" she said.

"What?"

"You heard me. *The* arm. I'm staring at it right now."

Yancy splashed out of the tub. "Stripling's arm? No way."

"Get your butt in the car," Rosa said.

Fourteen

Grave robbing was not uncommon in South Florida due to a thriving underground market for human bones, prized by Santeria priests and practitioners of extreme voodoo. The crime required muscle and nerve though no special stealth, as most cemeteries refused to spring for nighttime security guards.

Flaco Chávez and his partner, whose street name was Delta Force, were robbers by trade and had never before cracked a coffin. They'd met in prison and later shared an inattentive parole officer. Delta Force claimed to be an ex-army commando and he sometimes broke into gyms after hours to work out with the weights. Flaco Chávez specialized in mugging elderly ATM patrons, although he spoke vaingloriously of graduating to armored cars.

One night, while scouting for carjacking prospects at a BP station, the men were approached by a couple with an enticing offer: Six hundred dollars for robbing a grave – half the money up front, half when the grisly contents were delivered to a Denny's restaurant on Biscayne Boulevard. It sounded like an easy job to Flaco Chávez and his partner, who promptly stole a late-model Tahoe from a pregnant nurse and struck out for the St. Lazarus Gardens and Water Park in North Miami. Along the way they stopped to burglarize an Ace Hardware store, acquiring two shovels, a pick, canvas gloves and a flashlight.

The most challenging aspect of the heist, it turned out, was finding the correct target. Delta Force was ripped on coke and lacking in focus, so it was Flaco's chore to locate the burial plot of Nicholas Stripling, whoever the fuck *he* was. Once the site had been isolated, the excavation took barely an hour, Delta Force digging like a dervish while Flaco Chávez feigned a hamstring cramp. Heading back downtown, their stolen SUV was spotted by a county police officer, who deftly swung his squad car into a U-turn and lit them up like a disco ball. Flaco Chávez spoke out in favor of a low-key surrender but Delta Force, facing multiple parole violations and a long bus ride back to Starke, stomped on the accelerator.

Neither man could be bothered with seat belts, so their skulls spidered the windshield at exactly seventy-one miles per hour when Delta Force – showing misplaced faith in the performance-enhancing attributes of cocaine hydrochloride – attempted a cinematic off-road evasion and crashed into a banyan tree. The impact ejected from the Tahoe's rear hatch a navy-blue golf bag belonging to the husband of the pregnant carjacking victim. The golf bag spilled a full set of Callaways, three sleeves of Bridgestone balls, a speargun and an embalmed human arm, which was sent in its own ambulance to the medical examiner's office.

Ironically, the stream of emergency vehicles sped directly

past the Denny's on Biscayne, where a couple armed with a stolen 12-gauge shotgun (strictly for protection) was waiting in a rented compact for the grave robbers.

After another hour passed with no contact, Eve Stripling said: "I can't believe those assholes took the three hundred bucks and bailed."

"What part can't you believe?" grumbled the man beside her, the man who was now officially a boyfriend.

"We should've offered 'em five on this end," she said.

"Or maybe we should have said you two shitheads get *nada* till we get the arm."

Eve puffed her cheeks irritably. "Okay, honey, so they ripped us off. What the hell do we do now?"

"Call the pilot is what we do. Tell him we're on the way."

Neville's friends on Andros said he was crazy not to take the money from the sale of his family's property and build a fine new beach house on another stretch of seafront. They couldn't understand his militant opposition to the future Curly Tail Lane Resort, which they gullibly believed would bring new jobs and a geyser of tourist dollars. Words didn't flow easily from Neville and he struggled without success to explain his churned feelings, the gutting sense of loss. His three girlfriends sniped relentlessly on the subject of his stubborn foolishness, to the point that he began to miss the sulfurous company of Driggs.

The monkey had been sighted around Rocky Town in the Dragon Queen's motley entourage of spurious half cousins and walleyed supplicants. Meanwhile the unwanted American, Christopher, showed no effects of major voodoo. Neville was distraught to see on his former homestead a tall pile of casuarina trees that had been felled in order to widen the beach;

their scraggly dead roots looked like unclenched claws. Neville was halfway over the chain-link fence when Christopher's hired goon burst from the trailer swinging a cricket mallet and snorting like a gored hog.

Neville hopped on his bicycle and rode off shaking a fist. He hurried to confront the Dragon Queen but his angry knock on her door went unanswered. Through an open window he spied on the table an empty rum bottle and a puddle of hardened yellow wax where a candle had melted. Mingled with a smell of cigars was the familiar funk of unwashed simian.

He aimed his bike toward the wharf and wound up at the conch shack cooling his palms around a bottle of Kalik. Like many native-born Bahamians, Neville wasn't intractably aligned against progress, yet he was wary. Despite its nautical proximity to South Florida, Andros hadn't been overrun like Bimini or Freeport because its long western coast was inconveniently shallow and short of natural harbors. The island's vast middle interior was mostly boggy wilderness, a stifling outback. A slender Andros economy relied on vegetable farms, which fed most of the Bahamas, and on scattered coastal fishing settlements such as Rocky Town. One overabundant resource was fresh springwater; seven million gallons a day were shipped from Morgan's Bluff to Nassau, a place that many Androsians were content to avoid.

In Neville's view, the Curly Tail Lane extravaganza looked like another crooked Bay Street deal. That some people (his own half sister included) had been bought off was a certainty. The traditional outcome of such high-flying enterprises was, of course, bankruptcy. Christopher would be jacked up and jerked around until he ran out of patience and then money. Thereafter he would bitterly abandon the Bahamas and his half-built tourist trap, which would sit moldering in the heat until another foreign sucker came along. Green Beach was destined to be a perpetual construction site unless Neville could act swiftly to regain dominion.

A third beer was sweating on the bar before him when he spotted the Dragon Queen. Trailed by a handful of scrofulous attendants, she was motoring down the main road on a tricked-out wheelchair that gave the appearance of a mobile throne. Balanced on the steering yoke was Driggs, festively grinding his diaper against one of the rearview mirrors. He tolerated a batik head wrap that matched a flamingo-pink number worn in cool regality by the Dragon Queen. As they drew closer Neville could hear her singing low and froggishly. Her expression was governed by a style of wraparound shades once favored by the Haitian secret police.

"Madam! Stop!" Neville sprung off the bar stool and ran toward the approaching procession. "Madam, it's me!"

The monkey barked once and the Dragon Queen's ushers shifted themselves into a protective wedge around the still-rolling scooter. Neville was roughly turned away; there were filthy oaths and the threat of a stomping. Again he called out to the voodoo priestess, who dismissed his plea with a backhanded wave. The group proceeded past him along the path toward the conch hut, the Dragon Queen gliding ahead on rubber wheels.

Stunned, Neville crossed the street and sagged against a shaded coral wall. Momentarily a covered golf cart hummed into view, and out stepped the pinheaded security guard from Curly Tail Lane. He glanced at Neville long enough to scowl in recognition; then he strode directly to the palm-thatched restaurant, where the ragged assembly parted. Neville watched the goon kneel beside the electric dolly and plant a kiss on the Dragon Queen, a bobbing lip-lock that lasted long enough to draw saucy cheers. The stereo was engaged and soon the two of them were dancing to Jimmy Cliff. As the security guard pranced gaping and bear-like, the Dragon Queen used the joystick on her nimble chariot to spin fanciful circles around him. Throughout these maneuvers, Driggs – jouncing like a miniature stagecoach driver – cheeped in accompaniment.

Neville was stricken breathless from anguish. What a wretched mistake he'd made! The whore-witch Dragon Queen had taken him for both his money and his monkey.

Now she was screwing the white devil's hired man.

Sonny Summers said: "Let me tell you about my day."

"Wish I could make it better."

"Maybe you can, Andrew."

Yancy noticed some additions to the sheriff's desktop display: a photo of his wife wearing a snorkel and hoisting a distressed lobster, a brass toothpick holder from the chamber of commerce, and a small chintzy replica of the *Pilar*, Hemingway's fishing boat.

"Remember ... you know ... that little solid you did for me?"

"Babysitting the dead guy's left arm," Yancy said.

"Right. It was my understanding you delivered it to the widow."

"Absolutely."

"Who gave it a decent Christian burial."

"Yes, I can personally attest."

Sonny Summers slid forward. "So, this morning, I get a call from Dr. Rawlings, who says the ME's office in Miami needs the DNA swab he took off the arm."

That request would have come from Dr. Rosa Campesino, doing her job.

With false innocence Yancy said, "Maybe they found another body part from the same corpse."

"Exactly what I was thinking. Hoping for, to be honest. But then later Rawlings calls back and says guess what. You won't believe this, Andrew. They've got the actual arm in Miami. *The* freaking arm! From the *Misty*!"

Yancy of course had ID'd it himself at the Miami-Dade morgue. The distinctive watch stripe was still visible on Nick Stripling's mummifying wrist, although the embalmer had decorously retracted the middle finger. The county police were still trying to figure out how the severed limb of a drowned fisherman had ended up in the possession of two career felons, their stoved selves now occupying adjacent autopsy tables. Yancy had theorized to Rosa that Caitlin Cox had blabbed to her stepmother about the incriminating hatchet and the bone fragments he'd removed from the condo. Fearing a homicide investigation, Eve had recruited two random nitwits to dig up her husband's arm so there would be nothing for a coroner to exhume and examine.

Meanwhile, Rosa had to be careful what she told detectives. She might get fired if it became known that she was surreptitiously assisting a rookie restaurant inspector on an out-of-county murder case.

"Andrew, what the hell?" Sonny Summers threw up his hands.

"Give me back my old job and I'll get to the bottom of this."

"Christ, why would I want to get to the bottom of it? I just need it to go away."

The sheriff had come to the office in a pressed blue blazer with the requisite American flag lapel pin. He appeared to have put on a few soft pounds.

"We were dealing with a routine accident, right? Guy goes fishing, flips his boat, the sharks show up, whatever . . . and then his arm gets snagged by a tourist. See, I don't understand how we got from there to here."

"Because it wasn't an accident, Sonny."

"You're still pissed about getting canned. Is that what this is all about? Stirring the shit pot?"

Again Yancy thought of Rosa, who was definitely in the line of bureaucratic fire. Now she had real work to do, a case number and everything. Still, she hadn't urged him to retreat or even move to the shadows. A true champ, Yancy thought.

To the sheriff he said: "You're the one who wanted the guy's arm to go up the road in the first place. Now you got your wish, so what's the problem?"

"Channel 7, Andrew."

"You're killing me."

"They'll get a whiff of this. Don't think they won't."

"Who cares?" Yancy asked. "You haven't done anything wrong."

"And the fucking *Herald* will be all over it, too. My wife, she wants me to run for state attorney general year after next. She's already looking at private schools in Tallahassee."

Yancy found himself improbably touched by the sheriff's grandiose fantasy.

"Don't you get it?" Sonny Summers said. "Everything bad's gonna come out now. Weeks ago, when that goddamn arm first showed up, I told the media that Miami had taken over the investigation. That's what Rawlings put in his report, except it wasn't true. The thing was in your—"

"Freezer."

"—personal custody. And you're not even a cop anymore."

"That you can fix," Yancy said. "Just hand over my badge."

"They're gonna say I ditched a human body part and then lied about it. That's tampering with evidence, obstruction, whatever. Now the whole damn mess looks like a cover-up."

"Naw, it's just a jurisdictional snafu. Blame it on me – no, wait, don't."

"Hang on." Sonny Summers was jotting down the phrase "jurisdictional snafu."

Yancy decided it was wiser to keep the sheriff on edge. He said, "You should be aware, however, that Stripling was murdered here in Monroe County, not in Miami."

Sonny Summers looked up, blinking like a toad in a puddle of piss.

"Chopped to pieces at his condo on Duck Key," Yancy reported heavily. "The guy was a thieving shitbird but, still, a dreadful end. I know exactly how the killing went down."

"You do?"

"The wife and boyfriend did it. Hacked up Stripling's body and sunk the boat."

Sonny Summers bit his lower lip. "Where's the rest of the corpse?"

"Who knows? Gone forever."

"But, then, the arm she had the funeral for – how'd it get back to the Miami morgue?"

"Grave robbery gone bad."

"Oh, fuckeroo." The sheriff covered his ears.

Yancy mildly raised his voice: "I'm betting they hired some mopes to dig it up."

"For God's sake, why?"

"Because," Yancy said, "yours truly was hot on their tail. The widow Stripling and her man are running scared."

Sonny Summers kicked back from the desk, the chair squealing under his fresh lard. "But you're not in homicide, Andrew. You're on roach patrol!"

"Once a cop, always a cop," Yancy said fraternally.

Given the frequency with which body parts turned up in Miami, the discovery of another hacked-off arm usually didn't draw much attention from local news outlets. However, most severed limbs were found in Dumpsters or roadside canals, not in Callaway golf bags. Such a colorful detail, if leaked to a reporter, would almost surely produce a headline. After that it would take only a bit of digging to learn that Nick Stripling had been a big-time Medicare fraudster. Next stop: *Dateline NBC*.

"I wasn't the one who said it was a boat accident," the sheriff protested. "That was the almighty U.S. Coast Guard!"

"Sonny, please let me finish this off. I'm so close."

"No way."

"Here's your story: You had me working on the case from day one, okay? On special assignment. Why? Because you're a lawman's lawman. You always had private doubts, a gut feeling there was foul play. That's what you tell the press after I bust Eve Stripling for first-degree murder – then you'll look like a star."

"Slow down, Andrew."

"I'm the only one who can put it all together!"

187

Sonny Summers wouldn't budge. "You can't be anywhere near this case, or any case, because you're not on the damn payroll anymore. You're an ex-detective, and you got that way by violating a prominent dermatologist with a household appliance in the middle of the business district! It made all the papers, my friend."

Yancy had one more card to play. "Remember that fishing mate who got shot? It's a city case. Charles Phinney was his name."

"Sure, I remember. The robbery near the Raw Bar."

"Wrong."

"Or was it the Turtle Kraals?"

"It wasn't a robbery, Sonny. The kid was killed because he knew too much about the arm."

"You're giving me a cluster migraine."

"Stripling's widow set him up. Her boyfriend was the shooter."

"Guess what? Let's stop here."

"That's three murders," Yancy said, "almost four. They tried to kill me, too."

The sheriff lowered his lamentation to a rasp. "This is *not* a productive conversation."

"Let me make it all better."

"Take a vacation, Andrew. I'll clear it with Lombardo."

"But I don't need a vacation. I need my job back."

Yancy had to cool down so he bought a ticket on the Conch Train and took a slow tour through town. A pleasant couple sat down near him, confiding a fervid interest in the polydactyl cats that roamed the Hemingway House. One of the animals was reputed to have at least twenty-six toes, and for a glimpse the Whitlocks had traveled all the way from Ashtabula, Ohio. Yancy hopped off the train near the Mallory docks and strolled to the X-rated T-shirt shop, where he emphasized to Pestov the importance of Madeline's well-being. He was able to make his point without the Glock, which he'd chosen not to wear to his meeting with Sheriff Summers, who was a chronic stickler and worrywart.

Back at Big Pine, Yancy found his home reoccupied by Cody and Bonnie Witt, who now wished to be addressed by her pre-fugitive name of Plover. The summer rains had made a swamp of the couple's camping adventure, and Cody was suffering from chiggers and an oral yeast infection. Yancy walked them next door and helped them erect their pup tent in the spacious master bedroom of Evan Shook's unfinished spec house. Although the plumbing in the structure was connected, a semi-rustic experience was guaranteed by the raw plywood flooring, unscreened windows and lack of air-conditioning.

Rosa Campesino drove down after work and met Yancy at a Thai restaurant that he extolled as sanitary. Whenever he took her out, his appetite rebounded. Afterward they went to Duck Key, where the night watchman refused to open Stripling's condo until Rosa weighed in with her Miami-Dade pathologist laminate, which was visually more impressive than Yancy's restaurant-inspector ID.

It was clear that Eve Stripling had gutted the place in anticipation of a search warrant, confirming Yancy's suspicion that Caitlin Cox had told her about his earlier visit. Rosa remained on the balcony while Yancy returned Stripling's hair and bone chips to the shower drain; the hatchet he wiped down and wedged behind the water heater, making sure its wooden handle protruded far enough to be noticed by any half-competent CSI tech.

Earlier, over noodle soup, Rosa had reported three important forensic findings, two of which Yancy had been expecting: The Duck Key bone fragments had definitely come from Nick Stripling's arm, and the odd notches on the stump of the humerus matched the blade bite of the hatchet.

"But here's the best part," Rosa said. "The hatchet isn't what severed the victim's limb."

"Then what the hell did they use?"

"A surgical saw, Andrew."

"No shit?" Instantly he thought of O'Peele, the dead orthopedist.

Rosa said, "After the amputation they whacked at the arm with the axe to obscure the saw marks."

"And make it appear that a boat propeller did it."

"The wounds really don't look much alike, but they wouldn't know that. Same with those shark nibbles – they neglected to find the right species."

"Amateur hour."

"Yeah, but they nearly pulled it off," Rosa said, "so to speak."

"The sheriff's wigging. How're things in your shop?"

"So far, so good. From now on I'll be sticking strictly to the science. Whatever else I might have heard about this case, it's only hearsay. For instance, I have no official knowledge of the hair and bones we're now illegally transporting."

"What hair?" Yancy said. "What bones?"

After reinstating the crime scene at Duck Key, he drove back to Big Pine; Rosa followed in her own car. Wheeling up to his place, Yancy looked next door and saw through the top-floor windows the yellowish glow of a kerosene lantern that he'd loaned to Cody and Bonnie-slash-Plover. He had also coached them about what to say when Evan Shook showed up, and he regretted that he wouldn't be there to observe the man's reaction.

He led Rosa into his house and put on some jazz and poured two glasses of red wine. Then he told her about his forced furlough. "Sonny strongly recommends time away. He believes my relationship with Stripling's arm is problematic, and he'd like me to be unavailable for potential interviews and depositions."

"I bet I know where you're going, Andrew."

"Can't you take some vacation days?"

"Ha, not right now. The death business is booming."

Yancy pulled his travel duffel from a closet and tossed in some swim trunks, boxers and a stack of fishing shirts. He said, "Listen, I've been having this super-kinked-out fantasy, better than the autopsy slab. Promise not to freak."

"Oh brother."

"Me. You. King-sized bed at the Biltmore."

"You are *so* warped. Cable porn?"

"And French chocolates on the pillow."

"Here, let me help you pack."

In the morning they enjoyed a room-service breakfast before Rosa left for the morgue. Yancy wrapped up a left-over slice of smoked salmon, checked out of the hotel and drove directly to the retirement residence of corrupt Miami police sergeant Johnny Mendez. Sunning on the front walk was the ex-officer's rotund Siamese. Yancy displayed the fragrant morsel of fish and the cat trailed him to the Subaru.

Next stop was the Venetian Pool, where he parked under a ficus tree and called Mendez's house. "Say, how's that bovine nut sack of yours holding up?"

"Who the fuck is this?"

"Detective Andrew Yancy from Monroe County. Good news, sir: I found Natasha." The name was embossed on the animal's collar. "She was wandering the alleys like a dazed hooker, poor thing. Lucky I came along."

"Are you nuts!"

"Don't deny that you love this critter more than your wife. What's your cell number, Johnny Boy?"

Yancy took an iPhone snapshot of the Siamese licking salmon juice off his fingertips. He texted the photo to Mendez along with a note: "She doesn't seem to miss you."

Mendez called right back and said, "You're a sick hump, Yancy."

"And you are a larcenous fuckstick. However, I need a favor – and you should view this as an opportunity to become an authentic Crime Stopper, partial atonement for all that money you embezzled."

"What kinda favor? I'm retired, you asshole."

"Yeah," Yancy said, "but I bet you can still get me a police badge."

"What happened to yours? Ha, don't tell me you got canned again."

"I guess Natasha and I will be taking a road trip."

"Jesus, you need a badge like right now? All I got is my old one."

"That'll do, Johnny Boy. Put it in your mailbox, go back inside and stay there until you hear me honk three times. That means Empress Natasha is home. Try something stupid, like calling the real cops, and you'll never lay eyes on your darling inbred feline again."

"You hurt her, you're a dead man."

Yancy, who was allergic to cat dander, sneezed volcanically. "I'd never do anything to harm Natasha, preening diva though she is. What I *would* do, Johnny, is throw away her collar and leave her with some kindly souls I know who'd find her a good home with a higher class of human companions than you and Mrs. Mendez. Now go put the fucking badge in the mailbox."

"Christ, gimme some time to look for the damn thing."

"Twenty minutes," Yancy said. "I've got a plane to catch."

Fifteen

Neville was in no condition for romance, so he tried to break up with all three of his girlfriends on the same afternoon. Each of them said he was stupid and crazy and no damn good – yet they wouldn't throw him out. Neville suspected that the women still clung to hope that he'd change his mind about the mountain of money he was refusing to accept for his family's land. They harbored dreams that he would warm to the role of rich boyfriend.

He went snapper fishing near the submarine base and caught enough for dinner, breakfast and lunch. A friend who worked at the Lizard Cay bonefish lodge, which was closed for the summer, opened the kitchen and let Neville fry up his catch. That night he slept on his boat anchored off Green Beach, where he got soaked by a squall. Shortly before dawn he guzzled two lukewarm Kaliks and a quart of water. Then he waded ashore and hid among the remaining casuarinas, where he slapped mosquitoes and waited for his bladder to fill.

Unbeknownst to Neville, the white man Christopher had responded to the first incident of diesel contamination by equipping his earthmoving machines with locking fuel caps. Therefore the tank of the Cat 450E backhoe that Neville hoped to disable with beery urine was sealed from intrusion, and the spout lid held fast under a vigorous bashing. Soon Neville's bloated gut began to ache, so he climbed to the cab, unbuttoned his fly and let loose on the gauge cluster. In his heart he understood it was an impotent gesture, the sturdy backhoe plainly engineered for all-weather operation.

In a drained state he stepped to the ground, where he was jumped by the fetus-eared security guard, who wordlessly began to pummel him. The goon's name was Egg, or so Neville had been told by a boy cleaning conchs on the waterfront. Egg outweighed Neville by fifty pounds and his sweat smelled like fermented lobster. The weapon was a short aluminum bat of the type used by offshore charter mates to subdue billfish and tuna that are dragged aboard green. Neville flopped around in the freshly turned dirt, shielding his head and moaning at every blow. The man called Egg lugged him to the beach and kicked him into the water and walked away laughing. Neville remained on all fours in the sandy shallows until he vomited. It took all his strength to swim out to the boat and pull himself over the gunwale.

The next morning, despite a fear of flying, he caught a plane to Nassau and went shopping for an attorney. None of those who met him would initiate a lawsuit without a retainer, which Neville couldn't afford. They seemed disappointed to learn he wasn't seeking any monetary compensation, only the return of family real estate that had been lawfully sold by his half-sister. The prevailing opinion was that he stood virtually no chance of winning in court.

Neville stayed overnight with a nephew who wanted to take him to the Atlantis resort for a big time, but Neville declined. He was sore and unsteady after the beating by Egg. When his nephew asked what was wrong, Neville said he'd gotten into a fight over a girl.

"Oh mon, did you hot get broke?"

"No, suh."

"Because I know plenny women kin fix dot."

"I'm okay," said Neville.

The following day he bought a pair of sunglasses at the Straw Market and rode the mail boat back to Andros.

Yancy breezed through Immigration and Customs in Nassau. All he carried through the checkpoints was his duffel and a Sage fly-rod tube that falsely announced him as a free-spending American sportsman, always a welcome breed. He took a taxi to the general aviation terminal and told a handsome woman behind the counter he was looking for a pilot friend.

"This is what he's flying," Yancy said, and showed her a picture of the white Caravan. He'd printed it out from the flight-tracker website. "I was told to meet him here."

"Are you sure, sir? That plane left a couple hours ago."

"No way. He was supposed to take me fishing!"

"They went to Lizard Cay," the woman said. "Same as usual."

"That sonofabitch. He promised to wait for me."

"There's usually a three o'clock flight on Tropical. I'll give you the phone number."

Yancy smiled. "Darling, you just saved my vacation."

It was from his father that he'd gotten not only his passion for fishing but also a love of small planes. Every year the park service would conduct aerial counts of eagle nests in the Everglades, and after turning eighteen Yancy was allowed to ride with his dad and the pilot in the government Beechcraft. He always brought his own binoculars.

While he waited for his flight Rosa called to say that she'd FedExed to Key West police the slug from the gun that killed Gomez O'Peele. Yancy was confident that ballistics tests would prove it was the same .357 used on Charles Phinney. Rosa hadn't provided the details of the doctor's death to the detectives.

"But I'll have to tell them what I know," she added, "if the bullets match."

Yancy apologized for putting her in a dicey situation. She said she was a big girl and she knew the ropes. He asked if any news reporters had called the medical examiner's office to inquire about the severed arm in the golf bag.

"Well, we might have lucked out," she said.

"I like this 'we' business."

"The man to thank would be the late, great Dawkins Brophy. The same night the grave robbers stole Stripling's arm, Mr. Brophy—"

"I thought Brophy was his *first* name."

"Whatever, Andrew. It's not even my case," Rosa said. "Anyway, the same night our severed limb reappeared, Mr. Dawkins Brophy – or Brophy Dawkins – washed down three Ecstasy tabs with a half pint of Bombay gin. Then he went racing through Government Cut on a turbocharged Wave-Runner until he drove full speed into the stern of the *Duchess of the Caribbean*, killing himself and his date, a Belorussian lingerie model whose name I can't possibly pronounce."

"In other words, splat."

"Big-time splat."

"Damn," Yancy said.

Brophy Dawkins was a burly country-music star whose hit single was "Jesus Don't Speak Jihad," a defiant post-9/11 anthem. *The Duchess of the Caribbean* was one of the world's largest passenger cruise ships.

"It was a collision only in the sense that a june bug collides with a Buick," Rosa said. "Mr. Dawkins was decapitated and, consequently, his remains weren't fully recovered for a day or so due to tidal factors. Since then the media have taken an interest, Andrew. Rabid would be one way to describe it."

"Rule one: A celebrity head always trumps an anonymous arm."

"Sick but true," said Rosa. "Can I ask you something? I've been thinking about this Andros trip."

"I'll buy you a ticket. Please come."

"No, listen. Say you track down the murderous wife and her boyfriend – then what? You can't make a legal arrest over there. And the Bahamian cops won't do it without U.S. extradition papers, which you don't have in your possession because those documents don't freaking exist. The risk-reward ratio seems low, Andrew."

"Everyone needs a project."

"Soon as I hang up, know what I'm googling? Three words: 'Nassau bail bondsmen.'"

"Come on, girl, have some faith."

In the olden days Claspers smuggled weed and later cocaine. He never got busted though he didn't stay rich for long. Now the shit was coming in on freight trucks across the Mexican border, or by air from Haiti, where Claspers refused to fly. But after four thousand hours in the cockpit, on and off the books, he could still find lawful work. The Bahama Islands he knew well, from Bimini to the Exumas. These days in small planes he delivered wealthy tourists and expats to some of the same bleached airstrips upon which he'd once landed overloaded DC-6s at night, guided only by automobile headlights.

As a legitimate aviator Claspers was doing okay – not gangbusters, but he made enough money to cover the rent on his duplex, a car payment, child support and weekly visits to a club in Lauderdale called Marbles, where a bartender one-third his age pretended to be interested in him. Claspers didn't mind being strung along. The bartender had stellar fake boobs and a quick sense of humor. He considered telling her about his years as a big-time smuggler, but he doubted it would improve his odds of getting laid. Once upon a time, sure, absolutely – but hers was a generation that grew up on homegrown or Humboldt and thought Panama Red was a merlot. Claspers suspected the young bartender would have been more impressed to meet a guy who worked for Apple, or maybe a professional skateboarder. He over-tipped her anyway, because it brought back memories that made him feel good.

Lately Claspers had been piloting for a shady duck named Christopher Grunion, who disliked the formalities of the U.S. Customs service. Sometimes Grunion asked Claspers for clandestine transport between Andros Island and the lower Florida Keys. For these high-risk endeavors Claspers was decently compensated – not doper-league pay, but enough to sustain his loyalty. A secondary enticement was the opportunity to dust off his outlaw moves.

The aircraft leased by Grunion was a Cessna floatplane, a ten-seat Caravan that cruised at 160 knots. From Andros – either Congo Town or Lizard Cay – Claspers would steer a southeast course toward the Ragged Islands until reaching a singular quadrant where the seas belonged to the Bahamas while the airspace belonged to Cuba. Basically it was a neutral zone for law enforcement, and that's where Claspers would drop to four hundred feet, below radar, and swing sharply back across the Florida straits. Coming in low over the waves was the only way to cross undetected, because on Cudjoe Key the U.S. government tethered a famed surveillance blimp known as Fat Albert, which had been effectively used by the DEA to bust some of Claspers's colleagues in the aerial import trade.

Christopher Grunion seldom spoke during these flights. Often he appeared to doze with his forehead pressed against the window, causing Claspers to wonder if he was loaded, drunk or possibly ill. The girlfriend, Eve, was a nervous chatterbox who spewed questions. *Are we still in the Bahamas? What's that island down there? How fast are we going? Do we have enough fuel? What're you gonna do if the Coast Guard spots us?* Her yammering made Claspers long for the days when he flew the starry tropics in solitude, accompanied only by silent herbal tonnage and a terse Hispanic voice on the headset.

Bringing in the Caravan required a stretch of calm water, typically on the leeward side of an island. Daylight was also helpful, particularly during lobster season when the channels and bays of the Keys were clotted with small buoys that could tear up the floats and ruin a perfectly fine landing, even flip the aircraft. Once they safely touched down, Eve would call a taxi to come fetch her and

Grunion. Then the two of them would inflate the rubber raft they always brought as cargo (along with a small outboard engine), and from the plane they would putt-putt to shore.

Claspers thought the well-fed couple might benefit from rowing, although Grunion would need to shed the orange weather poncho that he always wore. Surely he sweltered like a pig beneath the plastic pullover; Claspers figured he kept it on because of some weird phobia or unsightly medical disorder. A pilot friend of Claspers's had been morbidly afraid of centipedes and refused to remove his heavy woolen socks, even while bathing. Eventually the poor bastard ended up on crutches, grounded. Later a photograph of his ravaged feet was featured in an illustrated atlas of fungal infections.

Claspers enjoyed sneaking in and out of the States, but much of his flying for Grunion was routine, Andros to Nassau and back. Grunion was breaking ground on an upscale tourist resort at Lizard Cay, so Claspers would bring in architects, designers, contractors, bulldozer mechanics and even the real estate agents to whom Grunion was pitching his project. About once a week Eve would ride the seaplane to Miami but there was no cowboy stuff – it was straight into Opa-locka or Tamiami, strictly legal, her passport open and ready for stamping. Claspers looked forward to those trips because he got some time to go home and chill. Nassau wasn't hard duty, either, though he always blew too much cash at the clubs and casinos.

The toughest part of the Andros gig was cooling his heels for days at a time, waiting for Grunion or his girlfriend to call with a flight in mind. Rocky Town was the nearest settlement to the construction site, and there wasn't much to do except eat conch, drink rum and ruminate about growing old with a prostate the size of a toadstool. Marley and the Wailers were all over the radio, yet even that got stale after a while.

Grunion and the woman were renting a house on the ocean but not once had they invited Claspers for lunch or even a cocktail. He would have hired one of the local kids to take him snorkeling or grouper fishing except that Grunion insisted he hang within fifteen minutes of the plane, which stayed chocked on the tarmac at what they called Moxey's airfield.

That's where Claspers was, drinking a flat Fresca, when the late afternoon flight from Nassau landed. Three Bahamian women got off lugging shopping bags and next came a rangy guy in his late thirties, early forties. He was carrying a duffel and a fly-rod tube. Claspers knew he was American because of his tan; the Brits and Canadians were white as milk when they stepped off the planes and pink as shrimp when they left. The American paused on the apron to look at the Caravan; then he ambled up to Claspers and asked, "Do you know who owns that seaplane?"

"Private charter."

"Too bad," the American said. "I want to fly down and wade the Water Cays. I was looking for someone to take me."

Claspers told him not to get his hopes up, because there weren't many floatplanes for charter. "Wish I could help, but I'm stuck here."

"So you're the pilot."

"That's me."

The American held out his hand. "My name's Andrew."

"I'm K. J. Claspers."

"You got time for a drink?"

Claspers said thanks anyway but he had to work. "I gotta do a run for the boss."

A dented blue van pulled up and Grunion's hired man got out. He was a dome-headed hulk with shriveled-looking ears. They called him Egg but the name on his papers was Ecclestone. He wore a bleached white T-shirt that by contrast made his skin shine like onyx.

"Let's go, mon," he said to Claspers.

"In a minute." Claspers wasn't afraid of Egg and he didn't care much for him. The guy was your basic pea-brained muscle, straight from central casting. Claspers said, "I gotta take a leak. Go wait by the plane."

Egg sneered and headed across the baking tarmac toward the Caravan.

The American said, "That's some boss."

Claspers snorted. "Not him, no way – he's just the help. Poor baby's got a toothache so I've gotta take him to a dentist in Nassau. Talk about the glamour life."

The pilot went to the restroom and propped himself at the only urinal, where he spritzed and dribbled for what seemed like an eternity. A doctor back home had prescribed some heavy-duty pills but half the time Claspers forgot to take them. Maybe if that hot bartender at Marbles ever gave him a real shot, he'd get with the program and tend to his plumbing.

Claspers wanted to ask the man with the fly rod why he'd come to the island during the hottest, deadest time of summer, when the bonefish lodges were closed. It was rare to see tourist anglers so late in the season, and even more uncommon for one to arrive alone. Typically they fished in pairs to split the cost of chartering a skiff.

When Claspers emerged from the head, he tugged down the bill of his cap against the glare of the sun. He looked around and there was Egg, sitting truculently on one of the airplane's pontoons.

The American was gone.

Sixteen

Evan Shook was surprised to see a muddy Toyota parked out front. The Oklahoma tag didn't make sense; the Lipscombs had said they were from Virginia. Plus they weren't supposed to arrive for another forty-five minutes.

Inside the house Evan Shook encountered two squatters, an attractive woman with frosted blond pigtails and a flabby guy who looked younger.

"Please don't get mad," the woman began.

"Clear out right now, before I call the cops."

The man said, "Bro, we took a major hit. This is *not* where we want to be."

It was the woman doing most of the talking, some hard-luck story about her purse being stolen, all their cash and credit cards. Evan Shook wasn't even pretending to listen.

"And this was supposed to be our second honeymoon," she concluded sadly.

That part Evan Shook heard, with vexation; the woman was way too hot to be sleeping with such a zero. Evan

Shook was unaware that people said the same thing about his mistress. Recently she'd been harping at him to leave his wife, demands inflicted at the cruelest bedroom moments. He couldn't afford a messy divorce, just as he couldn't afford to diddle for another six months with the Big Pine spec house. Between the construction loan and the property mortgage, the bank had him by the short and curlies.

"We tried camping," the male squatter piped up, "but, dude, the fuckin' skeeters!"

Evan Shook checked around. Except for the strange couple's tent, the place was in good shape for the Lipscombs. The menacing pentagram on the floor had been painted over by a select member of the construction crew, a Sikh carpenter who took no stock in silly Western superstitions. It was also he who'd disposed of the icky Santeria artifacts, lobbing the stiffened rooster into the canal and granulating the rodent skull with a belt sander.

The cute woman in pigtails said, "We weren't trying to make trouble. We just needed somewhere dry and safe."

"This'll be a cool-ass crib when it's done," her companion added for ingratiation.

Evan Shook nodded brusquely. "Yup. A real cool-ass crib."

Over the phone the Lipscombs had sounded like long shots. The guy claimed to be a retired hedge funder who was now raising trotters. He said he was driving all the way to Florida because the wife refused to fly ever since their Lear 45 had clipped a cow elk on the runway at Jackson Hole. He said they already owned a seaside spread at Hilton Head and a cottage up on the Boundary Waters. Evan Shook responded with cordiality but not gushing enthusiasm. It was his experience that people with serious money didn't broadcast their real estate portfolios to strangers who were angling to peddle them another property.

But maybe the Lipscombs were real. Maybe his luck would change.

The woman said, "I'm begging you, don't call the police. We have nowhere else to go."

Evan Shook opened his billfold and peeled off two, three, four hundred dollars. "Pack up your stuff and go get a room."

When the woman leaned forward to kiss his cheek, Evan Shook caught a heartbreaking glimpse down her blouse. "God bless you," she said.

What God? he thought. *In half an hour she'll be balling this slob in a hotel I'm paying for.*

Her lump-faced boyfriend solemnly took his hand. "Thanks, dude. I mean, duuuuude."

It's so tragic, thought Evan Shook. *So wrong.*

The phone number for Christopher Grunion obtained by Rosa – the last number dialed by Dr. Gomez O'Peele – was disconnected. Yancy had planned to call Grunion out of the blue, pretending to be an insurance broker or maybe a Republican pollster. He'd just wanted to hear what the prick who tried to kill him sounded like.

His room on Lizard Cay was fine; the AC was anemic but he had a striking view of the white flats, veined with tidal channels shining sapphire and indigo. Offshore Yancy could see a slow-chugging mail boat; otherwise the horizon was empty. He heard the Caravan lift off from Moxey's airstrip and pass over the motel on a slow turn toward Nassau. The pilot seemed like an okay guy although his bullet-headed passenger was bad news. Apparently the thug was connected to Grunion in a capacity of sufficient importance to warrant use of the seaplane for a dental crisis.

Yancy checked his phone and found a snide message from Caitlin Cox:

"Listen, *Inspector*, I think you oughta know what just happened. That judge in Miami declared my dad officially dead, whatever, so can you please leave us all alone and get back to your annoying life?"

The court's decision didn't surprise Yancy. Nick Stripling's mangled arm was sufficient evidence of death. That it had been unearthed later from the grave and then ejected from a stolen vehicle would have no bearing on the judge's ruling as to whether or not Stripling was in fact deceased. How he got that way – by mishap or homicide – was likewise irrelevant. Yancy wondered how long it would take Caitlin to get her slice of the insurance payoff, and whatever else Eve Stripling had promised.

He picked out a bicycle from the motel's rusty selection and rode to Rocky Town. It was critical to avoid Eve and her boyfriend, either of whom might recognize Yancy even in yuppie fishing garb. Unfortunately, he was the only white man on the streets, and the only white man at the seafood shack where he stopped to eat. A woman dicing conch behind the bar was so friendly that Yancy took a chance and said he was looking for a fellow American named Christopher. She gave a roll of the eyes and then one of those fabulous island laughs. Before long she was telling Yancy all about Grunion's ambitious project, the Curly Tail Lane Resort.

"Yeah, mon, dey gon have a spa and clay tennis and a chef dot's from some five-star hotel in Sowt Beach."

"Sounds spectacular," Yancy said.

"You friends with Mistuh Grunion back in Miami?"

"I am. Where does he usually hang out around here?"

"Ha, he dont hang no place. You see 'im drive sometime tru town but mostly he stay at Bannister Point. 'Im and his lady rent dot Gibson place. She come by every now 'n' then to pick up some chowder. Wot's your name, mon? Have another rum."

Yancy ordered one more Barbancourt with his meal. He dealt with the conch salad painstakingly; each incoming bite was picked apart by fork and then scrutinized for insect pieces. The locals who were witnessing this dour procedure snickered among themselves, but Yancy carried on. It seemed unlikely that Rocky Town was large enough to have a full-time health inspector, if such a job even existed on Andros. The conch shack was just that, an open-air bar next to a hill of gutted mollusk shells. No government health certificate was posted on the plywood menu board, only the boozy jottings of sailboaters and tourists.

Still, the food was excellent. After he finished eating, Yancy climbed on the clattering bike and set off in the starless night for the motel. At the bottom of a hill his front tire caught a pothole and he spilled sideways, landing on his back. He was sitting on the broken pavement and swearing aloud when he heard a motor.

From the crest of the roadway a single white light descended slowly. It was too small to be the headlamp of a motorcycle. Yancy leaned his bike against a utility pole. The white light weaved on its approach, the hum of the squat vehicle growing louder. Yancy still wasn't sure what he was looking at, though now he could hear a smoky voice, singing and laughing.

It was a woman piloting some sort of souped-up wheel-chair, which she braked to a halt when its narrow beam fell upon Yancy. She was dressed flamboyantly and followed by heavy-lidded matrons who clapped softly and rolled their heads. On the steering bar of the motorized scooter perched a monkey wearing a doll's plastic tiara and an ill-fitted disposable diaper.

"You hoyt, suh?" the throned woman asked Yancy.

"I'm good. Took a tumble off the bike is all."

"You a white fella? Don't lie. Where you from?"

She looked bony and harmless, yet Yancy experienced a spidery chill. The woman wore a wrap of pink batik on her head and swigged from a tall glass that barely fit in the cup holder. Although it was too dark on the road for Yancy to see her features, the gleam of a gapped smile was unmistakable. Something about her pet monkey didn't seem right.

She said, "Dot's Prince Driggs. He's a movie star! You two handsome boys shake honds."

"No, that's okay."

The monkey growled and thrust out a brown paw.

"Better do it," the woman warned Yancy, "or he fuck you up bod."

Yancy shook the moist little fist and said, "Well, I'd better be going."

"Take a ride wit me, suh. I'll sit on dot strong monnish lap a yours."

"Thanks, anyway. That's a spiffy wheelchair, though."

"Ain't no fuckin' wheelchair! You tink I'm a cripple?" To display her agility she hopped up, causing her attendants to flutter and fuss.

Indignantly the woman said to Yancy, "Wot dis ting is, boy, is lux'ry transport. Even got a iPod dock!"

"Sweet." He leaned closer to read the label on the mobile chair. It was a Super Rollie, the same brand that Nick Stripling's company had billed to Medicare in imaginary numbers.

"Can I ask where you got this?"

"From a friend. Woman like me has plenny friends." She resettled herself in the contoured seat and smoothed the folds of her colorful skirt.

Yancy said, "I'd really like to have a scooter like this."

"Maybe you lucky. Let's talk sum bidness."

The woman seized the fly of Yancy's pants and tugged him halfway on top of her. Zestfully she began to grope, her husky grunts reeking of rum and stale cigars. Yancy was shocked to feel the wiry old drunk fishing for his balls. He fought to get free but the monkey hooked three sinewy fingers through one of his belt loops. Only when Yancy pinched the hairless web of its armpit did the beast let go, screeching.

"No, no, don't hoyt my prince!" the woman cried. "Bey, I gon pudda black coyse on your soul! Black as det!"

Yancy pulled out of her grasp and jumped back from the scooter chair. The riled monkey hurled first his tiara and then the diaper, which landed in a sodden lump at Yancy's feet. As the matrons rumbled toward him, he kicked off his flip-flops and ran.

The last leg of the crossing got rough, and a few passengers began to throw up. Neville watched tall clouds building in the east as the breeze strengthened. The captain of the mail boat said a tropical storm was heading up from Hispaniola, which wasn't uncommon that time of year. He said the storm was called Françoise, which meant nobody would take it seriously. He said the hurricane forecasters in Miami should give scarier names to the storms – like Brutus or Thor – if they wanted people to pay proper attention.

Neville didn't own a television so his weather news came from the waterfront. Usually it was reliable. Some of the guides and fishermen had programmed their cellular phones to receive NOAA bulletins and radar loops; whenever they started moving their boats into the mangroves, Neville knew something big was coming. His own boat ran skinny, and he could take it up almost any creek on a low tide and tie off to the trees.

Still, he wasn't worrying about the tropical storm when the mail boat docked. Françoise could slide north or south, or fizzle to a squall line by the time it touched Andros. Neville was more concerned by what was happening at the family property on Green Beach. He needed a new strategy for halting the construction of Curly Tail Lane, his voodoo scheme having failed. By seducing Christopher's henchman the Dragon Queen had placed her own lustful urges ahead of her professional commitment to Neville. No crippling curse would be unleashed against the white devil; Christopher would have to be brought down by worldly means.

Neville's bike was at the airport so he passed on foot through Rocky Town, keeping a wary eye out for Egg. Still bruised from the beating, Neville longed to sleep on a real mattress instead of a boat deck. Among his three girlfriends the one named Joyous owned the softest bed but the hardest attitude. Neville decided he could endure another nagging if the payoff was a good night's rest. Joyous slept like a stump and seldom snored.

She lived near Victoria Creek, and the walk brought

Neville close to the property on Bannister Point where Christopher and the woman were staying. On a whim he left the road and made his way to the shoreline. The wind had swung southeast, pushing white-topped surf. Neville sat down on a coral outcrop with a rear view of the Gibson place. From behind him came a soft rustle in the bushes – two plump lizards humping in the last of daylight.

Neville was thirsty and tired from the slow rolling ride on the mail boat. His chin dropped to his chest and his eyelids closed as he pondered the difficult path he'd chosen. People said he was mad not to walk away from Green Beach and take the money. They laughed about it at the conch shack and called him a simpleton, which stung. By nature Neville wasn't a troublemaker; just the opposite. Never in his life had he thrown a punch in anger or caused a scene, but here was a fight from which he couldn't turn away.

What would he ever do as a rich man that he couldn't do now? Where would he go, and for God's sake why? He already lived in the loveliest place imaginable and, besides, he didn't like to fly. That's why he took the mail boat back from Nassau, seven hours by sea being more tolerable than twenty minutes by air.

Neville couldn't think of anything to buy with all that dirty wealth. His old bicycle carried him everywhere a car could go, and it didn't cost six damn dollars a gallon. Nor did he need a new fishing boat. The one he owned ran like a champ; the motor was a Yahama 150, way past warranty, but never had it stranded him, not once. He wondered if something was mentally wrong with him for being content with what he had ...

When he opened his eyes, night cloaked the shore. The lights were on inside Christopher's house. Neville got up from the rock and crept closer, approaching the landscaped edge of the lawn. Music came from speakers on the screened veranda – American rock. *Baby, we were born to run!* Neville brushed a mosquito from his nose. Through the windows he saw no movement inside the rooms. By an outside wall stood the plastic garbage can from which he'd pilfered the items he'd given to the Dragon Queen for use in her curses.

Something soft brushed against Neville's legs and he hopped backward. It was a young tabby cat, probably a stray. As he leaned down to pet it, a man spoke from the darkness behind him: "Don't move, nigger, or I'll blow your fuckin' head off."

Neville rose slowly and turned. "Don't do dot please." The gun pointed at him had a long double barrel.

"Who the hell are you? Why you sneakin' around here?" Christopher's face was difficult to see in the shadows though his orange poncho practically cast its own light. It made him appear tall and caped and spirit-like.

"I juss chasin' offer my cot," Neville said.

"That's not your fuckin' cat."

"Respeckfully, sir, it looks true like 'im."

Unfortunately, the tabby wouldn't play along. It ran off when Neville reached to pick it up. Christopher laughed.

Neville could see the whites of the man's eyeballs but not his nose or mouth. He perceived that Christopher was wearing a clinging fabric mask similar to what the local bonefish guides used to protect their faces from sunburn.

"Okay, beach nigger, what's your name?"

"Neville Stafford."

"Where you from? How old are you?"

"I'm sickty-four."

"No shit? You're in pretty good shape for an old fart."

"Dot I cont say." Neville wished he was younger and quick enough to grab for the gun. Then he would have pressed the muzzle to the man's forehead and told him to take his goddamn earthmoving machines back to Florida.

Now all Neville could do was stand still and plead for his life. In his head he said a prayer; then he asked Christopher to please kindly let him go.

"So you wanna make it to your next birthday, is that right?"

"Yah, mon," said Neville.

"My country, you get free insurance when you hit the big six-five. Government pays damn near all the bills, you get sick. They got the same deal here in the islands?"

"Dot I cont say. I ain't been sick."

Again Christopher laughed through the mask. "Good for you, nigger." He raised the barrel of the gun. "That means you can still run like a goddamn chicken."

He aimed five feet above Neville's head and a bolt of blue-gold fire punched a hole in the night. Neville ran and ran.

Seventeen

Nobody on Andros seemed especially worried about Tropical Storm Françoise. For a day the system had stalled down near Grand Turk; now it was sidling northwest again. The National Hurricane Center said atmospheric conditions were favorable for cyclonic growth. At this announcement, a TV weatherman in Miami began jabbing in febrile excitement at the floridly rendered "cone of doom" – a forecast map illustrating multiple possible pathways of the storm through the Bahamas chain and across toward Florida.

Yancy was watching on a flat-screen television in a second-story restaurant overlooking the Tongue of the Ocean. After the weather update he turned his attention to a bowl of chunky red chowder; submerged insect fragments would be hard to detect among the diced onions and celery. Yancy probed with a teaspoon. The night before he'd squashed seven adult-phase German cockroaches in his motel room; the largest was a flier that had alighted on his forehead as he slept.

The restaurant owner, an American expat with a white-streaked ponytail, asked, "What are you doing, mister?"

"Taking my time," Yancy said.

"It's only the best soup on the island. I use fresh-growed tomatoes."

Eventually Yancy took a sip. He bowed at the man and said, "Outstanding."

"Damn right."

"How's the bonefishing?"

"Super, if you can stand the heat."

"I love the heat," Yancy said.

A plane passed overhead, the pitch of the engine dropping during descent. Yancy hurried from the restaurant and pedaled his borrowed bicycle through gusty winds to the airstrip, where he found the white seaplane parked near the small terminal building. Claspers, the pilot, was talking on a cell phone while he set the wheel chocks. Standing alone by the fence was the beefy pinhead with the crumpled ears. He wore a brown guayabera, wet moons under the armpits. One side of his mug was shiny and swollen, testifying to an eventful dental appointment.

Yancy propped the bicycle against a shaded wall of the terminal. Soon a taxi van rolled up and the pinhead squeezed himself into the front passenger side. Yancy opened the sliding door and plopped down on the bench seat behind him.

"My bike's got a flat. Can I ride back to town with you?"

"I ain't gon dot way," the big man said.

"Then we'll drop you off first. My name's Andrew. What's yours?"

It was the driver who answered. "Egg's wot dey call 'im."

The goon stared ahead, rubbing his jawbone. He told the taxi man to take him to Curly Tail Lane.

"You mean Green Beach?" the driver asked.

"Ain't wot de sign say."

"N'how 'bout you, suh?"

"Conch shack," Yancy said.

The driver chuckled. "Almost lunchtime."

Egg took a prescription bottle from a pocket and tapped out three oval pills. "Fuck lunch, mon. Juss drive."

Yancy said he was from Florida. He said he loved the Bahamas and was thinking of buying a place on Andros, maybe a time share. Egg ignored him.

The van stopped at a construction site. Egg paid the driver, unlocked the chain-link gate and disappeared inside an Airstream trailer that looked like it had been rolled off a cliff. Yancy didn't see any signs or billboards on the property.

"Is this Curly Tail Lane?" he asked the driver.

"Yah."

"I heard it's going to be a five-star resort."

"Dot's de plon."

"They're just getting started, huh?"

The taxi driver laughed. "It's not like Miami. Tings move lil' slower here."

"You hungry?" said Yancy.

The driver's name was Philip and he was from Nicholls Town, on the north end. Yancy bought him fritters and a beer at the conch shack, where he flirted equitably with the two women behind the counter. Afterward he gave Yancy a motor tour of Lizard Cay, through the quiet old settlements of Elizabeth, Pindling's Bluff and Weech Harbor. Along the way Yancy saw a few families boarding their windows, but the prevailing mood was leisurely. When the taxi began to jerk and sputter, Philip pulled over by the ferry dock on

Victoria Creek. A squall blew in while he was beating with a wrench on the carburetor, so he scrambled back into the van.

While they waited for the rain to let up, Yancy described for Philip his unsettling encounter with the old woman on the motorized wheelchair. The driver frowned and told Yancy to be careful – she was a man-eater.

"A true sex witch, mon."

"What do you mean?"

"Wonna my uncles sleep wit her and tree months later he drop dead," Philip said. "She feed 'im poison coz he won't screw her no more. Wicked bod lady – you stay 'way."

"What's the story with that monkey?" Yancy asked.

The driver said the animal starred in the Johnny Depp pirate movies until he turned rowdy and got fired – the rumor was that he had been caught masturbating on wigs in the costume trailer. Later the monkey was won in a domino game by a local man named Neville Stafford, who'd been working hard to rehabilitate his new pet. Nobody was sure why Neville had gifted him to the old voodoo hag.

"Dey call her Dragon Queen," he added.

"Where'd she get those crazy wheels?"

"From her new boyfriend, mon. He won't lost long. Nonna dem do."

Yancy suspected that her Super Rollie was a demo left over from Nicholas Stripling's Medicare-fleecing operation. Christopher Grunion could have conned the "personal mobility device" from Eve and given it to the Dragon Queen, though it seemed far-fetched that he – or any fully sighted male – would start a romance with such a revolting loon.

"Is the lady's boyfriend a white American? About my age?"

Philip cackled. "No, bey, you already meet de fella! It's Egg."

"Oh, come on."

"Yah, dot's true. I tole you she's a witch, dot Dragon Queen. No cock is safe!"

"You know a man named Grunion?"

"Yessuh. Egg's boss."

"Show me where he lives," Yancy said.

"Why?" Philip seemed amused.

"Because ... he's a friend?"

"Dot's your story, I guess. What if I say no?"

Yancy took out the Miami police badge belonging to retired sergeant Johnny Mendez and held it up briefly for Philip to see. The shield featured a lush palm tree but not the officer's name, which was convenient for Yancy.

"You cont 'rest nobody here in de Bahamas," the driver said mildly.

"I was hoping for some friendly cooperation, that's all. Wouldn't you at least like to know what crimes I'm investigating?"

"No, mon."

"Three homicides that took place in Florida. Murders."

Philip sucked in a breath and said, "God o'mighty."

Yancy gave him some cash. "I'm not here to make trouble. I didn't even bring a gun."

"Too bod. He's a mean mottafuckah."

"You're talking about Christopher."

"Egg, too. You needa be cool."

"My middle name," Yancy said.

On the return trip to Rocky Town, Philip slowed the van

as they passed the oceanfront house Grunion and "his woman" were renting. Yancy saw a yellow Jeep Wrangler in the driveway but no activity. When he got to his motel room, he placed a box of bonefish flies and a water bottle in his fanny pack. Then he grabbed the tube holding his fly rod, selected another bicycle and rode back toward Bannister Point.

The tide was coming in, so the depth was fine. Under an overcast sky Yancy buttered his nose and cheeks with greasy white sunblock. Then he put on wide Polaroid sunglasses and a long-billed fishing cap with cotton neck flaps. This Unabomber style, tweaked for the tropics, ensured that neither Eve nor her boyfriend would recognize him from a distance.

He assembled the nine-foot rod, strung the peach-colored line through the guides and picked out a credible fly. Slowly he waded down the shoreline, occasionally pausing to cast at fish that weren't there. The wind was strong but he quartered slightly into it and double-hauled for more distance. It was a graceful exercise; anyone watching from a dock or a porch would have pegged him as a serious angler, not one of the usual goobers.

As he came within sight of Eve Stripling's place, Yancy spotted the widow herself. She was dragging a red kayak through the backyard toward one side of the house, where she stowed it beside a wall. Yancy continued wading, pretending to be focused on the flats. Next Eve went after a barbecue grill, which she rolled to the same sheltered location. Evidently she'd been following the TV weather reports.

Yancy put the fly rod under one arm and began the

ceremony of tying on a new tippet. He took his time, hoping for a glimpse of Grunion roaming the property. The water felt warm on his bare legs, and the wind kept the ruthless doctor flies at bay. Out of nowhere a Stratocaster started twanging in his brainpan – an old Dick Dale surf riff. Offshore was a misting reef break, and Yancy could hear the waves plowing the coral ledges. Whatever he was doing on the flats of Andros Island, it sure didn't feel like work.

From land came a yell. Eve Stripling stood on a rock outcrop waving her arms. Yancy's first impulse was to flee, though the effort would be doomed to play out in slow motion. The human knee wasn't engineered to sprint hundreds of yards in three feet of water.

How the hell did she know it was me? Yancy wondered dejectedly.

Then the wind dropped, and he was able to make out Eve's words: "Help Tillie! Help her!"

He squinted at something in the water between him and the widow, something alive. To no one he grumbled, "Are you shitting me?"

A puppy no larger than a muskrat was swimming toward him like a laser-guided clump of mattress stuffing. One of those urban teacup breeds, the dog had a stunted tail that drew a pencil-thin wake in the chop. It was a brainless expedition.

"Barracudas!" Eve shrieked from the rock. "Save her! Hurry!"

"Yeah, yeah."

"Sharks!"

"I heard you," Yancy said to himself. He advanced in long splashy strides toward the weary pooch and scooped it up.

Now what? he wondered. If he carried the animal all the

222

way to Eve, she would surely recognize him despite the sun-glasses and SPF 75 war paint. And instantly she'd know why he was there – to build a murder case against her.

"Thank you, mister! Thank you!" she bleated across the shallows.

Yancy responded with a modest-seeming wave. He set Tillie back in the water and pointed her toward the spot where Eve awaited: "Now be a good little rodent and swim to Momma."

But the pup wouldn't go; it spun around and thrashed its way back to Yancy, nosing into the crotch of his shorts. He tried a second launch with the same outcome. Tired Tillie was done for the day.

Now Yancy had no choice. He couldn't abandon the dog to a certain drowning, nor could he take her ashore and risk exposing his identity. So he turned and headed up-island across the flats. In one hand was the fly rod; in the other sat Tillie.

"Hey! Hey, you! Where are you going?" Eve cried.

The wind resumed blowing and her voice faded. Yancy glanced back and saw that she'd been joined by her boy-friend, glowing like a harbor buoy in his orange poncho. Together the couple was stork-stepping along the rocky ledge, trying to keep parallel with Yancy. It wasn't difficult to do; the water was now up to his thighs. Shells and sea urchins crunched beneath his wading booties, and once the bottom skated out from under him – a half-buried stingray, streaking seaward in a gray plume of marl.

As soon as Grunion reached a sandy stretch, he broke away from Eve and began to run, his poncho flapping like an unzipped tent. Yancy knew what was coming. Fifty yards down the beach, Grunion veered ninety degrees and sloshed into the shallows on a course of certain interception. Both of Yancy's escape options were problematic – returning the opposite way, toward Eve's house, or heading out to the deep, rough water. He wasn't blind to the irony of his dilemma; he didn't even *like* runty dogs. A pertinent question was whether pet-napping would be considered a felony or a misdemeanor in the Commonwealth of the Bahamas.

Yancy elected to stand his ground, submerged though it was. He secured Tillie in his fanny pack and rapidly stripped line from the fly reel. As Grunion splashed closer, Yancy spoke up in a defective Irish accent: "Git away from me, y'arsehole!"

Then he began arcing the tapered line in fluid loops back and forth over his right shoulder, using the robust breeze to extend his distance. Visually this motion recalled the virtuoso fly-casting scenes in *A River Runs Through It*, his father's favorite movie, except that Yancy's target was a human being, not a rainbow trout.

Shining on the end of his leader was a saltwater pattern called a Gotcha, size 1/0, tied on a stainless steel hook honed to surgical efficacy. Yancy stung Poncho Boy on the bridge of his nose, drawing a dark comma of blood. Grunion swore and backed off awkwardly. The next cast pricked an unshaven cheek and the one after that whipsnapped just shy of his left eyelash. Grunion, who showed no sign of recognizing Yancy, became preoccupied with self-protection. As if buzzed by hornets, he flailed one beefy arm in front of his face.

And on that arm was the large gaudy watch Yancy had seen before, on the wrist of his assailant on Big Pine. He was sure it was the same Tourbillon missing from the severed limb of Nick Stripling.

"Call yer dog to come!" he huffed at Grunion.

"What?"

"Ye heard me, dumb shite. Gawn and call yer bloody mutt!"

Yancy deftly kept the fly whistling through the air and with his left hand reached back and lifted the clueless canine from the fanny pack. He plopped her in the water and nudged her toward Grunion. On the beach, a hundred yards away, Eve Stripling paced and whinnied.

"Tillie, come!" Grunion commanded.

The addled pup swam in circles.

"Tillie! Over here! Tillie, yo!"

Pitiful, Yancy thought. He stopped casting and tickled the dog's rump with the tip of the rod. To Eve's boyfriend he said: "Try'n whistle, ye eejit."

Grunion whistled and Tillie's cornflake ears pricked.

"Now clap yer hands," Yancy said.

The man didn't clap; he whistled again. This time the puppy turned and paddled on a zigzag course toward the sound. "Good girl! Good girl!" Grunion hollered. Minutes later he was gathering Tillie from the waves.

Yancy resumed shooting casts at an imaginary point between Grunion's eyebrows. Flinching and ducking, the killer slogged back toward the sandy mound where Eve fretted. For extra coaxing, Yancy thwacked the Gotcha against the nape of Grunion's crispy poncho, and on the subsequent cast he stuck him in the right earlobe – a keen display of aim from seventy feet in a crosswind. Yancy set the hook using a sharp strip that broke the tippet and caused Grunion to bellow vituperatively. The pink-and-white fly remained loyally embedded, sparkling in the cocksucker's punctured ear like a dainty shrimp-shaped stud.

Once safely on land, Grunion pushed the dog at Eve and, cupping his wound, stalked back toward the house. Eve followed a few paces behind, cradling Tillie and pausing intermittently to glare across the flats at the would-be abductor of her precious princess.

Yancy hurriedly waded north, reeling in his line. The homicide investigation that he'd hoped would resurrect his law enforcement career was foundering, torpedoed by bad luck and a deficit of careful planning. He expected the bright yellow Wrangler to appear any moment on the coast road, an enraged Grunion tracking him toward a fateful landfall. The man would have armed himself, probably with the 12-gauge Beretta he'd swiped from Yancy's home in the Keys. Yancy himself was a sitting duck. A graphite fishing wand, no matter how artfully deployed, was useless against a screaming load of buckshot.

However, Grunion never returned. Nor, evidently, did Eve summon the island police, for Yancy came ashore unmolested. Riding the bicycle through a fresh rain toward Rocky Town, he concluded that the widow Stripling and her consort must have dismissed him as a crank, fly anglers being notoriously irascible if their solitude is violated.

He was on his way to the motel when a thunderclap chased him off the road, into an open carport attached to a small abandoned house. The slab floor was littered with rusting Red Bull cans and green shards of Kalik bottles that threatened his bicycle's bald tires. Still, the place was dry and its roof offered material protection from the sudden electrical storm, a summertime sensation that Yancy had learned to fear and respect during his Florida childhood. One afternoon, while camping at Cape Sable, he and his father had witnessed a lightning bolt incinerate a flock of turkey buzzards roosting in the boughs of an old pine, which then flared like a sparkler and split down the midline.

The sky over Lizard Cay had closed in and the rain began to slant. Cars passed every few minutes, slowing for puddles, though none of them were yellow Jeeps. Yancy set his fly rod against a wall and stayed perched on the bicycle, pondering what to do. The sensible move would be to return to the Keys and construct his homicide case the old-fashioned way, with forensics, paper trails and dodgy self-serving witnesses.

To remain on Andros was to risk spooking Eve and Grunion, which would screw up a prosecution beyond salvation. The trip certainly hadn't been a waste – Yancy had established that the couple was hiding out together, apparently investing the late Nicholas Stripling's Medicare plunder in a resort development remote from the noses of U.S. authorities.

In the downpour Yancy no longer could see the road except during bursts of lightning. Overhead the beams of the carport began to drip so he adjusted his position, clearing away more broken glass and clutter. From somewhere inside the house came an unhappy squeak and the sounds of scuttling, which Yancy attributed to rats. His shoulders tensed when he caught a whiff of spiced tobacco smoke.

Peeking through a rotted-out doorway, he spied an unexpected shelter mate – the voodoo woman's monkey, bedraggled, sopping, undiapered. The animal squatted in a corner sucking on a meerschaum pipe that he clutched blowgun-style with four tiny fingers, the dirty kernel of a thumb clocking in an agitated motion. The whitish bowl of the pipe was carved into a miniature topless angel of the voluptuous style found on bowsprits of old sailing ships.

If the taxi driver's story was true – that the monkey was featured in the *Pirates of the Caribbean* movies – his descent from stardom had been steep indeed. Yancy hoped the little bastard had forgotten the painful pinch he'd inflicted upon him the night before during the scuffle aboard the voodoo skank's scooter chair.

The animal's expression betrayed nothing as he sucked on the pipe. Then a boom of thunder – or perhaps Yancy's stare – caused the mangy desperado to bark sharply and flash brown-stained chompers.

"Chill out, little man," Yancy said.

The monkey spat the meerschaum and flew at him, snapping and scratching at his kneecaps and bare shins. From the superior height of his bicycle Yancy kicked back in a fevered defense until the heavy toe of his wading boot caught the beast flush on his crusty chin, launching him tail over head through a charred window frame, into the squall.

With blood-streaked legs Yancy pedaled out of the carport and down the road. His visibility was so foreshortened by the deluge that there was no opportunity to dodge the endless potholes, and by the time he reached the motel he'd bitten through his bottom lip. After a hasty dismount Yancy also realized that he had left behind his fly rod, a long-ago birthday present from Celia. Disconsolately he trudged across the soggy lawn toward his room, pulling up short when he spied the door ajar.

For a time Yancy waited in the raw wet dusk, rows of fat droplets pouring off the bill of his fishing cap. *Was it Grunion himself who had come, or had he given the job to Egg?* Yancy thought. *Hell, does it really matter?*

He uprooted a cane tiki torch, unlit, and rushed through the doorway swinging like Barry Bonds. Two matching lamps and a tray of decorative sand dollars were demolished before the torch broke to pieces. Dr. Rosa Campesino stepped from the bathroom wearing lace panties and a look of consternation.

"What on earth, Andrew?"

"Oh shit. I thought you were somebody else."

"It was supposed to be a surprise. I even brought some slutty red lipstick."

"Babe, you look fantastic."

"I caught the last plane in."

"Let's light some candles."

"The last plane before the hurricane."

"What?" Yancy said.

"Take off your clothes, dummy. You're dripping all over the rug."

Eighteen

"Are you in hedge funds?" Ford Lipscomb asked without glancing up.

Evan Shook said no. He was watching with equal measures of rapture and incredulity while Lipscomb wrote out a check.

"You say fifty grand'll hold it? Call it good faith – we've still got some wrinkles to iron out."

"Fifty's just fine." More than fine. Exquisite.

"Tell me the name of your lawyer again. On the escrow account?"

Evan Shook repeated it for Lipscomb. "He's up in South Miami. Does all my real estate work."

"Stay away from hedge funds, friend. Those giddy days are over," Lipscomb went on. "I tasted the best of it, then I bailed in the nick of time. Where the heck is Jayne?"

"Upstairs enjoying the view," Evan Shook said.

"Gold is the way to go. You ever listen to Glenn Beck? Maybe he's got a few shingles loose, but that weird little crybaby is right about gold."

Evan Shook wanted to pinch himself. After only two walk-throughs, the Lipscombs were actually buying his spec house! Ford and Jayne Lipscomb from Leesburg, Virginia, on their first-ever trip to the Florida Keys, arriving in a wine-colored Bentley convertible, its rear seat backs of hand-tooled leather splattered with fresh pelican shit – a rude souvenir from their Overseas Highway crossing.

Yet these remarkable Lipscombs, these brisk and purposeful Lipscombs, acknowledged with only the mildest of frowns the pungent bird goo on their expensive import. Handsome they were as a couple, married forever, their kids surely all grown up, well-schooled, well-bred and prospering. Evan Shook suppressed a pang of envy as Ford and Jayne approached the house hand in hand, smiling the way they might have smiled on their very first date, forty-some years ago. They were eager to tour all seven thousand square feet, and they absorbed Evan Shook's sales pitch with a genial attentiveness that unnerved him at first.

Such anxiety was understandable given his run of black luck with the property – the bloating raccoon corpse, the deranged bees, the gory witchcraft altar and then that nut job Yancy, sprawled naked as a jaybird to greet the Turbles. Next came the squatters, a depressingly mismatched twosome who had cleared out only minutes before the Lipscombs' first visit.

So now, on pivotal day two, Evan Shook couldn't be faulted for anticipating another sale-killing calamity – perhaps the ghostly pack of rabid mongrels that Yancy kept nattering about. In Evan Shook's mind flashed a gothic vision of the Lipscombs being taken down by the heels – first Jayne and then Ford – while sprinting for the Bentley.

He considered himself a rational person, but part of him had begun to worry that the spec house truly was jinxed, a word used by both his wife and his girlfriend in separate conversations.

Yet there was no sign of Yancy or wild dogs, and the Lipscombs' second tour was as uneventful as the first. Sweating, slapping at bugs, they remained at all times polite and uncomplaining. The few questions asked by the husband seemed deliriously naïve coming from an ex-Wall Street slick, until Evan Shook reminded himself that he was dealing with a man who'd never before witnessed a Gulf sunset, a man who'd habitually vacationed in Bridgehampton or Breckinridge before squandering the first act of his hard-earned retirement downwind from a goddamn horse barn.

Before long, Evan Shook had set aside his native wariness in order to nurture Ford Lipscomb's fantasy, which was the boilerplate back-nine fantasy of so many ultra-successful, ultra-resourceful American males: to live by the sea in perpetual sunshine, in a state with no income tax.

Jayne Lipscomb came down the stairs to report a pair of ospreys diving for fish in the tidal creeks.

"They're here every day," Evan Shook said. "Are you a birder?"

"No, but that's a thought."

"We've got a very active Audubon chapter down here."

"Did Ford tell you he's selling the trotters?"

Her husband broke in: "*We* are selling the trotters. Mutual decision."

Jayne Lipscomb sighed. "Gorgeous animals, but so much drama. My goodness."

"You'll love living in the Keys," Evan Shook said.

Ford Lipscomb handed up the check. "I'd like to buy a boat. Do a little fishing once I get the hang of it."

"First let's talk about window frames," his wife said. "Also, a skylight in the master bedroom? Is that doable, Mr. Shook?"

"Anything's doable."

A skylight inevitably would leak during the rainy season, as did all skylights in Florida, but Evan Shook felt unmoved to mention this because every whimsical add-on served to pad his wispy profit line. By the time the silicone sealant began to disintegrate, in two or three years, he'd be back in Syracuse, probably ass-deep in divorce papers.

Recently his mistress had delivered a curdling ultimatum: Dump the wife or else.

The else being a musician-slash-poet with whom she'd shared a cannabis vaporizer at the bluegrass festival – a mandolin player, she'd informed Evan Shook, knowing he would find that more threatening than a perky banjoist. The young man was *tall*, his mistress had added cruelly. Six-one in his socks.

Ford Lipscomb said, "When's the last time this island took a direct hit from a hurricane?"

Evan Shook chose to narrowly interpret the term "direct hit."

"Never," he declared. "Anyway, the building codes are much tougher now than in the old days. Heavy-duty glass, reinforced trusses – it's the law."

Jayne Lipscomb asked if he'd been keeping track of Tropical Storm Françoise on the Weather Channel. "Because this house, no offense, it's wide open. No windows, no doors, the roof could fly off to Cuba—"

"Oh, we'd board up the place," Evan Shook said with a

patient-looking smile. "That storm isn't coming this way, don't you worry. It's rolling straight up through the Bahamas."

"Just what I told her," said Ford Lipscomb.

"But look at what Katrina did!" The wife, tracing an elaborate S in the air.

Evan Shook inconspicuously touched the breast pocket into which he'd tucked the couple's check, and he was comforted to feel the crisp paper rectangle beneath the fabric.

Ford Lipscomb rose. "There *is* one important detail we need to discuss."

An unpleasant contraction commenced in Evan Shook's colon.

"Fire away," he croaked, bracing for the deal breaker.

"Sewer or septic?" Ford Lipscomb said.

Evan Shook went blank, such was his apprehension. He saw the husband's lips moving but he heard not a word. Helplessly he shook his head.

"The house," Jayne Lipscomb intervened, from behind tortoiseshell frames. "Is it on a sewer main?"

Evan Shook nearly gurgled with relief. "No, no, we have state-of-the-art septic, totally aerobic," he said. "Come outside and I'll show you where the tank's buried!"

Neville took his boat up Victoria Creek ahead of the first band of heavy showers. He tied off in some mangroves, threw out an anchor, tested the bilge pump and crossed back to shore in a skiff run by some conch boys from the South Bight. The thought of being confined with Joyous for the storm's duration was withering, so he decided to walk back to Rocky Town and surprise one of his less surly girlfriends. On the way he avoided Bannister Point, feeling lucky to be alive. The white man Christopher could have shot him dead as a thief instead of firing over his head, and Neville wondered why he'd been spared. After giving it some thought, he decided there was no mercy at play; Christopher simply didn't wish to draw attention to himself.

For an American businessman needing favors from the Bahamas government, killing a local fisherman would be foolhardy and counterproductive. Neville's death would have brought the top police authorities from Nassau, generating an inquest that would have stalled the Curly Tail Lane development and poisoned public sentiment. All this Christopher must have known. Still, the ugly confrontation was a close call that had left Neville shaken and doubt-ridden. Never before had he been called a "beach nigger," and he wasn't sure what that meant beyond the obvious slur. Did Christopher know it was Neville's home that he had leveled on Green Beach? That it was Neville who'd pissed in the fuel tank of the offending backhoe, Neville who'd been stomped by Egg?

No, he cont know dot was me, thought Neville, *or he would hoff say sum ting more den juss 'hey beach nigger.' He would hoff warn me stay offa dot property, mon, or next time Egg, he gern break your goddamn arms and leg bones too!*

The rain was falling harder by the time Neville approached the settlement. He worried about the angry look of the ocean, a deep muddy purple, the furling wave tops sheared by the rising wind. Hurriedly he hiked up the hill to the shack belonging to the Dragon Queen. The wooden shutters had been lowered and through the crooked slats came the sounds of a man and woman singing, or trying to. Neville selected the outside wall that was exposed most directly to the thumping raindrops, the noisiest wall, where his breathing wouldn't be heard by the occupants. There he positioned himself at a window and peeked through a gap between the sagging shutter and the warped pine frame.

Inside, the Dragon Queen was astride the broad lap of Egg, who had squeezed his ebony bulk into the pilot seat of her motorized scooter chair. The vehicle was rolling in tight circles around the dank little room – doing doughnuts is what the wild boys with cars called it. Neville could tell that Christopher's henchman and the hag were dizzy from their drunken orbits. Egg wore a sweat-soaked undershirt and possibly nothing else, his long yet oddly unmasculine feet protruding from beneath the Dragon Queen's rainbow skirt.

Neville muffled a gasp when his eyes fell upon Driggs, his former ward and companion. The haggard primate stood on the table amid empty rum bottles and plates of half-eaten fruit that was twitching with flies. He was holding his face over the yellow flame of a candle, lighting the bowl of a pipestem clenched in dingy teeth. Neville was appalled by this coarse new habit, and his anger swelled as the monkey studiously exhaled a train of smoke rings that dissipated in a swirl as a fresh gust rattled through the shutters. Driggs extended the pipe to arm's length and the Dragon Queen grabbed it as the scooter chair sped by, Egg cackling as he worked the joystick. The old woman got one heavy drag before losing her prize on the very next lap, Driggs reaching out to swipe it from her mottled lips.

The back of Neville's T-shirt was drenched, but the rain was warm, hurricane rain, and he didn't shrink from his spy post at the window. Inside the darkening room, Egg halted the motorized chair and snapped two fingers at the monkey, who blinked aloofly and spat into an upturned tambourine.

A small commotion began, and bile rose in Neville's throat – the Dragon Queen and her new boyfriend were attempting to screw!

To and fro rocked the shiny scooter, its tires carping on the smooth-worn planks. The entanglement progressed clumsily, and soon the shack filled with adenoidal moans and raspy howls that melded into a lurid, tuneless yodel. Neville slapped his palms over both ears and turned away, the raindrops slicking his cheeks.

What is the awful nature of this woman's power? he wondered.

Thunder crashed and Neville dove to the ground as the shutter by his head banged open. Out leaped Driggs, still mouthing the pipe. Clutched in his paws were a Bic lighter and a tin of Dunhill tobacco. He never glanced Neville's way, pausing only to shed his lumpy diaper before loping down the road through the squall. Neville called the monkey's name but another thunderclap smothered his doleful cry. He sprang to his feet and gave chase, although in the downpour he soon lost sight of his fleet quarry. Spurred by guilt, Neville continued his blind pursuit, shouting miserably for the small friend he'd sold to the terrible voodoo priestess.

Sold for nothing.

His lungs were burning by the time he reached the old Cooper place, which had been empty ever since Virgil Cooper went to Havana and fell for a tour guide named Miguelito. Neville ducked into the carport to rest and wait out the lightning. He was dripping like a horse. In a puddle at his feet floated an empty tobacco tin, which Neville picked up and examined solemnly.

Of course the brand was Dunhill.

"Driggs?" he piped excitedly. "You come out!"

But the monkey wasn't there. Neville checked every

room, every closet, every cupboard of the dilapidated house. So leathered were the soles of Neville's feet – he seldom wore shoes – that he was unbothered by the rubble of broken glass and splintery planks. He found no other trace of Driggs, although upon returning to the carport he spotted something he'd previously overlooked – a fly rod propped upright in a dry corner.

It was an expensive piece of fishing equipment, too fancy and specialized for the locals. There was no rust on the metal guides of the rod, and Neville tasted wet salt when he touched his tongue to the cork. He wondered if the wealthy tourist fisherman who owned the outfit had crossed paths with the bedraggled monkey, and perhaps out of pity had adopted him.

An hour passed until the wave of thunderstorms rolled by and the rain quit. With fly rod in hand, Neville set out at full stride in the deepening night.

Rosa said, "I've always wanted to do it in a hurricane."

"Technically, this is pre-hurricane."

"Don't be a spoilsport, Andrew."

"It's six hours away, you said."

"So, consider this a warm-up."

Yancy kissed each of her nipples, then he rested a cheek on her tummy.

"If only the storm wasn't named Françoise. That is *so* weak," Rosa said. She ruffled his hair. "Hey, what was that catchy little tune you were humming earlier?"

"When?"

"While you were going down on me. You don't remember humming?"

"Oh, that was 'Yellow Submarine.'"

"So you think of me as basically your sex kazoo."

"I only hum when I'm happy," said Yancy. Sometimes he just floated off into a zone; it had happened once with Bonnie – a Paul Simon song – and she'd boxed his ears saying, "You and Julio get out of there!"

Rosa whistled. "Listen to that wind blow. Holy crap!"

"Andrew wasn't the most ferocious name for a hurricane and look what happened."

"Andrew's a fine name, Andrew. You kidding?"

"Too preppy for a killer storm. That's what they said before it hit Miami."

"Who said? Some girl you were dating?"

"Her name was Mariah."

"Oh, she was just jealous," Rosa said. "'They call the wind Ma-rye-ah' – don't you remember that one? The poor baby wanted a storm named after herself! Tell me your age at the time of this romance."

"Twenty-two." Yancy was beginning to think in a serious way about Françoise, wondering if he and Rosa might possibly use the heavy weather to their advantage.

"When I was twenty-two I went to Paris," she said. "Graduation present from the folks. One day I went to the Rodin museum and I got totally turned on by all those sexy sculptures. You ever been there? He had a thing for nymphs and minotaurs. Incredible stuff. Anyway, I meet this semi-cute exchange student from Boston and we end up having a quickie in the bathroom."

"At the Rodin."

"There was a window. You could look out at the garden and see *The Thinker*."

"I want to believe this story," Yancy said, "with all my soul."

"Swear to God, Andrew. First and only time in a museum."

Yancy had never been to France. He imagined a misty rain falling at the time. "How was the flight today?" he asked Rosa.

"Not fun. The poor thing sitting next to me said two whole rosaries – one in English, one in Creole. Lord, what happened to your legs?"

"A monkey assaulted me."

"You mean her husband assaulted you."

"It's no joke. This was a horrible creature."

She remarked upon his recent travails with animals. "First some deranged dog in Miami practically chews your ass off, and now this. Lucky you're banging a licensed health-care practitioner."

"I did nothing to provoke the little bastard."

"Clearly it's all payback for abducting Johnny Mendez's cat. Surely you believe in karma – I never met a cop who didn't," Rosa said. "There's some goop in my kit bag. We should dress those wounds."

"The least of my problems. I capped off an otherwise productive afternoon by flogging Eve Stripling's boyfriend with a fly rod."

"And that would be your idea of stealth. Very slick."

"I'm pretty sure he didn't know who I was, but still it was a tight spot."

Rosa took a deep breath, lifting Yancy's head.

She said, "I'm afraid I've got some lousy news."

"Not right now. Please?" He blew softly into her belly button.

"I didn't mention it earlier because I didn't want to spoil the mood. Andrew, don't deny that you're susceptible to untimely distractions."

"I am," he said, "cursed with an overactive mind."

"The bullet that killed O'Peele came from the same weapon that killed Charles Phinney – the .357 they found in the doctor's condo. I saw the ballistics this morning."

"How is that bad news? It's exactly what we expected."

"The Key West police also think it's marvelous," Rosa said. "In fact, they're so overjoyed they want to close the Phinney case, ASAP. They're saying O'Peele shot the kid over drugs, then drove in a haze back to Miami. Once he sobered up and realized what he'd done, he blew his brains out. That's their story and they're sticking to it."

"Jackoffs!" Yancy sat up. "Is there any evidence that O'Peele and Phinney ever met?"

"Nope. I asked the same thing."

"Or that the doctor was down in Key West that night? Did he buy a poncho and a sun mask? Did he rent a moped on Duval Street?"

Rosa shook her head. "All they've got is the matching slug from the gun."

"And a dead boat mate that nobody cares about."

"How do you think I feel? I'm the one who sent them the bullet."

Yancy said, "They can't close the Phinney case without you ruling that O'Peele was a suicide. Otherwise their lame theory falls apart."

"It's easy to pull the plug on an investigation without officially saying so. Somehow the file just crawls into a drawer."

"Yeah, I know." Yancy put on a clean shirt and a pair of khaki shorts, Rosa cocking an eyebrow as she watched.

"Where do you think you're going, Inspector, on such a dark and stormy night?"

"I left my favorite fly rod in a vacant house up the road."

"We'll go get it tomorrow. Right now I'm craving a beer and conch salad."

"I happen to know just the place."

Rosa smiled and kicked off the sheets. "Kindly toss me my panties."

"But here's the deal – anybody asks, we're married, okay? We came to Andros to do some fishing and look around for a second home. Now we're stuck here because of the storm."

"Do we have any children? And where are we from?"

"Boca Raton, obviously. You're still a doctor – let's say a thoracic surgeon."

"Close enough."

"Our son, Kyle, just made the traveling lacrosse team at Pine Crest. We have twin daughters in the gifted program. Our dog is an incontinent pug named Cheney."

"Perfect," said Rosa, "and we all live in a yellow submarine."

She went into the bathroom and began brushing her hair. "What's your fictitious line of work, Andrew? Should anyone ask."

"Investments, meaning I mooch off an obscene family trust fund. Shale oil – no, better, microprocessors." Yancy used the corner of a sheet to wipe the sand off his feet.

Rosa reappeared waving a crinkled white tube. "Bring me those mangled legs of yours. By the way, I demand to see your alleged assailant."

"They say he was in the Johnny Depp movies but got the axe."

"These days every movie has a monkey," she said. "Monkeys are the bomb."

"Not this mangy little psycho. Hey, Doc, take it easy."

"Hold still, please. Do you have an actual plan for trapping Eve and her murderous beau? Or are we basically flying blind?"

"Of course I've got a plan," Yancy said.

"An intelligent, fully formed plan?"

"Define fully formed."

"I knew it," said Rosa.

"Ouch, that stings! Be careful."

Yet secretly he marveled at her touch, so tender for a coroner.

Nineteen

Claspers thought it was crazy to leave the Caravan chocked on the tarmac at Moxey's in the path of a hurricane. He wanted to fly it back to Florida, but Christopher Grunion said no way, amigo, are you stranding me and my old lady on this fly-turd island. When Claspers had suggested they all leave Andros before the storm drew close, Grunion said he and Eve weren't going anywhere. He said their house was built like a goddamn fortress.

"Where I'm staying, it's a death trap," Claspers had remarked.

Either Grunion hadn't gotten the hint, or he didn't want Claspers as a guest. In any event, Claspers was stuck. Maybe the storm would miss Lizard Cay entirely, or maybe it would smash the place head-on, in which case that lovely seaplane would end up as scrap aluminum.

Claspers said, "But what do I know, sweetie? I'm only the pilot."

"Yeah, mon, dot's you. Sky King." The pretty bartender brought him his third drink of the evening.

244

"Is it still a Category Two?"

"Dey say trey, mebbe four."

"Lively," muttered Claspers.

The wind clawed at the palm thatching over the conch shack. No music was playing but the radio remained the center of attention because it was tuned to the Nassau weather station. The gusty conditions had disabled most of the TV dishes in Rocky Town – Claspers had seen one lying upturned in the roadway – and many residents seeking storm updates had come to the outdoor restaurant. The young Androsians, who'd never been through a hurricane, laughed and joked. The older ones positioned themselves closer to the radio and kept their voices low. Françoise was reported to be roaring along the Exuma chains; even if Andros escaped a direct hit, the island would take a battering. By daybreak it would be over.

Claspers held his glass with both hands, admiring the miniature wavelets on the coppery surface of the scotch. He was one of a half dozen white customers, including the rangy American he'd met at Moxey's airport. Andrew, the fly fisherman. Sitting next to him at the bar was a Latin woman who probably smelled as heavenly as she looked. Claspers had a serious buzz going, a down-island buzz.

The woman at the fisherman's side made Claspers think of another beauty he knew in Barranquilla, back in the old times, a woman he would have married if she hadn't already had a husband and if the husband hadn't been a macho hot-head who liked to shoot people in the mouth.

Which Claspers well knew because he was working for the man at the time, running loads of grass up to South Bimini.

Donna had been the wife's name. By now she'd be in her

245

fifties and more lovely than ever. A few years ago Claspers picked up a rumor that her husband was machine-gunned on his way to a bordello, which is what happens when you hire a half-wit cousin to armor your Escalade. On some nights Claspers fantasized about flying back to Colombia, showing up at Donna's doorstep with a grin, a hard-on and a bottle of Dom. The airstrip he remembered well, and also the Moorish-style villa at the north end; in particular, a second-floor bedroom with a balcony overlooking the valley.

To the bartender Claspers said: "Buy those two sweet-hearts a round on me."

Afterward the couple returned the gesture and motioned for the pilot to move down the bar and join them. Andrew introduced the Latin woman as his wife, Rosa, and said she'd arrived on a flight that afternoon.

Claspers chuckled. "Your timing sucks, no offense."

"Oh, we'll find something to do," Rosa said. "You ever flown through a hurricane?"

"Naw, but I've slept through a few. It's easier than you think." Claspers took a hearty sip, demonstrating his pre-storm preparations.

The woman said she was a surgeon. "Hopefully nobody'll get hurt, but I always travel with a kit of instruments."

"On this island," said the pilot, "that makes you the whole freaking hospital."

Somebody turned up the radio. The somber voice from Nassau reported that Hurricane Françoise was now "pack-ing" winds of 105 miles per hour. Movement of the storm continued north-northwest.

The fisherman set a hand on Claspers's shoulder. "Can I ask you something? We heard your boss is the one who's building Curly Tail Lane. Grunion is his name?"

"That's him," said Claspers.

Leaning in close, Rosa confided that she and her husband were looking to buy in the Bahamas. "Andrew really loves this place," she added, "and I do, too."

"You should see it when the sun comes out."

"Point is," the husband went on, "do you think Mr. Grunion would mind if you introduced him to a potential customer?"

"I think Mr. Grunion would be fucking thrilled."

"We'd rather not deal with any Bay Street realtors. And we'd be paying cash, if that matters."

"Cash is never bad." Claspers liked these people, and briefly he considered telling them the truth: that Grunion's resort project wasn't exactly advancing at a breakneck pace; that Grunion was still getting hassled and tossed by the bureaucrats in Nassau; that a vandal had targeted the job site; that only two other buyers – one from Taiwan and the other from Dubai had put down actual deposits for time-share units.

However, even in a semi-trashed condition the pilot perceived there might be something juicy in it for himself, a commission from the boss, if a sale was forthcoming. Who was Claspers to stand between this earnest young couple and their balmy vision of paradise?

Rosa said, "What about tonight? It's not raining anymore."

Claspers cast a skeptical eye skyward. There would be a few hours of lull until the next storm band, but he wasn't in the deferential mode necessary to deal with Grunion. "Now's not a real good time," he said.

The man shrugged one shoulder. "We'll be on the first plane outta here after the hurricane. I got the whole damn trust committee waiting on me back in Boca. Maybe it'll work out on another trip, if there's anything left of this place."

Claspers stood up. "Let me make a quick call. Sorry, I didn't catch your last name."

"Gates," said Yancy, "as in cousin Bill." He flinched when Rosa jabbed his ribs.

The pilot didn't notice. He took out a waterproof radio phone and stepped through the puddles toward the tall pile of conch shells by the boat ramp. Eve, the girlfriend, answered on the other end. After listening to Claspers's pitch, she accused him of being wasted.

"What are you doing? There's a hurricane coming, you idiot."

"It's just I think these folks are for real. I didn't want Mr. Grunion to miss a good opportunity is all."

"How would you know if they're real or not?"

Claspers said, "I didn't know such things, I woulda been dead a long time ago."

Thinking: *Jesus, I am drunk.*

Next Grunion got on the line and chewed him out.

"Okay. Forget I called," the pilot said.

"This guy, so where does he get his money?"

Claspers told him about the trust-committee remark. "His name is Andrew Gates, as in Bill."

"Horseshit," Grunion said.

"Fine, I'm going back to the tiki bar. See you after the apocalypse."

"Wait, tell me about the wife."

"Cuban girl, a solid nine-point-eight out of ten. Rosa's her name. Seems super smart."

"They all seem smart when you're toasted."

"Not all of 'em, trust me," Claspers said with a damp hack. "This one's a doctor."

"Whatever. You think you can find the house or should I send Egg down?"

"Christ, don't send Egg."

When the pilot returned to the bar, he informed the couple that the meeting with Grunion was on. "If we can find a damn cab," he said.

Andrew said no problem and waved to a fellow in a Rasta cap who was playing dominoes at a side table. "That's Philip, my wheelman."

Claspers recognized him from the regulars at the airport. Philip was unenthusiastic about making the run to Bannister Point, but a twenty-dollar bill from Andrew improved his outlook.

The taxi van was parked in the fluttering halo of a streetlight. Claspers sat down in the second row and Mrs. Gates got in beside him. Her husband, the fly fisherman, didn't.

"What's up?" Claspers asked.

"Rosa's taking it from here. For now I'd prefer to hang back. Don't worry – she knows what's what in the real estate game."

The pilot grunted. "Mr. Grunion will be pissed."

"Mr. Grunion will have his hands full." The fisherman winked and shut the door.

Philip stomped the accelerator and off they went. Claspers sipped from a go-cup and chatted with Mrs. Gates and thoroughly enjoyed every minute of the ride.

It had been Rosa's idea to meet the couple alone because Yancy couldn't possibly accompany her. Nick Stripling's widow would recognize him face-to-face. Yancy hadn't argued about Rosa's decision though he should have. Possibly his judgment had been softened by tequila; Rosa had brought a bottle of Cuervo from Miami, and they'd had a celebratory taste in the motel room while she treated his monkey wounds. She'd been so jazzed about getting a chance to play cop, selecting for the occasion a pair of egregious Christian Louboutin sandals that were certain to catch Eve's eye and establish Rosa as a serious shopper for condos.

"Go big or go home," Rosa had said. "That's my motto." For earrings she'd chosen teardrops of pure jade, a past-life gift about which Yancy knew better than to inquire.

The plan was far from foolproof, but the start had been promising. It didn't take an FBI profiler to predict that Grunion's lonesome pilot would be down at the conch shack – where else in Rocky Town would he go when grounded by weather?

As for Grunion's receptivity to a cold call, Yancy had counted on a condition known among developers as acute hurricane anxiety. If Françoise flattened Lizard Cay, the Curly Tail Lane project would be in deep trouble. Grunion would have a wretched time trying to attract new buyers – especially those willing to overpay, a key demographic in the vacation-home market. Hurricanes being only slightly less damaging to real estate values than volcanic eruptions and leaky nuclear plants, Grunion was now probably glued to the Weather Channel with his gut full of refluxed acid, wondering how in God's name to build and promote a five-star island retreat if the island's one-star infrastructure was destroyed.

Yancy didn't know whether Eve and Grunion had tapped out Stripling's Medicare loot and paid cash for the Green Beach property, or whether they'd been brazen enough to apply for a bank loan. It didn't really matter; without pre-construction sales, Curly Tail Lane would fail, which is why Grunion didn't hang up on Claspers and blow off the young American couple who were waiting out the storm in Rocky Town.

Rosa's mission was to set a trap. An acting job, as she said; no superhero shit. She'd simply let it be known that her "husband" Andrew was determined to own a piece of this gorgeous tropic isle, no matter what the hurricane did. Better still, the couple was interested in purchasing two or three condos, not just one.

Then she'd explain to Eve Stripling that, because of the family's complex asset structure, the fund transfers and contract signings must take place back in Florida. There Yancy's pal in Homeland Security would have agents waiting to detain Eve and her boyfriend, based on allegations of previous illegal border entries. The incriminating testimony would come from none other than K. J. Claspers, desperately hoping to save his pilot's certificate from revocation. It would be Yancy's task to see that Eve and Grunion remained in custody until prosecutors could assemble at least one of the murder cases.

That was the plan, anyway. By now Rosa was at the house on Bannister Point, and Yancy was worried.

Ever since the night she seduced him on the autopsy table he had wondered how to satisfy such an appetite for excitement. Sending her off to meet with a pair of murderers was one way to spice up a date weekend, but experimenting with variable-speed sex toys in a bounce house would have been safer.

Yancy knew nothing about Christopher Grunion beyond his homicidal capacities; there wasn't a trace of the man in the public records or state crime computers. That Eve

Stripling's companion might be using an alias wasn't surprising, but it heightened Yancy's anxiety about Rosa meeting with the man. If she didn't return by ten sharp, Yancy would go to Grunion's place and check on her. His watch now said eight forty-six.

The wind blew a fat palmetto bug from the thatching and it landed on the opposite bar, next to a plate of cracked conch. A tourist woman who'd been enjoying the native entrée emitted a shriek and nearly tumbled backward. Her companions, all sporting ripely sunburned cheeks, joined in the squealing and pointing. The six-legged intruder composed itself and with probing antennae began to stalk the drippings of a half-finished piña colada. Hysterically the patrons appealed to the bartender, who indicated an unwillingness to intervene.

Yancy couldn't stand the racket. He walked around to where the first woman had been sitting, and with a bare palm he flattened the insect. The crunch sounded like a boot heel on a pistachio. There was a smatter of tipsy applause and one or two supportive shouts, which Yancy didn't acknowledge. If it had happened back in Florida, he'd be writing up the place.

He used a cocktail napkin to wipe the roach bits off his hand as the aggrieved female patrons gathered up their pocketbooks and scrunchies. They departed in an ungrateful flock just as a frayed-looking older fellow walked in and propped a fully assembled fly rod against the bar rail.

"Who is that gentleman?" Yancy asked the bartender.

"Dot's Neville Stafford. Poor mon bin out all night lookin' for his monkey."

"We've all been there. Let me buy him a beer."

*

252

The American sat down beside him and Neville said thanks for the Kalik.

"Rough time?"

"Yeah, mon."

"I ran into your flea-bitten buddy," said the American.

He showed Neville the bite marks and scratches on his legs. Neville felt bad. The American said the monkey had run off in a rainstorm after a fracas at the abandoned house.

Then he said: "Mr. Stafford, I believe that's my fly rod."

Neville nodded and set it by the man's stool. He told him the errant monkey's name was Driggs and mentioned the Johnny Depp connection. The American said he'd first seen the animal riding a motorized wheelchair with the Dragon Lady.

"Queen," Neville corrected him. "Dragon Queen."

"She sort of freaked me out."

"She freak everbotty out."

"Isn't her boyfriend that huge bald dude works for Christopher Grunion?"

Neville said, "How you know Mistuh Chrissofer?"

"I heard he's building a fancy tourist resort down on the beach."

"Yeah, mon. *My* beach." Neville stopped talking and finished his beer. The American ordered him another one.

"You sell him that land?"

"He tore down my house and put up a fence with a gottam padlock. Ain't no hoppy situation, mon. It was my hoff sister made the deal. Nobody axe me." Neville went through the story of the sale. He couldn't tell if the American, like others, thought he was crazy.

The man finished listening and said, "That's a lot of money, Mr. Stafford. You could have been rich."

"In wot way?"

The American broke into a warm smile. "Exactly. My name's Andrew."

His grip was firm when he shook Neville's hand. He said he lived on Big Pine Key, in the southernmost part of Florida. Neville said he had been twice to Miami and once to Fort Lauderdale, to have a mole on his neck removed. The American told him about his own house, about the hot-pink Gulf sunsets and the small wild deer that roamed the island. The deer were no larger than dogs, the man said, which Neville found fascinating.

"Every evening they'd come into this clearing to eat sprouts and twigs," the man named Andrew said. "I'd sit on the deck and watch them do their thing until it got dark."

"Ain't no deer on Andros dot I ever saw," Neville remarked. "Only pigs."

"But then some guy named Shook from upstate New York, he bought the lot next to mine and started putting up a huge house, a ridiculous fucking house. It's way too tall for the building codes but obviously he paid off somebody," the American went on. "Worst part? He doesn't even intend to live there, Mr. Stafford. Can't abide the heat and mosquitoes. All he wants to do is unload the monstrosity on some clueless sucker, take the money and go back north."

The American seemed deeply bothered by what his neighbor was doing to the land. Neville had never run into a tourist like Andrew, although he'd met a few like Mr. Shook.

"Wot 'bout dose lil' deer?" Neville asked.

"They don't come anymore. They can't eat plywood."

The man went still. Neville asked him what he was going to do.

"What are *you* going to do?" the American said.

254

Neville told him about recruiting the Dragon Queen to put a voodoo hex on Christopher Grunion. "But it dint woyk," he added. "And, at de end, she trick me outta my monkey."

"I'm not sure she got the best of that deal."

"Dot's true." Neville had to laugh.

"Movie stars, right? Nothing but trouble. Can I show you something?" The American took out a gold badge and held it close to his lap, below the bar counter, so that no one but Neville could see it.

"You police?" Neville whispered.

The man named Andrew put the badge away. He said, "Law enforcement authorities in the U.S. are very interested in Mr. Grunion – and that's not his real name. We believe the Curly Tail Lane project is being financed with moneys obtained illegally, by fraud. We also believe he's quite dangerous."

Neville nodded. "Yeah, dot asshole shodda gun at me."

"Really? When did this happen?"

"Big fucking gun, mon. Outside his house up Bannister Point."

"Shit." The man anxiously glanced at his wristwatch.

Neville drained his beer bottle thinking he and the American had something in common. Both were beset by greedy intruders destroying something rare, something that couldn't be replaced.

The light bulbs hanging from the beams of the conch shack flickered and dimmed; soon the island would lose electricity. Neville wondered where Driggs would take shelter during the hurricane. Not with the voodoo witch, he hoped. What kind of demon skank would teach a monkey how to smoke?

"Foyst time I gon see de Dragon Queen, I bring a private ting belong to Chrissofer."

"What was that?" the American asked.

"A sleeve from a fishin' shoyt like you got on dere, 'cept it was blue. Dragon Queen supposed to pudda coyse on de mon and take care my prollem on Green Beach. But den notting hoppen—"

"It was a sleeve?" The man named Andrew planted his elbows on the bar and pressed the knuckles of his hands together. To Neville he looked a bit pale.

"Yeah, a sleeve dot been toyn off. It was in Chrissofer's garbage."

"Torn off or *cut* off?"

"I tink cut." Neville made a scissor motion with his fingers.

"Oh Jesus."

"Wot's mottah?"

"Do you have a car, Mr. Stafford?"

"No, mon. I got a boat, but—"

"Never mind." The American slapped some cash on the bar and disappeared up the road, into the swaying shadows.

Neville picked up the man's expensive fishing rod and made his way to Joyous's apartment where after a quick poke he lay awake, listening to the coconut trees shake and wondering if the American was really a policeman, and if the things he'd said were true.

Twenty

Agent John Wesley Weiderman, five pounds lighter after his bout with spoiled shellfish, had intrepidly returned to Florida on the hunt for Plover Chase. He was armed with a promising new lead supplied by the fugitive's husband, a retired dermatologist who'd contacted the Oklahoma State Bureau of Investigation.

Dr. Clifford Witt had uncovered a series of credit card charges made by the suspect under the alias of Bonnie Witt and posted on a Visa account to which Dr. Witt had access (online password: nookyluv2). The purchases, all made in Key West, included groceries, lip gloss, blond hair coloring, domestic beer, condoms, dental floss, a car rental, four jerry cans, ninety-seven dollars' worth of gasoline and a room-service charge at a Best Western on South Roosevelt.

"We run out of cash so we had to go plastic," explained the man inside the hotel room, number 217.

He gave his name as Clyde Barrow, and he seemed unflustered by having a lawman at the door. Then again,

Agent John Wesley Weiderman adhered to a low-key approach.

"Do you know a woman named Plover Chase?" he asked.

"She left me, dude. Hit the bricks."

"Where'd she go?"

"Back on the run, I guess. Once an outlaw, whatever."

"Let's start with your real name."

The man said, "Okay, okay, you got me."

He was doughy and sunburned. He wore a black muscle shirt that said: OLD KEY WEST – A DRINKING VILLAGE WITH A SLIGHT FISHING PROBLEM!

"I'm Cody Parish," he said.

Agent John Wesley Weiderman didn't respond immediately. He was assessing the judicial prospects of his case, which were suddenly dimmer.

"Yo, as in Cody Parish the victim?"

"Got it," said John Wesley Weiderman.

It was the person with whom Plover Chase had notoriously swapped sex in exchange for good school grades. Now he was all grown up. He was, in fact, losing his hair.

"Ms. Chase and me, we hooked up again after all this time. Actually, she tracked me down on Facebook. Talk about a true-life fairy tale – it's all in my diary, I mean *everything*."

"May I read it?"

"First I better get with a lawyer," said Cody. "See, it's gonna be a book and then probably a movie. That's why I need to be careful nobody steals the good stuff and leaks it."

The agent asked Cody if Plover Chase had abducted him against his will. Cody said, "She's got something way more lethal than a gun. You know what they say – pussy is undefeated. That's from Merle Haggard himself."

"So she didn't threaten or physically harm you."

"Stompin' my heart to pieces, doesn't that count?"

"It was her English class where you first met, right? Back in the day."

"Not regular English but AP English," Cody said. "That means, like, super advanced."

"Got it." John Wesley Weiderman didn't have a sarcastic bone in his body.

"I love her the same now as I did back then. It's like nothing ever changed, time standing still, whatever."

"Why do you think she left you this time?"

"Dude, come on. Why do they do *anything* they do? Yesterday she shows up in a green convertible, packs her shit and off she goes up the highway. Monster hormone attack is my theory."

The agent didn't doubt that Plover Chase was gone; there were no women's clothes in the closet, no lipstick tubes or makeup items in the bathroom. On the unmade queen-sized bed lay a sad stack of men's magazines, raw jerk-off material that even a loser like Cody would have concealed had a female been in the vicinity.

"Any idea where she went?"

"Not really," said Cody. "Home maybe?"

"Was your family aware that you two re-connected?"

"Dad passed six years ago and Mom's in assisted living, thinks she's Shirley MacLaine. And guess what, bro, I'm thirty years old and I can bone whoever I want, long as she's legal age and says yes. And Ms. Chase, she said yes, yes, yes, and *more* yes, please, Cody baby! Bottom line, I didn't break any laws."

John Wesley Weiderman pointed out that it was illegal to aid and abet a wanted criminal.

"Only thing I abetted was rockin' her world. They gonna send me to the penitentiary for that?" Cody was striving to appear indignant.

"A jury might see it your way," said the OSBI agent, "but good lawyers cost money. Maybe by then you'll be rich from selling your journal, right?"

Cody Baby didn't appear to be emotionally pulverized by his lover's abandonment. He was, however, troubled by the possibility of being prosecuted.

"Listen, I just remembered," he said. "There's a guy lives on Big Pine Key, Ms. Chase had a thing with him for a while."

"I spoke with the gentleman. He used to be a police detective." John Wesley Weiderman wouldn't soon forget Andrew Yancy baring his ass to present his alleged wild-dog bites.

"Well, that's where she might be," Cody said without rancor. "With *him*."

"He told me their affair was over."

"Maybe he's not the one calling the shots. Obviously you never met Ms. Chase."

"Someday," said the agent.

"She wasn't too jazzed about the dude gettin' another girlfriend, okay? She acted all like isn't-that-nice, but I could tell she was seriously frosted."

"So you think she went to win him back."

"You know how whacked chicks can get. The guy's new girl is a doctor, 'kay? Ms. Chase couldn't deal with that, is my theory. It's all in the diary. I do a hundred words every night, not longhand but on my iPad. That still counts, right?"

"For sure."

Agent John Wesley Weiderman fully realized that pursuing Plover Chase was an unfair burden on the taxpayers of Oklahoma. Her capture would not make the state a safer place. It would instead make a tabloid celebrity of the ex-schoolteacher, and possibly a best-selling author of her now-grown-up victim, whom John Wesley Weiderman perceived as a grubby oversexed slacker. What a circus that would be, Plover Chase returning to Tulsa in handcuffs. Plus the waste of a perfectly good jail cell.

But Agent Weiderman was a follower of orders, and there were worse places to be sent than the Florida Keys. He'd diligently scouted the health department's website and located a relatively clean seafood joint, where for lunch he had eaten grilled mahi served with Cuban plantains and black beans. It was maybe the best meal he'd ever eaten that wasn't a rib eye.

"What about those jerry cans?" he asked Cody Parish.

Parish gave a loose-jointed shrug.

"On the Visa bill were four six-gallon gasoline containers from Ace Hardware."

"Weird." Cody said Ms. Chase must have purchased the items on a day she went out alone.

"Have you ever known her to be violent?"

"No way," Cody said. "But, like I told you, we were in major love."

"Maybe she feels different about Mr. Yancy."

"There's a wild streak, for sure. It's all in my diary."

"We'll be in touch about that," the agent said. He headed toward the door.

"You catch her, don't let on it was me that told you where to look."

"Of course not. We protect our sources." Which is what

John Wesley Weiderman was trained to say, and almost always they bought it.

Flip-flops slapping on the floor, Cody Parish trailed the agent to the stairway. "Twenty gallons' worth of gas cans, what do you figure that's all about?"

"Twenty-four."

Cody's spotty lips moved as he redid the math in his head, six times four. "Maybe she's just stocking up for the drive home. Doesn't wanna waste time stopping at service stations."

John Wesley Weiderman said, "I didn't think of that."

Because only a chowderhead would think of that. People used jerry cans for fueling lawn mowers or ATVs, but there was no good reason to carry four of them unless you had a bigger job in mind.

Rosa Campesino seldom thought about Daniel, her ex-husband. What brought him to mind now, while she sipped wine with Eve Stripling on the porch of an Andros Island beach house, was a whiff of syrupy men's cologne.

Beast Down it was called, Daniel's favorite. She'd never met another man who wore the stuff. However, Rosa knew it wasn't Daniel talking on the phone in the next room because Daniel was dead, having witlessly steered his two-thousand-dollar mountain bike over a cliff. The autopsy had been performed with competence in Bozeman, Montana. As a professional courtesy the report had been faxed to Rosa, who'd made copies for the paddleboard instructor and each of the three other women Daniel had been fucking during the marrriage, the lubricious details unearthed by Rosa's divorce attorney.

"I really like those shoes," Eve Stripling said.

"Thank you. They're seriously comfy."

"What happens when all that shiny red color comes off the bottoms? Do you have to, like, get 'em spray-painted?"

Rosa said, "That's a darn good question."

This was when light chatter filled the air, before things fell apart. Eve was holding a tiny cinnamon-colored dog, probably the same runny-eyed furball that Andrew had saved from drowning.

"How much longer will Mr. Grunion be on the phone?" Rosa asked.

"He's tied up on a business call," said Eve. "How about some more wine?"

Rosa said sure. She looked at her watch – still plenty of time.

"Maybe you could tell me how the units at Curly Tail Lane are priced, pre-construction. My husband and I are interested in a couple of two-bedrooms facing the water. We'd pay cash at closing."

"No financing?" Eve looked more amused than excited.

"We'll have to do the deal back in Florida," Rosa continued, "at the office of Andrew's trust managers. They're the ones who move the money around."

"I don't think so."

"Oh, we can Skype your people in from Nassau."

"That's not what I meant," said Eve. "I don't think we're interested."

Rosa held steady. "Not interested in an all-cash deal? Seriously?"

"Honey, there's nothing serious about any of this, and we both know it."

The dog jumped down and curled up in a corner. Eve opened another bottle of merlot. Waves rumbled out across the reef line, the wind thrashed the palms and Rosa tapped the toe of one of her French sandals.

She said, "My mistake, Eve. I thought you and your husband were in the business of selling condos."

"Thing about this place, it's easy to make friends if you treat the right people right. I'll give you a for-instance. We made a good Bahamian friend at the Immigration office, and guess what? She says nobody named Rosa Gates cleared through Nassau the last few days. Not Fresh Creek or Congo Town either. There *was* a Rosa Campesino—"

"I kept my maiden name," Rosa interjected, although she knew it was over.

"Did your 'husband' keep his maiden name, too? Because there's no Andrew Gates on the entry list, either." Eve with her stretched white jeans and tanned feet was rocking on a wooden swing, not in a lazing tempo.

She said, "Guy named Andrew Yancy came through Nassau on his way here to Lizard Cay. He used to be a cop down in the Keys. I've met the man, so just cut the bullshit."

Rosa set down her wine glass. "Tell Mr. Grunion I'm sorry to have wasted your evening. Clearly there's been a misunderstanding."

"Oh, give it up."

Calmly Rosa reached for her handbag and rose. "Too bad," she said.

Eve Stripling cocked her head. "Honey, you're not goin' anywhere."

At that moment a door to the house flung open, uncorking a fresh gust of Beast Down mixed with sweat. The smell was so strong that Rosa feared she might gag.

*

Against the wind he ran; uphill, downhill. Yancy was no athlete, not anymore. His lungs heaved, his legs cramped. The pocked pavement was strewn with sharp pebbles that gouged his feet.

Simple pain he could take; blood, too. It was the fucking up that was unbearable to contemplate, his own potentially disastrous failure to see the obvious.

An approaching vehicle turned out to be Philip's taxi heading back toward town, reggae thumping from the open windows. The van was dark except for the glow of a joint that Claspers the pilot was smoking in the front next to Philip. Yancy waved both arms but he was too gassed to shout. As the taxi sped past, Yancy noticed a hunched dark shape on the roof – Mr. Stafford's monkey, clinging grimly to the luggage rack.

Yancy ran on until he spotted a kid's bicycle lying beside a chicken pen in front of a cinder-block house. The windows of the place had been boarded for the storm, and through a crack Yancy saw light and heard voices. Uprighting the bike, he pedaled away on half-flat tires, his knees bumping the handlebars.

Egg loomed as a foremost concern when Yancy approached Bannister Point. Yancy reviewed his own rudimentary disabling skills, cop skills, understanding that he'd never fought a man of Egg's size whose reflexes hadn't been slowed by drugs or booze. Tonight Egg would be on full alert and sober as a hangman, not easy to surprise and bring down. In consideration of the goon's recent dental woes, Yancy planned to aim first for the jawbone.

A lead pipe or a marlin gaff would have been helpful, but he settled for a hefty pine bough that he found where he ditched the bicycle, a quarter mile from the house. Under low purple clouds he walked the rest of the way. The property was lit up like a used-car lot; Yancy heard the rumble of a gasoline-powered generator, a luxury in the out-islands. It meant that one could spend the duration of a major hurricane in air-conditioned comfort listening to Puccini or Van Halen, as long as the walls didn't blow down.

Yancy scouted swiftly, his footfalls muted by the noise from the shuddering trees. Egg wasn't lurking out front; the backyard looked clear, too. Eve Stripling could be seen alone on the porch, untangling some wind chimes. Yancy snuck along the perimeter of the house peering in windows; no sign of Rosa, no sign of anyone. He felt a hot coal in his gut.

Then Eve's mutt started barking madly, and he thought: *Oh, what the hell.*

He opened the front door and walked inside.

Standing in the foyer clutching a broken tree branch, expecting the absurd little canine to come lunging for his ankles, a creature that would have drowned or gotten gobbled by sharks if he hadn't rescued it . . .

This is what I get for one minor act of decency.

The yapping stopped.

Yancy took a couple of steps. Paused to listen.

Peeked around a hallway corner – nothing.

A voice said, "Up here, asshole."

Yancy climbed the stairs and there the man sat on a slick burgundy Super Rollie scooter, Yancy's 12-gauge Beretta angled across his lap. Hanging from a brass hat rack in a corner, next to a full-sized print of the famous Audubon spoonbill, was a dirty blaze-orange poncho and a couple of camo sun masks. Outside, a broken shutter banged and banged.

"Where's Rosa?" Yancy said.

"Sit down." He motioned toward a straight-backed chair.

"Where is she?"

"I've got a shotgun and you've got what – a piece of fuckin' firewood?"

"Nick, I asked you a question."

"Eve said you'd figure it out right away. I said you're not that bright."

"And I say you're bright enough not to shoot a cop." With his free hand Yancy took out the police badge on loan from Johnny Mendez. "See? I'm back on the force."

"First place," Nicholas Stripling said, "there's no law says a man can't cut off his own arm."

"Maybe not."

"I know for a goddamn fact."

"There's a law against murder," Yancy said. "You killed Charlie Phinney and Dr. O'Peele, and you tried to kill me."

"Ha, try to prove *any* of that shit."

"I will. In the meantime let's start with the Medicare rip-off," Yancy said. "Hey, guess what happens when the feds find out you're still alive."

"Who's gonna tell 'em? Not you, because you'll be disappeared."

Stripling wore a vented tan fishing shirt that was missing the left sleeve. The opening had been sewn shut to cover his empty shoulder socket. One of his ears was bandaged where it had been snagged by a bonefish fly, although Stripling obviously didn't know that the angler who'd wounded him was Yancy.

The air in the den was rank with cologne that smelled like apricots and linoleum wax.

"I remember the *Herald* didn't run a photo with your obituary," Yancy said.

"That's because we didn't give 'em one."

"Good call. They see the paper in Nassau, you're toast."

"Sit down like I told you."

"I guess I could've pulled up your mug shot," Yancy said, "but that was taken, like, twenty years ago."

"The picture on my driver's license was new. How come you didn't think of checkin' that in your God-almighty computer?"

"It didn't matter to me what you looked like because I thought you were dead. I was busy trying to catch your killer."

Stripling smiled crookedly. "That's pretty fuckin' funny, I gotta admit."

"Does your daughter know you're alive?"

"Don't worry about Caitlin. I'm gonna tell her when I'm ready."

"Make it in time for the holidays," Yancy said, "so she can order a big enough turkey."

"Is that a joke? Are you seriously standing here doing *jokes*?"

"For what it's worth, I took extremely good care of your arm. I kept it in the freezer of my refrigerator with the vodka and Popsicles. Didn't Eve tell you?"

"Thanks for nothing." Stripling's hand moved toward the trigger of the shotgun. Gleaming on his hairy wrist was a garish rose-gold Tourbillon.

"Nick, I've been very patient. Now, where's Rosa?"

Something beeped on the console of the Super Rollie. The padded footrest began to ascend, and with it rose the blue-black barrels of the Beretta, braced between Stripling's knees and pointed at Yancy's chest.

"You're right about one thing. Which, I'm not dumb enough to murder a cop." Stripling said. "But I got no problem killing a goddamn roach inspector."

Twenty-one

The decision to have his own arm amputated, a perfectly healthy arm – well, first you needed jumbo-sized *cojones*. Nobody facing a Medicare rap had ever tried it before, Nicholas Stripling was certain. Faking one's own death, sure, that happened all the time. The fuckwits usually got caught, too, whoring around Mexico or Costa Rica. Thinking they could just go missing without a trace on a whitewater raft or a solo desert hike, and the feds would say oh well and forget about them.

Which, how stupid can you be? The only way to foolproof the scam was to disappear *with* a trace. Give the bastards something to bag up and truck to the morgue, actual human remains. So when they do the DNA, when they stare at your mauled rotting stump, there's no doubt in their minds that this poor fucker is dead as a doornail.

Because who'd be crazy enough to cut off his own arm?

Eve had begged her husband not to do it, but he had no intention of going to prison, not even a country-club joint.

The feds in Miami were going hard-ass on fraud cases, and three guys Nick knew were doing heavy time, meaning double digits. One of them was an old Cuban gentleman who'd billed Uncle Sam for eighty-two hundred physical therapy sessions that he'd never performed. Stage 3 lung cancer and still they wouldn't let him out early! Nick Stripling told his wife that he couldn't do the flu in lockup, and that jail was *not* a goddamn option.

During the red-hot years of Midwest Mobile, he'd socked away eleven-plus million dollars – and don't forget this was South Florida, the Medicare-fraud capital of America, where the most experienced dirtballs came to gorge. Stripling had found himself competing against the slickest and slimiest – former mortgage brokers, identity thieves, arms dealers, insider traders and dope smugglers, all who'd switched to home-care durables because stealing directly from the government was so much easier, and the risk so small. Lots of Medicare scammers got richer than Nick Stripling, but still he'd raked in some sweet bank from all those fake orders for Super Rollies (also walkers, electric hospital beds, blood-pressure cuffs, bariatric commodes, wander alarms and sitz baths).

If he got caught the feds would demand full restitution, which wasn't going to happen in this particular universe. Stripling had made sure his ill-gotten loot was on the wing, moving it from Barbados to Luxembourg to Geneva, then finally back to a Nassau bank account belonging to one Christopher Grunion. The name had been invented by Stripling to enable an unscrutinized investment of his swindled fortune in some prime oceanfront on Lizard Cay. Eve was skeptical until he showed her an article from the *Nassau Guardian* predicting a flash turnaround of the luxury real estate market, wealthy Asians having discovered the sun-drenched charms of Bahamian life. Which, the Chinese and so forth? Nick was still waiting for the big stampede to Andros, trying to remain patient and optimistic.

The hardest part of his plan, what scared him the most, was letting a twitchy, shot-out pillhead like O'Peele perform the operation. Again, not much choice – no legit surgeon would have agreed to the job. Man walks in says please cut off my left arm. Doctor says what's wrong with it – gangrene? Melanoma? And the guy says nothing's wrong with it, I just don't need it anymore, could you please saw it off?

O'Peele said okay because Stripling was his boss and also because he needed the money. Percocets aren't cheap when you gobble 'em like Cracker Jacks. And by then Midwest Mobile was going down. Some of the geezers whose ID numbers had been stolen got around to reading their benefit statements, and they started calling Medicare saying they'd never ordered a Rollie scooter chair but they'd sure like to try one. As soon as the FBI began sniffing around, Stripling closed the office and promised new positions in future health-care enterprises to all his loyal staff, including Gomez O'Peele.

Who was grateful for the opportunity to pocket an extra five grand, which is what Stripling offered him to cut off Stripling's left arm and then beat on the bone stump with a hatchet to make it look like a boat propeller caused the wound.

The operation was performed at the couple's vacation town house in the Keys, Eve acting as nurse, her husband blitzed on pills and hooked to a morphine drip. The surgical saw and other implements were brand-new – Stripling had

272

made sure of that. Before they got started he had O'Peele pee in a cup, one of those drugstore kits, to prove the doctor was clean for the day. Also: blow into a portable booze tester of the style favored by suburban parents with teenage drivers.

Admirably, the doctor had arrived totally sober, his hands steady, and he came through big-time. Afterward the town house looked like they'd been butchering hogs, but the floors had been covered with Visqueen – Nick's idea – so that all they had to do was roll up the mess and cram it in a Dumpster.

Eve sobbing behind a hospital mask flecked with her husband's blood, O'Peele chugging Gatorade pretending it was Ketel One. Stripling lying there thinking, okay, during the Civil War? Medics had to do this shit on open battlefields, hack off arms and legs. These were fucking kids, most of 'em – no anesthesia, no antibiotics. For sutures they'd rip the stitching out of boot soles, for bandages they'd tear up filthy uniforms, maggots crawling in the open wounds.

So I'll be fine is what Stripling assured himself, not that his raw shoulder socket didn't hurt like a motherfucker. Holy Christ did it hurt! But he was a new man, a free man.

This was the day after he'd sunk the *Summer's Eve*, the fuel tanks topped out, the coolers packed with ice and bait. Just like a real fishing trip. His wife had followed him off-shore in a rented SeaCraft, past Sombrero Light, rough as a cob and no other vessels in sight. First he pulled the plugs and then he got her sideways in a trough and gunned her in reverse, the mighty blue Atlantic pouring over the transom and filling the cockpit. Stripling used a 5/0 hook to put a hole in the skin of the life raft (in case anyone wondered why he hadn't used it). Then Eve motored up in the

SeaCraft, he jumped aboard, and together they watched the *Summer's Eve* sink: a whorl of bubbles and seat cushions and not much else, owing to the whitecaps.

The next morning Stripling went under the knife of Gomez O'Peele, and by nightfall his severed left arm was staked on a mud flat near Vaca Cut being gnawed by sharks. That's what happens when a person drowns in the Florida Keys, which is a shark's version of a Golden Corral – all you can eat, all the time.

Which, the Tourbillon? That's one reason Stripling didn't leave it on his severed left wrist after the operation. Why not, Eve had said, just drive a Rolls-Royce off a pier? Besides, you love that watch, she said, which he couldn't deny. The Tourbillon was a work of art, far as Nick was concerned. He didn't want it to end up in a hammerhead's stomach.

Some mistakes along the way, no question.

First: choosing Phinney, the pothead mate from the *Misty Momma IV.* Eve had gone to the docks and scoped out the crews and personally picked him out. Showed him the arm and said the plan was to punk her cousin, who was chartering the *Misty* the next morning. Eve said the limb came from a med-school cadaver so no worries, Charlie, everything's cool. Her cousin's crazy fraternity brothers, she said, they're the sickos who dreamed this up. And Phinney fell for the whole story, practically came in his pants when she counted out the three grand.

But then he couldn't keep his trap shut about the wad, buying rounds all over Key West, and Stripling knew it was only a matter of time before he got stoned and blabbed about the arm, too. So Nick rented a moped and ambushed the guy after he and some hooker walked out of the Half

Shell. To make it look like robbery Nick even snatched Phinney's wallet – seven hundred and two bucks was all the kid had left from the biggest score of his life.

If Stripling had to do that part over again ... but, see, it was the best way to make sure the fucking arm got found – arrange for some tourist to reel it in while he's trolling for tuna, whatever. At first Eve had suggested they put the limb on the shore behind somebody's house, as if it washed up with the tide. But Nick feared the coons or pouch rats might drag it off, even a stray dog. Remember, the whole plan depended on the thing being recovered and positively identified as belonging to him. Being indisputably dead would get the feds off his case, not to mention bring a sweet payoff on the life insurance.

Stripling had flapped his empty left sleeve and said to Eve: I didn't go through all this misery just for sport! Like my secret dream was to be an amputee.

So they'd recruited Phinney to do the old sailfish scam, only using Nick's arm instead of a fish. And everything would have turned out great except Phinney couldn't keep a secret. Dumbass.

Mistake number two: waiting too long to deal with the Caitlin problem.

Again, Nick's call. He and his daughter had been on the outs ever since he'd married Eve. Caitlin had a big mouth, too, and don't forget she's married to Mr. Simon Cox, ex-military. The man was so straight he'd once turned in his next-door neighbor for watering the lawn on Thursday instead of Tuesday, some lame county law, a fifty-dollar fine.

If Caitlin ever told Simon about Nick's scheme to vanish, the buzz-cut sonofabitch would be down at the FBI in two minutes flat. So Stripling had chosen to keep his daughter out of the loop, planning to wait until she got bored with Simon and divorced his hopelessly square ass, which was inevitable. Then, when the time was right, Nick would send the seaplane to Miami and surprise Caitlin on her birthday, some sappy move like that.

Meanwhile there had to be a funeral, and – Stripling learns later – that's where his daughter starts talking to Yancy, the cop who had custody of the arm. Only Caitlin doesn't know he isn't a cop anymore, which was all over the Keys newspapers except Caitlin doesn't read anything besides price tags and horoscopes. Into her greedy little skull has crept the notion that Eve murdered Nick and is trying to screw Caitlin out of her inheritance. This she apparently tells Yancy. Puts him on the trail of Midwest Mobile Medical, which leads him to Gomez O'Peele, which results in the junkie doctor calling Stripling one night demanding more money, this time for keeping quiet.

Some detective came to see me, O'Peele said in a low voice, asking all kindsa questions about the Medicare stuff! I wrote down his name, you don't believe me.

The surgeon swearing on a stack of Bibles that he didn't say boo to Yancy about the Super Rollies, or about all those illegal prescriptions and 849s, and especially not about surgically removing that arm to help Stripling stage his own death. But honestly I don't know how long I can hang tough, the doctor says, you sitting pretty and me with the law knocking on my door. How about another five grand, Nicky? I know you can swing it.

And Stripling tells him okay, sit tight. Then he puts on a latex glove and drives straight to Gomez O'Peele's condo and gives him the same surprise as Charles Phinney, only this time setting it up like a suicide.

Next move is to address the Caitlin situation as any loving parent would, by offering the scheming bitch some cash up front and half the life insurance payout. Eve isn't thrilled about sharing, but they agree it's the fastest, cheapest way out. And sure enough, Caitlin hops on board, the sorrow over losing her father dissipating like a fart at the prospect of becoming a millionaire.

Which, all her nutty talk about Eve being a murderer? Miraculously forgotten. Caitlin can't wait to call Yancy and tell him she was wrong about dear Eve, out of her head with grief and so on. My dad died when his boat sunk, end of story, says Caitlin.

Not knowing, to this day, that he's alive and well. Stripling being in no hurry to inform his one and only offspring, with her track record of indiscretion and Simple Simon on the scene.

Mistake number three – possibly the worst – was Nick trying (make that *failing*) to kill Andrew Yancy.

Eve had met the guy once, the night she went to fetch the arm. Thought he was flaky but harmless. Later they find out he got demoted from sheriff's detective to roach patrol, the Key West *Citizen* reporting it was because he'd attacked his girlfriend's husband with a vacuum cleaner in front of hundreds of tourists, which didn't strike Nick as all that harmless. But Eve said trust me, honey, the man is not a threat.

Then he showed up at Dr. O'Peele's, asking questions, after which Eve said you're right, he's gotta go. Stripling planned to thump the sonofabitch and dump him in a canal. Set it up like an accident – the man went fishing off the bank, drank too much, took a fall. Made way more sense than shooting him point-blank, because even an ex-cop? The authorities wouldn't let that slide.

But that night, when Yancy disappeared under the water, sunk like an anvil, Nick had gotten a little anxious. Like, what if I didn't hit him hard enough? What if the fucker woke up on the bottom and swam off into the mangroves?

Which, turns out, is exactly what happened. Yancy pulled himself out of the canal, now sure that Caitlin's story about Eve was true because obviously Eve had sent her new "boyfriend" after him. And what does Yancy do next? He turns up at Nick's place on Duck Key, finds the hatchet and some bone fragments in a drain – this Yancy tells Caitlin, who immediately calls Eve, who in a cold panic calls her husband.

Now they've got another problem: how to retrieve Nick's left arm from Nick's grave before Yancy obtains a court order to exhume it. Because, with all the new CSI technology, a clever coroner could aim some type of super-ionized laser-imaging ray at the putrid limb and see that the amputation wasn't accidental.

And then Eve would get arrested for murdering a spouse who wasn't even dead.

So they end up paying two random shitbirds to dig up Stripling's coffin and snatch his arm, a job Nick would have done himself except it would have taken all fucking night, a one-handed man trying to shovel packed dirt. But the grave robbers never show up at Denny's, so Nick and Eve take off.

Dawn, they're on the seaplane to Andros. That afternoon, Eve receives an urgent email from the cemetery saying her husband's gravesite has been "disturbed," please call us right away. Luckily the cemetery people don't find any incriminating clues, just a hole in the ground and a pried-open casket.

Which, the arm? Who knows what those sick bastards did with the goddamn thing after they dug it up. Long as it was gone, Stripling didn't give a shit where. He had no attachment, emotional or otherwise.

Now his main concern – on top of this rotten weather – is the unexpected appearance in the Bahamas of Andrew Yancy, whom Nick is preparing to blast with the man's own shotgun.

Actually, though, the timing for a body disposal is pretty convenient. People often disappear during hurricanes, just blow the fuck away.

" . . . I got no problem killing a goddamn roach inspector," Nick is saying, intending for those to be the last mortal words Yancy ever hears.

Then Eve walks into the room.

"Hello there, Mrs. Stripling," pipes Yancy. "Nice to see you again."

"Don't do it here," she says sternly to her husband.

"Why not?"

"The mess is why. We'll lose our security deposit."

Stripling, barely able to contain himself. "Are you serious? So we buy 'em a new rug!"

"But meanwhile who has to clean it up? The only person in this household with two hands, that's who. Me! So, no, Nicky, you take him outside to shoot him."

Stripling is so fucking pissed off, he's having trouble steadying the shotgun. He tells Eve to go downstairs and turn up the stereo full blast.

"Wait, she's got a point," Yancy interrupts. "Bloody entrails everywhere, then you've gotta drag the body out of the house, which tends to leave a forensic trail."

"Shut the hell up."

"It's so windy outside, nobody would hear the gun go off. But you're the boss, Nick." Yancy shrugs. "Eve, where's Rosa?"

"Don't say one word," Stripling snaps at his wife.

However, he sees the benefits of doing the murder outdoors, the hurricane rains washing away the splatter. So he rises from the Super Rollie and pokes Yancy down the steps, through the foyer, out the front door. He tells Eve to switch on the floodlights – thank God for the generator – and briskly he walks Yancy to the north side of the house, Eve joining them under a pair of coconut palms.

"This'll work," Stripling says.

Yancy looking more worried now, raindrops pelting his face.

From the shadows comes a high-pitched bark, like a squirrel, then Eve is saying, "Tillie, you bad girl, come here right now."

Her spoiled runt of a dog, manically scooting between everybody's ankles.

"Get her outta here!" says Nick.

Eve pleading: "Tillie, heel! Tillie, calm down!"

Then Yancy whistles once. Real simple, like a bobwhite quail.

And the retard mutt jumps into his arms.

"Nicky, wait!" Eve cries.

Yancy smiles, clutching the dog to his chest. "Shoot me, Nick, you shoot Tillie."

Eve starts to lose it. "No, Nicky, don't!"

"Unfortunately, that's how shotguns work – big noise, big crater," Yancy says in a calm expository tone.

Stripling is grinding his unshaven jaws, blinking the rain bubbles from his eyelashes. Which, the Beretta? It wasn't designed to be aimed with one arm. Beefy as Nick is, the gun's getting heavy. Slippery, too.

"Drop that goddamn dog," he says to Yancy.

Tillie's rose-petal tongue is lolling, Yancy holding her at center mass, patting her matted, spud-sized head. He matter-of-factly advises Nick to put down the gun, Nick snorting: Guy must be out of his mind.

"You really don't want to kill this scrumptious little puppy," says Yancy. "It would break your bride's heart. Clumps of bloody fuzz all over the lawn?"

"I'll buy her another one. This is not a problem."

"You bastard!" Eve shouts, and jumps between her husband and the smart-ass restaurant inspector.

Which, Nick Stripling's plan? All of a sudden it turns to shit.

Twenty-two

Tillie remembered him!

Yancy shouldn't have been so surprised. Once he'd dated a veterinary assistant who told him that dogs never forget a person's odor, even after one fleet sniff. She said the canine memory was headquartered in its nostrils, and this was as true for arctic wolves as it was for designer diva breeds. Still, with Stripling poised to blow his guts out, Yancy had been caught off guard when, in a show of improbable athleticism, Tillie bounded into his arms. He sentimentally accepted the animal's forwardness as affection, possibly even gratitude for Yancy plucking her from shark-filled waters on his faux fly-fishing visit to Bannister Point.

For him now to employ Tillie as a shield against the loaded Beretta was understandably distressing to Eve, but not for a moment did Yancy believe Stripling would vaporize the family pet in order to kill him. It wasn't a measure of compassion but rather the fear of domestic bedlam; Eve never would have forgiven Nick, and without her loyalty he couldn't sustain the complicated artifice of his new life.

Still, instead of a dog Yancy would have preferred to be holding the Glock, which he'd left at home in Florida knowing the Bahamian Customs officials took a dour view of firearms in one's luggage. Even with Tillie in his arms Yancy's kneecaps remained vulnerable to a shotgun blast. The pup would be airborne before Yancy hit the ground, giving Stripling clear aim for a kill shot.

That option seemed to dawn on Nick just as his wife stepped in front of Yancy and the dog. The span of her hips, worthy of Rubens, made it practically impossible for her husband to shoot around her.

"Tell him to drop the gun," Yancy said to Eve, "or I'll pop poor Tillie's head off."

For drama he flexed his fingers around the stem-like neck of her pooch.

"He's lying!" Stripling boomed.

"What do you care about her, anyway?" Eve cried. Then, spinning back to Yancy: "Don't hurt her, please, she has a renal condition. Let's talk this through."

"You heard what I did to Dr. Clifford Witt, the noted dermatologist. It was all over the internet." Yancy wanted her to believe he was capable of blithe atrocities. "Eve, I'm going to ask one more time – where is Rosa?"

"Rosa's fine. Maybe we can make a trade."

"Shut your goddamn trap!" Stripling said to his wife, an unproductive approach.

She flipped him off, a robust salutation over one shoulder. Then she told Yancy that she'd lead him straight to Rosa if he freed her treasured companion.

"Only when I see Rosa alive," Yancy countered. It was

difficult to preserve a threatening countenance, as Tillie was now licking his knuckles.

Craning to see past his wife, Stripling swore wildly and proclaimed that Yancy was a lying cocksucker. Stripling was hollering to be heard over the wind, which in a matter of moments had accelerated to a gale that wobbled all of them. Yancy firmed his hug on the dog to keep her from sailing away. Eve was backlit by one of the floodlights, her reddish hair dancing like an electric mop; she cupped both hands binocular-style around her eyes, for protection. The rain beat down in gusting, horizontal lashes.

"Get out of the way!" Stripling bellowed at Eve.

"No, Nicky, we're gonna do a trade!"

"The hell we are!"

Yancy wasn't surprised that Stripling refused to go along with the hostage exchange. His thoughts shifted toward escape, knowing he could outrun the lopsided mook. The shotgun had a limited range of lethality that wouldn't be improved by the fierce weather conditions.

Yet Yancy hesitated to flee, thinking: *Once I get away from here, how do I save Rosa?* Most likely she was being confined somewhere inside the Striplings' house.

If they hadn't already killed her.

The opportunity to bolt was lost when Stripling, on the edge of rage, used the twin barrels of the Beretta to somewhat firmly prod his wife. She slipped on the wet grass and fell, the sight causing Tillie to begin yipping in dismay.

Stripling shouted his intentions to shoot Yancy's legs off, at which point Yancy lowered the miniature dog from chest level to groin level. Nick's expression never changed, even as he strained with his lone arm to keep the weapon level.

He seemed fully committed to pulling the trigger, Tillie or no Tillie.

Meanwhile Eve was on her knees frantically clapping at the dog, imploring her to jump. The waterlogged lump began to wriggle and whine in Yancy's arms.

"Oh fine," he said, and he placed her on the ground.

Tillie faithfully scrambled into the emotional clinch of Eve, who shouted up at Yancy: "Thank you!"

Then, to her husband: "Okay, Nicky, now kill him!"

Among Yancy's final regrets, the most unforgivable was allowing Rosa Campesino to meet alone with a pair of known murderers. She'd been so amped about going under-cover like a real cop, so calm and radiantly sure of herself – still, he should have said forget it, baby, we'll try something else. But he'd never learned to say no to the women in his life, even on those occasions when he was right – a fatal weakness, it turned out.

One lame, last stall for time: Yancy pointed at the drip-ping Beretta and yelled through sheets of rain: "Nick, I bet the shells got wet!"

"Let's find out, asswipe." The man looked unfazed, unworried.

Taking a breath, Yancy braced for the flash of the shot-gun. He considered shutting his eyes, but that seemed like something a doomed monk would do. Yancy wasn't so spir-itual or serene; nothing about death appealed to him.

So he folded his arms, directed a necrotic glare at Strip-ling and said: "Fuck you, Stumpy."

The response from Eve's husband was a gummy grin that showcased flawless white veneers, top and bottom, doubt-lessly paid for by the Medicare trust fund. As an honest restaurant inspector Yancy could never afford a smile so luminous, and he dolefully assumed this would be the last thing he ever saw – the ill-gotten, high-end dentition of his killer.

Next came a loud crack, though it wasn't from the Beretta.

And it wasn't Yancy who went down hard in the rain.

The Lipscombs had decided on real oak floors, a thrilling development for Evan Shook. He wrung a sweet price from an outfit in Deerfield Beach, the owner himself schlepping all the way to the house to measure the interior. Evan Shook let the construction crew take an early lunch, clearing the place for the flooring dealer and his helper. Evan Shook stood in the doorway smiling to himself because he knew the square footage so precisely that he'd already calculated his inflated surcharge to the Lipscombs.

A car he didn't recognize pulled up in front. A broad-shouldered man in a dark suit got out and approached the house. Evan Shook hoped he wasn't a new building inspector. The one he'd been dealing with for months was a very reasonable guy who, in exchange for two nights at the Delano and box seats at a Marlins game, had agreed to overlook the unlawful height of Evan Shook's spec house and other flagrant code violations.

"My name is John Wesley Weiderman," the visitor said. "I'm with the Oklahoma Bureau of Investigation."

A dry handshake followed. Evan Shook couldn't imagine what a lawman from the Midwest might be doing on Big Pine Key, on the unfinished brushed-marble doorstep of the soon-to-be estate of Ford and Jayne Lipscomb.

"I'd invite you inside," Evan Shook said, "but, as you can see, it's not quite finished."

"Nice place," said Agent John Wesley Weiderman. The temperature outdoors was ninety-one degrees and he was sweating through his suit jacket. "I came here to ask if you'd seen your neighbor lately. Mr. Yancy."

"Not for a couple days." Evan Shook thinking: *Oh shit. What now?*

"Are you two friends?" the agent asked.

"Actually, I don't know him very well." Evan Shook was tempted to say Yancy was a stoned flake, but trashing one cop to another cop could be dicey. The blue brotherhood and all that.

John Wesley Weiderman said, "I have reason to believe he might be in danger."

"You're joking. Danger from who?"

"A fugitive I've been hunting."

Evan Shook felt a familiar tremor of apprehension. First wild dogs in the streets, now a murderous psychopath on the loose.

"Let's chat in the Suburban," he said to the lawman. "It's got killer AC."

The interior of the vehicle was quiet and cool. John Wesley Weiderman commented upon the ample leg room and the suppleness of the leather. He inquired about the gas mileage and seemed undaunted by the EPA estimates.

"Will you be driving north," he asked Evan Shook, "if the hurricane comes?"

"Nah. We'll have some rain and wind from it, no biggie. The Bahamas are getting clobbered, for sure."

Evan Shook had been tracking Hurricane Françoise's progress as relayed by the high-strung meteorologists on Miami TV. In the unlikely event that the storm made a hard westward turn toward South Florida, the spec house would have to be zippered up hastily. The fretful Lipscombs had been phoning Evan Shook every few hours seeking reassurance that the place wouldn't be reduced from villa to slab.

To the agent from Oklahoma he said, "Tell me about this fugitive."

Evan Shook wasn't worried about Yancy's safety but rather the tranquillity of the neighborhood and, by extension, the finalization of his real estate deal. As excited as they were about their new house, the Lipscombs would probably walk away from the closing should a gruesome homicide occur at the residence next door. Evan Shook wondered what Yancy had done to place himself in mortal jeopardy – maybe some low-life gangster he'd once busted had escaped from prison and now was vengefully pursuing him.

"Her name is Plover Chase," said John Wesley Weiderman, "most recently using the alias of Bonnie Witt. You know her?"

"I don't." Evan Shook thinking: *Yancy's desperado is a chick?*

"They were romantically involved for a while," the agent added.

"Oh no," Evan Shook said, though it was hardly shocking that his neighbor would date a nut job.

"Here's a photograph provided by her husband. Did Mr. Yancy ever introduce you to any of his girlfriends?"

"Never." Evan Shook looked at the picture and said, "She was here the other day. Some younger guy was with her, not the sharpest knife."

"They've since parted ways," reported Agent John Wesley Weiderman.

"They were squatting in my house – tent, sleeping bags, the whole deal. She said they drove all the way from some-

where and got ripped off. I gave them money for a motel."
Evan Shook looked once more at the photo before handing
it back; definitely the same woman. "But she never once
mentioned Yancy," he said.

The lawman told him that Plover Chase had jumped bail
from a sex-crimes conviction in Tulsa County.

"What kind of sex crime?" Evan Shook's imagination
began to tingle.

"Sir, I'd rather not get into that."

"But she's dangerous, you say?"

"Evidently she's upset with Mr. Yancy because he's dating
someone new, a doctor. It's possible she intends to harm
both of them," said John Wesley Weiderman. "However,
you should also know Ms. Chase doesn't have a history of
violence. Her past offense was one of . . . I guess you'd call
it exploitation."

Evan Shook clicked his tongue in fake consternation. In
fact he was deeply intrigued. Never had a woman exploited
him in a sexual way, but it sounded exhilarating compared
to the listless bedroom comportment of his wife and even,
in recent months, his mistress.

"These triangle situations can get messy," the agent from
Oklahoma was saying, "and you can never predict how indi-
viduals might react. I was told Ms. Chase might be coming
here to settle a score. Arson is a possibility."

"Holy Christ," Evan Shook said, although privately he
felt that losing Yancy as a neighbor would be good for the
subdivision; the man's dumpy-looking house definitely
dragged down property values. Should the fugitive set the
place ablaze, Evan Shook would manufacture a milder story
for the Lipscombs – it had been a sad accident, Yancy falling
asleep with a lighted cigarette or whatever.

"Please let me know if you see anything unusual going on next door," said Agent John Wesley Weiderman.

"Absolutely. Do you have a card?"

"Of course."

"And may I see her photo again? Just in case."

"Here, keep it. I've got copies."

"Thank you," said Evan Shook, trying to mask an excitement he knew was inappropriate.

Neville couldn't sleep because he couldn't stop thinking about the man named Yancy, hurrying off to the house rented by Christopher Grunion and his woman. Why had Yancy gotten so worked up when Neville told him about finding Christopher's shirt sleeve? Neville had been hoping that the American policeman – if that's what he really was – would be an ally in the fight to save Green Beach.

Yet what could Mr. Yancy accomplish tonight, all by himself, with a damn hurricane coming? Was his intention to go arrest Christopher? Egg would beat him senseless first, maybe even kill him.

So Neville put on his clothes and took Yancy's fly rod and left Joyous's place through the back door. He borrowed her daughter's bike and pumped as fast as he could toward Bannister Point. Soon headlights appeared in front of him – a car weaving recklessly, forcing Neville to veer off the road.

It was Christopher's yellow Jeep. In the driver's seat sat Egg; one massive hand was holding the steering wheel while the other gripped the hair of a frightened dark-haired woman. Neville thought she looked Cuban or maybe from Puerto Rico.

By the time he reached Christopher's place, Neville was wind-beaten and drenched to the skin. Silvery needles of rain cut sideways through the broad wash of floodlights. The coconut palms heaved and shook like wild-maned giants. To Neville these visions appeared other-worldly though not hellish, for he'd been through hurricanes before. Drawing closer he heard back-and-forth shouts and he darted forward, careful to remain in the shadow lines.

At the north corner of the house stood three figures holding a triangular formation while the weather raged around them. One was Mr. Yancy; he was facing the others. The second person was a woman, Christopher's woman, clutching a piglet or some sort of small critter. The man with his back to Neville was large enough to be Egg but he had too much hair. It had to be Christopher, and the thing he was pointing at Yancy had to be a gun.

Unfolding in a slice of light, the scene confirmed to Neville the ruthless criminality of Christopher and also the importance of the American. Christopher wouldn't go to the trouble of shooting a man unless he posed a serious threat.

Neville had no time to search for a heavy rock or a limb. He snapped Yancy's fly rod over one knee, rushed up behind Christopher and stabbed him hard with the broken stub. The impact splintered the rod's graphite tubing down to the cork grip and unseated the reel, which fell into a puddle.

Neville wasn't a young fellow, but his arms were strong from years of conching and boat work. And while the fly rod was designed to wiggle at the tip, the butt segment was stiff and inflexible. Christopher Grunion dropped face-forward with the smallest of cries, the shotgun pinned beneath him. His woman began to caw and hop about on her knees.

Neville grabbed Yancy by the arm and said, "Come along, mon."

"I can't."

"Run!" Neville was now pushing the American ahead of him, through the hedges and trees, away from the floodlit house, down the road into the teeth of the wind.

After a hundred yards Yancy halted abruptly and bent at the waist.

"Rosa," he gasped.

"Who's dot?"

"My girlfriend. She's still back there."

"No, she ain't," Neville said.

Yancy straightened. "But she's alive?"

"Yeah, mon, I seen her."

"Okay. Okay." The cop was still panting, fists on his hips. In the sky lightning flared, giving Neville a metallic glimpse of the American's face, exactly what he was thinking.

"Tell me where she is, Mr. Stafford."

"I tink I know," said Neville, waiting for more thunder.

Twenty-three

Driggs was a white-faced capuchin born into a show-business clan. His father had worked for a few seasons on a popular television comedy called *Friends*, and an older female cousin had appeared with several look-alikes in *Ace Ventura: Pet Detective*, a high-grossing feature film starring Jim Carrey. Swinging deeper into the family tree, a great-great-grandmother of Driggs's had played the organ grinder's sidekick in an edgy Parisian musical about the Nazi occupation, the cross-dressed primate sporting hand-polished jackboots and a Hitler-style mustache clipped from Belgian broom bristles.

Born Baby Tom, Driggs was reared among other domestic capuchins on a ranch outside Santa Barbara. He showed none of his forebears' gifts for acting – his disposition was prickly, his attention span fluttering. Unlike his camp mates, he failed to outgrow an adolescent preoccupation with his own genitalia, and this too hampered his career.

A scrotum-grooming reverie, broadcast live on the

stadium Jumbotron, brought an end to a short-lived stint as the official "Rally Monkey" of the Los Angeles Angels. The next morning, his team of exasperated trainers sold Driggs to a freelance animal wrangler named Martell, who hoped to cash in on the monkey boom that was sweeping through cinema and television.

Thanks to an improbable connection at Disney studios – Martell had succesfully housebroken a dwarf lemur belonging to the senior comptroller – Driggs was allowed to audition for a series of action movies based on a popular theme-park ride called Pirates of the Caribbean. The part naturally called for the garb of a pint-sized swashbuckler. Knowing Driggs was averse to costuming, Martell prepped his would-be star for the audition by spiking the animal's noontime Snapple with a shot of Wild Turkey. No more relaxed performer ever set foot on the Disney lot. Two months later, he was in the Bahamas with Johnny Depp.

Driggs had been hired as a backup to another capuchin, Dolly, who was docile, obedient and attention-loving. Martell hoped she and Driggs might become off-camera playmates, and that Driggs would begin to chill in her company. It didn't happen.

Because some of the film's stunts were staged to occur on a ship's rigging – no place for a drunken monkey – Martell had halted the palliative dispensation of bourbon. Predictably, Driggs reverted to the execrable antics that had cost him the Angels gig. From remote shooting locations on Great Exuma came reports of unprovoked biting, wanton vandalism, wardrobe destruction and of course feces throwing, the signature method of protest for unhappy simians. Depp was spared only because Driggs tolerated him, but several other actors and even one of the stuntmen refused to come on the set unless it was Dolly's turn to work.

Her demure presence, far from calming Driggs, pitched him into a state of fiendish priapism that literally came to a head when an assistant director caught him jerking off on a rack of brunette wigs. Driggs and, by association, Martell were fired within the hour. The studio agreed to pay the trainer's airfare back to Nassau though not the expensive connecting segments to Los Angeles. No return ticket was provided for Driggs, not even in cargo.

Worn out by his dissolute trainee, Martell unloaded Driggs for seventy-five Bahamian dollars to a sponge fisherman from Andros, who was bloodied and soiled by his new pet on their homeward passage. That winter, kind fate appeared as a casual game of dominoes in which the sponger happily took a flop in order to divest the horrid creature on a gullible fellow named Neville Stafford from Lizard Cay.

Neville was a gentle, patient man, and the capuchin did not despise him. The name change from Tom to Driggs was an easy adjustment, as was the dietary switch from healthy seedless fruits to batter-fried chicken, conch fritters and coconut cakes, which Driggs soon learned to crave. His skin grew scaly and then inflamed, and thereafter he began losing his fur in handfuls. The unattractive condition was worsened by the tropical heat, and by the nonstop feasting of doctor flies and mosquitoes. Wild capuchins smash millipedes and smear themselves with the guts as a natural insect repellent, but Driggs was too far removed from his Central American roots to innately know that trick. Consequently he remained wretched and welted during the summers, which possibly explained why Neville cut him so much slack.

Throughout Rocky Town the animal became notorious for his crudities and hotheadedness. The only people who thought he was cute were rum-dented tourists and of course the daffy Dragon Queen, who remained convinced he was an unusually small boy, not a monkey. No sooner had the strange old woman taken ownership of Driggs than he began to miss life with Neville. Unsentimental by nature, capuchins do possess keen memories – and Driggs was quite aware that his situation had taken a downward turn.

Never once had Neville teased or prodded Driggs the way the voodoo witch did. The animal hated human diapers but at least Neville had been diligent about changing the dirty ones; the lazy Dragon Queen would let Driggs sit for a whole day in his own shit unless he caused a scene. She also dressed him in cheap doll clothes that made him snarl at his own reflection in the coffeepot. The shack in which she lived was smelly and vile even by monkey standards, whereas Neville had always kept his house tidy and open to the sea breezes.

Driggs did enjoy riding up and down the road on the old woman's motorized scooter chair, though he disliked the capering dances that she made him perform; to defy her, however, meant there would be no fritters. And no pipe, either.

Smoking had been taught to him by the Dragon Queen as a comic stunt, diabolically reinforced with ladles of peanut M&Ms. The loopy witch never told him not to inhale, so in short order Driggs became addicted to the Dunhill blend provided by the hag's companion, a hulking hairless figure whose jealousy of Driggs was as plain as the fungus beneath his toenails.

Some nights, after the Dragon Queen passed out, the

man called Egg would leer at Driggs and whisper harrowing taunts. The monkey would bare his teeth and squeal until the old woman stirred; once he even hurled an empty liquor bottle that Egg deflected with a forearm. The bottle shattered on the floor and roused the Dragon Queen, who punished Driggs by lashing him with his own leash, something that had never occurred during all his time with dull, reliable Neville.

That's when Driggs began plotting an escape. An opportunity came the very next day when the old lady and her companion became tangled on the scooter chair during a braying act of human sex that the monkey mistook for a terrible fight. Swiftly Driggs made his move, snatching a pipe, lighter and tobacco stash before leaping from a window. Off he ran through a soaking rain that seemed different from other summer squalls, as did the galloping surge of the clouds.

A wild capuchin might have intuited a hurricane was coming; if not, he surely would have been alerted by senior members of his troop, who would have organized a collective refuge in heavy limbs below the forest canopy. Driggs, however, was a city monkey by birth and upbringing. He understood only that he preferred to be dry, cozy and shielded from the quaking thunder, which literally scared him shitless.

The few covered hiding places he found also attracted humans; trusting no upright species, Driggs loped on. By nightfall he was tired and famished, and he'd lost his cherished pipe during a dustup with a white man. The road was mostly empty but Driggs came upon a van that stood idling while one of the occupants urinated in the bushes. Silently the monkey climbed to the top and rode the luggage rack through buffeting gusts back to the outskirts of Rocky Town, where he hopped off and made a downcast return to the shack of the Dragon Queen.

Squeezing through a loosely hinged shutter, he entered the candlelit hovel squinting. He was surprised to see, in addition to the witch and her boyfriend, a stranger – a younger, long-haired woman, trussed with belts to a chair. The man called Egg scowled at Driggs, but from her scooter the Dragon Queen sang out his name and joyfully welcomed him. With equine snorts she nuzzled the soggy capuchin while steering the wheelchair in gay loops until it hummed to a stop. Egg said the battery ran out and the old lady ordered him to put in another one, which he refused to do.

Driggs vaulted from the stalled scooter to the lap of the younger woman, who was unable to speak due to a gag made from one of the voodoo hag's bright scarves. The new woman's clean odor was pleasing, and Driggs pressed his face to her bosom and inhaled deep monkey breaths as a respite from the rankness in the room. Casually he foraged inside the woman's blouse for M&Ms or other hidden treats. Seeing fright in her eyes, he began combing his doll-like fingers through her soft shiny hair.

An outcry rose from the Dragon Queen: "Get 'way from dot whore, my lil' prince!"

Driggs clung to the newcomer's clothing, but Egg seized his tail and yanked him away. The monkey landed on the table, where he spied another pipe and snuck a hit that made his teeth freeze. He peered into the pipe bowl and saw a foreign paste of white crystals, which confused him. The Dragon Queen rose from the scooter chair and began flapping her skirt at the tied-down woman, who looked away.

Egg came around from behind and turned the woman's head with a hard slap, further upsetting Driggs.

Egg wore no clothes, the long brown thing between his legs reminding the monkey of his own. The Dragon Queen started to bob and clap while her naked boyfriend, shining with sweat, circled their prisoner. A frightened cry came from the bound woman.

Driggs heard himself chitter in agitation, meaning now he didn't want to be there, didn't want to see whatever was about to happen. The animal felt panicky and cornered. Yet outside the wind was roaring, the trees kept snapping – where could he run?

The Dragon Queen snatched him from the tabletop and buttoned him into a tiny tuxedo vest stained with coffee. She held him by the collar while shouting encouragement to Egg, who hurried to loosen the belts from the chair holding the younger woman.

"Do it! Gon now!" the hag crowed.

Once their captive was untied, Egg turned back to the Dragon Queen and struck a vulgar pose, flexing his arms. The Dragon Queen moaned theatrically and with her free hand fanned herself. When Egg took hold of the younger woman, still gagged, she began punching at his wide chest. The Dragon Queen chortled though the scene had an opposite effect upon the capuchin, who broke from the voodoo witch's grasp and launched himself in authentic jungle fury at her boyfriend.

A scream shot out from Egg – a high, full-throated scream that overrode the low drone of the storm. The door of the shack flew open but it wasn't the wind. Standing there was a white man Driggs recognized from previous altercations.

But behind the white man, looking over his shoulder, was ... Neville!

Driggs would have grinned had his incisors not been so deeply implanted in Egg's fleshy thing, to which the monkey clung as if it were the bough of a mahogany tree.

Yancy needed a moment to absorb the scene.

"Jesus," he said. "The man's got a monkey on his dick."

Neville was thunderstruck. "Dot's Driggs," was all he could muster.

Egg cast Rosa aside and feverishly commenced slapping at the capuchin, causing him to chomp down harder. Blood was dripping all over the thug's feet. He stopped flailing to appraise his tormentor, seven fuzzy pounds that might as well have been cast-iron tonnage.

The Dragon Queen railed at Driggs and hawked rheumy gobs at the intruders. Yancy shoved her backward into the seat of the Rollie scooter; then he pulled off Rosa's gag and firmly guided her toward the doorway. Neville refused to depart without his pet, who remained tenaciously attached to Egg.

From the goon came a seething croak: "Git dot fucker offa my cock or you dead mon." He was holding motionless under the most delicate of circumstances.

Once more the Dragon Queen lunged to intervene, crooning more voodoo nonsense. This time it was Neville who pushed her back onto the wheelchair.

To Driggs he gently appealed, "C'mon, boy! Poppa got fritters bok home!"

These were irresistible words to the hungry vagabond. Driggs spat out Egg and jumped to the top of Neville's head, his old riding perch. They hurried out the door behind Yancy and Rosa, chased by the fevered remonstrations of the voodoo woman.

By the time the hurricane struck, they were more or less safe – Yancy, Rosa, Neville and the monkey – inside a small house rented by another of Neville's girlfriends. Coquina was her name, and Neville fondly introduced her as half Cuban. She'd lighted two kerosene lanterns after the power went out; the windows she had boarded earlier that day with Neville's help.

The house was near the shore, the waves breaking hard enough to interrupt conversation. Coquina handed out dry clothes and a small towel for Driggs, who had torn off the tuxedo vest and was stuffing himself with johnnycakes and orange slices.

Neville pulled Yancy to a corner and said, "You tink Mistuh Chrissofer be dead?"

"I don't know. What'd you hit him with?"

"I didn't hit 'im, mon. I stob 'im wit your fishin' pole."

Yancy said, "The fly rod?"

"Yah. In de bock." Neville demonstrated how he'd broken it and used the point of the butt section as a lance. "Wot if I hoyt 'im bod? Maybe killed 'im."

"I didn't see a damn thing," said Yancy.

"Wot 'bout his woman?"

"It was raining. It was dark. She was drunk."

"She was?"

"If anybody asks me," Yancy said. "You bet."

Outside something heavy crashed to the ground. Across the room, Rosa and Coquina were feeding Ritz crackers to Driggs. They all looked up because of the noise. Coquina said it was probably a utility pole falling in the backyard.

Yancy told Neville he had done the right thing at Bannister Point. "The man's a criminal, a murderer. All you did was save my life, Mr. Stafford."

"Dot might be so."

"His real name is Stripling. Can you remember that? It'll be important if they come to ask you questions. The woman is his wife – did she get a look at your face?"

"No," Neville said. "Who gonna come axing questions? You mean from Nassau or Miami?"

"Remember that name – Nicholas Stripling. He shot two men dead back in Florida."

"Got-tam!" said Neville.

"Before he came here, he had a surgeon take off his left arm. That's why he always wore the poncho. That's why you found the cut sleeve in his garbage – his wife stitches up his shirts to fit the nub."

Neville's voice jumped two octaves. "Why a mon get his own arm cut off? 'E muss be stone crazy!"

"No, Mr. Stafford, he did it for money. This is one cold-blooded sonofabitch."

Rosa walked over carrying a lantern. She and Yancy went into a bedroom and shut the door.

Neville sat down to think. Anyone who for pure greed would give up an arm . . . a true white devil, like the Dragon Queen said. Maybe her voodoo had worked, after all. What if she'd given Neville a role in the curse, and set the stabbing in motion?

He looked up at the shuddering rafters. Then he turned back to address the monkey: "You con stay wit me like before, but tings got to change. No more smokin' and nonsense."

Coquina rolled her eyes and told Neville he was a fool.

302

Driggs blinked impassively and sucked an orange rind. It felt good to be out of the storm.

Yancy held Rosa close and said, "Baby, I'm so sorry."

"Totally my fault. Rule number one: Never conspire under the influence of tequila."

"Did they hurt you?"

"Not really, but it was definitely on the agenda," Rosa said. "Crazy old bat, first thing she did? Tore off my bra and poured Bacardi in the cups. The bald dude, he was just laughing and playing with himself."

"What the hell happened before that, at Stripling's house?"

"Oh, great meeting. She and the boyfriend knew we weren't for real – they've got a woman on the payroll at Immigration in Nassau. They knew 'Andrew Gates' was really you, they knew I wasn't really your wife – and they knew we were trying to set 'em up."

Yancy sat her on the bed. He kept apologizing until she told him to hush.

"Eve's boyfriend isn't a boyfriend," he said.

"I never saw him – he was in another room. The bald guy's the one who grabbed me. He's not a gentleman, either, Andrew. God bless that nasty little monkey for showing up when he did."

"What I'm trying to tell you," said Yancy, "is that the boyfriend is really the husband. Nick Stripling's alive."

Rosa flopped back on the covers. "Okay. What?"

"He had his own arm sawed off to make everybody think he was dead. It was Dr. O'Peele who did the wet work, right after Nick and Eve sank the boat."

"While Immigration has her in Nassau."

"Right. That's the beauty of the seaplane."

"They used the condo on Duck Key for the surgery, which explains the bone chips."

"Right," said Yancy. "Then, after they get some shark bites on the arm, Eve drives it down to Key West for the switcheroo on the *Misty Momma.*"

"Wow. Talk about a plan."

The wind against the ceiling beams sounded like a downhill locomotive. Yancy could feel the pressure in his eardrums.

"After the surgery," he said, "Nick came to hide out on Andros. He and Eve had already rented the house and started their big real estate project. They bought that sweet stretch of beach, probably using what Nick stole from Medicare. But he wasn't through with Florida. He snuck back to take care of Phinney and then O'Peele, and then me. Nick's the dude in the orange poncho, Rosa. He wears it to hide his stump."

Rosa ran her hands through her hair. Yancy noticed raw scrapes on both knuckles, from fighting the two freaks in the shack.

She said, "The man had his own arm amputated, Andrew. That's impressive."

"I've heard of doing a finger before."

"Oh, sure. The old Wendy's scam."

"I thought it was Burger King," Yancy said.

"Whatever. Customer starts gagging and there's a big scene. Somebody calls the local TV station. But you know it's a setup because what turns up in the cheeseburger is always a pinkie. That's the one you don't really use. An actual meat-rending accident, it's the thumb or forefinger that gets severed because those are working fingers."

"Sure, the ones nearest the blades and grinders."

"Exactly," Rosa said. "But pinkie cases are automatically suspicious. Somebody claims they found one in a bun, always check the hands of their friends and family. It's amazing how many dirtbags will chop off a pinkie just to get a piece of a lawsuit."

"You've got to admire the commitment."

"Because these fast-food companies, they'll settle almost every time. They don't want to go to a jury," she said. "Even if they know they're getting hustled, they can't take a chance."

"Not in South Florida, no way."

"Even a little finger, Andrew, that's pretty hard-core. But to give up your whole arm – that's a new one."

"We're blessed to live in such times," Yancy said.

"You think Caitlin knows?"

"Nope. Only Eve."

"And where is the fearless Mr. Stripling?"

"Not sure if he's dead or alive. He was about to shoot me when my new hero Neville stabbed him with my six-hundred-dollar bonefish rod."

"It just gets better and better," Rosa said. "And now we're in a hurricane!"

"Named Françoise, for Christ's sake."

"Don't spoil it, Andrew. Take off your pants."

The eye of the storm stayed out in the Tongue of the Ocean, feeding on the warm waters. Still there was substantial damage and disruption across Andros as it passed to the east. The winds on Lizard Cay reached seventy-one miles per hour, gusting to ninety.

Yancy found himself struggling to focus on what would

have been, under calm heavens, an act of carefree and delicious reflex. The din from even a small hurricane is
nerve-racking, and Yancy was additionally distracted by
thoughts of the evening's frenetic events. Rosa told him to
relax; Neville and his girlfriend wouldn't be able to hear
them from the other side of the door, which Yancy had
locked in case Neville's monkey got nosy.

It was during light-spirited foreplay when Rosa confided
that she'd been reading a smutty novel in which an inexpe-
rienced woman becomes enthralled by a lover who bosses
her around the bedroom with the same tone one might hear
from the nail-gun operator at a slaughterhouse. The woman
sportingly signs an enslavement contract, after which the
fellow forces her to put on Day-Glo wetsuits and perform
contortions that would daunt Olga Korbut.

Rosa said she was sort of enjoying the book. Yancy tried
to act intrigued though he'd never been good at fantasy sex;
it was difficult to stay in character and not make smart-ass
remarks. One time Bonnie made him play the shiftless
hitchhiker while she was the naïve Mary Kay associate who
got lost in her imaginary pink Lexus. Yancy couldn't keep a
straight face, or anything else, and Bonnie ended up steaming mad.

Adopting the role of ruthless dominator in Rosa's day-
dream would require some stagecraft, and in Yancy's
experience there was a hazy line between daring and dis-
gusting. Usually when making love he strived for a purely
sensory, uncomplicated experience. Incorporating a game or
a skit seemed too much like a class assignment.

For Rosa, however, he'd try anything – first in a morgue
and now in a hurricane, the whole damn house heaving on
its foundation. Fine.

"Thad always speaks to Juliette like a Russian," she was saying, referring to the characters in the novel.

"I can't do a Russian."

"Any Eastern bloc nation should work."

"Bad Irish is all I've got," said Yancy.

Rosa kissed him and said, "All right, let's hear it." In the lantern's light she looked lovely, but this wide-eyed Juliette thing she could never pull off, not with her butterscotch skin and those South Beach bikini stripes.

She said, "Ready? Now call me a mean name and order me to put my feet behind my head."

"You can actually *do* that?"

"Come on!"

"Kay, ye wortless bitch, do wutcher told or I'll spank yer arse with a boogie whip."

She broke up, giggling and kicking at the air. "It's like screwing Shrek!"

"Did I not warn you about the accent?"

"Give me some Daniel Craig."

Yancy slid over and pinned her arms. "Don't move," he rumbled.

"Oooh, baby, that's pretty good!"

It took a little time but Yancy's mind began to untorque, despite his almost having been shot point-blank and then escaping through a tropical gale to rescue his date from a voodoo den. All the heavy stuff faded as he rolled around with Rosa and finally let go. The storm made the intimacy more exotic – they were trapped but also tucked safe. When the lantern died they found their way by touch, and the knocking from a loose porch plank became their rhythm.

Later, when they had time to think about it, their recollections differed as to exactly when the top of Coquina's house blew off. Yancy thought it had happened a few moments before they finished, as Rosa's fingertips began to dig into his arms. But she said no, it was the precise instant she came that the roof had peeled away, the nails popping like firecrackers.

Yancy had known without turning what the loud noise meant. Suddenly he could see Rosa beneath him and she could see the clouds, because even at night a hurricane brings its own particular light. The wind came wailing into the open room yet the rain flew dead sideways over the gap where the boards had been, and not a drop fell upon the bed.

Rosa had laughed deeply, shaking Yancy by the shoulders and saying, "*That* is what I'm talkin' about, mister!"

Which is the part they both would remember the same way.

Twenty-four

By dawn the weather had broken and the wind dropped to nine knots. Hurricane Françoise was gone. The landing strip at Lizard Cay was littered with trees, coconuts, plywood, two-by-fours and sheets of brittle plastic roofing from a nearby chicken farm.

Along with the other debris Claspers removed two dead roosters as he walked the runway with a couple of other pilots and some neighborhood kids. Three small planes had flipped during the heavy winds, but Claspers had done a good job securing the Caravan, anchoring the tie-down stakes in a rocky patch off the edge of the tarmac. The aircraft was untouched by Françoise except for a goatee of shredded palm fronds on the propeller.

By invitation the other pilots had spent the storm inside the well-built vacation homes of their wealthy clients, while Claspers in his underwear had huddled in the shower stall of a leaky motel room expecting the entire structure to implode. Although his gutsy aviating was extremely valuable to Christopher Grunion – who these days would fly a float-plane under the radar into South Florida? – Claspers never got the call from Bannister Point inviting him to come take shelter with Grunion and his girlfriend.

Assholes.

Like they don't have a spare fucking bedroom.

Even when Claspers had delivered a potential customer for their unbuilt condos – that pretty Cuban woman, the doctor – he didn't get past the front door. Grunion's girlfriend had handed him a Heineken and said: "Here, K.J., take one for the road."

Had the motel walls crumbled during the hurricane, good luck finding another pilot who would do for Grunion what Claspers did. For the risks he'd taken he could lose his certification, or even go to prison. And where was the appreciation for all those daring moves? Where was the respect?

Claspers didn't know exactly what type of scam Grunion was running, but he knew enough to sink the man if it came to that. Like most good pilots Claspers kept a detailed log of his flights in and out, where and when – solid tracking information that could be handed over to authorities if ever he were questioned about his work for Grunion.

Because you don't earn loyalty by treating your best people like peons, not the man who flies your motherfucking airplane.

So long, K. J., have a nice hurricane!

Well, screw you, thought Claspers.

His nerves were wrung from the storm. Even half-stoned he'd been terrified to hear the windows buckle and moan. Back home he would've swallowed some pills and gone to sleep, but back home there were custom-fitted aluminum shutters and impact-resistant glass and strapped trusses. The building code on Lizard Cay was more lax, which was to say it existed only on paper. Consequently, Claspers spent the night hugging the tiles in the shower. After Françoise passed he stumbled to his bed and found the mattress soaked, clammy rain dripping from a crooked seam in the plaster ceiling. At the first light of day Claspers was out the door.

Without electricity he was unable to recharge his cell phone, and at any minute he expected to see the yellow Jeep speeding up to the airstrip, Grunion primed to bitch him out for not taking his calls. The man would want to go to Miami until Andros Island was up and running, or maybe he'd just send Claspers back for groceries and DVDs. Grunion's girlfriend was a major fan of Matt Damon and once directed Claspers to fly low over the actor's house on Miami Beach so she might catch a glimpse. Claspers had no clue where the guy lived, so he'd randomly chosen a bayside spread with an infinity pool and buzzed the place at four hundred feet. Grunion's girlfriend had been thrilled – she couldn't wait to tell Grunion that she'd seen Matt Damon's Irish setter taking a dump on the putting green.

As Claspers removed the straps from the Caravan he thought about quitting and finding another gig. In the old days even his hard-ass cartel bosses would ask him to swing by the *finca* for drinks. Great food, late-night guitars, good times – that's how Claspers remembered it. That's how he'd first met Donna, one of the wives. The Colombians treated Claspers like an important member of the enterprise, which he was, because bales need wings. Never would they have let him hunker alone in a crackerbox motel during a hurricane.

The only bad thing about dumping Grunion – that seaplane was really fun to fly. Claspers loved it.

"You fueled up?" somebody called.

Claspers turned and saw Andrew, the American trust-fund fisherman, walking with his handsome Latina wife across the tarmac. They were carrying their bags.

"How'd the real estate meeting go?" Claspers asked.

The wife said, "Not too good. We were hoping to hitch a ride home with you."

"If I got two open seats, no problem. All depends on who else is coming. And if it's cool with the boss."

"Nobody else is coming," the fly fisherman said.

"Is that from Grunion direct?"

"We'd like to leave right now," the wife said. "Basically as soon as you can pull those chocks."

Claspers was amused by the couple's boldness. Maybe they'd been rattled by the hurricane, or maybe they'd had a brush with that caveman Egg.

He said, "It ain't my airplane, *señora*. Wish it was."

The fisherman took out a gold police badge and held it in front of Claspers's nose. "So you can appreciate the sense of urgency, Mr. Claspers. We'll pay for your gas, but the earliest possible departure is what we need. Like in five minutes."

"You're a cop?"

"The clock is ticking. Seriously," said the woman.

"You, too?"

"She's a forensic specialist," the fake fisherman explained. "We're working two homicides in which your employer is suspect *numero uno*. Also an attempted homicide, I almost forgot. Plus there's a pile of heavy federal charges that I can tell you about on the flight back. Unlike Mr. Grunion, the doctor and I don't mind the lines at Customs and Immigration, so you can take us straight to Miami International."

Claspers was feeling off balance. "I dunno what the hell you're talking about."

"It's simple. You either get this fucking plane in the air right now, or your license gets yanked back in the States and you find another profession, like driving an ice-cream truck. That's not too ambiguous, is it? Nothing fuzzy about the scenario I'm presenting. The man you call Grunion and his female companion? On several occasions you flew them nonstop from here to Monroe County, Florida – in this very same aircraft – without officially clearing at Tamiami or Key West. That's a crime, and the look in your eyeballs tells me you're aware of the possible shitstorm in your future. If you've never had the opportunity to interact with Homeland Security, you're in for a treat. I'm Inspector Yancy, by the way, and this is Dr. Campesino."

All the pilot could say was: "Grunion killed somebody?"

The pretty doctor patted his arm. "We really need to get moving."

The hurricane stayed out over the Bahamas until meandering away. It rained heavily for a day in the Lower Keys but now the sun was shining and Evan Shook's construction crew had returned to the job site. He was parked in front of the spec house talking on the phone with Mrs. Lipscomb. The topic was crown moldings.

A green Sebring convertible driven by a blonde pulled up next door at Yancy's place. Evan Shook told Jayne Lipscomb he'd call her back.

"Will you check those prices? Ford thinks we can do better."

"Sure. Right away," Evan Shook said absently.

From the glove compartment he removed a stun gun he'd purchased just in case Andrew Yancy hadn't hallucinated the wild dogs. Agent John Wesley Weiderman had said the woman didn't have a violent past, but Evan Shook pocketed his new Taser, just in case.

Before stepping from the Suburban he looked at the photo once more – there was no doubt it was the same person. She entered Yancy's house and Evan Shook moved closer to the fence separating the properties. His phone was in one hand; in the other was Agent Weiderman's card. Evan Shook knew he should make the call immediately; it would be the responsible thing to do.

Before Plover Chase burned his neighbor's house to the ground.

What a sight that would be, he thought. *A bona fide inferno.*

The fugitive came out the back door and stood on Yancy's deck. She noticed Evan Shook watching as she tied her hair in pigtails. He waved and she nodded back pleasantly. Evan Shook couldn't help wondering what sort of elaborate sex crime she'd committed – ropes? whips? manacles? – and what man in his right mind would press charges.

Back home at his club, Evan Shook was dependably conservative during law-and-order discussions: Lock up the bastards and throw away the key! Don't do the crime if you can't do the time! One quick phone call and Miss Plover Chase would be prison-bound. Possibly there was a cash reward. Agent Weiderman would know.

Then again, it was difficult for Evan Shook to imagine how such a sunny-looking soul could be a menace to society. That was his dilemma as he tapped Agent Weiderman's number into his smartphone. He was about to press Call when Plover Chase took off her cotton beach dress, under which was revealed a candy-striped two-piece swimsuit – not a bikini, yet still . . .

After dabbing sunblock on her nose, she stretched out on a plastic lounge chair that must've cost Yancy all of eleven dollars. To Evan Shook she seemed extremely laid-back for a would-be arsonist.

"Hi, there! I remember you!" Now she gave him a full-on wave.

Evan Shook tucked away the phone and Agent Weiderman's card as he approached the fence. Conscious of his shortness, he stood straight as an aspen. The heel lifts in his loafers helped.

"Where's your boyfriend?" he asked.

"We broke up," she said, "but thanks for the motel room."

"No problem."

"I didn't break into this place, don't worry. I've got a key." Her lips were a faint shade of pink but her toenails were the color of tangerines.

"Have you seen Andrew?" she asked.

"Not for a few days. Maybe he's out of town."

"I'm a friend of his. Really I am."

"Then he's a lucky guy. What's your name, friend of Andrew?"

"Bonnie," she said. "I tried his cell but he didn't call back. Usually he's good about returning his messages."

"My name's Evan. You want some water or a soda? It's hot as blazes out here."

"No, thanks. There's beer in the fridge."

Plover Chase had a nice figure and her legs looked naturally tanned, a feature Evan Shook appreciated. His wife got herself sprayed twice a month at a salon in downtown Syracuse, and she came out looking vinyl. Also, the stuff tasted like insecticide.

"Andrew's the one who told us it was okay to crash at your house," the fugitive confided. "Sorry about that."

"I think he likes to play practical jokes."

"Have you met his new girlfriend? The surgeon?"

Evan Shook heard himself say, "Yes, she's down here a lot."

Which was untrue.

"What's she look like?" Plover Chase asked.

"Good. She looks good." Evan Shook had never set eyes on the woman, but he said it anyway. "She's got long brown hair."

"Scale of one to ten?"

"Eleven."

"Whoa, daddy."

"They seem pretty serious," Evan Shook added.

The fugitive was looking at him over the tops of her sunglasses. "Like, how do you mean? Move-in-together serious, or get-married serious?"

"Well, you know Andrew."

"Yes, I certainly do know Andrew," she said.

Behind them, the construction site was a cacophony of hammers and table saws and sanders – even a boom box playing salsa music from Miami, heavy on the horns.

"Where you from, Emmett?"

"It's Evan." He spelled it. "I live in New York State."

"So you're down here really just to get that house built," Plover Chase said. "All by your lonesome."

"My family's up north, that's right. I fly back and forth most weekends."

Yancy's stalker crossed her killer legs, and Evan Shook found himself sidetracked by unwholesome fantasies.

"So this mansion you're putting up, Evan, it's basically a real estate investment?"

"When I'm here, I stay at the Casa Marina. That's down in Key West."

"And that's where you go at night," she said, smiling, "after a long hard day at the job site."

"They have a nice bar. Cool and private." He pointed. "Watch out, there's a horsefly on ... well, right *there*."

"That would be my décolletage." She flicked the insect away, and with a knuckle wiped the blood dot. "How old do you think Andrew's girlfriend is?"

"I don't know. Young for a doctor," Evan Shook said. "Want to come by the Casa later for a drink? They've got a country band that's not bad."

Plover Chase sat up and swung her lovely feet to the deck. "Andrew's somewhat famous around Key West. But you probably know that already. Infamous, I should say."

"For what?"

"You don't read the papers when you're in town? Shame on you."

"There's a place on Duval where I buy the *Times*. But, really, I don't pay much attention to the local news," Evan Shook said. "So tell me what Andrew did to get his name in the headlines."

The woman laughed and said never mind, it's water under the bridge. Then she said good-bye and picked up her beach dress and disappeared into Yancy's house.

Evan Shook walked back to the Suburban thinking about the justice system. The prisons of America had become so overcrowded that hard-core cutthroats were being turned loose daily, only to strike again. Where was the logic of locking up a hot-looking babe like Plover Chase for a crime of "exploitation," whatever *that* might be?

So Evan Shook didn't dial Agent Weiderman. He still had some mulling to do.

In the meantime he called Mrs. Lipscomb back at the Pier House. He told her that the price for the carved poplar moldings was as low as he could go, regretfully, without taking a loss on the order. She put her husband on the line, and Evan Shook listened to him whine and huff about switching to fiberboard before he eventually surrendered and said okay, what the hell.

"Give her what she wants," Ford Lipscomb sighed.

"Sir, I feel your pain. But it's gonna look special when we're done."

After hanging up, Evan Shook made a U-turn in the Suburban and drove past the house next door, where the pigtailed fugitive was unloading from her car's trunk a set of red jerry cans that are normally used to transport gasoline.

Clearly she was struggling with the fact that Yancy had a brainy, beautiful new girlfriend.

Evan Shook pretended not to look at Plover Chase as he rolled by, goosing the accelerator. Sometimes it was best to let nature take its course.

Eve Stripling removed from her prone, moaning husband a broken piece of a composite-fiberglass rod blank manufactured by the Sage company. The jagged point had perforated the disc sac between the fifth lumbar vertebrae and first sacral vertebrae, at the base of Nick Stripling's spine, leaving him in bald agony, unable to stand.

Eve rushed inside to fetch the Rollie scooter chair, into

which Nick one-armedly hauled himself, spitting mud and cursing his wife for not letting him shoot Andrew Yancy in the den. She guided Nick into the house and spent an hour icing his wound, which failed to restore the functionality of his legs. There followed an animated discussion that ricocheted between the subjects of urgent medical care and Eve's gross culpability for Stripling being ambushed.

Which, the guy who attacked him? Nick had no goddamn idea who it was. Never saw the man's face. Eve insisted she didn't get a good look, either.

Some black dude, is what she said – a gem of a clue, here in the Bahamas. Very fucking useful.

Eve told Nick to quit yelling and let's figure out where to find a rock-star spinal surgeon, soon as we get off this stupid island. Miami was out of the question because Yancy might beat them there and tip the feds that Stripling wasn't dead, triggering a full-on manhunt.

Yancy, who should have been safely out of the picture, a steaming pile of guts. Instead he was likely hunkered somewhere nearby on Lizard Cay, waiting for the weather to clear.

One thing Stripling had in his favor was a counterfeit U.S. passport bearing the name of Christopher Joseph Grunion. It was a superior counterfeit that had cost him nine grand – some wiseguy who ran a lunch truck in Little Haiti. The passport would remain usable for maybe three days max, depending on how long it took Homeland Security to process Yancy's information and enter Stripling's alias in the computer.

"We're going to England," Nick declared hoarsely to Eve.

"All right, honey. There's a nonstop from Nassau."

"They've got fantastic doctors. Good as New York."

Eve agreed. "I'll call British Air soon as we get cell service."

This was during the heavy part of the storm, rain hammering the roof, the electric generator grinding like a cement mixer.

To his wife Stripling said, "I better not be fuckin' paralyzed. This is all on you."

"Knock it off, Nicky."

"You know I'm right."

He couldn't stop railing about what had happened. Which, what are the odds of getting randomly stabbed in your own yard during a hurricane?

While holding a loaded shotgun.

The pain was worse than anything Stripling had ever experienced, worse even than post-amputation. Breathing hurt. Blinking hurt. Talking hurt even more.

His suspicions turned to a certain sketchy freelance employee, Mr. Carter Ecclestone, otherwise known as Egg. The meathead was supposed to return to the house after taking care of Yancy's girlfriend. However, Egg hadn't been seen since before the hurricane struck. The Jeep, however, was back in the driveway . . .

Maybe Egg *was* here, Nick thought, only now he was working with somebody else. Like that nutty old crone he'd been balling – what if she'd talked him into killing Stripling and robbing the place? Maybe she put a voodoo spell on that pea-brained motherfucker.

Or maybe it was Eve who'd made Egg a better offer. Lately she'd been riding Nick's case about how boring it was on Lizard Cay, how she'd go batshit crazy living here all the time with nothing to do. She'd gotten downright surly when Nick had told her to quit bitching and get a hobby, take up snorkeling or kiteboarding. He'd said the two of them were in this thing together, up to their shiny white asses, only maybe Eve was thinking: *Not necessarily.*

Except the Egg theory didn't add up. He wouldn't have tried to murder Nick with a spindly goddamn fishing rod. He would have disemboweled him with a knife, or cracked his skull with that fish billy, or snapped his neck with those gorilla paws.

Everything about the night ambush seemed unplanned and frantic. A total amateur, but who? Stripling had made a point not to know a soul on the island.

"Oh great," he muttered. "Now I gotta take a leak."

"You can still void?" Eve said buoyantly. "That's a super healthy sign, Nicky. And I see your toes moving, too!"

"Yeah, that's right, they're dancing a tango. Now bring me something – a jar or a bowl, I don't care."

Eve went to the kitchen and came back with an empty wine bottle.

Stripling scowled. "Get serious. My dick won't fit in there."

"Sure it will."

"It's bigger than a goddamn cork!" Wretchedly he pounded on the armrests of the Rollie.

"Honey, chill. I didn't mean anything," his wife said.

"Gimme your glass before I wet my pants!"

She was holding a Waterford tumbler full of ice, peach vodka and soda. It came from a table set belonging to her maternal grandparents, now deceased. Nick could sense that Eve was reluctant to deploy the sentimental heirloom for urine collection.

Or possibly she just didn't want to pour out her cocktail.

Stripling was better at forging orders for Rollies than he was at driving one. Impatiently he toggled the joystick until the motorized chair clicked and surged forward. As it passed by Eve he made a swipe at her precious tumbler but she pulled it away. The scooter thudded hard into a wall, jarring Nick's damaged spine and also his distended bladder, which yielded a warm sour flood. With it came well-founded gloom.

Once the FBI learned he was alive, his days of freedom on Andros Island were numbered. The Curly Tail Lane project would be done, of course, as would Grunion Global Realty, Nick's mishandled stab at legitimacy. Although he still had a few million liquid, he could easily waste every penny on lawyers and bribes trying to fight extradition to the United States.

Or he could pack up and run. Purchase a new identity, find another place to hide and start over as an international fugitive. Which, talk about exhausting. He didn't want his face on the Interpol website. He wanted to stay dead.

It wasn't impossible for a clever person to get lost and stay lost in the Bahamian out-islands – if you were blessed with a spouse who was content to sit around weaving straw hand-bags or painting kindergarten faces on coconut husks. Keeping Eve settled would require a locale that offered shoe shopping, Pilates, sushi bars, a hair salon and a dog groomer.

A city, in other words. And living in a city would be risky.

Plus, Stripling had already ordered another Contender to replace the one he sank in the Keys. The new boat was a thirty-six-footer, sky blue, with beast triple Mercs and a sixty-gallon bait well. Delivery was due any day. He was naming it *Lefty's Revenge*, in honor of his lost arm. A god-damn fish-slaughtering machine is what it was – Nick would be able to run from the east side of Andros all the way to Cay Sal and back on a single tank.

But not if he was hiding out in Geneva or São Paulo.

He could think of just one major move that would solve everything and keep the status quo: Silence Andrew Yancy before he got to Florida and met with the feds.

It was the only way Stripling could stay officially deceased, safe on Lizard Cay. Yancy and his Cuban girlfriend, or whatever she was – they were the only ones besides Eve who knew enough to bring Nick down.

"We gotta find that cocksucker," he said to his wife.

"You can't even walk, Nicky. And, please, it's a hurricane outside!"

"In the morning I'm talkin' about. First thing."

She said, "You're hurt. We'll need to get out of here."

"Where the hell is Egg? That's who we get on Yancy's ass. Call Egg, okay?"

"He's not answering the two-way. Here, let me find you some dry pants. Not even the radio's working, honey. We should get some sleep and wait for the storm to blow through."

Stripling said, "It's all your fault, this whole clusterfuck. Now put down your drink and roll me to the damn bathroom."

In the morning Nick felt even worse. The puncture in his lower back was oozing a fluid that didn't resemble blood. So severe was the pain that his facial muscles had seized into a grimace. But the cell phones still weren't working and there was no internet connection, making it impossible to contact British Airways. Eve proposed that Claspers should fly them to Nassau right away, so they'd be certain to get seats on the first flight to London.

323

But all Nick could talk about was hunting down Yancy before he escaped. Which, no way was that shithead going to sneak out of Andros today. Bahamasair was still grounded from the storm, and none of the local boats were crossing to Florida, not with the Gulf Stream running fourteen feet.

As long as Yancy was stuck on the island, Nick said, Egg would be able to track him down and kill him. Now just find Egg!

Eve said, "First things first, honey."

She dosed her husband with Clorazepams and Tylenol 2s, left over from a knee operation, before assisting him from the Rollie to the Jeep. On the back seat sat a pair of Louis Vuitton suitcases and Tillie the dog, fussing inside her tartan travel case. During the ride to the airfield Stripling sustained a bitter monologue about people who said white-collar criminals were soft, pussies, when here he was an amputee, possibly crippled from the waist down, staring at life with no parole if he got busted.

Say the word "outlaw" and everyone thinks bank robber, but did John Dillinger cut off a limb to trick the FBI into thinking he was dead? No, sir, he went to the movies and got shot full of lead. Which, these days, any fuckwit with a ballpoint pen and a Halloween mask could rob a bank. The average take was a whopping four grand, less than Stripling spent every year on periodontics.

Despite the hordes of health-care scammers working in South Florida, Nick rated his felonious speciality as elite. Defrauding the United States government of millions of dollars was no job for morons, he said. The Medicare system was chaos times ten.

Faking all those claims required cunning and precision that was foreign to the thug world. Every patient name and

Social Security number had to belong to some real person, which meant hacking a medical data bank or paying off a clerk. Then the stolen names had to be transcribed correctly down to the middle initial, no typos! Same with the Socials, otherwise a government computer in Atlanta or Bethesda would spit the forms right back. Just the paperwork would make you nuts, sixteen fucking copies of everything – and, Jesus, you had to be sharp with the math.

Stripling, growing fuzzy from the pills, rambled on to Eve. Said he'd proved himself a heavy hitter. Reminded her that he wasn't some gutless boiler-room hack who'd copped a plea, paid back the money and ratted out his brother scammers. No, he'd given up a healthy arm and committed two cold-blooded murders so he could keep his riches and stay clear of prison.

He was the real deal, an epic badass!

Yet when they pulled up to Moxey's airstrip and he saw the white seaplane rolling toward a takeoff, Yancy blowing a kiss from behind a port window, Stripling pitched sideways out of the Jeep and began to jabber.

Twenty-five

When the roof blew off, Neville was in the bathtub with Coquina and Driggs, covered with sofa cushions. Coquina was crying while the monkey quivered and mewled. Neville wrapped his arms around them for two hours. He knew by the ebbing pitch of the wind that the hurricane was moving away, so he wasn't afraid.

Not of the storm.

But he couldn't stop worrying about Christopher, wondering if he was dead or alive. Yancy had said Neville didn't do anything wrong, but Neville was aware that the police paid more attention when the person who got killed was rich and white. On the other hand, if Yancy was right about Christopher being a dangerous murderer, a wanted man, things might turn out all right. Maybe Nassau would reward Neville for his bravery at Bannister Point by returning the family land at Green Beach.

Then he could rebuild his house, and go back to life the way it was.

At dawn they got busy – Neville and Coquina along with Yancy and Rosa. Together they packed up Coquina's belongings and in the wilting heat carried them to her mother's place down the road. The mother wanted nothing to do with Driggs, who two Saturdays earlier had snatched a silver bracelet from her ankle outside the straw market. Neville said the monkey's manners were much improved. Coquina's mother reluctantly agreed to let the creature stay while Neville borrowed her car to drive the two Americans to the airport.

"But I hoyd ain't no Bahamasair today," she said.

The American man said, "We're flying private, ma'am."

On the ride to Moxey's, Yancy once again thanked Neville for saving his life. Neville asked what would happen next.

"Soon as I get back to Florida, I'll speak with the FBI," Yancy said. "Tell 'em where they can find Mr. Stripling – the guy you call Grunion."

"Wot if he's dead from the stobbin'?"

"Then all that's left is to arrest his wife and find the rest of the money."

Rosa spoke up: "No, Andrew, that's not all. Mr. Stafford might have to deal with the authorities here."

"Yeah, they could be a pain," said Yancy, "but I'll fly back and tell them exactly what went down. How you stopped Stripling from shooting me."

"You'd do dot?" Neville said.

"It's a promise, man."

Neville felt better. Having an American policeman on his side would be good.

"Wot about my beach?" he asked.

Yancy said he wasn't sure. "If Stripling bought it with the

Medicare money, prosecutors in Miami might file a claim on it."

"But the land's mine." Neville was perplexed. "Egg stayin' dot trailer. I cont move back till he's gone."

"Egg's heading to prison, too," Rosa said. "For what he did to me."

Neville didn't know all that had occurred at the Dragon Queen's shack, but he'd never forget what he saw when he and Yancy opened the door. It would be fitting for Egg to spend time at Fox Hill as a prisoner instead of a guard. Neville pictured him being taunted in the showers by the other inmates, the ones he'd hurt with the marlin billy. Much sport would be made of his monkey wounds.

After they arrived at the airport, Yancy asked Neville to call as soon as he got information about Stripling's condition. "Dead or alive, I need to know. Meanwhile don't talk to anybody about last night at Bannister Point. You already tell Coquina?"

"No, mon."

Rosa said that was good. "For her and you."

"I dont won hafta move 'way. Home is home, you unnerstahn."

"You won't ever have to leave," Yancy said.

"I be hoppy 'f dot's true."

"It's true, Mr. Stafford."

Rosa went to the ladies' room. Neville asked Yancy about his own difficult situation back in Florida, about the large house being constructed on the land where the little deer lived – the deer that were no bigger than dogs.

"You gon stop dot fella and make 'im rip de place down?"

Yancy smiled in a tired way. "Wish I could, but it's probably too late."

"I hope not," Neville said.

Yancy said good-bye and shook his hand. Rosa did the same when she came back. She told him to take good care of Coquina, and to put Driggs on a strict fruit-and-fiber diet – no more conch fritters! Yancy said it was time to go. He and Rosa picked up their bags and went inside the terminal building.

Standing at the chain-link fence, Neville saw several overturned planes on the turnaround section of the tarmac. He also noticed, undamaged, the single-engine seaplane belonging to the man he knew as Christopher. A few white men and some local teenagers were out clearing the landing strip of hurricane litter. Soon the American policeman and his girlfriend would be able to take off, if they had a pilot who would fly them. The weather out west, toward Florida, looked all right.

The car belonging to Coquina's mother was a rust-freckled Taurus with a Salt Life decal on the back window and a fickle alternator. Neville tried the key seven times before the ignition turned over. Then, barely a mile from the airport, the engine quit. Neville got out and popped the hood hoping for something as simple as a loose wire. He fiddled with various connections but nothing worked.

Neville heard a car coming the other way and decided to flag it down. As the vehicle came into view he noticed first that it was yellow, then that it was a hardtop Jeep Wrangler, of which there was only one on the island. Neville stopped waving and backpedaled for cover behind the broken-down Taurus.

But the Jeep was moving too fast. Both occupants looked squarely at Neville as they swerved around the stalled sedan and sped on toward the airport. The bastard that Neville had stabbed in the back sat upright in the front next to his woman, who was driving. Their taut expressions displayed not a flicker of recognition, only annoyance at the roadway obstruction.

Once they were out of sight, Neville placed both hands over his heart and thanked the Lord Almighty for his good fortune. Obviously the murderous fugitive had no idea who'd speared him from behind with a fishing rod.

Minutes later Neville heard an aircraft lifting off from Moxey's. He looked up and saw the floatplane, as white and graceful as a gull. The man known to him as Christopher wouldn't have had enough time to make that flight, no matter how fast his woman was driving.

So it had to be Yancy, the American policeman, on board. Yancy and his girlfriend.

The fact was confirmed minutes later when the yellow Jeep reappeared, racing back from the direction of the airfield. This time Neville didn't wave at the Striplings as they passed, but he didn't bother to hide, either.

Rosa fell asleep on Yancy's shoulder but he kept awake, his eyes on the pilot. The flight to Miami was only forty-five minutes through a light chop. To the north, beyond Grand Bahama, towered a bank of muddy clouds, the last tailings of Hurricane Françoise.

Riding on small planes never failed to put a tune in Yancy's head, and this time it was "Mozambique." Claspers didn't ask for details of Stripling's crimes or say much of anything at the controls. Yancy figured he was preoccupied devising a story for Nick or the FAA, depending on which way he decided to play it. After the Caravan touched down at Miami International, Yancy offered him a one-hundred-dollar bill for fuel. Claspers shook his head and pointed to a gold AmEx clipped to the sun visor. The name imprinted on the card was Christopher Grunion.

When the plane taxied to a stop, Claspers tugged off his earphones.

"So, what are your plans?" Yancy asked.

"I'm not sure. Too old for prison and, man, I do like to fly."

"It won't be my call. The feds can be prickish, as you know."

Claspers said, "I had no idea he murdered anybody. Swear on the Bible, the Koran, whatever."

"Hey, I believe you."

"Then I was thinking maybe you could help. Put in a good word."

"Sure, but here's the situation," Yancy said. "Technically I'm not a cop. I'm a restaurant inspector."

"Fuck a duck!"

"It's just a temporary reassignment. The badge I borrowed from a colleague."

"Other words, you count dead flies at the Pizza Hut. This is who I got for a character witness."

"I'll be a detective again in the very near future. Meanwhile, let's not disparage the tireless civil servants who keep our public dining establishments free from vermin."

"You don't mind," said Claspers, "I got a shitload of paperwork."

Yancy woke up Rosa. They climbed out of the plane and jumped from a pontoon to the tarmac. A brief snag occurred upon re-entry when a Customs officer asked Yancy to unzip his footwear, tight nylon booties that were tailored for water wading though not ideal for travel. The fishing shoes smelled vile but the Customs man intrepidly probed their sweaty interiors in search of contraband.

Afterward Rosa called a cab to take them to the parking garages, where they kissed good-bye and set out separately to locate their cars. Twenty minutes later Yancy was in his Subaru heading up the interstate to the FBI office in North Miami Beach. He wasn't dressed for the occasion, and in fact looked like a man who'd spent the night in a hurricane. Again the booties were a liability.

Getting past the reception desk required dropping the name of a well-regarded Miami police lieutenant for whom Yancy had once worked. Eventually he ended up in an interview room with the two humorless street agents he'd encountered at Nick Stripling's funeral. They remembered Yancy with manifest unfondness, so he rather enjoyed dropping the bomb.

"Mr. Stripling isn't dead. I just left him in the Bahamas, bleeding from a fresh hole in his back."

The posture of the agents improved. They began to fashion questions. One of them asked who stabbed Stripling. Yancy said he didn't know; it was a drunken dispute.

The other agent asked if Yancy had traveled alone to the islands.

"Yep," he said, which was technically true. Rosa hadn't told him to leave her out of the recap, but that was his intention. The FBI needed to know only the basics, beginning with Stripling's whereabouts.

The taller agent was Strumberg and his partner was Liske. Their suits weren't the same shade of gray but the cut of the lapels looked identical. When Yancy told them about Stripling's self-amputation, they tried to act as if they heard such stories every day.

However, Yancy knew they were stoked because they called in an assistant to take down what he was saying. The assistant's laptop needed recharging so there was a period of lame small talk while she got on the floor to locate an electric outlet. Strumberg asked how Yancy had lost his detective job.

"Aw, come on. You guys know what happened. They let you have free internet, right?"

"The media can exaggerate."

"Not this time," Yancy said. "In defense of a woman's honor I waylaid her husband with a portable vacuum. The gesture was unappreciated and, unfortunately, witnessed by the proverbial throngs."

The assistant's laptop beeped to life, and the important phase of the interview continued. At one point Liske asked Yancy to draw a map of Lizard Cay. Yancy politely suggested that a satellite photo would be more accurate. The assistant found one on a classified government website and zoomed in on Bannister Point.

Yancy placed a fingertip to the screen. "That's the house your subject is renting, but he won't be there much longer. You should call whoever you need to call and have him arrested. But that's probably not going to happen this afternoon, is it?"

"There's a strict diplomatic process," said Liske, "we're obliged to follow."

"Then you might lose him."

"Not for long," Strumberg asserted. "How badly was he hurt?"

"This morning I saw him in a car at the airfield. And if he's well enough to ride in a car, he can ride on a plane."

"How do you know he hasn't already left the island?"

"His pilot flew off without him," Yancy explained, "at my instruction."

"You hijacked his aircraft?"

"Not with a weapon – and I prefer the word 'commandeer.' The pilot didn't know who Stripling was until I told him. He might be in a mood to cooperate."

"We'll see." Liske looked at Strumberg. "Stripling could charter another flight to Nassau. From there it's a straight haul to London or New York."

"Or even easier to come here," Strumberg said. "Hell, we know the man's got brass balls. If he cut off his own arm, as you say."

Yancy informed the agents that the Nassau airport had gotten trashed by the storm. "But I'm guessing the runways will open by midafternoon, tomorrow morning at the latest. I were you guys, I'd be putting on my Bluetooths and workin' those phones, because that fucker's probably got a fake passport. Ask Immigration to look up a Christopher Grunion."

The quick-typing assistant piped, "Could you spell that name for me, please?"

Overall Yancy thought the debriefing went as well as he could have hoped. Although the FBI agents were riveted on the Medicare case, they showed more than polite interest in the two murders committed by Stripling in Florida. Such heavy allegations could boost him to the top of the fugitive list and, in Liske's priceless phrasing, "incentivize" the Bahamian government to apprehend him. It would help if a homicide warrant was waiting in Monroe County or Miami-Dade, the jurisdictions where the shootings took place. That would be Yancy's next project.

Back in the car he plugged in his phone and called Rosa. She was already at work, elbow-deep in an autopsy. The spare key to her house was hidden inside a fake cactus next to the back door. Yancy let himself in, fed the fish, showered and fixed a peanut-butter-and-cucumber sanwich. He left messages for Rogelio Burton and Sheriff Summers, telling them that he had big news and that he was on his way back to the Keys.

The cell rang in his hand – Tommy Lombardo at the health department.

"Hey, I know you're supposed to be on vacation and all—"

"No, I'm working," Yancy said.

"What, they got a roach emergency in the Bahamas?"

"That's hilarous, Tommy. It's a murder case."

"Sure, it is."

"I'm back in the States. What do you need?"

"You, Andrew. There's been, huh, a complaint filed on Stoney's. Worse than the usual, okay? Some widow from Ponte Vedra wound up in the ER with a three-aught hook in her watchamacallit. That pink wormy thingy hangs down in your throat?"

"The uvula," Yancy said. "She got a fish hook stuck in her uvula. I'm betting she ordered the Cuban yellowtail."

"Man, that's amazing. How'd you know?"

"Brennan doesn't check the gut for hooks when he cooks a fish whole."

"How come?"

"Because he's a bumblefuck."

"I need you pronto back in the saddle, Andrew. This one made the *Citizen*. The widow lady, she's got an in with the governor."

"Let's have lunch later in the week. Pick a place that won't poison us."

Rosa got home from the office at five-thirty. They didn't go out for dinner and they didn't make love. The autopsy she'd completed was that of a girl who had died on her birthday. Only eight years old and the parents had left her alone while they went to play the slots at the Miccosukee casino, way out on Krome Avenue. The girl was doing laps in the backyard pool when her appendix ruptured, no one there to hear the cries for help. She made it back to the shallow end but the pain doubled her up, and that's where they'd found her – the parents, so shitfaced they couldn't remember where they'd left their car keys.

Yancy spent the night holding Rosa on the bed. She cried and said not every day at her job was so awful, and all he could say was close your eyes. At dawn she was sleeping when he kissed the top of her head and slipped out the door.

First he drove to Johnny Mendez's residence and placed the crooked ex-sergeant's gold badge inside the mailbox. The Siamese was licking its paws on the hood of the Lexus, while the gargoyle visage of Mrs. Johnny Mendez watched him from the porch. She wore inappropriate heels and a sheer morning robe that revealed a gruesome topography of misspent liposuctions. Yancy felt a prick of sympathy for Mendez; embezzling from Crime Stoppers might have been the only way to pay for his wife's cosmetic overhauls. Yancy honked once and sped away.

In Homestead he steered off the turnpike at the speedway exit and drove to the apartment building where his grandmother had lived. From the road he could see the window the burglars had broken on the day of her funeral. Whoever lived in the unit now had a small child; a tricycle stood on the walkway by the front door. Yancy called his father in Montana and left a message asking how the fishing was. He didn't mention where he was calling from.

On the drive to the Keys he kept the radio off. His thoughts tumbled in the quiet, and the miles slipped away. A fender bender on the Snake Creek drawbridge had backed up traffic, so Yancy stopped for a grouper sandwich at a café he knew to be clean. His muted phone showed two more calls from Tommy Lombardo, though nothing from Neville Stafford on Lizard Cay.

As soon as the highway cleared Yancy was back in the car, still thinking of Neville and the incident at Bannister Point. Yancy worried that Eve Stripling might have recognized the old man from Rocky Town, and that her husband would send Egg to murder him. Yancy wondered how long it would take the FBI to make a move.

His backup choice was Sonny Summers, despite the sheriff's fear of the severed-arm case. Yancy thought Sonny might be persuaded to speak with the Bahamian authorities if he saw a chance for down-range glory – assisting the capture of a runaway murderer.

Halfway across the Seven Mile Bridge Yancy heard a siren. A ladder truck loomed in the rearview, and he slowed to let it pass. Fires were so infrequent in the Keys that Yancy assumed the emergency was another head-on.

He was coming over the pass at Bahia Honda, leaving a second voice message for the sheriff, when he saw a churning spire of black smoke. It was rising on the Gulf side of Big Pine, far from the highway, which meant it wasn't a car crash. Some poor bastard's home was ablaze.

Yancy wondered if it was somebody he knew.

Twenty-six

Dear Diary,

All these years I've been wondering what ever happened to her, and tonight she walked into the Olive Garden and re-stole my heart.

She said, "Cody, you can do better than this."

I said, "You look awesome, Ms. Chase."

And she did look awesome, even hotter than I remembered from school. I'm pretty sure she got her boobs done.

"Can we go somewhere private to talk?" she asked.

I told Arnelle the hostess I was taking a ten-minute break, but there was no way. Ms. Chase grabbed my hand and led me to her car. We drove to the Bank of America near Oral Roberts, and I got the most epic BJ of all time. She parked in the tellers' drive-through so nobody could see us, and I swear I almost kicked out the windshield.

After zipping me up she told me how she'd walked out on her husband and drove all the way from Florida just to find me. She said she couldn't stay long in Tulsa because there's still a warrant left over from what happened all those years ago between me and her.

She said, "I'm a big-time fugitive, Cody."

Right away I started getting hard again, but she acted like she didn't notice.

I told her I had a girlfriend but it wasn't serious. "She's a teacher, too. AP English, same as you. Only it's a charter school."

Ms. Chase smiled and gave me a long kiss. I had a joint so we smoked it. The car smelled like McDonald's fries because that's all she ate the whole way from Sarasota. She said she didn't waste time in sit-down restaurants – she wanted to get to Oklahoma as fast as possible and track me down.

Her hair looked different because she got platinum highlights so nobody would recognize her from the Wanted poster, which I'd never seen but then I hardly ever get to the post office.

"There's a big wild world out there, Cody. Are you ready to take the ride?"

"See, they just promoted me to assistant manager."

"Congratulations."

"But the boss, he's a major dickbrain."

She said, "Life is but the blink of an eye. This is what you'll learn."

I apologized for how the trial went down, what I said about her on the witness stand. Ms. Chase said she understood and forgave me totally. I was under major pressure at the time – it was my parents who made me testify and turn over all the stuff I wrote about our love affair. My mom read every page of the diary but she didn't get most of it, thank

God. She literally asked me what a "back-door job" was. I made up something about sneaking into a club.

Ms. Chase wanted to know if I'd ever got married, and my answer was almost but not quite. She told me her husband's a retired doctor with gobs of money. He knew she was running from the law but he proposed to her anyway, which I totally understand. She said he's much older than her and also he's kind of a perv. He likes to beat off while he's got a belt or electric cord around his neck, which I've heard of but sure never tried.

"Who are you reading these days?" she asked.

I told her I've sort of gotten away from books and more into Xbox.

"Oh, Cody," she said, and I took it as a cut.

She told me it was time to start thinking big, so I pointed at my all-world woody and asked, "You mean big like this?" She laughed and gave it a squeeze, which got my hopes flying, but then she started talking about inner journeys and the hand of fate.

I kept trying to pull off her skinny jeans but she wouldn't go for it. She did unbutton her top, which was pretty sweet. There were more freckles than I remembered but who cares.

"Don't you have any big dreams?" she asked, but offhand I couldn't come up with any.

"Well, you should, Cody. You're a sharp young man, an A student back in the day."

It's not easy to have a seriously deep conversation when you've got a purple hard-on that could cut a diamond. I told Ms. Chase there was a new Chipotle's opening up on North Utica and I was thinking about putting in for day manager.

"No," she said. "You're coming with me."

And that's what I did.

Yancy handed the transcript back to Montenegro, who said the sheriff's office was holding the iPad on which the diary was stored. One of the road deputies had confiscated it from the rental car.

"I knew that fuckwit was keeping a journal," Yancy said. "Should I go see Bonnie?"

The lawyer said he didn't care. "Bonnie's not her name, dude."

"Well, 'Plover' is unacceptable. I can't bring myself to say it."

"And you had no knowledge of her true identity while you were balling her?"

"The last time we were together is the first time she told me."

"And of course you felt no obligation to notify the police – or your long-suffering counsel." Montenegro rubbed both hands on his shaven orb. He was more expansive than usual but no less jaundiced. "I probably could get her six months and probation for the arson, if she wasn't already on the lam for a sex felony. Oklahoma hasn't decided whether to extradite, but I spoke to an Agent Weiderman—"

"Yes, we've met," Yancy said.

"Not a bad guy. We discussed the problems with the Tulsa case, now that Mr. Parish intends to become a published author. This new diary of escapades won't be helpful to the prosecution."

"Listen, should I go see her or not?"

"You're not as pissed as I thought you'd be."

"I am highly pissed. Supremely pissed."

"She's determined to plead insanity," Montenegro said. "Says she torched the house only because she was deranged by her passion for you. Another celestial mystery, but there you fucking have it."

"For Christ's sake, Monty, she's not insane."

"How would *you* know? I mean, of all people." The lawyer yawned. "See what you set in motion, Andrew, by sleeping with this unreliable person. The dominoes continue to fall – on my desk, unfortunately."

"Have you talked to Bonnie's husband?"

"The board-certified physician you assaulted at Mallory Square? Seems like eons ago. No, I haven't spoken to Dr. Witt because he's presently in ICU at Sarasota Memorial Hospital exhibiting the cognitive capacity of an artichoke. He was found nude from the waist down, hanging from a peewee basketball hoop at the local Kiwanis park. This was four-thirty a.m., some rookie cop called it in as a suicide attempt, which it wasn't. The bottle of virgin olive oil being a key clue. Also, the cashmere choke collar."

"Is he going to die?" Yancy asked.

"The family says the doctor's chances for recovery are about the same as the chances of him paying for his estranged wife's legal defense, which is to say remote. Go see her if you want but, here, read this first."

It was more lovesick rubbish from Cody Parish.

Dear Diary,

Ms. Chase is gone! She left the Best Western to take a walk, and came back in a rental car. I begged her to stay but I could only watch helplessly as she packed her bag.

"Don't you love me anymore?" I cried.

She touched my cheek and said, "Darling, where's my shampoo and conditioner?"

"Darling"? Seriously?

My whole world was crashing down. How could she take my heart in her hands and choke it like a baby bunny rabbit?

The last time we made love I knew something wasn't right because she didn't make a sound. Also, she didn't move her butt very much, which isn't like her. I asked what's wrong, princess, and she said nothing's wrong, everything's beautiful.

But that night in bed I had a horrible feeling she was thinking about someone else. It had to be Andrew, the man she was with before she came back to Tulsa and took me away. He's got some hot new girlfriend now and I think Ms. Chase is jealous. Supposedly the girlfriend is a doctor, like Ms. Chase's husband, and maybe that screwed with her head, too.

Or maybe it's something else. Maybe she just went batshit crazy which can happen when the monthly hormones take over. I've seen it before, and watch out!

All I know is I've lost my true soul mate. Yes, she was an outlaw and a schizo but I loved her anyway – and I would have stayed glued by her side until the law hunted us down. Every day on the road with Ms. Chase was wild lust and adventure, and I don't regret one single moment.

If she showed up on my doorstep tomorrow I'd take her back in a heartbeat, and no man alive would blame me. I'd go through the fires of Hell and follow her anywhere, except back to Tulsa because I am seriously done with the Olive Garden.

Like the book says, you can't go homeward angel. And by God I'm not.

Yancy drove out to the detention center on Stock Island, a place where as a detective he'd interviewed numerous inmates though never a former lover. He was friends with the duty officer, so he and Bonnie had a room to themselves. She was excited to see him and disappointed by his chilly reponse.

"Andrew, why are you looking at me like that? It's just a fire. Nobody died."

"You're right. It's not like you burned down an orphanage."

"Please, there's no cause for sarcasm."

Her county jumpsuit was the same blaze orange as Nick Stripling's poncho. She wore the braided pigtails but the jailers had taken away her lip gloss.

"You think they're recording us?" she said, looking around for a video camera.

Yancy said no. The phone calls usually got taped but he wasn't sure about visitations.

"Cody wants to come see me, too, but Mr. Montenegro says absolutely not."

"Why did you do this, Bonnie? So much drama."

"Oh please. It was all for you. Don't pretend like you don't get it, or I'll really be upset."

"But I truly *don't* get it."

"You were right about Cody," she said. "He was keeping a secret journal of everything we did, just like before. His notion is to do a book and get rich. He thinks he can write, which I suppose is my fault for building him up so much in class. But isn't that what teachers are supposed to do? I didn't know he would peak in eleventh grade! At first I was livid about the new diary, but then Mr. Montenegro said it's good for my case in Oklahoma because they'd have to charge him with aiding a fugitive, which would be messy for the prosecutors."

"Because he's supposed to be the victim," Yancy said.

"Exactly, Andrew. The boy I supposedly corrupted."

"Here's the thing: They don't need Cody's testimony to convict you for bail jumping. Also, Bonnie, this arson? Major felony. Nobody gets a free pass if they torch a home."

"Insane people do. Eighteen months of treatment, then we can be together again. I've done my research."

"Insanely jealous isn't the same as clinically insane." Yancy impatiently drummed two fingers on the table. "Why am I even bothering with this conversation? You *are* somewhat nuts, I'll give you that. But no judge in Florida would let you walk."

"I miss you so much, darling. Did you hear about Cliff strangling himself?"

"Yes, it was an inconsiderate choice of venue. The Kiwanians do good work."

"He probably took me out of his will when I ran off with Cody. Not that I care about the money."

"You and the doctor are still legally married. He dies tomorrow, you'll get half the estate." Yancy winked at her. "Not that you care."

"God, when did you get so mean?"

"Ever since I drove down my street and saw flames shooting into the sky."

She reached across the table and pinched him hard. "Why are you being like this? It was your idea – don't you dare say you don't remember. I did this for you!"

Yancy said, "Okay, now you are officially in lunar orbit."

"It was that night at your place when we were lying out on the deck. You put the blanket down – that wool blanket that smelled like a wet puppy – then we smoked a number and drank a bottle of cabernet." Bonnie's jaw was working and she was squeezing her hands together.

"We went out there to make love and watch the moon set over the Gulf, right? You said it was the most peaceful sight imaginable, a golden spring moon. But then it turned out that guy's new house was in the way."

Yancy lowered his forehead to the table. "You can't be serious."

"It was so tall it blocked out the whole arc of the moon," she went on. "You got real sad and then super angry, and that's when you turned to me and said—"

"I oughta burn that fucking house down."

"See, you *do* remember!"

"Word for word," Yancy muttered to the tabletop.

The worst day of Evan Shook's existence began when he sent a text message to his wife that read: "See you in Miami tonight. Don't forget to bring our little friend!"

Mrs. Evan Shook was perplexed because she had no plans to visit him in Florida, engrossed as she was with hosting a cocktail party (including finger food) for the Republican Women's Club of Greater Syracuse. Nor did she understand her husband's reference to "our little friend," which was actually a jackrabbit vibrator belonging to his mistress, the intended recipient of the text.

Only when his wife called to accuse him of arranging illicit threesomes did Evan Shook realize his calamitous typing mistake. She said she'd been hearing lurid rumors of his cheating ways, and now she had proof! It so happened that one of the most feared divorce lawyers in the tri-state region would be attending that night's fund-raiser, and Evan Shook's wife said she planned to fuck him and then hire him.

Against such a blindsiding Evan Shook rustled up what he regarded as a passable defense: The text had been meant for Ford Lipscomb, the "little friend" being a cashier's check to cover construction overruns on the Keys house. This yarn was rejected with savage derision. Evan Shook's wife advised him to hang on to his shriveled little nuts because she and her new attorney were coming with a blowtorch.

"And a Brink's truck," she added, and hung up.

So it was understandable that Evan Shook was preoccupied as he headed to Big Pine for a meeting with a landscape architect retained by Mrs. Lipscomb, also en route. On the highway his Suburban was passed by two speeding fire engines that normally would have aroused his curiosity, but he remained fogged with gloom. No internal alarms went off as he turned onto Key Deer Boulevard and saw the smoke; he thought it was just some redneck burning tires.

A green Sebring convertible went flying past in the opposite direction, and that's when Evan Shook's senses stirred: The woman at the wheel of the car was his next-door neighbor's stalker. Suddenly the billowing plume held promise, and Evan Shook drove faster. He'd never made that pledged phone call to Agent John Wesley Weiderman, never reported his encounter with the pretty fugitive on Yancy's backyard deck.

And he never would.

By the time he came around the corner of the block, Evan Shook was completely prepared to see a house on fire. He was not, however, expecting the house to be his own.

The first words from his lips were "Fuck me!" It was not an unapt metaphor for what had occurred, and he would repeat it often to no one in particular. The spec house was, in the parlance of professional firefighting, fully engulfed.

Impressive were the efforts to save it but everything except the slab was raw fuel, from the wooden baseboards to the wooden trusses. Evan Shook positioned himself upwind, leaning against one of the fire trucks and watching in a funereal stupor as the walls of his island investment buckled and turned to ash.

Mrs. Lipscomb showed up sobbing in the company of her landscaper, whose shared grief was triggered by the loss of a lucrative contract. Next to arrive on scene was Agent Weiderman, who provided the police with the name, description and automobile information of the suspected arsonist. Twenty minutes later Evan Shook was informed by a sweaty road sergeant that Plover Chase had been captured at a roadblock on Summerland Key. Four empty jerry cans smelling of gasoline were recovered from the trunk of her rental.

In the growing crowd Evan Shook recognized his insurance agent, who was scampering around snapping photographs. Although the site was covered for fire loss, Evan Shook couldn't recall the numerical terms of the policy, specifically the payoff limits. He was morbidly aware of how much of his own money he'd sunk into the property, and additionally what he owed on the mortgage and construction loan. Even with the insurance check he could lose his ass. All that remained would be a pile of charred rubble and a bare lot, which Evan Shook undoubtedly would be forced to surrender in the divorce.

The future was nauseating to contemplate. Evan Shook wished he were a clueless bystander, not the victim, so he could enjoy the blaze for the crackling spectacle it was. At some point Agent Weiderman asked if Evan Shook could think of a reason why Plover Chase would torch his house instead of Andrew Yancy's.

"No idea," said Evan Shook. "Only thing I ever did to the lady was rent a hotel room for her and her deadbeat boyfriend."

"Strange. Wonder why she picked you."

"There's the one you should ask!" Evan Shook was pointing at Yancy, who'd just stepped out of his car. He looked genuinely astounded by the sight of the fire.

Evan Shook squirted past the much taller Agent Weiderman and rushed toward Yancy yelling, "This is all your motherfucking fault! Your lunatic girlfriend burned down my house!"

Yancy surprised his neighbor by pinning him somewhat forcefully to the hood of the Subaru. "In the first place," Yancy said nose to nose, "she couldn't possibly have done this because she's in Miami. Secondly, she's not a lunatic, but on her behalf I'll accept your heartfelt apology."

"Not the doctor girlfriend," Evan Shook wheezed. "The fucked-up blonde. You know which one."

Yancy righted Evan Shook and set him on the ground like a lawn jockey. Agent Weiderman wedged the men apart and led Yancy away to brief him on the improbable particulars of the crime. Evan Shook was so upset that when the phone vibrated in his pants, he pulled out the stun gun by mistake and nearly Tazed his own ear.

After successfully extracting his cell he heard the voice of Ford Lipscomb:

"Jayne told me what happened, Evan. It's so terrible, truly awful." He was calling from the Gulf Stream aboard the *Misty Momma IV*, which he'd chartered for the day.

"It's heartbreaking for us," he continued, "but poor you! Good God, man, you must be in shock."

"Something like that," said Evan Shook.

"Jayne's completely devastated. I just spoke with her and she says the place is still burning – they couldn't save anything."

Evan Shook whimpered to himself. Three firefighters were chopping at a smoldering portico. "Is this about your deposit, Mr. Lipscomb?"

"No rush," he said. "Tomorrow's fine. Whenever the banks open."

Twenty-seven

Claspers didn't come back. The following day, the Striplings enlisted another pilot to fly them out of Andros – a local guy with a dubiously maintained twin Beech, but Nick said go for it. The new pilot advised them to be ready at noon.

Cell service on the island was working again, so Eve phoned British Airways in Nassau and booked two business-class seats to London. Her next call was to a spinal surgeon on Devonshire Street whose patients had awarded him four and a half stars on the internet, which was insufficiently stellar for Nick but Eve made an appointment anyway.

While she was repacking for a longer, possibly permanent stay, Egg showed up. He was haggard and limping; Nick chewed him a new one anyway. The goon offered no apology for disappearing the night of the storm. He said he'd had a medical problem, so he'd brought back the Jeep and walked to the trailer at Curly Tail Lane. He didn't say what had been done with Yancy's girlfriend, and the Striplings didn't ask.

Eve told Egg to look at the Super Rollie, which had been malfunctioning since Nick crashed it into the wall. Egg said the automatic steering was fucked up. Nick started hollering and cussing again because how else was he supposed to get through Heathrow if he couldn't walk. Eve said all airports offered wheelchairs.

"Not with motors!" her husband railed. "Not with a goddamn iPod dock!"

He was in ragged shape despite the painkillers. Eve told Egg to roll him outside while she finished filling the suitcases. In the hurricane's aftermath Bannister Point was an obstacle course – branches and coconuts and two-by-fours all over the place. Egg in his hobbled condition did a poor job of dodging the rubble, and even the Rollie's pneumatic suspension couldn't spare Nick from the bumps. Between groans he rehashed for Egg the saga of his ambush.

Then he asked: "It wasn't you who tried to kill me, was it?"

"No, mon. Why I do sum ting like dot?"

"You'd have to be brain-dead," Stripling agreed. "But who could it be? I don't have any enemies on this fuckin' island. I don't *know* anybody on this fuckin' island."

Egg reminded him about the vandal who'd peed on the backhoes at the construction site.

"I thought you took care of that sonofabitch," Nick snapped.

"Yah, I hoyt 'im putty bod but he ain't dead. I saw 'im utter night."

Stripling wondered aloud if the stealth urinator was the same man he'd caught snooping outside the house, the old beach nigger he'd run off with the shotgun. Which, who'd be crazy enough to come back after somebody fired a twelve-gauge over your head?

Egg made no response. It wasn't a daily occurrence that a sober white person used the n-word in his presence, but the boss man seemed clueless.

"You gotta find out who crippled me," Nick went on. "That's your number one job."

Egg said he'd ask around town.

"Yeah, right. Be careful not to work up a goddamn sweat." Nothing annoyed Stripling as much as lack of initiative. "Maybe your woman can help," he needled Egg. "Do some of her voodoo shit and pull a name out of some dead chicken's asshole."

"Dot ain't funny."

"What's with the limp?" Nick could see that the brute was hurting.

"Monkey fucked me up bod."

"No shit?" It was Stripling's first laugh in days.

Eve caught up with them on the road. When her husband saw she was out of breath, he asked what was wrong.

"You-know-who at Immigration just called," she said. "Honey, it's already in the computer – somebody in Miami flagged your passport!"

Stripling deflated in the scooter chair. "That fuckin' Yancy got to the feds."

Eve was jumpy and distraught. "So what now, Nicky? You-know-who said they won't let you out of the country, and there's nothing she can do. She said don't go near the Nassau airport."

"So screw Nassau. We'll stay right here until I line up another way out. The Bahamians can't arrest us till they get a warrant from the States, and that could take weeks.

Months even. Meantime Mr. Ecclestone'll keep an eye on Moxey's for us, right? In case a chopper full of uniforms shows up."

Egg sniffed noncommittally.

Eve said, "Arrest *us*? My passport's clean. You're the one with the fake."

Sometimes she could be so thick it drove Nick nuts. "Yes, baby, 'us' as in Mr. and Mrs. Stripling, co-conspirators. You think Yancy left you out of the story? Like maybe he didn't hear you telling me to go ahead and blow his brains out? Or maybe the Cuban babe forgot you were the one told Egg to put a gag in her mouth and get rid of her?"

"Yeah, but, Nicky—"

"Just shut up."

Worse came to worse, he and Eve could escape by water. The new Contender would be arriving soon – the boat was a damn rocketship is what it was. He could run it straight down to Grand Turk.

Nick commanded Egg to take him back to the house. Eve walked on ahead. She didn't speak again until they were alone and the new pilot had been dismissed and the bags were unpacked.

"We could fly a spine doctor over from Miami or Palm Beach," she said.

"Really. And he'll bring his own MRI and a CT scanner? Hell, all we gotta do is lease a 747 and he can haul the whole friggin' OR. That's genius, Eve." Stripling chuckled mordantly. "It's like you forget I was in the business."

"Quit being an asshole, Nicky. You weren't in the medical-care business, you were in the stealing business."

Which, he would have run over her ungrateful ass with the Rollie except the motor didn't work because Egg had removed the battery to lighten the vehicle for pushing. After Eve stormed upstairs Stripling stewed in the scooter chair for a long time. The ice melted and turned lukewarm in the towel she'd placed upon his puncture wound. The liquid sensation caused him to squirm.

Egg had slipped away again and Eve wasn't responding to Nick's yells, so he pitched forward out of the Rollie and worm-crawled to the nearest bathroom, where he struggled to seat himself. He noticed that his pee stream grew weaker whenever the pain got worse, which, according to MyBedsideMD.com, could be a troublesome indication. Unfortunately, his wife was in possession of the codeine Tylenols, meaning Nick would have to suck it up and apologize or spend the remainder of the day in deepening misery.

He swung open the bathroom door and called out, "Eve, I'm sorry! Come downstairs!"

No reply.

"Eve, baby, please! I said I was sorry."

An astringent dispatch from the second floor: "Go blow yourself, Nicky."

Damn, he thought. *She's really hacked off.*

One benefit of working in a violent metropolis such as Greater Miami was superior crime-lab technology, which had advanced by leaps and bounds during decades of extreme homicidal misbehavior. The .357 Smith & Wesson found by Gomez O'Peele's body was tested, at Dr. Rosa Campesino's request, for the presence of a cornstarch mixture commonly used on the inside of powdered latex medical gloves. Sometimes, when fitting a nervous hand into such a glove, a criminal might externally disperse microscopic particles of the cornstarch formula. That's what turned up on both the handle and the trigger of the weapon that killed Dr. O'Peele.

It was a significant finding because a person who purposely shoots himself typically doesn't worry about fingerprints, and therefore doesn't don gloves before putting the gun barrel to his temple. In any event, the hands of Gomez O'Peele were bare when his body was discovered, and the only latents on the .357 came from two of the doctor's right-hand fingers, which was instructive because his sisters reported he was left-handed.

Cumulatively the evidence was more than enough for Dr. Rosa Campesino to classify O'Peele's death as a homicide, and she signed her name on the certificate. To surprised North Miami Beach detectives she conveyed her opinion that the doctor had been shot by a person other than himself who'd staged the crime as a suicide and had worn hand protection available at any medical-supply outlet. Rosa didn't identify Nicholas Stripling as the likely killer because it would have jeopardized both her job and the case; the Bahamas excursion ranged far outside the accepted investigatory parameters of an assistant medical examiner. Yancy had to be the one to provide Stripling's name.

Rosa's ruling on O'Peele's nonsuicide was an untidy development for the Key West Police Department, which had named the dead doctor as Charles Phinney's killer since the same pistol was used in both shootings. The *Citizen* had already run a story saying the Phinney case was being closed due to the prime suspect's self-inflicted demise. Now a new story had to be written announcing that the murder of the young fishing mate remained unsolved.

Rosa emailed her summary of O'Peele's autopsy to

numerous interested parties, including at Yancy's suggestion Agents Liske and Strumberg at the Federal Bureau of Investigation. Afterward, while Rosa was eating a tomato salad at her desk, a hearse arrived at the morgue to pick up the body of Lindy Schultz, age eight, who'd died of drowning after her appendix ruptured in the family swimming pool. Nothing complicated about the postmortem, but Rosa was having difficulty writing the report.

She got home at six p.m. and took off her lab clothes and poured a glass of white wine. When Yancy called, she told him she'd gone ahead and closed O'Peele as a homicide. He was all gung ho, saying it cleared the way for murder charges against Nick Stripling – if the police could patch together a case.

Rosa was doubtful. Yancy had been the last person to see the doctor alive, a fact any semi-competent defense attorney would exploit to cast suspicion Yancy's way. There were no known outside witnesses to O'Peele's killing and probably no physical evidence placing Stripling at the doctor's apartment. Unsurprisingly, the serial numbers had been scraped off the .357, making it impossible to trace a chain of ownership.

"And anybody can buy surgical gloves," Rosa said.

"What gave you the idea to look for that powder?" Yancy asked.

She could tell he was impressed.

"Couple years ago I had a case where a urologist down on Brickell shot her boyfriend dead. Instead of using a regular medical glove to handle the weapon, she put on those latex finger cots – five of them – because she did a lot of prostate probing and that's what she had at the office. It goes without saying she wasn't the brightest bulb in the chandelier.

The techs pulled a flawless palm print off the gun but also some cornstarch from the fingerlets. She wound up pleading to murder two."

Most of the time Rosa enjoyed her work, although she was increasingly aware of the mental toll. She never watched *CSI: Miami* or any of the TV shows featuring buff forensic investigators; in fact, she didn't look at much television except *Morning Joe* and the Tennis Channel. Her now-deceased former husband had been a decent mixed-doubles partner even with a spazzy backhand.

She asked Yancy if he was glad to be back in the Keys, and he said there was never a dull moment. "The westward view out my window has been dramatically enhanced. I can't wait for you to see."

"Oh shit. What did you do, Andrew?"

"Not a thing! However, I may have unwittingly inspired a bad deed. I'll tell you all about it this weekend. You're still coming down, right? If not I might get maundering drunk and take a spill on Duval Street."

"I'll be there as promised," Rosa said. "Oh, major update on Stripling's traveling arm: It's been returned to the warm bosom of Mother Earth. The cemetery sent a man to fetch it this morning. He was dressed like a freaking Blues Brother, I swear. Said his boss sprung for a new coffin because the grave robbers 'marred' the other one. That's the word he used."

"But isn't Eve required to sign a release?"

"They got verbal consent. He said the funeral director called her this morning."

"In the Bahamas?"

"I'm not sure, Andrew."

Yancy didn't know it but Rosa was soaking in the tub.

She'd been there for an hour, so the water was beginning to cool. She'd pinned up her hair and lit a candle that made the white wall tiles shine pink. It was a small candle, like the ones used for offerings in the back of the church except Rosa's was huckleberry-scented.

Yancy said, "So, how are you doing? Tell the truth."

"I'm okay, honest. But you know they're going to get away, right? Both murder cases are impossible – O'Peele and your boy Phinney. Basically zero evidence, which leaves the Medicare fraud. It'll take the feds forever to indict Stripling and get a fugitive warrant, and by then he and Eve could be in Marrakech. What the hell were we thinking, Andrew?"

Yancy said, "Look, you had a rough day."

"I suppose you've already dreamed up another plan."

"According to my new chums at the FBI, nobody calling himself Grunion has tried to leave Nassau. They believe Nick and Eve are still on Andros. And no, there isn't a new plan. It's the same ballsy, brilliant plan as before."

"For God's sake," Rosa said.

"See? I made you laugh."

"You most certainly did." She poked one big toe out of the water and found herself picturing it with a tag.

Wow, she thought, *that's pretty fucked up*. Definitely time for a career re-evaluation.

"Don't forget," Yancy was saying on the phone, "Stripling tried to kill me, too. As his only surviving victim, I intend to present myself to the county grand jury as a well-groomed, credible witness. Attempted murder is also an extraditable offense."

Rosa didn't want to derail Yancy's enthusiasm, yet she feared that his value to prosecutors would be small given the messy circumstances leading to his demotion from the detective squad to roach patrol.

"You heard from Neville?" she asked.

"Not yet," Yancy said. "I'm hoping he's just laying low."

"I feel terrible about Coquina's house. The whole roof blowing off – that was insane."

"It's what hurricanes do."

"It wasn't the hurricane, Andrew. It was us."

Rosa said good-bye and put down the phone and closed her eyes. She was smiling when the candle burned out.

Neville wasn't worried for himself. It was Driggs who was in danger.

"Some bod mon lookin' to kill you so do wot I say. Now get in!"

The monkey made a fuss but eventually he curled up inside the backpack, which Neville zipped up snug. He threaded his arms through the straps and rode his bicycle to the conch shack. Half the thatching was gone, so he sat on the shady side of the bar. A muffled chitter came from the backpack when Neville set it on the stool beside him.

Everybody in the place was talking about the storm, sharing damage reports, gossip, whose husband spent the night with who. Neville ordered fritters and out of guilt he slipped a small one to Driggs. The air was thick as glue, like always after a hurricane.

Egg came limping down the road, but Neville didn't get up to leave. He was from Andros and Egg wasn't. The others sitting at the conch shack were locals, too. If Egg got a notion in his fat skull to start trouble, he would be heavily outnumbered.

Like a half-wit he sat down squinting in the hottest patch of sun. When he finally spotted Neville he hitched around to the shade.

"Mon, I shoulda kill you down on de beach," he said.

Neville stayed cool. He was still sore from the beating outside the trailer.

"Utter night at my old lady's place, 'member dot? She say it was your fucking monkey did a number on my cock."

"Wot! Ain't my monkey, mon. I give 'im up as pay fuh summa her big woo-doo." Neville snuck a glance at the backpack. He prayed Driggs would stay quiet.

To Egg he asserted, "Dot monkey belongs legal to her, not me."

"When I find 'im I'm gon rip 'is head off."

"No way! He wort good money. She dint tell you he was in de movies with Johnny Depp?"

Egg was conscious of his outsider status on the island. He lowered his voice. "I seen dot wicked ape run off wit you. Don't lie. Give 'im up and we be done wit dis foolishness."

"Mon, wasn't fuh me you'd still have his filty teet in you! Lucky f'you I walked in dot shack when I did." Neville was startled by his own strong words. The plastic fork in his hand was shaking.

"Okay. I guess you wanna die," Egg said.

"Dot's *you*, mister! You beeda one must wants to die coz dot's wot hoppen to men who lay in bed wit de Dragon Queen."

"Oh bullshit."

"Axe anybotty on Lizard Cay! Go on," Neville said. "Lisbon Jones. Duncan Roxy. Lightbourne Carter, too. All strong young fellas come under her spell and now dey stone dead. Go look in de graveyard up Prince Hill, you dont believe me."

"I ain't under nobody's spell," said Egg, without much zip.

"Listen to some hard truth, mon."

Egg said Neville was a lying sonofabitch, but he didn't hit him.

"Somebody stobbed my boss in de back and put 'im in a wheelchair. Wot you know 'bout dot?"

"Mr. Chrissofer got stobbed?" Neville acted shocked.

"And why you hongin' wit dot white mon, anyhow?" Egg asked.

"Wot white mon?"

"One you was wit at de old lady's place. One who took off yest'day in boss's plane."

From the corner of his eye Neville caught movement – Driggs fidgeting inside the zippered satchel. Egg didn't notice.

"Who I choose to hong wit is my bidness," Neville said.

"Had de hawt Cuban girlfriend."

"Yah, I know who you mean. Dot white mon? He a cop from Florida."

Egg frowned. "A cop? No way." Sweat was beading on his prunish little ears.

"He gon put your boss mon in a U.S. prison," Neville said ominously. "I was you, I'd get my ahss back to Nassau look f'nudder job."

Egg gimped off at a brisk clip. Neville finished his fritters and paid the bill. On the bike ride to the dock he stopped to open the backpack. Out squirmed Driggs, funky-smelling and carping as he climbed to Neville's shoulder. He was having a bad time kicking the nicotine.

One of the conch boys in a Whaler took them up the skinny creek where Neville had left his boat during the hurricane. For bailing rainwater Neville had brought two bisected milk jugs. He handed one to Driggs, who hurled it back at him. He grabbed the monkey by the scurfy ruff and said, "Stop dis shit, or I drop you at Mr. Egg's. He boil you in a goddamn stew!"

It took more than an hour to empty the water and mangrove leaves from the boat. The engine kicked over on the first try and before long they were in open water, needlefish scattering like shooting stars ahead of the bow. In a drooping diaper Driggs stood all the way up front, a single upraised paw shielding his wide eyes from the glare.

The tide was high, so Neville was able to run the flats all the way back to Rocky Town. He kept his face turned away, toward the ocean, as he passed by Christopher's house.

Twenty-eight

Caitlin Cox was in the shower when she heard the phone ring. She hoped it was her stepmother calling to report a bounteous transfer of funds into Caitlin's checking account. Caitlin and Simon had already listed their house and were looking for a much bigger place down in Palmetto Bay.

Two hundred grand was the amount Caitlin had been led to expect from her late father's offshore stash. A fatter chunk would be coming a bit later, when the life insurance company paid off on Nick's $2 million policy. Half of that was going to his one and only daughter, who could expedite its delivery (Eve had explained at their reconciliation lunch) if she quit making wild accusations about the manner of her father's death.

And Caitlin stopped, like, right away. The anticipated windfall had brightened her attitude toward all humanity; Simon said she was like a new person. When he got home from work every morning Caitlin would have two bagels thawing for him in the toaster oven. It was like being married to a geisha!

His job was night security on a movie shoot. *Swill* was the name of the film, about two guys and a hot vampire chick who open a juice bar on South Beach. As a surprise Simon brought Caitlin to the set, and the coolest thing happened – they asked her to play a customer who gags on a blood-and-banana smoothie. It was a short scene, no speaking lines, but still she was over the moon.

Although Simon earned a decent wage, he and Caitlin hadn't saved enough for a down payment on a fish tank, much less a house. For upward mobility they were relying on the money from Eve. But when Caitlin stepped out of the shower, she saw Simon holding her cell phone like it was a lit stick of dynamite.

"Is it her?" she asked.

"No, sweetheart, but you better take it."

Andrew Yancy was on the other end, and he got straight to the point:

"Caitlin, I've got a heart-stopping bulletin. Your dad's not dead."

"This is your idea of funny? You sick mother."

"He's hanging with Eve in the Bahamas – I tracked him down last week. He wasn't elated to see me, I won't lie. There were harsh words and gunplay."

Wrapped in a towel, Caitlin perched her bottom on the edge of a sofa. Simon was making inane hand gestures attempting to elicit information.

"I don't believe a word you're telling me," Caitlin said to Yancy. "Where in the Bahamas?"

"Andros Island. He's been using a fake name. They bought a beach, he and Eve, and they're trying to build a resort – I've given all this to the FBI, by the way. Don't waste a plane ticket, because they're going to haul your old man back here and lock his ass up. So this is sort of a good news, bad news call, but I did promise you we'd speak again."

Caitlin experienced an odd mingling of emotions, none of which was joy. "But I saw the arm in the coffin with my own two eyes. You're telling me it came from somebody else?"

"Oh no, the arm was definitely your father's. He had it removed by a surgeon. That was key to the whole scam, see? So everyone would think he's dead. The feds were getting ready to bust him, so he decided to have a quote-unquote boating accident."

"No. Way."

"Nick said he planned to let you in on the secret, when the time was right. But my feeling is that, being next of kin, you deserve to know now. I'm thinking you and Simon might want to scale down your financial plans."

Caitlin said, "Who *does* that? Cuts off their own freaking arm!"

Her husband waved at her and whispered, "I saw a really heavy flick about that! Rock climber fell down a crack—"

"Go, Simon! Get out!"

The cell phone sailed past his ear, and Simon retreated to his mini-gym. After Caitlin calmed down, she picked up the phone and spoke Yancy's name. He was still on the line.

"So, what about the money?" she asked. The deadness in her voice reminded her of how she used to sound in the heroin days. "The insurance part, I guess that's history."

"This is a lot to digest," said Yancy. "One day you're grieving for a lost parent, the next day for a lost inheritance."

Caitlin could hear the annoying clank of the weight machine in the other room. "So what happens to Eve? Sneaky lying bitch. We sat down together, just her and me, and she never told me Dad was still alive. What, like I'd rat him out or something? Know what I think? I bet it was her idea for him to give up a perfectly good arm. Sounds like her."

"Eve's in trouble, too," Yancy said.

"Good! You mean like jail?"

"Oh yes."

"Awesome!"

"We'll see."

"Then who gets all Dad's money?"

"The lawyers do," Yancy said. "Good-bye, Caitlin."

"Wait. Why are you laughing?"

Before putting his phone away he listened to a brief voice message from Neville Stafford saying Stripling was still on Lizard Cay, a big relief. Neville wanted to know when the police were coming to arrest the man. Yancy had been working to make that happen, but today he had a mundane job to do.

From the car trunk he removed his improvised roach-herding device and the portable vacuum. Alone he entered Stoney's Crab Palace. Tommy Lombardo, the coward, had texted to say he wouldn't be there; obviously he wanted Yancy to be the bad guy.

Brennan intercepted him at the door. "Not again. Are you kiddin' me?"

Shrimpy-smelling fingers twirled a hundred-dollar bill under Yancy's nose. He poked Brennan hard with the snout of the vacuum and ordered him to behave.

"But it ain't gotta be this way. Nilsson and me was like brothers!"

"Save your cash," Yancy advised. "I see oppressive legal fees in your future."

The widow who'd gulped the fish hook had tragically lost her uvula. A chopper hired by her offspring had flown her back to Jacksonville for follow-up treatment at Mayo. Brennan said that overlooking the hook had been a freak accident and he insisted that Yancy inspect his current stock of whole yellowtail snappers, seven fish. None featured honed tackle in the gullet, and Yancy made a terse notation before returning to his roach hunt.

"Aw, come on, what the fuck?" Brennan whined.

"This is coming from the top."

"Of Hotels and Restaurants? You mean like the director?"

"Higher still," Yancy said.

The downed widow was a Tea Party patroness who'd funneled ludicrous sums to the governor's election campaign. From her hospital room she had phoned the executive mansion and angrily warbled her story, and now Brennan was to be punished for serving barbed seafood.

Among many violations on the premises Yancy cataloged twelve live cockroaches, twenty-six dead flies, rodent droppings too abundant to count, a drum of rancid mayonnaise, a can of Comet stored beside the Parmesan cheese and, in a small bowl of slaw, one human toenail clipping. Over Brennan's objection Yancy wrote up another emergency closure of Stoney's.

"But we got a wedding party Saturday! Goddammit, I'm calling Lombardo."

"Take your best shot," Yancy said.

"It's that skinny chick who was dating Phinney. She's marrying that little Russian knob."

"Madeline? Oh, perfect."

Yancy drove to the T-shirt shop in town and saw an Out to Lunch sign on the door. Rogelio Burton met him at Pepe's for coffee. Yancy told his friend about the many twists in the Stripling investigation, and Burton was uncharacteristically blown away.

"Christ, I've heard of guys doing a finger before but never an arm!"

"It's trailblazing," Yancy said.

"So is you chasing this asshole through a hurricane. Best part is, you brought a date."

"That's not for general publication, Rog."

Burton advised him not to have high hopes for obtaining murder warrants on Stripling, as the evidence was less than overpowering. The detective also wasn't stunned to hear that the feds were still dicking around with the Medicare indictment, and that no decision had been made about how and when Stripling should be taken into custody.

Yancy told Burton about his latest Plan B – that he intended to give Key West prosecutors an affidavit about the night Stripling socked him and dumped him in the canal.

"That's an attempted murder, cut and dried."

"I'm not disagreeing," Burton said. "But, Andrew, you as the star witness? No offense, but the state attorney isn't what you call a risk taker. I don't see Billy Dickinson hanging a whole case on the testimony of a guy who sodomized a big-shot doctor at Mallory Square."

"It wasn't sodomy. It was a dry colonic."

"And now the doctor's wife, who you were boning behind

his back, torches the house next door to yours. Please tell me you didn't put the idea in her head, 'cause I know how much you hated that place."

"No, that was all Bonnie," Yancy said. "But I've got to say, the new view from my back deck is pretty fucking fabulous. You should swing by after work on your way home."

Burton sipped his coffee. "Plus she's a fugitive on sex charges. Wait'll *that* turns up in the *Citizen*."

"Dickinson won't have to lift a finger," Yancy went on. "All he's got to do is put me in front of the grand jury. Stripling gets indicted and then there's a warrant, which is all I care about right now. The Bahamian cops snatch his ass, put him on a plane to Miami. He's a flight risk, so no bond, and there he sits in jail while the FBI puts the heat on Eve, who'll eventually cave. She, not me, becomes the star witness against Nick. What?"

"Nothing. I hope that's how it goes down."

"They nail this fucker, Rog – the guy who shot poor Charlie Phinney on the streets of Key West, horrified tourists all over the place – what else can Sonny do? He's *got* to give me back my job."

Burton said, "I like to see you radiating positivity."

"Go fuck yourself."

Yancy returned to the T-shirt shop and in the thong aisle he cornered Madeline, reeking of cigarettes as usual. She explained that Pestov had offered her thirty-two hundred dollars to marry him. He'd popped the question one afternoon shortly after an Immigration officer had stopped by the store.

"Hey, I could seriously use the money," Madeline said. "And Pestov's an okay dude. I don't have to ball him or nuthin'." She was letting her hair grow, the roots showing brown and gray. "Charlie'd understand," she added. "He was into cash flow."

"Where's the proud groom?" Yancy asked.

"Out the back door. He saw you coming."

"Go get him, please. I need a favor."

"What kinda favor? Jesus."

"Tell him it's very important."

Madeline bit her lower lip. "Man, don't screw up this deal for me."

"Relax," Yancy said. "This one's for Charlie."

So far, the retirement years of Johnny Mendez had been uneventful, full of golf and JetBlue specials. His neighbors knew nothing of his corrupt past and treated him with the respect due a former police sergeant. That was more than Mendez could say for his wife, who had selfishly scheduled herself for yet another cosmetic procedure that his insurance plan wouldn't cover. This time it was a mentoplasty, commonly known as chin augmentation, which involved the surgical implantation of a small silicone module. In profile the face of Muriel Mendez would soon resemble a Hudson River tugboat, and her husband would once again be draining his pension account to pay for it. There was no point in arguing with her but he tried.

He was on the losing end of another shouting match when Andrew Yancy rapped on the door. It was a tailor-made opportunity to exercise the state's Stand Your Ground law and shoot Yancy dead as an intruder, and Johnny Mendez might have done it if Muriel could have been counted on to support an embroidered account of the incident.

"Hide the fucking cat," he said to his wife, who shooed the obese Siamese to another room.

"But Natasha loves me," said Yancy. "Come outside, Johnny, let's chat."

Mendez went to the bedroom and from the nightstand got his .38 Special, which he stuck in the waist of his golf shorts. Yancy was waiting on the porch. He said he was sorry for abducting the cat and thanked Mendez for the use of his sergeant's badge.

"I want to make it up to you," he said.

"No, you don't. You hate my fucking guts."

"Well, yes, that's impossible to deny. The truth is, I'm here because I need you to do something."

"What now? The answer's no effin' way. Are you serious?" Mendez couldn't believe this jerk showing up at his door.

"One phone call, Johnny. Five grand in your pocket." Yancy grinned and held up five fingers.

Mendez was suspicious, but there seemed no harm in listening. His wife came out complaining that the garbage disposal was jammed again. She was heading straight to Home Depot to purchase a new one, and for the errand she'd dressed in a short canary-yellow tennis ensemble.

Yancy said, "You are lookin' good, Muriel."

"Thank you. This is Stella McCartney – Johnny says it cost too much but I say he's a lucky duck." She laughed, a jungle hooting that spooked a pair of mockingbirds from the cherry hedge.

Yancy said, "He is the luckiest of lucky ducks. Don't let him give you any shit."

Mendez felt like shooting both of them. After his wife drove off he showed Yancy the pistol and told him to start talking fast, or else. Yancy punched him in the gut, shoved him inside the door and whisked the .38 from his pants.

"What kind of drooling moron threatens a man who's just offered him an easy five grand? Don't answer, Johnny Boy, that's rhetorical."

Mendez was bent double, huffing to catch his breath. Yancy helped him into a BarcaLounger and laid out the arrangement.

"Tomorrow there's going to be an item in the Key West newspaper – you should look it up online. It'll say Crime Stoppers is offering five thousand dollars for information leading to the arrest of the person or persons who murdered a man named Charles Phinney in Key West. I'd appreciate it if you call that hotline number, Johnny, and tell them who did it. Strictly as a concerned citizen, you understand."

Mendez, still clutching his midsection, was wary. "You know the killer, how come *you* don't call up for the reward?"

"Because I might end up as a witness in the case. It wouldn't go over so good with the jury if they knew I benefited financially from the defendant's capture. His lawyers would cut me to ribbons, am I right?"

"Only if you're dumb enough to tell 'em the truth."

Yancy emptied the bullets from the gun and tossed it back to Mendez, just like in the movies.

"Johnny, I picked you for three reasons: experience, experience, experience. Nobody can work Crime Stoppers like you," Yancy said. "The killer's name is Nicholas Stripling. He's hiding out in the Bahamas. It's all right here."

Yancy handed Mendez a paper that listed every important detail, from the suspect's DOB to his alias to the color Jeep he was driving. It was more like a dossier than a tip. Mendez knew that the cops in the Keys couldn't brush it off as a crackpot lead. There would have to be a follow-up.

He said, "They don't catch him, I don't get any money. You're aware how that works."

"Then what – you wasted a phone call? Big deal."

"I'm just saying."

"Stripling is the right man, Johnny. Everything I'm giving you is gold. Plus he's only got one arm, which is what the Wanted posters would call a noticeable feature."

"Okay, yeah. But I still don't believe you won't be takin' a cut."

"All I want," Yancy said, "is to see this shithead in handcuffs. That's it. That's all."

"Guy who died – he was a friend of yours or something?"

"Never met him. Just some kid worked on a fishing boat."

Mendez thought about it from all angles, and he really couldn't see a downside to making the call. He'd get a code number, like all the tipsters; nobody would ask his name.

And the five grand would cover most of Muriel's chin work.

"One thing you didn't tell me," he said. "Who put up the reward?"

Yancy looked amused. "You never cared before."

"Don't be a douche. Is it the dead kid's family came up with the money?"

"You'll love this," said Yancy. "It's the Russian mob."

Twenty-nine

The airstrip outside Barranquilla was stubbled with weeds from years of disuse, although the pale Moorish villa looked the same as Claspers remembered it. He circled back toward the coast and set the Caravan down on a flat sapphire bay. After mooring to a crab pot he dove from the starboard pontoon and swam to shore, where he flagged down a taxi, which took him first to a liquor store and then to the countryside.

His clothes were still damp when he knocked on the tall carved door. Donna was more breathtaking than ever, as he'd known she would be. He said he'd been shocked to hear of her husband's death, such a terrible crime, and then he asked if she'd remarried. She said no and invited him to come inside. Her English was still very good. He was careful not to throw his arms around her until he was sure she was alone. He iced the bottle of Dom and then she led him up the stairs.

Later, sitting in the twilight on the bedroom balcony,

they drank the champagne and watched a pair of emerald-colored parrots courting in the treetops. When Donna asked if he was still in the business, Claspers laughed and said no, not for a long, long time.

"Then what are you doing here?"

"Dropping off an airplane."

"When are you going back?"

"I don't know," he said. "You need a pilot?"

The next morning he phoned Palm Aviation Options in Boca Raton and told the leasing agent where the Caravan could be found. The man was displeased to learn that the aircraft was way down in Colombia. Sending a person to retrieve it would be inconvenient and expensive.

"Your client's glad to pay," Claspers said, and read off the numbers on his former employer's gold AmEx.

"Thank you, but I should speak directly with Mr. Grunion."

"He's a busy guy," Claspers said.

"And who are you? I didn't get your name."

"Nobody special. I'm fond of that seaplane is all."

The leasing agent put down the phone and turned to the men sitting in his office.

"Speak of the devil," he said. "The aircraft you were asking about is in South America when it's supposed to be in the Bahamas. Can somebody please tell me what the hell's going on?"

"Sorry," said Special Agent Liske.

"We appreciate your cooperation," added Special Agent Strumberg.

There was a fundamental disagreement about the future of Driggs. Egg wanted to twist the little monster's head off.

The Dragon Queen wanted him found and brought back alive.

"Dot's my sweet pink boy," she said warmly.

"Ain't no boy. Dot's a goddamn wild-ass monkey."

The Dragon Queen told Egg to quit talking that way or she would unleash a black curse on his soul. She ordered him to search the island and made him take one of the meerschaum pipes, packed with Dunhill, which she said Driggs would be unable to resist.

Now Egg sat by himself at the conch hut wondering what to do. He didn't strictly believe in Caribbean magic, but the woman possessed some kind of mystic power. What else would account for him being seduced by such a moldy-smelling crone?

Since the night of the storm Egg had been avoiding sex due to the tender state of his cock, which the monkey had mauled like an ear of corn. Tumescence was a hydraulic impossibility, yet the Dragon Queen gave Egg no sympathy, pestering him crudely whenever he stopped by. At first he'd been merely annoyed but now he was worried. The girl behind the bar had confirmed the eerie story told to Egg by Driggs's owner – three young men on the island had died shortly after breaking off a romance with the ill-tempered old witch. Poison was the rumor.

Egg decided the monkey man was right – it was time to move on. Soon he'd be out of a job, anyway. Grunion was in deep shit with the American authorities, his days as a Bahamas real estate tycoon running out. Even before the stabbing the man had been obnoxious, a loud racist bastard. Egg didn't care what happened to him.

Nassau beckoned – not only the girls but the air-conditioning. There was always a bar or a tourist hotel where you could cool off. Here on Lizard Cay the grip of deep summer was unbreakable; the conch shack's ceiling fan had only one blade. In the absence of casino income the puny island's infrastructure doddered; two-thirds of the power poles knocked down by the hurricane still lay where they'd fallen. Even when the electricity worked, the trailer on the construction site was a toaster oven, the prehistoric wall unit blowing warm, dog-fart air. Egg couldn't get any sleep there, and now he was too creeped out to crash at the Dragon Queen's.

So, after three beers and a shrimp hoagie, he made up his mind to fly home and valet cars at Atlantis, until something easier came along.

"Mr. Ecclestone."

Egg spun himself on the stool. "Wot hey, mon."

It was a fellow named Weech, who'd been a rookie guard at Fox Hill prison when Egg worked there. Now Weech was with the Royal Bahamas Defence Force, which Egg knew was more than a navy. The RBDF did big cases with the American DEA and FBI.

"You here chasin' druggers?" Egg asked lightly.

Weech wore full camos, boots, wraparound shades and a black beret. He was carrying an assault rifle with a jumbo clip. Egg noticed that he'd bulked up and lost his sense of humor. Weech said he'd received information that a suspected murderer from Florida was living with his wife near Rocky Town. The American was using the name Grunion and, although he was missing an arm, he was described as extremely dangerous.

"No shit?" Egg said.

"Dey say you woik fuh 'im."

"I juss quit."

"You smot fella," said Weech.

Three other RBDF officers appeared, every one as muscled and heavily armed as Weech. Egg looked toward the harbor but he didn't see the government patrol boat. They must have used a different dock.

Weech was studying a printout. "De house is on Bannister Point," he said. "He's up dere now? Don't lie."

"You gon grob 'im?"

"Yah, mon. Soon as my orders from Nassau come tru." Weech skimmed the paperwork again. "Where's his floatplane? It's not at Moxey's."

Egg said, "Plane's gone. He pissed off 'bout dot, too."

Weech and the other officers stepped away, into the sunlight, to converse out of earshot. Egg thought their balls must be roasting in those combat uniforms.

On the other side of the bar stood Philip, the taxi man. Egg waved him over and arranged a ride later to the airport. First he had to pick up a gold necklace he'd left at the Dragon Queen's place last night. Hanging on the chain was a miniature gold anchor inlaid with real diamonds. The piece was quite expensive, and Egg couldn't believe he'd forgotten it. The Dragon Queen had told him to remove it so she could lather him head to toe with some smelly green cream she'd said would stop the pain in his privates.

"Mr. Ecclestone, one more ting." It was Weech again, standing beside him. "Be wise you don't tell your boss we're here."

Egg said, "Mon find out soon enough. Dot's his old lady."

He jerked his chin toward the water. Eve was at the wheel of a gleaming new fishing boat idling toward the ramp at the conch hut. Egg recalled she was crazy about the chowder, seasoned with sherry. She'd piled her hair under a blue

379

ball cap, and she was wearing the flowered top of a two-piece swimsuit and white jeans. Her husband wasn't aboard.

The RBDF officers were hard to miss, and Eve spotted them right away. Instantly the three loud outboards began rumbling in reverse. As she spun the boat's bow toward the bight, the name painted on the stern came into view: *Lefty's Revenge*.

Eve gunned the throttles.

Weech said, "No prollem. She ain't goin' no place we cont find her."

Egg believed that to be true. He set the wicked monkey's pipe on the bar top and walked off.

Plover Chase already had received the Miranda spiel, but Agent John Wesley Weiderman recited it again.

"My lawyer advised me not to talk with you," she said.

"I'll leave the minute you ask me to."

"Cody said you seem like a decent sort. Open-minded. Straight shooter."

"I was sorry to hear about your husband," John Wesley Weiderman said.

"Oh, let's not go there."

"I spoke with the hospital. The nurses said he moved his right hand yesterday."

"I don't doubt it. That's how he got where he is," said Plover Chase.

The agent told her the prosecutors in Key West would agree to probation on the arson, but only with a guarantee that she'd go back to Oklahoma and do at least two years for the old charges.

"Two years for what?" she said. "This time around, Cody won't be testifying. He's saving it all for his book."

"We don't need Cody. You jumped bond, Ms. Chase. That's a separate crime."

"But I'm not going back to Tulsa. I plan to stay right here and be near Andrew." She pulled an orange thread from the sleeve of her jumpsuit. "I'm not scared of a trial. It isn't like I tried to kill somebody. Nobody was in the house when I lit the match."

She was something of a surprise to John Wesley Weiderman, the level way she looked at him, her poise and confidence seemingly unshaken by the grubby experience of jail. For some reason he'd been expecting despondency or a teary plea for lenience.

Instead Plover Chase came across as a strong, composed woman who'd just happened in a heartsick lapse of judgment to torch an unoccupied structure. Clearly she was rehearsing for court.

"I'm in it for the long haul," she added.

"Your lawyer will advise you that's a foolish choice. The judge in your old Tulsa case is deceased. The lead prosecutor is now farming soybeans. There's no longer much interest back home in making an example of you. The state just wants to close the file. Two years is a real fair deal."

"And lose Andrew forever? No, sir, I won't be going anywhere."

It was warm in the interview room. John Wesley Weiderman felt like loosening his necktie, but he didn't. After twelve years on the job he was still puzzled by people who were determined to live in turmoil. Plover Chase wasn't a career criminal, yet she was making it impossible for her to be treated as anything less. Oklahoma wanted her sent back as soon as possible, the arson having upended the assumption that she was harmless.

The agent explained to Plover Chase that she was fortunate to be offered basically a free pass out of Florida. It happened that the Monroe County state attorney was unenthusiastic about expending his limited resources on a flaky love-triangle case while a cold-blooded murder remained unsolved.

"I read about that," she interjected. "They're good about letting us see the newspapers."

"The young man – Phinney was his name – he was shot down in cold blood. There's heavy pressure to find the killer and put him away."

"God, I hope so."

"Point is," the agent said, "they're happy to ship you home and save the taxpayers here some money. However, if you insist on fighting extradition, forcing a trial, talking to reporters—"

"Hey, she called *me*—"

"—then you're going to aggravate these Key West prosecutors, and they'll come down hard on you. You could get five years for burning that house and, when your hitch is done, *then* they'll send you back to Tulsa to face the music."

Plover Chase was undaunted. "I plan on being acquitted of the arson," she said.

John Wesley Weiderman put forward his opinion that she wasn't insane.

"I was at the time of the crime!" She was a plucky one.

"That's a long shot with juries."

"Now you sound like Andrew."

It was time to go. The lawman stood up and buttoned his suit jacket.

"Well, good luck," he said.

She gave a little smile that wrinkled her nose. "How long have you been chasing me, Agent Weiderman?"

He was halfway to his car when a cab pulled into the parking lot of the stockade. The driver chose a spot in the shade of a tree, and a rear door was flung open. Cody Parish got out holding a brown grocery bag. He clutched the bag with both hands as he headed toward the front doors of the building.

John Wesley Weiderman thought it odd that the cab stayed to wait. Running the meter was expensive, and Cody Parish didn't give the impression of a young man with a bankroll. He braked like the cartoon coyote when the lawman called out his name.

"Oh. Yo!" Cody lifted one hand off the brown bag to wave, sort of.

John Wesley Weiderman crossed the parking lot unknotting his tie. The heat shimmered off the pavement like a vapor.

"I just had a visit with Ms. Chase," he said.

Cody was antsy, shuffling in his flip flops. "Yeah? That's where I'm goin' now."

"Bet you're wondering how all this will turn out."

"Sure, dude. Absolutely." His cheeks were flushed and his chubby neck was moist.

"Okay, here it is," said John Wesley Weiderman. "Ms. Chase is going back to Tulsa, no matter what she thinks. The prosecutors here will drag out the arson case for months and she'll wake up one day understanding that she's basically rotting in that cell, that Mr. Yancy is no longer infatuated with her, and that she might as well be in Oklahoma working off her sentence. Her lawyer here will be relieved that she came to her senses, and the very next day we'll be on a plane home, she and I."

Cody looked as if his face had locked in the middle of a sneeze. "Huh," was all he said.

"You all right?"

"Yeah, I'm . . . I'm good. Holy shit, it's like two hundred friggin' degrees out here."

"What's in the bag?"

"Books and stuff. She's a major reader."

"Me, too. May I have a look?" John Wesley Weiderman took the bag from Cody and opened it. He said, "See, this is what I was afraid of."

"Dude, come on. Don't, please . . . "

"Oh, I'm not about to touch anything," the agent said. "Neither are you."

There was a rubber Liberace mask and a chrome cap pistol. Cody had intended to bust his true love out of jail.

"I thought it'd be a super-cool thing for my diary, for when they make the book and movie. Her breaking out with some mystery man," he whispered. "See, all I got so far is fifty-three pages and this agent I called in New York? She said that's not enough. She said I need more material."

The lawman closed the paper bag and handed it back.

"And that taxi would be your getaway car?"

"I know, right?" Cody was about to break down. "Sometimes I can be, like, a total fucking idiot."

"That doesn't begin to cover it," said John Wesley Weiderman. "Get back in the cab and go straight to the bus station."

"Yes, sir."

"Buy yourself a ticket to anywhere."

"Okay, dude. Thanks, like, so much. I totally mean it." As Cody was stepping backward, he dropped the brown bag and kicked it away from his feet. "Yo, would you tell Ms. Chase I still love her like crazy?"

"If it ever comes up," said John Wesley Weiderman.

Yancy lay out watching a thunderhead bloom in the Gulf. Every afternoon it was a new show, now that the house next door was gone. Earlier a convoy of dump trucks had hauled away the rubble and ashes, Evan Shook watching blankly from his Suburban. He'd told Yancy that the insurance payoff was tied up in his divorce, as was the property. He and his future ex-wife couldn't even agree on a real estate broker. Meanwhile his mistress had dumped him for a blue-grass player who had his own fucking website. Yancy couldn't make himself feel sorry for Evan Shook. Bonnie shouldn't have burned down the man's house, but the house shouldn't have been built to start with.

Not nine feet over code.

Not big enough to block out a setting moon.

Rosa was caught in Miami traffic, so Yancy put in his ear-buds and smoked half a joint and opened a new bottle of Barbancourt. His name was in the papers again, thanks to Bonnie's birdbrain interview with the *Citizen*. The headline: FIERY CLIMAX TO SEX FUGITIVE'S ROMANCE. To the reporter Bonnie had decoded the arson as a misguided act of love for Yancy. Then she'd rehashed their whole affair, a lowlight being the foolishness at Mallory Square.

The article made a racy splash, and Yancy could hardly blame Sheriff Sonny Summers for not taking his calls. He would be more approachable after Nick Stripling was arrested and returned to Florida, and there was credit to be claimed.

Meanwhile, the toxic new publicity had demolished

Yancy's chances of testifying at the grand jury; his role in the capture and prosecution of Stripling would have to be strictly invisible. Under no other circumstances would Yancy have enlisted the thieving though adroit Johnny Mendez. It was a backdoor move, using Crime Stoppers, but Yancy had grown impatient with the deliberate, over-cautious duo at the FBI.

He downloaded the new Steve Earle and watched the high-stacked clouds turn purple. By the time Rosa arrived the bugs were insane, but she wanted to stay outside and see the crime scene next door. It had been a regular day at work, all grown-ups on the table, and Rosa was in a fair mood. The squall stalled offshore, so Yancy fired up the grill. Burton had dropped off some lobsters, most of them legal.

"Some men would be flattered," Rosa said playfully, "if a sexy woman did something that dramatic to win back their love."

"Oh yes, torching a stranger's house. Hallmark should do a valentine."

"Obviously she still cares for you, Andrew."

"All I want out of a relationship is neutral buoyancy. Is that asking too much?" He was lightly buzzed.

"Maybe she just missed being the center of attention during those boring years as the doctor's wife. Once you're in the headlines it's like a drug. That's what they say."

"Oh, is that what they say?" Yancy was grinning.

"Hey, I'm serious," Rosa said.

"You're adorable is what you are."

"Wow, how much did you smoke?"

The lobsters were excellent. After dinner they tossed the shells into the canal and watched a swarm of mangrove snappers go berserk. Then Yancy walked Rosa back to the house and in the dark they took a long bath, the faraway weather strobing through the windowpanes. While she was moving on top of him, her hair flying, Yancy spied a palmetto bug on the shower curtain. For once he kept quiet and stayed in the moment. Deep space was what it seemed like, weightless and slow motion.

At midnight he and Rosa were dancing in their towels when his cell phone rang. He didn't recognize the number, so he didn't answer it. Early the next morning it began ringing again; this time he picked up. It was Neville Stafford calling from Lizard Cay.

"Are you okay?" Yancy asked thickly.

"Yah, mon. How soon you come?"

"Why? What happened?"

Neville said, "Wot hoppen is Chrissofer gone."

"What do you mean 'gone'? Define 'gone.'"

"I try'n call loss night."

Yancy said, "This is un-fucking-believable." Except it wasn't.

"Tink you should come, mon."

"Right away." He put down the phone and looked hopefully at Rosa.

"Andrew, I love you," she said, "but not enough to go back."

Thirty

Key West homicide detectives reacted to the anonymous Crime Stoppers tip the way Yancy had expected they would. They didn't go through diplomatic channels in Nassau, as was required of the FBI, but chose the more direct and efficient approach. They picked up the phone and called Lizard Cay.

There the Bahamian police contingent consisted of a single easygoing officer named Darrick. He was rattled to learn that the reclusive American developer of the Curly Tail Lane Resort was a fugitive murderer. As soon as Darrick got off the line with Key West, he made an agitated call to his superior at Andros Town, who made a more agitated call to a nephew of high rank on the Royal Bahamas Defence Force. A patrol boat refueling at Fresh Creek was dispatched to Rocky Town, triggering events that neither Yancy nor Neville Stafford could have foreseen.

The authority to detain foreign nationals rested at higher levels of the Bahamian government and required a tedious exchange of paperwork. In the meantime, Nicholas Joseph Stripling was put under a military surveillance that was highly visible, the purpose being to discourage thoughts of flight. The presence of the Defence Force commandos produced in Stripling round-the-clock anxiety and improvident behavior, including the constant berating of his wife, Eve. In actuality she'd had little to do with the hell-bound spiraling of his fortunes.

On the deciding night, Neville went snapper fishing at the mouth of the bight. The sea was velvet, the stars tucked behind thick clouds. He carried a large flashlight that connected with rusty alligator clips to the boat's battery. Driggs was a reluctant crew; huddled in the bow, he crossly labored to peel off a nicotine patch Neville had affixed to a bald spot on his chest.

Near one of the navigational markers the channel bottom dropped off into a deep gouge. There were giant cuberas, too powerful for Neville's tackle, and also hogfish, excellent to eat but difficult to fool with a baited hook. Neville missed several strikes because he was too distracted, replaying in his mind a frightful finishing skirmish with the Dragon Queen.

It had happened on the road to the docks. The voodoo woman was drunk, slumped in her electric scooter chair and attended as usual by her murmuring matrons. At the sight of the monkey she began to keen, reaching for him with stained crooked fingers. Driggs yeeped and ducked behind Neville.

This rejection brought from the Dragon Queen a mortifying wail. Neville tried to dart past but she nimbly manipulated the joystick to keep the wheelchair in his path. She said Egg had gotten sick and she needed a new boyfriend, and she commanded Neville to come see her later for sex.

"You owe me, bey," she said.

"Fuh wot I owe you?"

The Dragon Queen huffed. "Fuh dot woo-doo. Ha! You'll see."

She held up a gold chain strung through a small, diamond-studded anchor. "Dis here fuh my lil' pink boy."

"No need, madam."

"Take it, mon, 'less you hungry fuh pain."

Neville was ashamed that he still feared her dark magic. He accepted the chain and handed it to Driggs, who began scratching at a scab with the prongs of the anchor charm. The Dragon Queen frowned and levered herself from the scooter. From the depths of her dress she produced a small meerschaum, which she waggled like a lollipop at Driggs.

"Don't!" Neville warned, but the monkey wore a rictus leer as it flew toward the old woman's ankles swinging the anchor necklace like a mace. She commenced a queer jig, kicking left and right at the frenetic creature while chanting in a voice as deep as pure evil.

Neville was not too preoccupied to notice Philip's taxi van jouncing at a loose clip down the hill. He tackled Driggs and in a tangle they rolled clear. The Dragon Queen's supplicants had also seen the speeding van and – rotund as they were – parted as fleetly as sparrows. Their excited shouts, loud enough for a tent revival, failed to pierce the voodoo woman's boozy trance.

The taxi slammed hard into her bony frame as Philip stomped uselessly on the brake pedal. In a sinusoidal path the van petered on down the road. Through its punctured windshield jutted the Dragon Queen's legs, her vivid raiments flapping like a broken beach umbrella. Terrified,

Neville lowered a shoulder and barreled through her cow-like retinue, Driggs galloping after him.

Now they sat in the boat solemnly waiting for a fish to bite. On shore Rocky Town looked smaller than usual because half the lights were still out from the hurricane. As the tide rose, the current grew stronger and the ripples ticked against the bow. Neville's rod bent, and he reeled in a good five-pound hogfish. He placed it inside a Styrofoam cooler, where it flapped loudly, startling Driggs. With a sigh the monkey pantomimed a pipe-smoking motion, which Neville ignored.

An hour passed without another nibble. Neville was preparing to move to a different spot when he heard high-powered engines. Initially he believed it was the Royal Defence Force patrol boat he'd seen earlier near the public wharf. Then he saw a bright light moving rapidly up the shoreline from Bannister Point – a foolhardy route in darkness across tricky water. The danger was grounding on the flats or smashing into a coral head. Nobody in the government fleet would make such a run, even with a spotlight.

Neville figured it must be drug smugglers, so he lay down flat on his seat. He groped for Driggs's silhouette and pulled the monkey to his chest. The sound of the fast boat got louder and louder. Driggs smelled awful but Neville didn't let go. He knew that his own small boat, with its low profile and dark hull, would be difficult to see on a starless night.

Abruptly the oncoming engines shut down. Neville waited a few minutes before peeking over the gunwale. Anchored on the edge of the shallows, perhaps two hundred yards away, was a sleek light-colored boat. Neville guessed the length at thirty-five, maybe thirty-six feet. It had a V-hull, three big outboards, and a pair of tall out-riggers for trolling. The finish on the sides of the craft looked bright and new.

A faint light glowed in the cockpit, and Neville discerned movement – a hunched figure emptying a bucket over the transom again and again. There was no conversation rising from the deck and no two-way radio crackle, which seemed odd. Voices carried a long way across open water and, in Neville's experience, dopers were always yakking to each other.

At Neville's feet, Driggs issued a sequence of warning chirps. Neville hastily snatched up the monkey and held him over the side for a pee. It was a small milestone in Neville's dogged campaign to housebreak his unruly pet, and his hushed praise for Driggs was heartfelt. He set the animal in the bottom of his skiff and returned his attention to the gleaming boat across the channel, where there was finally noise.

The person on the aft deck was grunting as if moving bales. Something heavy made a splash near the stern. Neville figured the smugglers were dumping their load, yet he counted no other splashes. Soon the triple outboards thundered and the boat sped away, cutting a long, foamy stitch in the sea.

Neville struggled to pull up his anchor, which had snagged on the ledge of the hogfish hole. He started the motor and backed upcurrent with the rope in one fist. When the anchor came free, Neville hauled it aboard.

Then he aimed his flashlight and chugged toward where the other vessel had been. It wasn't clear why the smugglers had spooked, but they were a jumpy breed. Neville expected to see a fifty-pound bale of grass or a bundle of cocaine floating in the tide. What he found instead was something else, and a dread turbulence of sharks drawn to the surface by buckets of rotting fish heads.

The following afternoon, when Yancy stepped off the plane, the first thing he saw on the tarmac at Moxey's was a pickup truck with a wood coffin in the flatbed. The driver said the dead man was called Egg though his real name was Ecclestone. He'd been found sprawled on Prince Hill, near the graveyard. Heart attack most likely, the driver said. The corpse was being flown back to Nassau, where Mr. Ecclestone was from. None of the freezers on Lizard Cay were large enough to hold a person that size.

Yancy said he was a friend of the deceased, and he asked the driver if he could say good-bye. The driver lifted the lid of the coffin. It was Egg inside.

He was stark naked, the monkey bites still visible on his sad-looking cock. Both his eyes were wide open and so was his mouth. Yancy could see that a chunk of tongue had been bitten off. From each of the goon's nostrils trailed a crust of dried blood. Whatever killed him wasn't a heart attack. Dr. Rosa Campesino could have solved the mystery if Egg had been lucky enough to die in Miami. For show, Yancy flicked one of the thug's crimped ears and said, "Adios, wild man." The pickup driver offered a respectful nod.

Down at the waterfront a crowd was collecting. Yancy didn't see Neville though it looked like most of the island's population had turned out to watch a Bahamian patrol boat escort a barge to the government docks. Upon the barge sat a light-blue Contender, outriggers drooping, the hull showing a stoved hole with the diameter of a garbage-can lid. The bridge of the damaged fishing boat had been covered with a yellow tarp, meaning the accident victim, or victims, were deceased and still aboard.

Yancy was working his way through the onlookers when he felt a sharp tap on one shoulder – it was Neville. He wore amber sunglasses and a faded Peter Tosh T-shirt.

"Come along," he said to Yancy.

"I'm right behind you, brother."

The ride in his skiff was choppy but the breeze felt good. Andros was so vast that it made its own weather, and a squall line thickened over the center of the island. Yancy was eager to hear Neville's story even though he knew the ending. He'd known it the moment he laid eyes on the monkey.

To manage the bumpy waves Driggs balanced up front in the hinged pose of a surfer, his ropey arms extended. Yancy smiled though he remained wary, for his shins still bore the beast's claw marks from the attack at the vacant house. Yet today Driggs wore a different look, and it wasn't just the new bling.

Near the channel marker Neville cut the engine and dropped the anchor and let the wind push the bow toward the cut of the bank. The tide was dead low. Yancy stood to snap a picture with his phone for Rosa.

The Super Rollie had uncannily come to rest upright on the flats, its spoked wheels glinting. As they looked out across the ocean, the empty scooter chair was the only object above the waterline all the way to the horizon. Yancy could envision his photo as an artsy advertisement in some medical-supply catalog.

Neville told him everything he'd seen the night before, everything he'd heard later in Rocky Town.

"It's big woo-doo, mon."

"Sounds more like Stripling seriously pissed off his wife."

"Was me who paid fuh dot coyse on 'im! Finally it hoppen!"

"What about Egg?"

"Dot I dint do," Neville stated somberly. "Dragon Queen got mod and spike 'is rum. I told 'im stay 'way."

"Well, she's done her last voodoo dance."

"Yah, mon," said Neville. "But Philip need a new toxie."

Yancy had a few questions but there was no one left alive to answer them. He asked Neville if they could take a ride down the coast before returning to the dock. He wanted to see the place where Eve Stripling, surely believing she was free, had at a fatal velocity steered the *Lefty's Revenge* into a coral outcrop known to islanders as Satan's Fist.

It had happened only a few minutes after she rolled her husband off the stern into night waters churned by sharks, the fatal splash witnessed by a local fisherman and his pet monkey. The makeshift ramp used to launch the scooter chair was discarded by puzzled authorities, who had no inkling of its purpose. It had been found on board the impaled Contender along with Eve, whose brains were splashed all over the interior windshield.

Neville couldn't picture the man he knew as Christopher going overboard without a fight, even having only one arm and a severely injured spine. Yancy surmised that Eve had incapacitated her husband with painkillers before wheeling him onto the boat. The sharks she'd chummed had finished the job, interrupted momentarily when Neville motored up on the scene and made his daring grab.

As they prepared to set out for Satan's Fist, Yancy remarked that Driggs looked like an honest-to-God movie star.

Neville craned forward. "Same ting as if I found it at de bottom of de sea."

"Absolutely. The maritime law of salvage."

Stripling's wrist was fatter than the monkey's neck, so with a jeweler's screwdriver Neville had removed several links from the watchband. Now the Genève Tourbillon fit Driggs splendidly as a collar.

Yancy said, "Nobody'll try to steal it, that's for sure."

"No, he fuck 'im up bod."

"It's a gorgeous watch, Mr. Stafford. This will do wonders for his self-esteem."

"Yah, mon. He hoppy fella."

The monkey did seem uncharacteristically mellow, as if his demons were lulled by the inner ticking of the rose-gold timepiece. He plucked leisurely at his nicotine patch as he eyed the marooned Rollie, its tires licked by the tide.

Neville said, "I dint tell a soul wot hoppen out here loss night."

"And why should you?" Yancy shrugged. "It's over. Everyone's dead."

"Yah, dot's right."

"I assume there was nothing left of the bastard."

Neville scratched the silvery stubble on his jaw. He looked uneasy.

"Don't tell me," Yancy said.

The fisherman flipped open the Styrofoam cooler. "Here's wot de shocks dint eat."

"Oh Christmas! Of course!"

It was Nick Stripling's other arm.

Thirty-one

The sheriff, not wishing to be seen with Andrew Yancy, insisted on an off-site meeting. They agreed that Yancy's house was the safest place.

"Is this any way to treat an international crime buster?" Yancy said.

Sonny Summers squeezed out a chuckle. "Walk me through this mess, okay?"

They sat in the cheap lounge chairs on the backyard deck. The sheriff was known to sweat like a warthog so Yancy had preemptively chosen a shady spot.

"The man who murdered Charles Phinney is dead. Would you like the official version first?"

Sonny Summers said, "Oh, why not."

"Nicholas Stripling and his wife perished two nights ago in a boating accident off the coast of Andros Island. Foolish Americans, sporting around in unfamiliar shallows."

"Okay. What really happened?"

Yancy popped a beer and delivered a nearly complete account.

"Oh, fuckeroo," the sheriff said, and grabbed a bottle for himself.

"There's a karmic symmetry you've got to appreciate. Not quite Shakespearean, but close."

"Were you on Andros when this happened? Did you – what's the word – contribute to these events in some way?"

"No, Sonny. I was here on Big Pine."

"Well, thank God for that."

Yancy set up his pitch. "If Stripling hadn't drowned he'd be going to prison. Nobody in the States knew where he was until I told them. Nobody had a clue he was alive."

The sheriff rolled the chilled beer bottle between his palms and stared at the scorched patch of land where Yancy's sex criminal ex-lover had torched his neighbor's extravagant spec house.

"Sonny, are you even listening? I flew to the islands on my own dime and found this shitweasel. He almost blew my head off point-blank, you understand? I risked my freaking life to solve this case."

"You want your badge back. I get it."

The muddy response reminded Yancy that he was talking to a politician. "But there's a big 'however,' right? I can smell it."

"However," said Sonny Summers, "the situation isn't that simple. Yes, you did some first-rate police work. Ballsy, man. *Scary* ballsy. But what you just told me, man, I can't put that in a press release."

"No kidding. Who said anything about a damn press release?"

"Oh, I'll need a good one," said the sheriff, "the day I

rehire you. See, you're what the media calls a controversial figure. And now Bonnie Witt's plastered all over the *Citizen* again, just when I thought this shit was fading away."

"Meaning Mallory Square."

"Everything, all of it," the sheriff said in a beleaguered tone. "Consorting with a fugitive, whatever."

"Like I knew? Come on, Sonny."

"Some people are saying this arson was all your fault. Just bar talk, but still. They say you put Bonnie up to it because that house" – Sonny Summers nodded grimly toward the burned lot – "was screwing up your precious sunsets."

"Absurd."

"Look, we're shipping her crazy ass back to Oklahoma. Maybe in a year or two, if you can stay out of the damn headlines, I'll bring you back on the force."

"But I thought you were going to quit and run for attorney general."

Sonny Summers shifted his bulk. "Then I'll be sure and tell the new sheriff to put you on the short list for detective. Same rank as before. Meanwhile, I hear you're tearing it up on roach patrol. Gangbusters is what Tommy Lombardo said."

"Did he now."

"He tells me you bring a firearm on these restaurant inspections. Is that true?"

"It sets a certain tone."

"But you haven't actually shot anything, right? Rats and so forth."

"Not yet, Sonny."

"Try not to. That's my advice."

"Thanks. You've always been like a father to me." Yancy was barely holding it together.

The sheriff said, "I've got to ask – where'd they find Stripling's other arm? I mean, after all the screwed-up shit that happened with the first one."

"I was there, remember? Chauffeuring it up the highway on your secret orders. That was the start of it all."

Sonny Summers wanly acknowledged the fact.

"Stripling's right arm," said Yancy, "was recovered in the water near the spot where the boat wrecked."

Where Yancy had dumped it from Neville Stafford's fish cooler, a detail with which he chose not to burden the sheriff.

"And the sharks ate the rest? They're sure about that?"

"Sonny, they were big fuckers. Bulls and lemons. Whatever was left of Stripling, you could probably scoop it with a guppy net."

"I'll call Key West homicide – they'll be jazzed about closing the Phinney case. We can set up a joint press conference tomorrow. Our prime suspect is dead, et cetera."

All of a sudden it was *our* suspect. Miraculously Yancy held his tongue.

He said, "The right arm is being sent back to Miami to be buried with the left one. There's plenty of room in the coffin." Caitlin Cox was handling the arrangements. Yancy had hung up on her when she'd asked whom she should call about her father's life insurance.

Sonny Summers put down his beer bottle. "Okay, then. Anything else?"

"Just my police career is all. My self-worth and future sanity."

"Be patient, like I said."

"You ever spent a day on your knees counting mouse turds?"

The sheriff winced. "Enough already. Good Lord."

400

Later Yancy trailered his skiff down to Sugar Loaf and poled the Gulfside flats. He'd forgotten to bring a fishing rod, but that was all right. The sun on the back of his neck felt good enough. A salty clean breeze on his cheeks. For a while he staked up to spy on a great blue heron wading along the mangroves spearing minnows and shrimp.

When he got back to Big Pine, the FBI men were waiting in front of the house. They'd made the trip in a new black Tahoe, pretty sweet for a government ride. Yancy remembered his dad always drove a puke-green utility vehicle, standard issue for the park service.

"Howdy, gentlemen," he said to the partners.

While he rinsed his boat they inquired about his latest trip to Andros Island. Agent Strumberg divulged that they'd spotted his name on a list of travelers provided by Homeland Security. Yancy explained that in the absence of prompt federal action he'd returned to Lizard Cay to check on Nicholas Joseph Stripling.

Agent Liske warned him that he was acting recklessly. "You could jeopardize our whole case. We're getting very, very close to making a move."

In a bombshell whisper Strumberg divulged that the seaplane Stripling was leasing had turned up in Colombia.

Yancy started laughing. The agents stiffened.

"What's so damn funny?" asked Strumberg.

"It's too late to catch that asshole!"

"Just watch us," Liske said.

"Guys, you're killing me." Yancy turned off the hose and dried his hands on his pants. "Your suspect, Mr. Stripling, is deceased."

"Shit," said the FBI men, one after the other.

Yancy brought them into the house and fixed a couple of

iced teas. For himself he unwrapped a grape Popsicle. The agents found the circumstances of Stripling's demise somewhat mind-bending. Strumberg walked out to the Tahoe and started making calls. Yancy put on some music, a Springsteen concert.

Liske surprised him by saying he'd seen Bruce twice at the Meadowlands. "The band can't be the same without Clarence."

"I hear it's still a great show."

"The gun – is that loaded?" He pointed at Yancy's Glock on the kitchen counter.

"I'm fully permitted," Yancy said. "The Russian mob is very active in Key West."

"Is that cannabis?"

Near the sink lay a half-smoked doobie.

"Medicinal," said Yancy. "Self-prescribed."

Strumberg returned, having confirmed the details of the fatal boat accident in the Bahamas. Eve Stripling's corpse had been identified at the scene. Fingerprints taken from the hand of the recovered arm matched those from Nick's long-ago arrest as a car-crash scammer.

"Incredible," said Liske. "Just when we're about to nail the son of a bitch, he really dies – and the exact same way he wanted us to think he died before."

Once more from Strumberg: "Shit."

The agents were bummed because there was nobody to arrest. Yancy felt their pain. After all, it was his case, too.

"You boys had him by the balls," he said, to boost morale. "It was a done deal."

Peevishly Strumberg reported that someone other than an authorized FBI official had tipped the Royal Bahamas Defence Force that Stripling was living on the island.

"Wasn't me," said Yancy. "You might check with the Key West police. They've been working the murder of that fishing mate pretty hard."

"Whatever. Our boy got sketched out by all the pressure. Word was that he and the wife were plotting to escape in their new boat. The RBDF thinks they were on a practice run the night they crashed."

Yancy saw no reason to enlighten the agents about what really happened. "What's your next move?" he asked. "Or do you have a next move?"

"Chasing the assets, of course," said Liske, "starting with his bank accounts in Nassau."

"Plus all that prime beachfront he was developing on Andros," Strumberg added.

"Don't get your hopes up," Yancy said. "Stripling had a silent partner in that resort deal. I don't know the guy's name but I heard he's got a Bay Street lawyer, the brother of an MP. Try to execute a property forfeiture over there, they'll tie you up in the courts forever."

The FBI men bore this setback stoically. In the absence of prolonged legwork they would never discover there was no silent partner in Curly Tail Lane, no high-powered Bay Street barrister.

Yancy said, "Stripling hadn't put up any buildings, anyway. Just chopped down some trees."

"It's way easier to go after the money," Liske muttered to Strumberg, who agreed with leaden resignation.

As soon as the agents drove away, Yancy phoned the conch shack in Rocky Town and left a message. He looked forward to telling Neville Stafford that it was safe to move back to Green Beach.

Rosa got in around seven. "Your tongue's purple," she said.

"But my heart is true blue."

"Take your hand out of there. I'm hungry."

They cruised down to Stoney's, which Yancy had cleared for reopening in time for Madeline's pre-wedding party. Madeline was glad to see him and Pestov was less furtive than usual, buoyed no doubt by the future upgrade of his citizenship status. Rosa and Yancy gave the happy couple a three-speed juicer, though a better gift was the news that Charles Phinney's killer had drowned in the Bahamas.

Madeline sniffled in relief, while Pestov emitted a chuff of glee that had nothing to do with seeing justice for the murdered charter-boat mate. Because Nick Stripling had died before he could be arrested, Pestov wasn't obligated to cough up the five thousand dollars he'd grudgingly committed to the Crime Stoppers reward.

And retired sergeant Johnny Mendez would have to find some other means to pay for his wife's new chin.

Brennan acted insulted when Yancy and Rosa departed before even the apps were served. They went to a pizza joint that always passed inspection, then back to Yancy's house, where they made love on Rosa's pink yoga mat, which stuck to Yancy's butt like an oversized Post-it note.

"What did the sheriff say about your job?" she asked later, after they showered.

"Be patient, he told me. Maybe a year or two."

"That sucks, Andrew. I'm sorry."

"Monday I'm doing an Italian joint down on Ramrod," he said. "Some customer, retired navy, you don't even want to know what he found in his calzone."

Rosa dried off. "I'm applying for a pediatric residency at Jackson. It's time."

"Uh-oh. What happened?"

404

She said, "I'm burning out is all. It'll be nice to have patients who can talk back."

"Did another kid come in today?"

"A child, Andrew. He stepped in front of the school bus. Eleven years old."

"Aw Jesus."

"You know what? Let's go look at the moon."

Outside they held on to each other. Rosa's hair was still wet, and the drops felt cool on Yancy's arms. The sky was clear and the air was still, though in the far Caribbean a new tropical cyclone had begun to churn.

Gerardo, for God's sake. Already the TV weathermen in Miami were fibrillating.

Rosa said she wanted to come stay with Yancy if the storm veered toward Florida. "Hurricane sex is the best," she whispered. "You'd better agree, by the way."

"Off the chart."

"Hey, I brought the movie."

"Finally," Yancy said.

His career troubles were placed in cosmic perspective by the sight of a barefoot woman in a Foo Fighters T-shirt popping popcorn in his kitchen. Beyond the window hung a crescent moon, lighting the Gulf of Mexico. Life was fine. All that stood between him and his detective badge was a few thousand cockroaches.

"The DVD's in my purse," Rosa said.

She'd rented the first of the Johnny Depp pirate films, which they'd both seen before. Yancy paused the action on a close-up of the scraggly buccaneer monkey, costumed in a velvet waistcoat and a bell-sleeved shirt.

He and Rosa edged forward for a close look.

"I don't think that's Driggs," Yancy said.

"But he was younger then. Before his fur fell out."

"Check out those chompers. What a psycho."

"Don't you dare," said Rosa, "talk that way about my little hero."

The next day Captain Keith Fitzpatrick took them fishing offshore on the *Misty Momma IV*. It was a free trip, Keith said, in honor of Yancy finding Phinney's killer. Rosa reeled in mahi until her arms got sore. Yancy caught a tuna on a gorgeous new fly rod that he couldn't afford but had bought for himself anyway.

That evening he fixed a plate of sashimi while Rosa grilled the fillets. They drank a manageable amount of tequila and made plans for Gerardo, just in case. As the sun slipped below the mangroves a Key deer – a grown buck, antlers in velvet – appeared in the yard. Not even three feet tall at the shoulder, the deer nosed silently along Evan Shook's fence line looking for shoots. Rosa was taken by its grace.

Yancy pulled out his cell phone and snapped a picture for Neville.